PRAISE FOR C.L. TAYLOR

'Claustrophobic and compelling.'
Karin Slaughter

'I was glued from start to finish!'
Shari Lapena

'She's done it again . . . what a brilliant read *Strangers* is.'
Cass Green

'*Strangers* is her best yet. Expertly woven and so pacy – my heart was banging at the end!'
Holly Seddon

'This is REALLY good. Read it in a day.'
Jane Fallon

'Stayed up to finish *Strangers*, unable to put it down. It's her best one yet. A joy to read, full of living, breathing characters, a compelling plot, humour and a killer twist.'
Mark Edwards

'Clever, surprising and nuanced – C.L. Taylor is at the top of her game.'
Gillian McAllister

'Brilliant characters and a jaw-dropping denouement. I swear I hardly breathed for the last 100 pages. This one is going to be HUGE in 2020.'
Claire Allan

'Clever and unsettling, with a brilliant cast of characters, I am sure this is going to be another huge success.'
Rachel Abbott

'A deep and dark tale of three individuals whose lives collide with such force, I'm sure I was holding my breath near to the end. Utterly sinister and compelling.'
Mel Sherratt

'Wonderfully devious, clever cliffhangers and utterly addictive.'
John Marrs

'A masterclass in character. Clear to see why she's a million-copy seller.'
Sarah Pinborough

'Highly original – kept me utterly enthralled.'
Liz Nugent

'Twisted, unbearably tense, and a shock ending.'
C.J. Tudor

'Has a delicious sense of foreboding from the first page, and a final, agonizing twist. Loved it.'
Fiona Barton

'Fans of C.L. Taylor are in for a treat.'
Clare Mackintosh

'Claustrophobic, tense and thrilling, a thrill-ride of a novel that keeps you guessing.'
Elizabeth Haynes

'A gripping and disturbing psychological thriller.'
Lucy Clarke

'Pacy, well written, and anxiety-inducing.'
Lisa Hall

'A compulsive read.'
Emma Kavanagh

'Kept me guessing till the end.'
Sun

'Haunting and heart-stoppingly creepy, *The Lie* is a gripping rollercoaster of suspense.'
Sunday Express

'A rollercoaster with multiple twists.'
Daily Mail

'Packed with twists and turns, this brilliantly tense thriller will get your blood pumping.'
Fabulous Magazine

'A real page-turner . . . creepy, horrifying and twisty. Intriguing, scary and extremely gripping.'
Julie Cohen

'A compelling, addictive and wonderfully written tale. Can't recommend it enough.'
Louise Douglas

See what bloggers are saying about C.L. TAYLOR . . .

'I devoured *Strangers*. Twisty and clever, utterly compelling characters and a superb edge-of-the-seat finale.'
Liz Barnsley, *Liz Loves Books*

'My eyes were simply glued to the page, I couldn't tear them away!'
The Bookworm's Fantasy

'An intriguing and stirring tale, overflowing with family drama.'
Lovereading.co.uk

'Astoundingly written, *The Missing* pulls you in from the very first page and doesn't let you go until the final full stop.'
Bibliophile Book Club

'Imaginative, compelling and shocking – *The Fear* is a highly engrossing read.'
The Book Review Café

'*The Fear* is a dark tale of revenge and just when you think you know where the story's going, the author takes you by surprise!'
Portobello Book Blog

'[*The Missing*] inspired such a mixture of emotions in me and made me realise how truly talented you have to be to even attempt a psychological suspense of this calibre.'
My Chestnut Reading Tree

'Tense and gripping with a dark, ominous feeling that seeps through the very clever writing . . . all praise to C.L. Taylor.'
Anne Cater, *Random Things Through My Letterbox*

'C.L. Taylor has done it again, with another compelling masterpiece.'
Rachel's Random Reads

'In a crowded landscape of so-called domestic noir thrillers, most of which rely on clever twists and big reveals, [*The Missing*] stands out for its subtle and thoughtful analysis of the fallout from a loss in the family.'
Crime Fiction Lover

'When I had finished, I felt like someone had ripped my heart out and wrung it out like a dish cloth.'
By the Letter Book Reviews

'*The Fear* is a gripping, fast-paced read.'
The Book Whisperer

'*The Missing* has such a big, juicy storyline and is a dream read if you like books that will keep you guessing and take on plenty of twists and turns.'
Bookaholic Confessions

'Incredibly thrilling and utterly unpredictable! A must read!'
Aggie's Books

'A gripping story.'
Bibliomaniac

'It's the first time I have cried whilst reading. The last chapter [of *The Missing*] was heart-breaking and uplifting at the same time.'
The Coffee and Kindle

'Another hit from C.L. Taylor . . . so cleverly written and so absorbing that I completely forgot about everything else while reading it. Unmissable.'
Alba in Book Land

C.L. Taylor is a *Sunday Times* bestselling author. Her psychological thrillers have sold over a million copies in the UK alone, been translated into over twenty languages, and optioned for television. Her 2019 novel, *Sleep*, was a Richard and Judy pick. C.L. Taylor lives in Bristol with her partner and son.

By the same author:

The Accident
The Lie
The Missing
The Escape
The Fear
Sleep
Strangers

For Young Adults
The Treatment
The Island

C.L. TAYLOR

Her Last Holiday

avon.

Published by AVON
A division of HarperCollins*Publishers* Ltd
1 London Bridge Street
London SE1 9GF

www.harpercollins.co.uk

HarperCollins*Publishers*
1st Floor, Watermarque Building, Ringsend Road
Dublin 4, Ireland

A Hardback Original 2021

First published in Great Britain by HarperCollins*Publishers* 2021

A catalogue copy of this book is available from the British Library.

ISBN: 978-0-00-846092-1 (HB)
ISBN: 978-0-00-846545-2 (TPB)

21 22 LSC 10 9 8 7 6 5 4 3 2 1

Typeset in Sabon LT Std 11.25/14.5pt by Palimpsest Book Production Limited,
Falkirk, Stirlingshire

Printed and bound in the United States of America by LSC Communications

To Laura Barclay

Chapter 1

Now – May

FRAN

Fran's rage has reached boiling point. The stifling heat of the tube carriage, the scrum of warm, sweaty bodies and the woman continually smacking her knees with her oversized shopping bag have pushed her too far. She's one tut away from combusting.

Her day started with an ominous burning sensation when she went to the toilet. Irritating. A UTI was something she simply didn't have time for, especially when her Year Elevens were weeks away from taking their ICT GCSE.

When she arrived at St George's Academy an hour later her mood wasn't helped by an email from Nigel Flemming, Deputy Head, informing all teachers that, owing to staff shortages, they would have to take it in turns to supervise the seclusion room for disruptive students. And it continued to sour when she lugged an armful of heavy textbooks to the photocopier only to discover an 'out of order' notice taped to the top. She sighed. A urinary tract infection, the loss of a free period and a five minute walk across school to find another photocopier would not unhinge her. These were minor irritations, not life-changing events. *If I can survive the last two years*, she told herself, *I can deal with this.*

Now all Fran wants to do is escape from the hell that is the London Underground, get home, use the toilet, change into her pyjamas and crawl into bed, but the carriage is packed and every time they stop at a station it takes at least three attempts to close the doors. As the train slows into Kilburn station, the woman with the enormous bag stops tormenting Fran and squeezes her way through the mass of bodies to the door. Simultaneously, the people either side of her shuffle to fill the space she left behind. Someone stands on Fran's foot, making her wince. She looks up sharply but if the grey-haired man in a suit registers her annoyance, he doesn't acknowledge it. Instead, he continues to gaze over the heads of the other passengers, wearing the weary, blank expression of a London commuter. Fran sucks in the warm, fusty carriage air, an objection forming on her lips. There's no excuse for a lack of manners and—

The thought evaporates.

One second ago, the grey-haired man had his right hand wrapped around a pole for balance and his left hand hanging loosely at his side. Now, that same left hand is gently stroking the bottom of the woman in front of him. Fran's heart gives a little jolt as she clocks the woman's dark hair and slim figure, but it's not Jenna – it never is. This woman is much younger, mid-twenties at a push. Her hair is held up in a pony tail and she's dressed casually in leggings, trainers and a T-shirt.

The young woman shifts her weight, a little wiggle of irritation at the waist to show her dislike at being touched, but she doesn't turn around. Did she assume a bag or a coat was brushing against her? It is a packed carriage after all. Or maybe she was too scared to glance over her shoulder and look into the eyes of a pervert. She's got nowhere to run, no means of escape.

Fran glares at the man as he casually drops his hand back to his side. He hasn't spoken to the woman the whole journey, nor she to him. They're no couple.

Nothing happens for a few seconds, and then the man inches forward, his face expressionless as he closes the gap between him and his victim. His hand slides away from his side, his fingers inches from the cleft of her bottom. Fran's spine straightens.

Don't you dare, she thinks as the train slows, approaching the next station. *Don't you bloody dare.*

The man dares.

The young woman gasps in shock and tries to escape the probing fingers, but there's nowhere to go. She is pinned on all sides by armpits, knees and hips. A smirk settles on the man's lips and Fran's rage erupts. She reaches out, thumb and forefinger extended, and grabs as much of his backside as she can. Then she twists. Hard.

The man jolts, rising up on the toes of his shiny black shoes, then he snaps round and glares accusingly down at her.

'I believe this is your stop,' Fran says as the doors open.

The man grimaces. He's torn between leaving the carriage and responding to Fran. The young woman he groped is no longer in the aisle; she's moved into the belly of the train. Her eyes meet Fran's. Other than a woman in a hijab and a couple of teenage boys they are now alone in the carriage with the grey-haired pervert. An urgent beeping fills the space. The doors are about to close.

'Ugly Bull Dyke!' the man shouts at Fran. Seconds later, he's gone.

There's confusion as Fran moves down the carriage towards

the young woman, and the young woman heads towards her.

'Did you see—'

'Are you okay?'

'What happened?'

'He's gone.'

'What did you say to him to—'

'I'm so sorry—'

There's an awkward pause as they wait for each other to finish.

'Stella.' The younger woman holds out her hand. 'Whatever you just said or did, thank you.'

There's a Northern tinge to her accent that Fran can't quite place. Leeds or Sheffield, maybe.

'Fran Fitzgerald.' She returns the handshake. Now the adrenaline's worn off she is desperate for the toilet again.

'It's a hate crime you know,' Stella says, 'what he called you.'

Fran tuts. 'To men like that we're either sluts or lesbians. Limited vocabulary. Tiny brains that match their tiny penises. And as he didn't want to ram his hand between my legs that makes me a . . .' She pauses as she registers the expression on the other woman's face. 'I'm not saying you're the slut. Not in any way, shape or form. You're no more a slut than I am a lesbian and' – she takes a deep breath – 'I'm sorry. I'm not expressing myself very well. It's been a long day and—'

'No, no. I get what you're saying. He's the dick.'

'Good. Because . . .' Fran shrugs off the rest of her sentence. Stella doesn't need to know that she's been reprimanded several times at work for saying something tactless to another member of staff. She doesn't mean the words to come out the way they do but she can't always stop herself. She does try though.

Yes Frances. She hears her mother's voice in her head. *You are very trying.*

'Because . . .' Fran repeats, distracted by her reflection in the mirrored doors. She looks small, and round, and old. How did that happen? 'Because what happened wasn't your fault. As I said, the man's a deviant and I would be more than happy to get off at your stop and report what happened to a member of the TFL staff. Or the police.'

As she looks back at Stella she is surprised to discover she's grinning.

'What?' Fran asks. 'What did I say?'

'Nothing. I just . . . it's refreshing. *You're* refreshing.'

Fran's not entirely sure she wants to know what that means so she doesn't question her further. Instead, she asks Stella where she's getting off and offers to accompany her to the nearest police station.

'West Hampstead.' Stella glances at the huge bag of books that Fran has left on her seat. 'And that's really kind of you but I think you can report this sort of thing online. Can I take your number anyway, just in case the police need to speak to you?'

'Of course.' Fran rummages in her bag for a piece of paper and a pen and scribbles down her mobile number and full name. 'Do you have family? At home. Can you get there safely?' Her throat tightens as she imagines Stella stepping out of the tube station and vanishing, never to be seen again. It happens; she knows that well enough.

'I'll be fine,' Stella says. 'I've got flatmates. I'm angry more than anything. If the tube hadn't been so packed, I'd—' She breaks off as the train crawls out of the tunnel and pulls to a stop at West Hampstead station. 'Shit, this is me. Thanks for this.' She plucks the piece of paper from Fran's fingers. 'And for doing what you did.'

Fran shrugs. 'Not a problem.'

As the train doors open Stella moves to get off then turns back. 'Hug?'

Fran stares at her in horror. What's the polite way of saying no? Is there one when the girl's just been sexually assaulted and is in need of physical reassurance? Should she just say yes and grin and bear it? A dozen different responses run through her head but the one that comes out of her mouth is, 'I'd rather we didn't.'

Stella laughs. 'Bye Fran, thanks again.'

As Stella bounds off the train, Fran's mobile vibrates in her handbag. She fishes it out and taps in the password. Her mum has sent her a WhatsApp message. Fran clicks on it and squints at the black and white image. It looks like a newspaper article. She digs around for her reading glasses and puts them on.

She recognises the face in the photograph – the dark hair, the strong jawline, the piercing grey eyes.

It's Tom Wade, the last man to see her sister Jenna alive. And tomorrow they're setting him free.

Chapter 2

Then – two years earlier

JENNA

Jenna sits back in her seat, fastens the belt around her waist and rests her arms on the armrests. She looks dispassionately at her hands, hanging loosely over the ends. Normally they'd be in her lap, fiddling with a ring or a bracelet. She mentally examines the rest of her body: her heart is beating steadily, her face isn't flushed and her feet aren't tapping out a frantic rhythm on the floor of the plane. It is as though someone else – Jenna Fitzgerald's unafraid clone – is sitting in seat 10A. She searches inside herself for the fear that accompanied her on previous flights. It's not there. She fires up her imagination and pictures the plane lurching in turbulence, exploding at 30,000 feet or hitting the ground nose first. She waits for her pulse to begin racing and her temples to dampen. Nothing happens. Her phobia of flying has vanished but not because she took a course or visited a hypnotist. She simply no longer cares.

She looks out of the window, the back of her head vibrating against the headrest as the plane accelerates. Erica, beside her, makes a soft whining sound as the plane lifts into the air. She's twenty-five, one of the 'babies' of the group.

'Are you okay?' Jenna asks.

'Could you . . . could I hold your hand? I hate flying.'

'Of course.'

The words have barely left Jenna's mouth when Erica grips her hand, squeezing it so tightly her knuckles knock together. Erica's eyes are screwed shut, her lips pressed into a hard, thin line, her brow tightly knotted. She looks like one of the Cabbage Patch dolls Fran kept on a shelf in her room. She wouldn't let Jenna play with it even though she must have been fifteen, while Jenna was only three.

Jenna pushes the memory away and places her free hand over Erica's. 'Breathe. Remember what Tom taught us. You are in control of your anxiety. Not the other way round.'

Instinctively, she glances in Tom's direction. He's on the other side of the plane and several rows ahead so she can't actually see him, but she knows he's there. He flashed a smile at her as she made her way onto the plane. As their eyes met, she felt something inside her twist. It was still there, the attraction she'd felt on the first day they met, the attraction she was certain was mutual.

'I . . . can't.' Erica forces out the words on short puffs of breath.

'Let go of your fear,' Jenna says. 'You're living a story you have created. It's not reality. Tell it no and push it out of your mind.'

Erica shakes her head minutely then squeals as the plane dips to the left.

'Look at me,' Jenna says. 'Open your eyes.'

Erica shakes her head again. Jenna waits. One second passes, two, three, then Erica opens her eyes and turns to look at her.

Jenna smiles. 'Good. Well done. Do I look scared?'

The younger woman's eyes rove her face. 'No.'

'That's because there's nothing to be scared of.'

It's a lie. But only a little one. There's plenty to be fearful of but dying in a plane crash is no longer on her list.

She gives Erica's hand a little squeeze as the plane levels off. 'That's the worst bit over. Now you get to relax for three hours.'

'Relax?'

'Read, watch a film. You can borrow my iPad, if you want?'

'Could I?' Relief floods Erica's face. 'Have you got anything funny? I don't think my heart could cope with anything scary.'

'Sure. It's in my bag.' She checks that the seat belt signs have been switched off then unbuckles her belt and shuffles past Erica and the man sitting in the aisle seat.

She hands Erica the iPad then glances across to seat 4C, where Tom was sitting. It's empty. Her gaze flits towards the front of the plane. The toilet engaged sign is lit up. Abandoning her bag, she moves down the aisle and hovers outside the toilet. One of the flight attendants, preparing a trolley with snacks, catches her eye and smiles. Jenna returns the smile then turns to look out of the window. Clouds. Miles and miles of white, fluffy, picture-book clouds. As a child, she told her mum that one day she was going to jump out of a plane just so she could lie on one. She was going to float around the world, she told her. She couldn't imagine anything more restful and—

'You're not planning on opening that, are you? I'd quite like to get to Malta in one piece.'

Jenna twists sharply. Tom is standing beside her, a smile playing on his lips.

'The door.' He looks meaningfully at her hand, gripping the handle of the exit door.

'I . . . I didn't even realise I was . . .' She snatches her hand away.

'It's okay, I was joking.' He strokes her arm from the shoulder to the elbow and back again. The warmth of his fingers on her skin pulls her back from the clouds and into her body. 'I'm sorry I startled you.' He drops his hand but his gaze lingers. He looked at her in the same way the first time they met – his head slightly tilted to one side, his body relaxed, his pupils wide and dark, his attention so completely focused on her it was as though the rest of the room didn't exist.

She edges away from him, to break the tension, then shifts the conversation to the reason she signed up for the retreat. 'I wanted to talk to you about the advice you gave me. I talked to my mum, as you suggested, but it really didn't—'

'Tom. Jenna. Everything okay?' Kate strolls towards them, her dark hair twisted into a messy bun at the nape of her neck, a notebook clutched in her right hand. She doesn't wait for a reply. 'Tom, we need to go over the itinerary again. I'm not sure whether the timings of the activities on day two quite work with—'

'We were talking,' Jenna says, irritated by the interruption.

Kate places a territorial hand on Tom's arm. 'There'll be plenty of time for that during the week. You have a one-to-one scheduled for . . .' She opens her notebook and runs a red fingernail down the page. 'For Wednesday.' She smiles brightly. 'We have lots of wonderful things planned between now and then. It's going to be a transformative experience, Jenna. Okay, Tom?' She pulls on his arm. 'Shall we?'

He turns back to Jenna and leans in, his breath warm in her ear. 'When we get to the hotel meet me at the entrance at seven o'clock, wear a swimsuit under your clothes and bring a dressing gown.'

Before she can reply he's gone, marched back to his seat by Kate. Sighing, she makes her way back down the aisle, forcing herself not to glance at Tom as she passes his row. She's two rows away from her seat when she stops abruptly. Someone just touched her on the leg.

'You okay, Jenna?' A man around her age with black hair, shaved around the sides with the top pulled back into a walnut sized bun on the back of his head, smiles up at her. On the tray in front of him is an open can of beer and several empties.

'Fine.' She smiles apprehensively. She only met a handful of people during the one day seminar in London and she's forgotten almost all of the names of the people she shook hands with in the airport. Kate had collected the group into a corner of the departure lounge and suggested they introduce themselves to each other.

'Damian.'

She shakes his hand and is about to tell him her name when she realises he's already said it.

'Flight okay?' he asks, and she catches a slight slur to his soft Scottish burr. 'Who are you sitting next to?'

'Erica.'

He frowns, not recognising the name.

'Blonde, beautiful, thin,' she prompts.

Damian shrugs, nonplussed. 'Do you think she'd swap?'

Jenna laughs. 'I doubt it. I'm her emotional support person. I had to hold her hand on take-off.'

'Right, right.' He runs a hand over his hair, although it's already slicked into place. 'Maybe we need to ask the other person on your row to swap places with me. That way you can sit in the middle and hold my hand too.'

'Are you scared of flying?'

'No.' He laughs, his gaze flicking from her face to her chest. 'I just want to spend some time with you.'

'How about you spend some time with Bessie instead? I'm sure she'll hold your hand.' She catches the eye of the woman sitting next to Damian. She's mid- to late sixties with pink hair, clashing red lipstick, enormous earrings and the most colourful kaftan Jenna's ever seen.

'Ooh, yes. Of course I will.' Bessie shoots out a hand, heavy silver rings glinting on every finger, and clasps Damian's hand. 'Where would you like me to put it dear?' She winks lasciviously at Jenna.

'I'd better get back to Erica.' She ignores Damian who's trying to catch her eye. 'Enjoy the rest of the flight and don't do anything I wouldn't.'

Damian snorts. 'I'd love to know what that is.'

But Jenna has already moved off. As she walks down the aisle she can feel him watching her; his gaze resting as heavily on her bum as his hand did on her thigh.

Chapter 3

Now

KATE

Kate touches the brake as the prison comes into view at the end of the road. Even from this distance she can see the mass of bodies crowding the entrance to the car park: journalists, photographers, a camera crew.

She knew the press would be waiting; Tom's face has been splashed all over the news for the last couple of days. Somehow she's going to have to angle him through the maelstrom without him saying a word. She's been schooling him for weeks. During every telephone call she's told him to keep his head down and say nothing, but she knows Tom; if a journalist presses the right button he'll respond.

As she pulls into the car park cameras are shoved up against the car windows and flashbulbs pop, forcing her to hold up a hand to shield her eyes. She wants to stop, to wind down the window, to scream that she's not part of their news story, that her life has been destroyed too. But she doesn't. She nudges the car through the mass of bodies then navigates around the car park until she finds the perfect spot to tuck her Volvo V70 out of sight. She turns off the engine and leans back into the headrest. Did the photographers get any useable photos? Did she look distraught or angry? How will the journalists caption them in tomorrow's papers? Will they paint her as a victim – the loyal wife, supporting her husband despite everything? Or the villain – a complicit accomplice in a terrible crime? The jury – the social media jury, anyway – was split when Tom was sentenced. Some interpreted the look on Kate's face as she climbed the steps to the courthouse as 'hard-nosed and cold'. Others thought she looked tired and sad.

She takes another steadying breath then glances at her watch. It's 8.57 a.m. Anthony Broadhurst, Tom's lawyer, said he would be released sometime between nine and ten a.m. She'd meant to arrive much earlier, eight thirty at least, but she dithered so long over what to wear – ditching the navy suit she'd selected yesterday in favour of a skirt and a cashmere jumper (softer, less austere) – that time had sped away.

She shifts in her seat to take another look at the press, wondering why they haven't followed her into the car park, and spots two flashes of yellow neon amongst the dark coats. Police, preventing the press pack from hounding her. She isn't sure whether to feel relieved or irritated at the sight of their yellow vests and black peaked caps. She can still remember how airless and cold it felt in the station's interview room, how dispassionately her interrogators looked at her and how bleak and broken she felt.

She stares instead at the closed gates of the prison. The press won't see when Tom walks through those gates, but she will. And if the police do their job she'll be able to ferry him across the car park to the safety of the car without a single journalist asking him a question. She's been worrying unnecessarily, worrying *him* unnecessarily. Within thirty to forty minutes they'll be home – their new home. Tom will want to eat, grab a drink, shower and sleep. Maybe have sex. She's thought about everything. She's changed the sheets, laid out new clothes and ordered in his favourite food and drink. Then, when he's fully relaxed, she'll show him her plan. Her stomach hollows at the thought – excitement and nerves mingling. For the last year she's done nothing but work on it, putting everything into it – time, passion, painstaking research. Two years ago, their world was shattered, but she's going to pull the pieces back together and, like the Japanese craft of repairing broken pottery with gold – their new life will be more beautiful for having been broken.

Movement at the gate makes her sit up a little taller. A man is walking from the prison to the gate, accompanied by a guard. She squints and leans towards the windscreen. Is it Tom? As the gate opens and the man, in a blue sweatshirt and black beanie hat, carrying a bin bag over his shoulder, walks into the car park, Kate slumps back into her seat. It's not Tom. The released man wanders towards the exit then freezes as the press rush towards him. The police officers skirt round them, shouting and waving their hands and the pack falls back. One of the officers approaches the man and they have a brief conversation while the other officer makes a motion with his arms for the crowd to part. He beckons the man through.

Kate jolts as she glances back at the gates. A second man is walking out to freedom. Even though she's visited Tom at least once a month for the last fourteen months it still takes her a moment to register that the chin length hair and the raggedy beard belong to her husband. Tom takes three or four steps outside the walls of the prison, then stops and looks around the car park. *He's searching for the Range Rover,* Kate thinks ruefully. *Not a ten-year-old Volvo V70. Keep walking,* she silently urges, casting a look towards the press pack. *Keep walking this way.* But Tom doesn't move.

In an instant, she's out of the car. Shock registers on Tom's face as she sprints towards him, but it quickly morphs into relief. Kate opens her arms wide and calls his name, mentally urging him to run to meet her. Still he doesn't move but then a jolt seems to pass through his body and he drops his bin bag and speeds towards her. As they embrace, Kate hears a roar of excitement from the entrance to the car park. She's almost certain she can hear the sound of the photographers' cameras firing, machine gun fast. She buries her face in the crook of Tom's neck and she smiles.

Tom stares out of the window as they drive through South London.

'You forget . . . about the small things.'

Kate glances at him. He's barely said a word since he got into the car. 'What was that?'

'Normal life. People going shopping, walking the dog, chatting, laughing . . .' He tails off.

Kate moves her hand from the gear stick to his thigh. 'You're part of all that again now. We can put what happened behind us.'

In the first few months in prison Tom would spend every visit going over and over what had happened, the 'crime' that had sent him away, trying to make sense of it, berating himself for what he did or didn't do. He sent her letters, filling page after page with his thoughts. He was so obsessed, so repentant, so desperately unhappy that Kate contacted their lawyer asking if he could arrange for her to speak to the prison governor. She was worried that Tom might need a psychiatrist. Anthony talked her out of it. It was the shock, he said. Tom was processing not just what had happened, but also his new reality. Once he got used to the routine, and accepted that his sentence had an endpoint, he'd begin to calm down. Kate protested but Anthony's years of experience were too persuasive, and eventually she backed down. He was right, of course. Over time Tom stopped mentioning his 'crime' and began sharing snippets from his daily routine instead. He had a job, he told her, working in the laundry, and he had become an unofficial life coach to many of the inmates. He sounded . . . not happy exactly, but accepting of the situation, which in turn made Kate feel more positive about the life they would have together when he returned home.

'Can we?' Tom asks now. 'Put it behind us?'

'Of course we can.' There's a forced cheeriness in Kate's tone that even she can hear.

'Oh,' Tom says as they park up.

Kate looks out of the window, seeing their surroundings through her husband's eyes: the crisp packets and plastic bags twisting in the wind, the bubble writing graffiti, the bike frame chained to the railings, stripped of its wheels, handle bar and seat. Then she looks up at the grey, concrete monstrosity that towers above them.

'Home.' She smiles tightly. 'It's not . . . you'll get used to it.'

Tom leans forward in his seat. 'What floor did you say we were on?'

'The eighth.'

He shrugs. 'I guess that's one way to stay fit.'

'I've tried to make it look nice. Inside.'

'I'm sure it looks lovely.'

Not as lovely as our old house, Kate thinks but doesn't say.

While Tom has a nap in the bedroom, Kate pours herself a glass of wine and sits down at the small table in the living room that she uses as a desk. It's where she heads every evening, after she returns home from whichever financial institute, legal firm or company the temping agency sent her to that day. It's where she studied, researched, and formulated her plan. She glances back towards the bedroom, logs into Twitter and then takes a sip of red wine.

@SoulShrink

Self-help for your soul. Tom Wade. Somatic Symptom survivor and Motivational Speaker. Lifelong solutions for stress and anxiety. I've been where you are. Let me help.

1,997 Following, 215k Followers

She'd set up the account ten years earlier, shortly after she and Tom got together, when someone in his ragtag little somatic symptom survivor group said their soul felt lighter after the meetings and someone else piped up, 'That's because Tom's a soul shrink.' Tom's eyes had shone when he returned home that evening. 'I feel like I'm doing something important,' he'd told Kate. 'This isn't just about me anymore. It's about helping others, setting them free.' A weight had lifted in Kate's chest. She couldn't remember the last time she'd seen him so happy and fulfilled. While he cooked dinner she'd crept off to the bedroom and pulled her laptop onto her knees.

'There you go,' she'd said, returning to the kitchen some time later, angling the screen towards him as he stirred the risotto on the stove. 'Your Twitter handle is SoulShrink and your description is self-help for your soul. Now you can reach millions and transform their lives too.'

He'd laughed. 'Followers? That makes me sound like Jesus.'

'Well, he had loads. You've only got one.'

Tom had raised his eyebrows. 'Someone found it already?'

'Yeah.' Kate smiled. 'Me.'

He'd wrapped his arms around her then, pulled her into his body and kissed her until the smell of burnt rice filled the air.

Now, Kate takes another sip of wine. 215,000 followers. Two years ago, Tom had nearer 600,000. But 215,000 is still a huge number. For whatever reason, those people chose not to unfollow him. Some probably follow so many people they've forgotten all about SoulShrink. Others might have inactive accounts. But some of them will want to hear from Tom again – certainly the ones who tried to balance out the slew of hateful tweets with compassion and understanding. She opens a new tab in her browser and types, 'Tom Wade released from prison' into Google. Dozens of news articles fill the page but Kate doesn't read them. Instead she clicks on the 'Images' link and scans through the pictures. She spots one of her, looking focused and pale, leaning over the steering wheel of her car. Another of her and Tom sprinting across the car park towards each other, arms spread wide. It's a powerful image, but it's not right. She continues to scroll through the photographs then lifts her finger from the mouse wheel as a close up of Tom appears on the screen. It's from when they were hugging; she can see strands of her straight dark hair behind his head. But that's not what caught her attention. It's Tom's face, crumpled with emotion, his eyes screwed shut. She clicks on the image, to see a larger version, and that's when she sees the tear. One single tear, rolling down his cheek.

She glances back over her shoulder and listens for any sound that her husband may be stirring but the pounding bassline of the music in the flat above makes it hard for her to hear a thing. She was going to wait for Tom to wake up before she explained her strategy for relaunching SoulShrink. She was going to take him step by step through her plan. But this can't wait. It's been three hours since Tom was released from prison and #SoulShrink is trending on Twitter. Her phone, set on silent beside her, has been lighting up all day with call after call, but she'd let them all go to voicemail. She's not speaking to a single journalist. Neither is Tom. She doesn't want anyone putting words in his mouth when she's perfectly capable of doing that herself. Her heartrate quickens as she right clicks on the photograph of Tom's face then opens the SoulShrink 2020 folder on her desktop and double clicks on the file called 'First tweet'. She's lost count of the number of different versions she's written over the last few months but this one, this final version, is as perfect as she's ever going to get it. She pastes the sentences into a tweet then adds the photograph. She moves the arrow over the blue 'Tweet' button and sees it turn to a hand. She rereads the text. Tom's first tweet as a free man is guilt-ridden, repentant, compassionate and human. It'll either restart their lives or destroy them for good.

Kate clicks the mouse.

Chapter 4

Now

FRAN

As Fran opens the gate, Trooper, her parents' ailing, arthritic Golden Retriever, hauls himself to his feet and barks twice. He makes no effort to move from the only patch of shade in the garden, the two-metre gap between the side of the cottage and the hedge. Fran casts an eye over her parents' home in a leafy suburb of High Wycombe. The thatched roof of the cottage, replaced several years earlier, still looks thick and sturdy; the lawn, either side of the path, is pale and sun-bleached but striped from a recent mowing. The ornamental shrubs in their concrete tubs are neatly trimmed, standing either side of the front door like leafy sentinels. Orderly, that's the word she would use to describe what she sees. Orderly, conservative and bland.

'Hi Troops!' Fran calls as she makes her way down the path.

The dog's eyes follow her but its tail is the only part of him that moves.

She pauses as she reaches the front door. Her instinct, and thirty years living in London, makes her raise her fist. She pauses, then turns the doorknob instead. Her parents only lock the front door when darkness falls.

'Mum?' She steps into the cool, flagstoned kitchen. 'Dad?'

She slips off her shoes, steps through the small dining room and pushes at the door to the living room. Her mum, sitting in a chair by the window, peers up at her from above her reading glasses. 'Oh, it's you.'

The phrase, and the dismissive tone of her mother's voice, act like a time machine. In a blink Fran's twenty again, home from university for the summer, and her eight-year-old sister is sitting on the floor cross legged, watching TV. As Fran hovers in the doorway Jenna looks up, an expression of studied indifference on her face and, mimicking her mother, says, 'Oh, it's you.'

Fran tries to push the memory away but her sister is everywhere she looks – on the mantlepiece, the window sills, and propped up in front of the hearth. Her mother used to say 'too many family photographs are uncouth', but the room has become a shrine to Jenna's smiling face. Fran looks back at her mother, almost swallowed up in the large, plush armchair. She's a small, slight woman; physically, at least.

'We did agree that I'd visit at 10.30 a.m.,' Fran says, touching her watch. 'And it's 10.32.'

'Always the pedant.'

Fran hears the soft shuffle of slippers on carpet behind her and turns to see her father Henry entering the room. In her mind he's forever in his forties, a towering man with thick dark hair and a booming voice, and it always comes as a shock seeing how old age and infirmity have curled him into himself, stealing not just his height and his hair but his spirit too. Initially, after his stroke two and a half years earlier, he was determined to regain his mobility and mind. He learned to walk again but, when he realised he'd never regain the use of his left arm, he fell into a deep depression. He withdrew into himself, refusing to go on the holidays Geraldine had dreamt of filling their retirement with, and made excuses not to leave the house or see friends. He became monosyllabic and sullen, a shadow of the man he'd once been. As his presence in the house diminished, Geraldine's grew larger and all the resentment, bitterness and anger she'd been smothering for years would come bursting out whenever she had a visitor. Any hope that Henry would recover – emotionally or physically – was extinguished when Jenna disappeared, and Fran barely recognises the man standing in the doorway, a cane clutched tightly in his right hand.

'Fran.' He nods, acknowledging her presence, then slowly, painfully, shambles across the living room to the sofa and sits down.

'How are you doing, Dad?'

'Same as always. Nothing changes.'

Her mother slams her book shut and stands up. 'I suppose you'd like a cup of tea, Frances.'

Fran raises an eyebrow in her dad's direction then follows her mother into the kitchen.

'Are you okay?' Fran asks, knowing she's not, as her mum clicks on the kettle and then reaches into the cupboard for two mugs.

'Yes. No.' Geraldine bangs two mugs on the work surface. 'No, I'm bloody not.'

In another life, with another mother, Fran would have placed her hand on Geraldine's shoulder or twisted her round for a hug. Instead, her hands hang loosely at her sides.

'Tom Wade?' she ventures.

'Of course bloody Tom Wade.' Her mother turns to face her. 'That bastard's only been out of prison for three days and he's already at it. Tweeting his bloody nonsense about compassion and regret and being . . . being . . . humbled and broken. Broken? What the hell does he know about being broken?'

'Mum . . .'

'And the replies . . . they're what make me more cross than anything. All his sheep-like followers falling for his crap.' She reaches around Fran and snatches an iPad from the kitchen table. 'Look!' She jabs at the screen several times. 'Listen to this one: *Please don't beat yourself up like this, Tom. You are a good man.* And this one: *It shows how honourable you are that you carry the burden of a terrible accident on your shoulders.* Terrible accident?' She looks up at Fran. 'No one stubbed their bloody toe. People died, for God's sake!'

'I know.' Fran gently takes the iPad from her mother's hands and returns it to the table. 'Stop looking. It's bringing everything back.'

'But it's not bringing *her* back is it? Jenna's still missing.'

The whistling of the kettle cuts through the strangled pause. 'I'll do the tea,' Fran says. 'You sit down.'

Even with her back turned to her mother she can feel the weight of her despair. It's like a car crusher, pushing her head into her shoulders, compacting her vertebrae, collapsing her organs, making her shrink.

'I've been googling,' Geraldine says as Frans sets the steaming cups of tea on the table, 'but I haven't found anything. You're going to have to help me.'

'Do what?'

'Find his address. You're an IT teacher, you should know where to look.'

Fran regards her mother over the lip of her mug. In her soft violet jumper, double string of pearls, puce painted nails, neat, white elfin hair style and full face of make-up, Geraldine still looks every inch the Colonel's wife.

'Why do you want Tom Wade's address?' she asks, although she's pretty sure she already knows the answer.

'To ask him where Jenna is.'

Fran puts down her mug.

'What?' Geraldine asks.

Fran says nothing, but a twitching muscle in her cheek betrays her.

'She's not dead,' Geraldine says. 'Don't start all that again. You can throw all the evidence in the world at me but I won't listen. She's my child. If she was dead I'd sense it. I'd know.'

'I looked for her. She's not—'

'Not that you'd understand, not being a mother yourself.'

It's a barb that was meant to stick but Fran doesn't so much as flinch. Her mother may see her childlessness as a sign of failure, of not fulfilling her feminine role in life but, for her, it's the opposite. Not having children was very much her choice.

'What difference will talking to Tom Wade make?' she asks. 'He's going to tell you the same as the police – Jenna jumped or fell off a cliff. She's not hiding, she's not being held against her will and she's not wandering around with amnesia.'

'How can you possibly—'

'It's been two years. If she was still alive she would have contacted us by now. Unless you said or did something that— Woah!' Fran leans back sharply as her mum flicks her wrist and hot tea leaps across the table. Most of it misses her but there are tannin-coloured splodges on her jumper, from her chest to her hips.

'My hand slipped,' Geraldine shouts as Fran rushes to the sink, grabs a dish cloth and soaks it in cold water. She dabs at the dark stains on her thin, cotton jumper then turns, the dish cloth still pressed to her stomach, to confront her mother.

'You blame me!' Geraldine shouts before Fran can speak. 'Everyone always blames me.' Far from looking repentant, Geraldine is sitting up taller in her chair, gripping the mug tightly. 'It's my fault Jenna's missing, my fault she went to Gozo, my fault you were bullied at boarding school, my fault Daddy had a stroke. It's all my fault.' Angry tears burn in her eyes. 'I raised you girls, I gave you the best start in life and I dedicated forty-eight years of my life to your father and his career and what did I get in return? A blissful retirement spent travelling the world and grandchildren playing at my feet when I return home? No, I got nothing. Nothing, nothing, nothing.'

Fran feels herself shrink further under the weight of her mother's self-pity. She's the size of a sixteen-year-old, a fourteen-year-old, twelve, ten, eight . . . She is eight years old, standing in the doorway of a large, Victorian school house, watching her mother walk away, down a driveway as wide as a river.

'Tears are for babies,' says the woman standing beside Fran. She's the size of a giant and smells like stewed plums. 'If Mummy looks back, give her a smile and a wave.' She clamps a hand to Fran's shoulder and digs too-sharp nails into the thin material of her new school blouse. 'This is harder for Mummy than it is for you.' Fran waits and she waits but her mother never looks back.

Chapter 5

Then

JENNA

As Jenna steps onto the minibus she scans around, looking for somewhere to sit. She keeps her gaze soft and unfocused to reduce the chance of Damian catching her eye. Everyone is paired up, most people staring silently out of the windows, the others chatting nervously. After the relative peace of the flight the volume level went sharply up when the plane touched down. Even before the seat belt sign went off, most of the passengers were up on their feet, scrabbling around in the overhead lockers for their belongings and filling the aisle; pressing up against each other, huffing and puffing, desperate to get off the plane. It was similarly frenetic at the luggage carousel; everyone desperate to grab, grab, grab and be gone. Jenna hung back by the toilets, watching and waiting. There was no hurry. Kate had said in her email that the coach to the ferry wouldn't leave until she had ticked everyone off her list.

Now, as Jenna continues to scan the minibus, a hand, waggling from side to side above everyone's heads, catches her attention.

'Over here!' It's Erica.

Jenna hurries through the bus and gratefully takes the empty space. As she pulls her handbag onto her lap she notices Damian, several rows ahead, craning round to look. Jenna slumps down in her seat.

'Thank you,' Erica says, her blue eyes sparkling beneath her clumpy mascaraed lashes, 'for being there for me on the plane. I feel a bit silly now, if I'm honest.' Her voice is clipped, sing-song, light.

'You were scared. I've been there.'

'Have you? You seem so together to me.'

Looking at Erica with her smooth twenty-something skin and glossy hair makes Jenna feel old. The others in the group look tired, uncomfortable and nervous, but Erica looks like she's about to embark on the most amazing adventure. But appearances are deceptive. Everyone on the bus is broken in some way. Even Damian. They wouldn't be going to the retreat if they weren't.

'Hello, everyone, and welcome to Malta!' Kate has appeared at the front of the minibus with Tom. 'I hope you all had a good flight. We've now got a twenty-minute journey across Malta to the ferry that will take us to Gozo. Take this opportunity to look out of the window and enjoy the wonderful view. If you have any questions you can ask me on the ferry.' She looks at Tom expectantly.

'Thank you, Kate. And thank you – all of you – for coming.' His gaze moves over the bus, resting momentarily on each of the group. When his eyes meet Jenna's she glances quickly away. 'I know many of you are feeling nervous and apprehensive. You're away from home, with a bunch of strangers, on the verge of a transformative experience. In seven days' time, when we're back on this bus heading to the airport, your outlook and your life will be forever changed. The burden on your soul will be lifted and when you arrive back in the UK you will be a brighter, happier, more positive person. There is nothing you cannot overcome. Nothing *we* cannot overcome' – again, his eyes rest on Jenna – 'if you put your trust in me and in each other.'

In the row to Jenna's right, Alan, a Welsh man in his early twenties with wildly curly hair and an infectious laugh, lets out a whoop of delight and punches the air.

'Quite.' Tom smiles. 'No more speeches from me for now. Sit back in your seats, enjoy the journey and don't forget to breathe.'

He takes his seat beside Kate and the driver starts the engine. Jenna gazes out of the window as the bus pulls away from the airport. The sky is a brilliant blue, dotted with soft fluffy clouds, and the May sun warms her skin through the glass. Malta is like no other European country she's ever visited. In the distance, the low domes of churches and the bent necks of huge metal cranes break up the clusters of cream stone, block-shaped houses. She feels as though she's speeding through a Greek or Arabic country, but all the English street names and supermarket signs make her feel like she hasn't left home. On either side of the bus the road is lined with squat green bushes, the leaves thick and spiky like cacti, and Catholic shrines inset into the low stone walls. She gets lost in the landscape, ignoring the familiar, concentrating on the unusual and new.

'I can't wait to get to Gozo,' Erica says, jolting Jenna out of her reverie. 'You know it's a mythical place? It's known as Calypso's Isle because apparently the enchantress Calypso kept Odysseus in bliss there for seven years.'

'I didn't know that.'

As Erica continues to warble on about Gozo and past retreats and how she's trying to come to terms with trust issues as a result of her father's multiple infidelities, Jenna tunes out. She hasn't got the headspace to deal with someone else's issues; she can barely cope with her own. Her phone vibrates in her bag and she subtly pushes it away, towards her knees.

'Someone's desperate to get in touch with you,' Erica says, as the phone continues to buzz.

Jenna doesn't reply. Instead, she opens the bag and tips the mobile towards her so only she can see the screen.

Twenty-one missed calls since she left Britain.

She turns the phone off.

Chapter 6

Now

KATE

Tom's black mood has filled the small flat like smoke. There isn't a single room where Kate can draw breath without tasting his anger. It's been five days since she posted the tweet and neither of them have had much sleep – not Kate in the bed and not Tom on the sofa. The first forty-eight hours were the worst. Journalists targeted their phones and then, when they turned them off, the doorbell. There is no doorbell now. Tom ripped it off the wall.

Kate sits on the bed staring at the long list of Google alerts for Tom's name. She's read dozens of news articles, hundreds of Twitter comments and as many emails as she can stomach but the SoulShrink email inbox has thirty-seven unread messages, all sent in the last seventy-two hours and all marked urgent. Her own email address has been targeted too, as has her

Facebook account, Instagram, Twitter and even her long-abandoned LinkedIn account. Everyone wants to talk to Tom – newspapers, magazines, breakfast shows, news programmes and documentary makers. And the requests aren't just coming from inside the UK. The German, Spanish, French, Maltese and American press are bombarding them too. The senders of the emails are trying every trick in the book to get Tom to talk to them: 'we want you to tell your side of the story', 'we're sympathetic to what you've been through', 'this is your opportunity to let the British public know that you're as much of a victim as the people who died.' Kate shuts her laptop, puts it on the bed beside her and drops backwards, arms spread, and stares at the ceiling. She knew this would happen; she factored it into her plan. What she didn't anticipate was Tom's flat-out refusal to talk to anyone. Why did she jump the gun and send that tweet without talking to him about it first? Why? She presses her hands to her face and breathes noisily through her nose. Because she's spent the best part of two years dreaming about restarting their lives and she couldn't wait a second more. And now she's screwed it all up.

'Kate?' She hears the floorboards creak under the thin carpet. 'We need to talk.'

She shakes her head, her hands covering the tears running down her temples into her hairline.

'We can't carry on like this.' She feels the mattress shift under her husband's weight as he sits on the edge of the bed. 'Kate, look at me.'

Still she refuses to remove her hands from her face. She has lost everything. The dream that life could return to normal has ended. This is her reality – this small damp flat, her mind-numbing job and her cold, resentful husband. She's been holding her breath for two years and her lungs have run out of air.

'I know you didn't do it to hurt me,' Tom says softly. 'You

were trying to help. I get it. But . . .' He sighs heavily. 'I hadn't even been out of prison for twenty-four hours. You don't . . . you have no idea where my head is at. I just needed some breathing space, Kate. To get used to this flat, to you, to being a free man again . . .' He tails off and, for several seconds all she can hear is the thumping of her pulse in her ears.

She slides her hands away from her eyes and turns to look at him. He's hunched over, his forearms on his thighs. She reaches a hand out to touch the curve of his back, an instinctive movement to comfort him, but her hand falls away.

'I'm sorry,' she says.

Tom says nothing.

'I wanted to help put things right.'

When he still doesn't respond she speaks quickly, desperately, filling the silence in the small room.

'There are still people out there who love you, who support you. It's not all hate.'

Her husband twists round so sharply it makes her jump.

'So?'

'So we start again.' She shifts position and sits up. 'There are still people out there who want your help.'

He stares at her, brow knitted, his eyes searching hers. 'I can't help anyone.'

'Of course you can. It's what you do.'

'What I *did*.'

'It wasn't your fault, Tom. They know that.'

'The jury thought otherwise.'

'They . . .' The words dry up on her tongue. They've had this discussion so many times she can't bear to go through it again. 'What the court decided and what the people who follow you think are two different things. They don't believe the stuff they read in the papers. They know you from your tweets, your YouTube videos and your events. They believe in you, they trust you.'

'Then they're idiots.'

She wants to shake him. To slap him. To crawl inside his skull and jump-start his brain. The despair in his voice and the despondency in his eyes is worse than the rage. At least when he was screaming at her and smashing the doorbell off the wall he looked alive. This man isn't her husband. He's not the person she fell in love with. He's a brittle, broken shell.

'So that's it?' She sits up. 'You're just going to give up? Not content with serving your time you're giving yourself a life sentence to go along with it?'

'No, I—'

'No? What are you going to do then, Tom? Stay locked up in this flat, hiding from the world while I go out and earn the minimum wage for doing data entry and filing divorce papers?'

'Kate—'

'You're going to abandon all those people who need you? Who look up to you? Because of an accident? Because of a terrible, tragic accident you're going to tell them to fuck off and deal with their shit alone because you're too busy licking your wounds to—'

'Stop it!'

A globule of his spittle lands on her cheek but she's so angry, so frustrated, so fucking incensed that she doesn't even pause to wipe it off. 'You saved people, Tom. You saved them from misery and guilt and suicide and pain and you're just going to walk away and let people suffer because you'd rather lick your wounds than—'

One second Kate is sitting on the bed, the next she's flat on her back, Tom's hands on her shoulders and his legs either side of her hips. As she gasps he presses his lips to hers and puts his tongue in her mouth, kissing her roughly, desperately, angrily. For a second, two, she is too shocked to respond. Then she kisses him back, moves her hands to the waistband of his jeans, slides her palms over his warm skin and pulls him closer. She looks up at her husband as he pushes himself inside her – to read his mood, to see if there's anger or passion in his eyes – but he's not looking at her. He's staring somewhere just above her head, his gaze unfocused, lost in a memory. She's seen that haunted expression before.

He's thinking about Jenna.

Chapter 7

Now – nine months later, February

FRAN

Fran sits on the closed lid of the toilet seat and takes her phone from her bag. There's a new text from her mum. All it says is *Well?* She scrolls back through the unanswered messages:

Do this for your sister.

You owe me, Fran. You owe Jenna too.

It's not like you've got anything else to do.

You can't let me die not knowing what happened to her.

She shakes her head as she rereads that one. Her mother might be seventy-three but, other than a broken hip, she's in robust health and, given the longevity of the Rotheram side of the family, she's unlikely to pop her clogs for at least another twenty years. Her mother's texts are emotional blackmail, pure and simple. Fran clicks on the link at the top of the tirade and shakes her head as Tom Wade's smiling face fills the top half of the screen.

In need of a psychological detox? it says beneath his photo. *Join motivational speaker and anxiety survivor Tom Wade aka SoulShrink in a beautiful, wooded hideaway in the heart of Snowdonia. Learn how to heal your trauma, free yourself from anxiety and face the future with optimism rather than fear.*

It's not the first time she's read that description but, unlike the last time, when she felt incredulous and angry, now all she feels is irritated.

She swipes back to her mum's messages and taps on the call icon. Geraldine answers almost immediately.

'Finally!'

No mention of the last time Fran visited, no apology for the outburst or swilling her with tea. It's the first time they've spoken. There have been texts, lots and lots of texts, but Fran's dad Henry was the one who broke the news, slowly and stiltedly, about Geraldine's fall.

'I'm at work,' Fran says. 'I was teaching. You can't just bombard me with texts and expect an immediate reply.'

'It was an emergency.'

Fran unlocks the door and checks for feet beneath the cubicle next door. 'You falling and breaking your hip was an emergency. The texts you just sent are emotional blackmail.'

'The retreat cost me two thousand pounds.'

'That was your decision. I told you not to book it.'

There's a sharp intake of breath then. 'How else was I going to get to speak to him?' She pauses long enough to let the unspoken sink in: *You didn't find his address on the internet.* 'And besides, it wasn't my fault I broke my hip. I've told your father on countless occasions to put his slippers on his side of the bed when he retires for the night. But does he listen? No. He probably left them at the end of the bed in the hope that I would trip and fall.'

'Well you didn't die, did you?' Fran catches sight of her reflection in the mirror and stops speaking. It's ridiculous – *she's* ridiculous. She's a fifty-one-year-old teacher having an argument with her seventy-three-year-old mother, during a free period at work, in the staff toilet.

'I haven't got time for this,' her mum snaps. 'Just tell me you'll go. I know you can make it. It's during your half term. I looked it up on the school website.'

Fran leans against the sink unwilling, or unable, to look at her own reflection for a second longer. 'Did it occur to you that I might want to spend half term doing something fun rather than going on some godawful retreat full of whingers, hypochondriacs and attention seekers? Not to mention—'

'That's not very nice.'

'What's not nice?'

'Calling people whingers and attention seekers. Jenna went on a retreat.'

Fran rubs a hand over her face. 'I know, Mum.'

'And we won't get anywhere if you walk in with that attitude.'

'You're assuming I'm going at all.'

'Fran.' In the pause that follows Fran feels the shackles of their fifty-one-year-old mother-daughter relationship wrapping around her heart. 'You need to find out what happened to your sister.'

'I tried to do that two and a half years ago. I went to Gozo. I—'

'You didn't speak to Tom.'

Fran's lips part but no sound comes out. They can't keep having the same conversation over and over again. Geraldine may have lost a daughter but Fran lost her sister. The last time she saw Jenna was in the school car park, two weeks before she disappeared. Fran had had a hideous day. She'd been told she'd be teaching ICT to Year Seven the next term (her least favourite year) and then she was reprimanded for rudeness when she objected. When she returned to her classroom she struggled to get the students to settle. It was windy outside, there was a storm forecast for later in the day and the kids were wide-eyed and super-charged. Their concentration spans were shot and they didn't complete even half the task she'd set for them.

When Fran returned to the staff room at the end of the school day she'd felt exhausted and flat. All she wanted to do was go home, run a bath and lose herself in a book. Instead, she had had an evening at the kitchen table ahead of her, with course work to mark and lessons to plan. She'd groaned as she checked her phone. She'd completely forgotten that Jenna had texted the previous evening saying she needed to talk, and now it was too late to cancel. Her sister was waiting in the car park, primed and ready to go to a nearby cafe – and not even a very nice one. Fran had picked up her bag, heavy with books and put it over one shoulder. Then she'd scooped up an armful of folders and slowly made her way down the stairs and out of the school. She saw Jenna immediately, hovering by her car. Fran's heart had sunk. It wasn't like Jenna, demanding a chat, and she couldn't remember the last time they'd met up alone. She didn't have the energy to listen to Jenna emotionally dissecting the end of her relationship with Nick. She'd overheard several barbed comments about him at Jenna's birthday dinner and it was obvious her sister wasn't over him. The only other thing she might want to discuss was their parents, and Fran certainly wasn't in the mood for that.

'Hi,' Jenna said, as Fran drew closer. She seemed as wired as the kids, stepping from foot to foot, her hands tapping lightly on her thighs. 'Good day at work?'

'Terrible, and it's only going to get worse.' Fran jiggled the folders in her arms. 'I need all this marked by the morning.'

Jenna held out her hands. 'Let me take them.'

'It's fine.' Fran heaved the folders onto the roof of the car then retrieved her key fob from her handbag and pressed the unlock button.

'Are you still okay to go for coffee?' Jenna asked as Fran loaded the book bag and folders into the boot. Fran had her back to her but she could hear the plaintive note in her sister's voice. She sighed, rather louder than she meant to, then closed the boot and rested a hand on the car.

'Is that a no?' Jenna's expression tightened. 'I came here all the way from East London and you're going to blow me off?'

'Can't you tell me now? Or give me a ring later? No, not later. I'll be marking and—'

'I can't believe this family.' Jenna steepled her fingers over her nose and took a long noisy breath.

Inwardly, Fran rolled her eyes. So it *was* about their parents.

'Is anyone dead?' she asked. 'Or dying?'

'No.' Jenna gave her an exasperated look.

'Then can't it wait?'

And that was it. Jenna had stalked off to her own car and Fran had shrugged, wondering why everything had to be such a drama. It was the last time she saw her sister alive.

'Well,' Geraldine says now, as Fran turns the cold tap off and on, checking to see if it drips. 'Are you going to go and confront Tom Wade or not?'

'What makes you think I'll get anything out of him?' There's a rough edge to her question but her resolve is fading faster than her irritation. She has no idea where her mother gets her energy from and it's sapping all of hers.

'Because you'll be able to look him in the eye,' Geraldine continues. 'You'll know if he's telling the truth or not.'

'Will you let this drop if I go to the retreat? You won't berate me for the rest of my life for asking the wrong questions or saying the wrong thing?'

There's a pause.

'Imagine you're me,' her mum says. 'And don't give up until he tells you the truth.'

'What if he refuses to talk to me about Jenna?'

'You keep on at him until he does. You're a teacher. It's your job to get people to do what you say.'

Chapter 8

Then

JENNA

Jenna stares in horror at the thick, gooey, red liquid covering most of the clothes in one half of her suitcase. 'What the hell?'

'What's wrong?' In an instant Erica is beside her. 'Oh!' She stares at Jenna with big round eyes. 'Is that . . .' She tentatively touches a finger to the liquid.

'Nail varnish.' Jenna picks up a white strappy vest top, the neckline sticky and red. 'It's ruined. And these . . .' She pulls out her favourite pair of jeans. 'And this.' A cashmere-blend grey jumper she's only had for two weeks.

She plucks out a few more items of clothing and throws them into the corner of the hotel room she's sharing with Erica. She might be able to save the jeans if she can find someone with nail varnish remover and some handwash but she'll have to throw away her jumper and several of her tops. She reaches back into the suitcase and, after some rummaging, removes a small glass bottle and a black lid with a brush attached.

'The top's come off,' Erica says. 'Was it the pressure do you think? Because you hadn't done it up tightly enough?'

'I wouldn't know,' Jenna says. 'It's not mine.'

'Sorry?'

'I'm a physiotherapist. I don't wear nail varnish.'

'How did it get into your case then?'

Jenna looks at her. 'I have no idea.'

There's no nail brush in the hotel room bathroom and, despite Jenna's best efforts, her fingertips are still tinged a deep pink as she steps out of the shower and pulls a towel off the rail. It's just her bloody luck that one of the airline's luggage handlers found a nail varnish bottle with a loosened lid on the ground and zipped it into her case. At least that's what she's assuming happened. The alternative is that one of the other guests at the retreat realised they had nail varnish in their hand luggage and, mistaking her case for theirs, popped it inside. But there was no mistaking her case for anyone else's. Even with all the suitcases squashed into the corner of the cafe where the guests met pre-check-in, her rainbow tag on the handle would have stopped most people from thinking it was theirs. Unless someone put it in there, lid loosened, on purpose? No. She dismisses the thought. She doesn't know these people. The only person she's really spoken to at length is Tom.

Erica, lying on one of the two single beds in the small bedroom, looks up from her book. Jenna feels her eyes following her as she crosses the room, plucks a jumper from her suitcase and pulls it on.

'Are we supposed to be somewhere? If you wait a sec I'll get my shoes on.'

Jenna pauses, her hand on the doorknob. 'No, no. You're good. Dinner isn't until eight.'

'So where . . .' Her roommate's gaze flits to the dressing gown in Jenna's arms. 'Oh, you're going to the spa.'

'Yes.' Jenna turns her face so Erica can't read her lie. 'I'll see you later. Enjoy your book.'

Jenna and Tom stroll along the dirt track that leads out of the hotel and along the cliff face. The sun is striping the sky red, purple and orange, and there's a chill in the air that makes Jenna wish she'd put a coat on over her jumper. She briefly considers putting her dressing gown on over her clothes then dismisses the thought. When she met Tom as planned, in the hotel lobby, he simply nodded and said, 'Great, follow me.' And so she did. He still hasn't told her what they're doing, or why, and she hasn't asked.

'I lied to Erica,' she says. 'About where I was going.'

Tom glances at her. 'Why?'

She tries to unpick it. Why did she lie? Because she knew Erica would ask her questions she didn't know the answer to? Because she didn't want her to tag along?

'I suppose I panicked.'

'Do you always lie when you panic?'

Affronted, she stops walking. 'What's that supposed to mean?'

'I wondered if it might be part of a pattern.'

'A pattern of what? Compulsive lying?' She stares at him, hurt and unsettled.

'Forget it.' She turns and marches back towards the hotel. As she walks she listens out for the sound of his trainers slapping against the mud and his voice calling her back. When she doesn't hear anything she turns sharply. Tom's not following her. He's not even looking her way. He's still strolling towards the cliffs, his dressing gown hanging from his arm. She wants to go back to her hotel room, crawl into her bed and pull the blankets over her head, but what would that solve? She needs to find a way to move forward, not stay in the same place.

'Wait up!' She runs after Tom, her trainers pounding the hard, dry mud.

She rejoins him, matching him step for step. His eyes flick towards her and he smiles.

'Are you laughing at me?' she asks, as they reach a rickety gate and Tom fiddles with the latch.

He opens the gate and gestures for her to pass through. 'Why would I do that?'

'Because I came after you.'

She feels as though he's toying with her, testing her somehow. It feels risky, being around him, but she's played it safe her whole life and it's only led to frustration and regret.

'Where are we going?' she asks.

He gives her a long look, his eyes searching her face. 'You need to trust me, Jenna. Can you do that?'

'I don't know.'

His smile widens. 'At least you're honest.'

With the sun so low in the sky Tom's face is all troughs and hollows: shadows beneath his eyes, under his cheekbones and bottom lip. As they walk she imagines drawing him, sliding charcoal over paper, leaving white highlights on his brow and the bridge of his nose. The thought surprises her. It's been a long time since she's felt the compulsion to pick up a pencil, paint-brush or piece of charcoal. The urge to create is normally smothered by the mundanity of everyday life: bills on the doormat, clients cancelling appointments, a leaky tap, a noisy neighbour, a bad night's sleep. She'd always wanted to become an artist – her GCSE art teacher said she showed real talent – but when she approached her parents about going to art school instead of sixth form they squashed the idea. 'It's not a proper job.' 'You need a job that uses your brain.' 'We didn't pay for Grammar school so you could spend a lifetime in debt.' She didn't fight them, as she assumed they knew best, but a small part of her died on the first day of the new A level term.

She drapes her dressing gown over her shoulders, shielding herself from the whipping wind. They've paused their walk a foot or so away from the edge of the cliff, and the hundred and twenty metre drop to the sea below. She wants to inch closer, to experience the dizzying sensation of being on the edge of the world but she doesn't trust herself to move. Tom, beside her, is gazing at the horizon, his pupils huge, dark pools beneath the low set of his eyebrows.

'We should carry on,' he says, 'before it gets too dark.'

He sets off again, following the curve of the cliff, stepping around pools of water, navigating the rocky terrain with confident steps, but his head remains bowed. Jenna remains on the cliff edge, watching him. His mood shifted when he was staring out to sea. He seemed troubled. She could feel it, as powerfully as the wind. As the distance between them widens she hurries to catch up.

They continue to walk in silence for several minutes and then Tom clears his throat.

'We're here.'

The cliff top path has led them down to a small pebbly cove, locked between two stony cliff faces. The sea is no longer a deep navy. Instead, the water is a soft turquoise, sea foam licking at the pebbles.

Jenna raises her eyebrows. 'That looks cold.'

Tom turns to look at her, a small smile playing on his lips. 'It is. Ready for a swim?'

Chapter 9

Now – February

KATE

Tom is nowhere to be found. He's not in the bedroom, the living area, the hot tub or the kitchen. Kate sweeps through the house, peering into empty guest bedrooms and communal areas, then steps outside. She follows the path up to the car park, fully expecting to see a space where her Volvo was parked, but it's still there. Where the hell is her husband? In less than two hours the first of the guests is going to arrive and she needs everything to be in place. It largely is. There's food in the fridge and the cupboards, easily enough for five days, and there are towels and welcome letters on each of the beds and toiletries in the en suite bathrooms. Everything that was on her list has been ticked off. She's even texted each of the guests (on Tom's behalf) saying how much he's looking forward to meeting them and reassuring them that it's okay to be nervous. But where's her bloody husband? He's the key to the retreat's success and he's gone AWOL with two hours to spare.

'Tom!' Kate heads back down the path at a trot, scanning the surroundings for any sign of life. Nothing. No Tom. She fishes her phone out of her pocket, taps a few icons, then presses it to her ear. Voicemail. What the hell is going on? Her mind swings between possibilities as she rounds the house and jogs through the garden – Tom's gone for a run, he's hurt himself, he's hitched a lift, he's . . . dead. She tries to push the thought away but her body has already reacted. Her pulse has quickened and her throat has tightened. She wouldn't be so worried if Tom wasn't so obsessed with the last retreat. The press may have moved on, but he still insists on searching Google daily, scouring each page for any mention of his name. He's punishing himself, using the internet to self-flagellate, and there's nothing she can do or say to stop him. It's why this retreat is so important. The guests aren't the only ones who have to learn how to heal.

'Oh for fuck's sake!' She spots three dark shapes at the far end of the field – two horses and a man, a thin chain link fence separating them from each other.

'Tom!' Kate cups her hands to her mouth but the house isn't called 'The Wind's Song' for nothing and her voice is whisked away.

She jogs towards her husband, her feet and calves caked in mud, her damp hair clinging to her scalp and her cheeks flushed pink, but Tom is oblivious. He's scratching the nose of a chestnut mare, murmuring something Kate can't hear. She steps closer, certain he must be able to hear her laboured breathing but his attention remains fixed on the horse. His attention is always elsewhere: TV, newspapers, his phone. He'll look at her if she's talking to him but he no longer glances over at her to see what she's doing or to check if she's okay. He used to look at her lustfully, his eyes bright, a playful smile on his lips, but she can't remember the last time he touched her, other than brushing past her in the cramped London flat. They haven't had sex since the week he left prison and even then he looked through her, imagining someone else.

'I've been looking for you,' she says.

Tom turns slowly, reluctant to abandon the mare. 'And now you've found me.'

He looks tired and drawn, his straggly shoulder length hair tucked behind his ears, the prison beard that she begged him to shave off wiry and unkempt.

'We've got less than two hours until our guests arrive.' She touches the damp sleeve of her coat that covers her watch. 'I thought you might want to . . . freshen up and get ready.'

'Get ready for what?'

'For the course.' She's not sure if he's being deliberately obtuse because he knows it winds her up but she's not going to rise to it.

'I'm not running the course.'

'Don't. Just . . . don't. I'm this far from breaking point and if you think—'

'I'm not running the course.'

'Of course you are. People are on their way here; they've paid!'

'Then text them, refund them, do whatever you have to do.'

He's deadly serious. There's not the hint of a smile on his face and no light in his eyes.

'I . . . Tom you can't do this. I've paid thousands to rent this place for the week, hundreds and hundreds on Facebook and Instagram adverts. I've literally . . . I've drained our bank account. There's nothing left. If we have to pay people back we're not even going to be able to pay the rent on the flat.'

'Where's it gone?'

'Where's what gone?'

'The money. We had over a hundred thousand pounds in savings when I went to prison.'

Kate searches his eyes. Is he . . . is he accusing her of something? Of squandering it? Of living the high life while he was inside?

'Don't you fucking dare,' she hisses. Tom's shrug and the impassive expression on his face make her want to slap him. 'When you went to prison I lost everything. My home. My friends. My job. My reputation. That money went on a tax bill, on paying off our credit cards, it went on a year's worth of mortgage. I tried everything I could to hang onto what we had. I—'

'You didn't work for a year after I went to prison.'

'Because no one would hire me! My name was mud. You're the one who went to prison but I paid too. God knows I paid. Christ, Tom. I can't . . . I can't believe you're saying this . . . doing this . . . after everything I've done.'

He shoves his hands deep into the pockets of his wax jacket and turns away, staring after the horses that have lost interest and wandered off. He mumbles something Kate can't hear.

'What was that?' She grabs his arm and turns him towards her, forcing him to look her in the eye. 'What did you just say?'

'I never wanted this. I've told you that over and over again, but you railroaded me and organised it anyway.' He looks back towards the house. 'Two people died. And you expect me to act like it never happened. To stand in front of broken, vulnerable people and ask them to trust me.'

'What happened was an accident, Tom!'

'You don't get sent to prison for accidents.'

'Well, you did! You didn't mean to kill those people, you didn't plan it. You're not a murderer. They wanted to make an example of you. They wanted to shame you, Tom. Like they shame celebrities that drink drive or hit their partners. But I've been doing research into that, into how you come back from public shaming. I listened to the audiobook by Jon Ronson and—'

'Fuck Jon Ronson!' Tom's spittle hits Kate on the cheek, the forehead, the side of her nose. 'And fuck you! I'm not doing this. It's not a business, Kate. It's not a money-making enterprise. It's not a way to get our old house back. This is people's lives we're talking about. And I'm not doing it. I'm never doing it again.'

Rage burns in Kate's chest as he pulls away from her and turns to walk back down the field.

'No.' She grabs his arm again. 'You don't get to walk away from me.'

'Don't I?' He glares down at her. 'And you're going to stop me how?'

'I'll . . . I'll . . .' Hot tears well in her eyes. She can't force him to do this. She can't make him do anything. Battling, arguing, cajoling, threatening – they'll all just make him fight back harder. She lets go of his arm and wipes the tears from her cheeks.

She hears a sound catch in Tom's throat. He was going to say something and stopped himself. She's staring at the wet, muddy ground but she can feel him watching her. The pause becomes loaded, swollen with emotion. Fresh tears spill down her cheeks.

'Give me one reason,' Tom says softly, 'one reason why I should do this that isn't to do with money or houses or building the business. Give me one reason.'

She takes a shuddering breath and raises her eyes to his. 'Because Jenna's dead, Tom. And I'm all you've got left.'

Chapter 10

Now

FRAN

Fran's audiobook ends at the exact moment she catches her first glimpse of Cân-y-gwynt and she can't help but gasp. She knew the retreat was luxurious – there's an indoor hot tub for goodness' sake – but it's the scenery, rather than the building itself, that wows her. The substantial nine-bedroom house is nestled in the hollow of a Welsh valley, surrounded by rolling hills painted in vivid shades of viridian, fern and violet and the grass is lush and long thanks to days of lashing January rain. She eases the car through narrow country lanes then parks up in a small car park, shielded from the house by tall, neat hedges, then makes her way down a small grassy path, through a white gate and down the gravel driveway to the house. It's a long low building – in an L shape apart from the porch in the centre – with a slate grey pitched roof. To the right of the porch is a wide window, revealing the hot tub inside. Anyone sitting in it has a lovely view of the lawn and hills beyond but the landscape isn't the only thing on view. No hot tub for Fran. If she wanted strangers to gawp at her flabby bits she'd have signed up for a naturist retreat, not a self-help one.

As she reaches for the door handle, the door swings open and a tall, well-dressed woman in her late thirties, with shoulder length glossy brown hair, shoots her a beaming smile. It's Kate. Fran recognises her immediately from the media coverage of Tom's trial.

'Hello, hello! Welcome to SoulShrink,' Kate says brightly. 'Tom said he thought he saw someone walking down the path.'

Fran imagines Tom Wade standing at one of the upstairs windows, staring out, his gaze fixed on the path; watching, waiting for the next gullible fool to join his cult of the lonely and desperate.

Kate holds out a hand. 'Lovely to meet you. I'm Kate.'

'Fra . . . Geri.' She could kick herself. She's been rehearsing this moment for the last four hours, convincing herself that she's Geraldine Rotheram (her mum was wily enough to book the retreat using her maiden name rather than her married name) and she's screwed it up at the first introduction. How the hell she's going to pull it off for the whole five days she doesn't know.

'Geri, of course.' If Kate caught the stumble she isn't letting on. 'How was your journey?'

'Fine.' Fran nods. She can't be arsed getting into the nightmare of the seemingly endless M40. 'Good. All good.'

'Excellent.' Kate shoots her another fake smile. 'Most of the other guests have arrived and are having tea and cake in the lounge but I'm sure you're desperate to see your room and freshen up.' She holds out a hand. 'Can I take your case?'

'No, it's fine.' Fran peers over Kate's shoulder. The interior of the building is largely white walls, oak beams, paintings of landscapes and what looks suspiciously like laminate flooring. It's pleasant and clean but Fran's got no intention of staying for the full five days. Her aim is to complete her mission as quickly as she can so she can salvage her half term. 'No sign of Tom? I was looking forward to meeting him.'

'Tom's . . . just getting a few things together. You'll meet him later on. I know he's really excited about meeting you all.'

'Right.' Fran matches Kate's smile then quickly adopts a more miserable expression. This is a retreat for depressives and anxious types after all. She can't look *too* cheery.

'Okay then.' Kate turns. 'If you'd like to follow me.'

Fran's behind has barely hit the cushion of the armchair when the overweight, bespectacled, curly haired young man sitting beside her reaches out a hand. 'Hello, I'm Phoenix. Pleased to meet you.'

'Geraldine.' Mentally Fran congratulates herself on getting her fake name right, then realises she was so fixated on getting it right she completely failed to register his name. 'Sorry, what was your name again?'

'Phoenix.'

'Like the city or the bird?'

'The bird.' When Phoenix smiles his eyes almost completely disappear beneath the rise of his cheeks: two dark slits hidden behind strangely old-fashioned glasses. 'The one that rose from the ashes. From Norse mythology.'

'Greek,' Fran says, then, spotting the blush of colour that's appeared at the base of his throat, adds, 'Although there are some particularly fascinating creatures in Norse mythology including Nidhug the dragon that feeds on corpses and Sleipnir, an eight-legged horse. It's very easy to confuse mythical creatures. I frequently got them confused as a . . .' She tails off before she says the word child. Phoenix is in his early twenties and she's fairly certain he wouldn't appreciate the comparison. She needs to steer this conversation onto a decidedly less awkward track.

She smiles warmly at Phoenix. She's met a number of oddly named children in her thirty years as a teacher. Her particular favourites are Aero (which always makes her think of chocolate), Jubilee (which makes her think of the Queen), Paizlee (which makes her skin itch because of the incorrect spelling) and, many moons ago, a poor child named Gordon Bennett.

'Are your parents hippies?' she asks.

'No.' He presses his glasses against his nose and clears his throat. 'Why do you ask?'

'It's an unusual name.'

The blush on Phoenix's neck creeps up to his jawline and Fran shifts in her seat. Now what's she said to make the poor lad feel uncomfortable?

'If I tell you a secret . . .' Phoenix leans a little closer as someone else – a tall man with a stoop – walks into the lounge area and slumps into an armchair. 'Will you keep it to yourself?'

Fran feels a little frisson of glee. She can't remember the last time someone shared a secret with her. 'Of course.'

'Phoenix isn't my real name. I changed it. Not by deed poll but I will, maybe when I get back home after this.'

'How does it feel?' Fran asks, admiring his gumption, then swiftly realising he's not the only one to have walked into the retreat with a pseudonym.

'Powerful,' Phoenix says. 'Well, it did, but now I feel a bit' – he swallows again – 'stupid.'

'Oh no. You mustn't feel that. It's a wonderful name and you must embrace it. What was your – if you don't mind me asking – what was the name you were known by before?'

Phoenix looks down at his hands. 'You'll laugh at me.'

'I most certainly won't.'

He glances up, looking at her from over his glasses, then whispers in her ear.

'Oh.' She presses her lips together, steadies herself and then says, 'Well, I think you suit Phoenix much better.'

'Thank you, that's the nicest thing anyone has said to me in a long time.'

He slumps back in his chair, relief flooding his face. Fran exhales softly and glances around the room as more people enter and fill the remaining chairs. She's not quite sure how she managed to save that conversation. It's a conundrum she can't solve – how she can be such a great teacher but such a terrible conversationalist. She can command a classroom like no one else, simplify complicated concepts and field questions. She can juggle different levels of ability, slow her pace if she starts losing students and analyse the mood of the room. But when it comes to social interaction with anyone over the age of eighteen she either manages to insult them, misunderstand them or else she finds herself in such an awkward conversation that her only recourse is to feign a coughing fit and swiftly leave the room. Not that she could do that now. Kate is standing in the archway that leads to the communal kitchen and, standing next to her, smiling nervously and twisting his hands together, is the man Fran has been waiting to meet. Tom Wade has finally appeared.

Chapter 11

Now

KATE

Kate sits forward in her armchair, her clipboard in her hands, watching carefully as Tom moves around the room, shaking hands, asking names and welcoming the participants to the retreat. It's a scene she's watched dozens of times before but her attention wasn't as focused as it is now, her grip on her notes never as tight. When she sent out the newsletter, tweeted the details, and posted the Facebook adverts, she felt sick with anticipation. She was braced for a deluge of negativity, trolling and abuse – and she certainly received plenty – and it wasn't until EventBrite forwarded her the first flurry of bookings that she started to relax. By the end of the first day there were twenty-seven confirmed bookings in her inbox; nowhere near the numbers Tom had attracted at the height of his career but it would be enough for them to cover the costs of a retreat and make nearly ten thousand pounds of profit. She wouldn't have to worry about paying the rent for six months and there would be enough left to plough into more advertising. She might even be able to hire a tech company to help whitewash the internet of the worst of the articles about Tom, or a PR firm to help repair his damaged reputation.

However, when she looked through the bookings she noticed an unusually high number of participants who'd registered home addresses in London, which was odd as her Facebook adverts had targeted people living less than two hours from the retreat. She recognised one name immediately – a tabloid journalist who'd hounded them after Tom was released from prison. She cancelled his booking then set about checking the other names. She cross checked the rest of the names in her inbox, found two more journalists and cancelled their bookings too. A Google search revealed three more. But what of the remaining twenty-one people? How many were journalists using pseudonyms? She spent hours searching social media, looking for Facebook pages and Twitter accounts, trying to ascertain who was a 'normal person' and who was trying to sneak under the radar. Her snooping reassured her that ten people on her list were safe – their Facebook pages were open to the public and she could see photos of family gatherings, gripes about the road closures and boring, mundane updates about work, health and the weather. That left eleven with question marks against their names. She emailed them, asking them to provide her a photo 'for her records' and ran them through a Google image search. The results didn't reveal any more journalists but she did discover a psychologist and an author who'd both registered using pseudonyms. She cancelled both bookings. Of the nineteen people left only nine of them paid. It's still enough to give her and Tom a few months of financial freedom but she's still worried there's a journalist in the room, someone who slipped through her net.

Kate adds to her notes as Tom moves around the room.

Joy O'Brien – small and round, rainbow jumper, gave Tom an adoring look as he approached her, stood for a hug when he offered his hand. Looks delighted to be here.

Peter Kitson – thin man in his early sixties, openly scowled when Tom hugged the woman beside him. Possibly journalist?

Priyanka Singh – Early sixties. Bereaved. Lonely. Wouldn't hurt a fly.

Geraldine Rotheram – reserved, sceptical look on her face as she watched Tom work the room. Looks ill at ease. Journalist?

She doesn't bother making notes on Renata Scanlon, Phoenix Bloom or Damian Strang, all of whom have been on previous retreats and certainly aren't journalists.

Kate continues to write as Tom greets the final two guests, noting down anyone who is gazing around the room as though they're mentally making notes. As Tom finishes speaking to the last guest Kate tries to settle herself. The chances are she's being paranoid and, even if there is a journalist in their midst, what are they going to say? There won't be any scandal or deaths at this retreat and anyone who tries to dig around in the past will find themselves given very short shrift.

'Right!' Tom settles himself into the armchair beside her. 'Thank you all for coming. I'll just give you a bit of background about me before we get going. Apologies to anyone who has heard this before, but I know a lot of you are feeling very vulnerable right now and it's only fair that I open up too. So . . .' He takes a slow, steady breath. A silence falls in the room.

'The elephant in the room,' Tom continues. 'Let's address it straight off. Nine months ago I was released from prison after serving a sentence for the deaths of two people.'

Kate scans the faces around the room and spots expressions of sympathy, awkwardness and sadness. They're the reactions that she'd expect but two of the guests are acting unusually. Peter, the older man, is sitting forward in his seat, staring intently at Tom, and Geraldine, the woman with the short hair in her early fifties, is frowning. She adds a star next to both of their names then tunes back in to what her husband is saying.

'I am responsible for those deaths,' Tom says. 'I was overconfident, too sure of myself, too trusting in the process. I made mistakes – terrible, terrible mistakes – and, as a result of my failings, two wonderful, kind, beautiful people are no longer with us: Tim Chambers and Bessie Grange. I failed them and I failed their families. I may have left prison but I will never be free of my guilt. I swore to myself that I'd never run another retreat but . . .'

A beat passes, then another. Several of the guests shift in their seats. Tom doesn't notice. He's gazing past them, out of the window, at the stretch of green lawn and the mountains beyond it. Kate clears her throat. The guests are swapping glances, growing increasingly uncomfortable with the prolonged silence. She puts her hand on Tom's arm and gives it gentle squeeze. He doesn't react. She's going to have to say something if he doesn't speak soon.

'But my mind was changed,' Tom says, making her jump. He taps the back of her hand then subtly pushes it away. 'I failed Tim and Bessie but there are still people who need my help. You want my help and if I can change even one life then what I'm doing, what I did, isn't in vain.'

He pauses to take a sip of water from the glass on the table beside him. Kate smiles encouragingly but he doesn't meet her eye.

'My own journey,' Tom continues, returning the glass to the table, 'began when I was involved in a car accident and the other party involved, a man around my age, was paralyzed from the neck down. I took time off work. I struggled to get out of bed and, when I did, I'd only make it as far as the living room. Sometimes I watched television, listlessly, not really taking it in. Sometimes I'd just lie on the sofa and stare at the ceiling. I stopped seeing my friends, I stopped exercising, I ate junk food – shovelling it down without tasting it – and then I stopped sleeping. I began to dread going to bed because I was afraid of the thoughts that would whirl around my head. I'd stay on the sofa until five or six a.m., staring at the TV, only sleeping when exhaustion finally claimed me. But I wouldn't sleep for long. I'd get three, maybe four hours sleep, tops, and then I'd be wide awake again.'

Kate spots several of the guests nodding, empathising with his story. He's pulled them back in, his uncomfortable pause forgotten. Joy, on the end, has her elbows on her knees, her face in her hands, gazing at him adoringly.

'One day,' Tom continues, 'I woke up and my left foot was numb and my calf was tight. I assumed I'd slept on it awkwardly, but the sensation remained all day. The next day I woke up with a numb right hand. I Googled my symptoms and when Multiple Sclerosis showed up on the first page I started to worry. I tried not to panic but, over the course of a week, my left leg became progressively weaker, collapsing under me several times a day. When I abruptly lost the vision in my right eye I made an emergency appointment to see my GP. She listened as I described my symptoms then examined me and ordered a blood test. I barely slept for the five days it took to get the test results back. I knew, from Googling, that the blood test wouldn't diagnose MS, it was to rule out other conditions, but I couldn't shake the feeling that there was something seriously wrong with me. My bloods were normal, my GP told me when she finally rang, but she wanted to refer me to a neurologist. I burst into tears. One day I was a young, successful, healthy man and the next I was facing an uncertain future alone with a degenerative condition. To say that was the lowest moment of my life would be an understatement.' He pauses, his face flushed with emotion. His audience is enrapt, staring intently at him, waiting for him to continue speaking. Kate feels a swell of pride. She wrote this speech and taught him how to deliver it, how to vary the tone of his voice and the pace for maximum impact. And now he inspires trust in people within seconds of meeting them.

'So,' Tom continues, 'I met with the neurologist. She examined me, testing my eye movements, the strength in my limbs, my balance, coordination, speech and reflexes. By this point I was walking with a stick and one side of my body was numb. She organised an MRI scan which was noisy and claustrophobic and, while I lay inside it, I prepared myself for the worst. All I could hope was that my condition, that had progressed so suddenly, would now slow. Afterwards, the neurologist gave me her diagnosis.' He pauses to gaze around the room, locking eyes with each of the guests. Kate knows how Tom's story ends but, even so, she can't help but hold her breath.

'She said there was nothing wrong with me,' Tom says. 'I didn't have MS. The MRI was normal and the physical exam had revealed that, despite the numbness in my left leg, my reflexes were normal. She asked if I had considered whether my symptoms might have a psychological cause.'

An audible gasp from Phoenix gives Kate a little jolt of joy. There's something so satisfying about the shock on the faces of the participants at this point in Tom's story.

'I was horrified,' Tom continues, 'and bloody angry. I could barely walk and there she was, accusing me of faking it. I demanded a lumbar puncture – something I'd read about online – and a second opinion, but the doctor was resolute. I showed no signs of muscle wastage and my reflexes were normal. What I needed wasn't a neurologist but a psychiatrist.'

Priyanka snorts in indignation.

'That was my reaction too,' Tom says, smiling kindly at her. 'So I arranged to see a second neurologist and begged for a lumbar puncture. By this point I was occasionally going blind in one eye.'

There's an audible gasp from several of the clients and Kate forces herself to look down at her hands.

'But again,' Tom says, 'it came back as normal. By this point I was at my wits' end. I was becoming progressively weaker and weaker every day and yet every doctor I saw was telling me that there was nothing actually wrong with me.'

Geraldine, sitting on the very edge of her seat, coughs lightly and raises a hand.

'Yes.' Tom nods at her to speak.

'That's not strictly true, is it?' Geraldine says. 'You were suffering from somatic symptom disorder which is a recognised mental health illness.'

Kate suffocates a sigh. Geraldine's just ruined the punchline to Tom's story.

'You're right,' Tom says with a smile. 'That was what was wrong with me and it's something the psychiatrist explained when I hit my lowest point and agreed to meet with her.'

'Quite,' Geraldine says. 'Then you started a self-help group with fellow sufferers in order to chat about your illness and you inadvertently became the group leader.'

Tom laughs: a proper, hearty, belly deep laugh. 'You've just shaved a good ten minutes off my talk there. If you needed a refreshment break you only needed to ask.'

A frown settles on Geraldine's forehead. 'I don't need the loo if that's what you're implying. I just—'

'Excuse me.' The round woman in the rainbow jumper on the end of the row leans around the man sitting next to her to glare at Geraldine. 'We've paid to be here and I'd like to hear what Tom has to say. It's rude to interrupt.'

Geraldine raises her eyebrows. 'Well, you just interrupted me.'

'Ladies, please!' As Tom holds up his hands in friendly protest, Kate sits up straighter. There's been friction between participants in previous retreats but never this early on.

'Ladies? Seriously?' Geraldine transfers her glare from Joy to Tom. 'Instead of sitting there patronising us maybe you could answer a question?'

Joy attempts to interrupt but Tom holds up a silencing hand. 'What's your question, Geraldine?'

'You mentioned that two people died at the retreat in Gozo.'

'That's right.'

Tom glances at Kate, panic in his eyes, but before she can help him Geraldine asks another question.

'What about Jenna Fitzgerald?'

Chapter 12

Now

FRAN

A shaft of bright sunlight creeps through the partly drawn curtains and illuminates Tom's face, spotlighting his discomfort. He rubs his lips together, licks them and swallows, his sharp Adam's apple clearly visible above the navy curve of his crew-necked jumper. Something inside Fran tightens. He knows something. It's radiating off him like heat. As she continues to wait for an answer she becomes aware of a sharp pain in her left arm and turns at the exact moment Phoenix jabs her with his index finger.

'What?' she snaps.

He holds a hand to his mouth, masking his lips from everyone else in the room. 'Why are you asking about Jenna?'

Fran tuts and looks back towards Tom who's having his own sotto voce conversation with his wife. Fran clears her throat. If they think she's going to let this drop then they're very much mistaken.

'Geraldine.' Tom rises from his chair. 'Shall we have a little chat?' He gestures towards the front door.

Fran gets up too then pauses. She's not sure she wants to be alone with such an odious, slimy excuse of a man. She'd much rather have this out in public where everyone can witness him sweating and stuttering but, before she can object, Kate announces that it's time for a refreshment break and suddenly everyone is on their feet and heading to the kitchen area.

'Geri.' Phoenix taps her on the arm, making her shudder. What is it with total strangers and their constant need to touch?

'What is it?' she snaps again.

'Are you okay? You're trembling.'

She lifts a hand. Her fingers are tremoring as though she's playing an allegretto tune on a piano. But it's not nerves that have given her the shakes, it's anger.

'Would you like me to get you some water?'

Fran's rage softens. 'That's very kind of you, Phoenix, but I'll be perfectly all right.'

'Have you got a coat?' Tom appears beside her. 'It's a nice day but it's cold.'

Fran plunges her hands into the pockets of her navy blue fleece. 'This will suffice. Thank you.'

She follows him out of the front door then matches him step for step as he rounds the house and heads towards a gate that leads to an eight or nine acre meadow. The grass is knee-high, speckled with yellow primroses and delicate white snowdrops. She grimaces as she steps into the meadow and her feet sink into the damp earth. The mud's going to ruin her favourite purple suede boots but she's not going to suggest to Tom that they turn back. Not yet.

Tom inhales deeply through his nose, holds his breath and

exhales noisily. Fran doesn't turn to look at him. He can indulge in that cleansing breaths idiocy as much as he likes but he's not going to convince her that he's some kind of spiritual guru.

But he had convinced Jenna. There was something her sister was desperate to talk about, that windy May afternoon in the school car park. Had she shared it with Tom instead?

Tom runs a hand through the grass, catching the flower heads between his fingers. 'What do you know about Jenna?'

'That she killed herself, in Gozo.'

Tom doesn't immediately answer. He keeps walking, keeps stroking a hand through the grass.

'Jenna was troubled.' His tone is softer, less defensive.

'In what way?'

'I can't tell you that I'm afraid. What we discussed is confidential.'

Damn. Bloody client confidentiality. She should have known he'd pull that one out of the bag.

'But was she suicidal? In your opinion?'

'She wasn't—' Tom catches himself. 'Do we ever know how someone else is feeling? Really?'

'I would have thought the leader of a self-help retreat would know exactly how his guests were feeling.'

Tom stops walking. 'What's all this about?'

The intensity in his gaze makes Fran's guts tighten. 'What do you mean?'

'I'm not stupid, Geraldine. If that is your real name.'

She's almost impressed. Has he figured it out? Maybe Jenna told him their mother's name. Or maybe he's done some digging of his own.

'What paper do you work for? From the way you speak and dress I'm guessing *The Daily Mail* or *The Telegraph*.'

Horrified, Fran makes a mental note to overhaul her entire wardrobe the moment she gets back home.

'I'm not a journalist,' she says. 'I'm a teacher. ICT. Ask me anything about data logging, digital imaging, networks or—' She catches herself mid-sentence. By rushing to defend herself from Tom's accusation she's inadvertently blown her cover story. She's supposed to be a widowed ex-receptionist. But it's too late for her to back pedal now.

Tom shakes his head dismissively. 'If you were a journalist you'd have prepared a cover story, including swatting up on your computer knowledge.'

'Ah, but there's a difference between swatting up and practical knowledge. Talking of which, your website is antiquated. Whoever built it did a terrible job of the CSS, the layout is all over the place and it's not responsive or accessible.'

'Okay.' Tom holds up his hands. 'Okay. Fine. Answer me this then; why are you, an ICT teacher, so interested in what happened to Jenna?'

Fran's ready for this question. It's the one part of her cover story that she hasn't forgotten. 'She was my physiotherapist. When I turned up to an appointment the reception told me that Jenna had died, unexpectedly, during a wellness retreat abroad. Then I saw the papers.' She takes a breath, her mind working frantically as she tries to reconcile her cover story with her outburst earlier. 'The reason I spoke up earlier, during the speech, was because . . . because Jenna should be remembered. She died in Gozo, too.'

The tension in Tom's face and the suspicion in his eyes softens. 'Of course,' he says, his voice rich with compassion. 'Of course she should. And I'm so sorry I didn't mention her. I suppose . . . I suppose I didn't want the new guests to think too much about suicide. Many of the people who come to see me are really very troubled.'

To Fran's horror, Tom places a hand on her shoulder and gently squeezes it. 'Outwardly, you seem very together, Geraldine, but that's an illusion, isn't it? You lock your emotions away and they boil within you and then explode in angry outbursts. It's how you push other people away.'

I don't *use* anger, Fran thinks. I *am* angry. People are imbeciles. You in particular.

'Gosh,' she says. 'You're very insightful.'

Tom smiles down at her. It's the type of gaze a parish priest might give an elderly parishioner offering up a soggy Victoria sponge.

'It would help give me' – Fran clears her throat – 'closure, if you could tell me the circumstances leading to Jenna's death.'

Tom's hand falls away from her shoulder. 'I'm not sure that would be—'

'Please.'

He puts his hands in his pockets and his gaze drifts to his feet. 'She was . . . troubled, as I said. But she was' – he swallows – 'a good person, a very good person. Funny, strong, opinionated . . .'

They're not the words Fran would have used to describe her sister. She'd have chosen obedient, neurotic, bland and infuriating. They were as different as it was possible for two sisters to be, although, Fran concedes, she might share the 'infuriating' trait.

'She was excited about the sweat lodge,' Tom continues. 'She happily shaved her head.'

Fran read about that in the papers – all the guests stumbling around the field and hotel grounds in swimsuits and bare feet, disorientated and dehydrated, their heads shaved. It was all part of the ritual apparently, the head shaving. They were abandoning their old selves, ready to be 'reborn' later.

'She lasted until almost the end,' Tom continues, 'but something prompted her to leave.'

'*Something*?'

He shakes his head. 'I . . . I couldn't say.'

Couldn't, Fran thinks, or won't?

'Did anyone go after her?' she asks.

'I don't know. I was . . . I had a duty of care to the others.'

His first lie. He didn't look after anyone. He fled at the first sign of trouble. So much for his *duty of care.*

'When did you realise she was missing?' she asks, knowing full well that he wasn't the one to raise the alarm.

'Kate . . . Kate rang me. She told me there was no sign of Jenna but her' – his voice thickens with emotion – 'her flip-flops had been found at the edge of the cliff and . . .' The words dry up and he turns away, swiping a hand under his eyes.

Crocodile tears. He did the same thing when he was interviewed outside the court before his trial. The man's a sociopath, mimicking the response he thinks is expected of him. It's ridiculous. She's wasting her time. Jenna took her own life. And this fraud of a man couldn't care less.

She looks at him, now openly sobbing, and shakes her head. She should lambast him for what he's doing, extorting money from the vulnerable and the mentally unwell but she can't be bothered. She wants to get back to her room, pack up her stuff, drive back to London and spend the rest of her weekend playing her violin and tending to her plants. The sooner she puts the whole sorry charade behind her the better. What a waste of bloody time.

She stalks back down the field, the sound of Tom's sobs still ringing in her ears, and lets herself back into the house. The others are gathered in the living room area, clutching mugs of tea and handfuls of biscuits. Phoenix calls her name but she doesn't acknowledge him. She continues on past the kitchen, through the corridor and into the bland, featureless room that's supposed to be her bedroom for the next five days. She hasn't unpacked much, just a book, her washbag, earplugs, a small reading light and her hypothyroid medication. She scoops them up from the bedside table, carries them over to her suitcase and places them neatly inside. She zips the suitcase up and is halfway to the door when she remembers she's left her mobile phone behind. It's on the carpet, near the head of the bed, plugged into the only socket she could find in the room. She looks at the first line of her mum's message – *Tell me EVERYTHING* – then spots a small, white folded piece of paper lying on the carpet. She unfolds it, expecting to find a shopping list or a cleaning rota but what's written inside isn't a stranger's idle musings.

> *Fran, Don't trust a word Tom tells you. Your sister DID NOT kill herself. Go for a walk after dinner and I'll tell you everything.*

Chapter 13

Then

JENNA

Jenna shivers beneath the soft fluffy cotton of her dressing gown as she steps carefully over the rocky waste ground, Hotel Ta' Cenc in her sights. The moment she gets back to her room she's going to jump into the shower and she's going to stay there until she's regained the feeling in her hands and feet. Tom, beside her, doesn't appear to be feeling the cold at all. He's talking nineteen to the dozen about the benefits of cold water swimming and how it's been clinically proven to help ease, or even cure, depression. She enjoyed their swim – when she finally plucked up the courage to jump into the icy cold water – if *enjoyed* was the right word to describe her breath catching in her throat, her heart pounding violently and every millimetre of her skin singing with pain. Tom treaded water beside her as she fought to pull air into her lungs, telling her not to panic, urging her to steady her breathing.

'Trust me,' he told her. 'You can do this. You're not going to die.'

And as Tom repeated his instruction her breathing returned to normal and her heartbeat settled. As he nodded at her, smiling with satisfaction, she threw back her head and shouted 'Fuckkkkk!' at the sky.

Tom laughed. 'That was my reaction too, the first time I went cold water swimming. Come on, let's swim.'

So she did. She matched him stroke for stroke as they headed into the choppier water, away from the stillness of the bay. They continued to swim, neither of them saying a word, until Jenna flipped onto her back and stared up at the pink-streaked clouds overhead.

'This is incredible and ridiculous all at the same time.'

Tom snorted softly. 'Do you feel better than you did on the plane? Less panicky?'

She twisted back onto her front, fighting to control her chattering teeth. 'All I can think about is how cold I am!'

'Good. Stop thinking and reconnect with your body. Mindfulness at its best.'

'Couldn't we meditate by a fire instead?'

He laughed then flipped onto his back, spreading his arms wide. He wasn't shivering and shuddering like her but the skin on his arms was pale and pinched. Jenna watched, hands sculling under the water, legs frantically kicking, as his body gently rose and fell with each gently undulating wave.

She'd got him wrong, she realised, heart sinking. He wasn't interested in her, not the way she thought he was. He was treating her like a client, as he was supposed to. The reason he'd touched her arm on the plane and whispered in her ear that they should meet later wasn't to show her how attracted he was to her, it was to reassure and ground her. They were bobbing around in the sea at sunset, not because it was a romantic rendezvous but because he felt she needed help. He was probably planning on doing cold water swims with all of the guests. No wonder he was so surprised when she'd admitted lying to Erica about where she was going.

'You're hard to read.' There was a hard note to her voice, a biro scribble over the soft pencil mark of her feelings.

'Am I?'

'Yes.'

'Do you try to read everyone you meet?'

She thought about the clients that visited her physiotherapy clinic, their expressions as strained as their bodies. She thought about Nick, her ex-boyfriend, carrying the stress of a tough day at work into a restaurant or pub, her friends' forced smiles when someone they didn't like walked into a room, her mother's exasperated eye roll, her father's stunted emotions and Fran's obvious discomfort when someone reached for a hug. 'Of course,' she said. 'Doesn't everyone?'

'You'd be surprised.'

'Do you have many psychopaths on your retreats?'

He laughed then twisted in the water so he was upright again. 'We need to get out before hypothermia sets in.'

She looked back towards the shore. 'That's fine by me.'

'Do you feel ready to talk?' Tom asks now. The sea is far behind them, the cliff tops too. In a couple of hundred metres they'll be back at the hotel.

Jenna stops walking and looks at him. The sun is so low in the sky the landscape, and Tom, have taken on a monochrome hue. 'About what?'

'You were trying to tell me something on the plane, and we were interrupted.' His eyes are so soft and compassionate that, despite her shame at mis-reading the situation, she feels drawn back in.

She pulls her dressing gown tighter around her damp skin

and tucks her hands under her armpits. 'Do you remember what I talked to you about after the London seminar? When I pulled you to one side?'

He nods. 'Of course.'

'Well . . .' She rubs the frozen toes of one flip-flopped foot against the back of her calf. 'I confronted my mum, like you said I should.'

'And?'

'She denied it, then she got angry, then she admitted it and . . .' She presses her hands to her face and looks at him over the top of her fingertips. 'I just . . . I can't believe it. I can't believe what she told me. I . . . I can't match the mental image I have of my parents with what she said.'

'You think she's lying?'

'No. I don't. And that's the . . . that's the thing that's really messing with my head. I believe her. I believe what she told me but I don't know who she is anymore, who Dad is. They feel like strangers. I don't know even who I am anymore.'

'You're still you.'

'No.' She shakes her head. 'I'm really not.' She stares up at him, this tall, handsome man with his wavy hair slicked back from the sea and his compassionate eyes, and she presses her lips together. She's going to cry. She can feel it, all the anger and frustration she's kept bottled up for so long, swelling inside her, desperate to escape. She hates that she's a crier. She wishes she was the type of woman to lash out, to scream and rage, instead of a weak, sobbing mess.

'What would make you feel better?' Tom asks.

'Nothing.'

'How about if you let it all out?'

'No.' She held it together on the plane, on the minibus, in her hotel room, in the sea. As long as she doesn't talk about how she's feeling she can control her emotions. But he's making it so hard for her. He's looking at her so sympathetically, acting like he cares.

'Scream,' he says. 'Shout. Hit me. Let it out, Jenna.'

'No.'

'Why not?'

'That's not the kind of person I am.'

'And how's that worked out for you?'

She hits out at him then, before she can talk herself out of it; shoves him hard in the chest with both hands.

Tom doesn't flinch.

'Do it again.'

'No.'

She does it again.

'Who are you angry with, Jenna?'

'You.' She shoves him again, as hard as she can and feels satisfaction burn in her chest as he's forced to take a backwards step.

'No you're not.'

'Yes I am.' She barrels into him again, and again and again, until her forearms ache and her breath is in her throat and her head is throbbing and then she collapses against him – exhausted, empty, spent. As he wraps his arms around her she wants to scream at him that she hates him for making her hit him but she's crying so much she can't speak.

'Okay?' Tom asks as they pass through the gate to the hotel and make their way towards the stone chalet bedrooms.

Jenna nods mutely.

'Jenna?'

She feels spent, as though every ounce of energy in her body has been drained away. 'I'm okay. I'll—'

'Tom?' a woman calls. She's standing on the path between the first two chalets.

'Kate.'

Jenna hears the tension in Tom's voice and when she looks at him his body is tense, as though primed for a fight.

'She sounds pissed off . . .' she begins, but Tom touches her arm, silencing her.

'I'll see you later, at dinner.'

He walks off before she can reply, heading for Kate. As he gets closer he steps off the path, swerving around her, but Kate grabs him by the wrist, forcing him to stop. Jenna watches their body language as they talk: Kate's staccato hand movements and Tom's dismissive shrug. They're arguing. Kate's voice grows louder. 'We'll talk about this in your chalet,' she snaps then she yanks at his arm and pulls him into the darkness of the complex. Jenna watches until they disappear from view, then she slips off her flip-flops and jogs after them, her dressing gown belt loosening and then falling away as her cold feet silently pound the smooth paving slabs. She's not sure why she's following them but she can't stop herself.

She jogs through the dark alleys between the chalets, slowing as she hears the shrill sound of Kate's voice and Tom's bass tones. She's nearly at the end of the path. There's one last chalet, set apart from the rest. She moves closer. Kate and Tom are just around the corner, and they're still arguing.

'You seem determined to screw everything up,' Kate snaps.

'How is helping out a client screwing everything up?'

Jenna's stomach clenches. He's talking about her.

'I saw how you looked at her. In London, on the plane, just now.'

'It's called compassion, Kate.'

'Compassion? Listen to yourself, Tom. It's me you're talking to here, not one of the guests.'

'I'm just trying to help her.'

'You're trying to fuck her.'

Jenna smothers a gasp with her hand. She didn't imagine it, the attraction between her and Tom; Kate noticed it too. It was there, the connection between them, the first time they met. It was after his London seminar and he was mixing with everyone in the lobby. A gaggle of women had congregated around him and Jenna had waited until they'd all drifted away before she stepped forward to say hello. She felt sorry for the other women with their tittering giggles and simpering smiles. They'd fallen for his onstage persona but she wasn't that easily charmed. She hadn't booked her place to fall in love with the man on the stage. She'd turned up because she was desperate. Her life had fallen apart, her family didn't care and she didn't want to share something so private with her friends. She didn't know who else to turn to.

She'd almost scrolled straight past Tom's advert when it appeared on her Facebook feed but five words caught her eye 'I Can Save Your Life'. It was gross, arrogant and offensive but she still clicked on the link. She read about Tom, his history and how he'd discovered the five secrets that could turn anyone's life around. She clicked away again. She wasn't desperate enough to turn to a stranger for help, and definitely not one that advertised his seminars on Facebook.

But later that evening, after a bottle of red wine, she found herself thinking about that line 'I Can Save Your Life' and she googled Tom Wade. She clicked on one of his YouTube videos, just to confirm to herself that she was right about him. Then she watched the next video. And the one after that. When she woke up in the morning, on the sofa, with two empty bottles of red wine on the floor beside her, she checked her phone. She had an email, confirming her place on the next SoulShrink one day retreat in London. She wasn't going to go. She really wasn't. But then she did.

'I'm not *trying* to fuck anyone,' Tom says now.

Kate gives a short, sharp laugh. 'So it's already happened, has it? Nice. What did you do, take her to the cliff edge and pound her as the sun set? How romantic of you.'

'Stop it!' Tom's shout bounces off the walls, followed by the sound of shoe leather scuffing against stone and grunts from between clenched teeth.

'Get off me,' Kate says.

'Not until you calm down.'

'You don't get to tell me what to do.'

'Calm down, Kate.'

There's a sound, the sharp sting of a slap, then a terrifying silence. Jenna breathes into her hand, too shocked to move. Should she step round the corner and say something, or run in the opposite direction?

'Say sorry.' Kate's sharp tones cut through the silence.

Tom doesn't reply.

'Say sorry,' she says again.

'Kate—'

'Say it.'

'I didn't—'

'Just bloody apologise. I'm sick of this shit. You went off with Jenna when I specifically told you that you weren't to do anything that wasn't on the itinerary. I have spent *months* planning this retreat. I haven't been eating, I've barely slept. I've dedicated every single waking hour of my life to making this a success. All I'm asking . . . *all* I'm asking . . . is that you stick to the itinerary. Can you do that?'

There's a pause and Jenna imagines Kate staring up at Tom, her green eyes narrowed beneath her black, winged eyeliner, one hand pressed to her cheek, the skin hot and tender beneath her palm.

'Fine,' Tom snaps. 'I'm sorry. Okay? I'm sorry. Now give it a rest.'

Chapter 14

Now

KATE

Kate swears under her breath as the front door to the retreat opens and Tom walks in. His leather shoes, the ones she spent an age polishing so they looked half decent, are caked in mud. He's taken off his jumper, revealing a crumpled blue cotton shirt with sweat patches under the arms. His eyes are red. So is his nose. He's been crying, she realises. For God's sake. Had Geraldine seen? She'd returned first, looking grim, and had headed straight for the ground floor bedrooms. Kate tried to follow but Peter, the sour-faced man in a shirt, tie and V-neck jumper, blocked her route. He had a terrible allergy to perfumes and deodorants, he said, and his roommate Phoenix had applied both so liberally he could no longer walk into their shared bedroom without his eyes streaming. As he continued to moan and whine, Kate zoned out. If Geraldine was a journalist she was probably phoning in a story to her editor at that precise moment. When Kate finally got rid of Peter, Tom walked in.

'What happened?' She intercepts her husband as he heads towards the kitchen.

He sighs, his eyes not meeting hers. 'She wanted to know what happened to Jenna. I told her I didn't know.'

'And then you burst into tears?'

'For god's sake, Kate.'

'Tom.' She grips the sleeve of his shirt. 'You've got to get it together. We've got five days to get through. If you're going to have a breakdown, have it after the guests leave.'

He laughs hollowly. 'You're all heart, aren't you?'

'One of us has to keep their shit together or we're going to end up on the streets.'

He snatches his arm back and brushes the sleeve of his shirt as though he's wiping her away. 'Firstly,' he hisses, 'I am not having a breakdown, and secondly, just let me get on with it. I said I'd lead this retreat and I will.'

As he moves to pass her she holds out an arm, blocking his way. 'Clean your shoes before you start the workshop. They're filthy. It looks unprofessional.'

He looks down at his feet then crouches, undoes his laces and slips off his shoes, and hurls them away. They hit the front door with a thud. 'There you go,' he says, 'no more shoes. I'll lead the workshop in my socks.'

Before Kate can comment, Geraldine casually strolls back into the room, her hands in her pockets. She makes her way to the kitchen area, takes a biscuit from the plate then watches the other guests retake their seats as she eats it in two bites. Kate tries to read the expression on Geraldine's face. Is she curious? Puzzled? Focusing in on one person in particular? What does she know?

'Okay everyone!' Tom retakes his chair. 'Back to business. Our first session is about listening without judgement. The temptation when someone opens up to you is to comment, give advice, or chime in with your own experiences, but we're going to learn the art of listening. For those that are doing the talking I want you to do so without censoring yourself or your story. Okay, I'm going to split you all up into groups of two and then . . .'

Kate can't help but be impressed at how quickly he can do that – switch from irritable and argumentative to confident and charming. Everyone in the small group is gazing up at him, rapt, hanging onto his every word. It's a cliché but he really can light up a room. It's what first attracted her to him, over ten years earlier, when she walked into the cold, damp church hall in North London. She'd never thought of herself as the type of person who'd join a self-help group but she was desperate. Asthmatic since the age of eight, she'd gone to her GP complaining that she was having trouble breathing, particularly in the evenings, and wanted to know if the doctor could increase the dose of her preventative inhaler. Her doctor listened to her chest and said she couldn't hear any wheezing or rattles. She monitored Kate's oxygen saturation and declared it normal. Kate pleaded. She could barely breathe in the evenings and she'd done everything she could to make her situation better – she was hoovering daily, she'd installed a portable air filter and she'd even invested in a machine to remove the dampness from the air (which seemed to collect a lot of water from her first floor converted Victoria flat). The GP agreed that they should try a new preventative inhaler and told her to come back if things didn't improve. They didn't, and ten days later Kate returned to the surgery saying that, if anything, her breathlessness was worse. The doctor listened to her chest and checked her vitals. Still normal. She prescribed Kate a tablet to help with her allergies and sent her away. The fourth time Kate sat in front of her doctor she begged for a chest X-ray. She didn't have a cough, she was in her early thirties and she'd never smoked in her life but breathlessness was a symptom of lung cancer and she'd become convinced that she had it. The X-ray results came back clear.

'Is there anything that might be provoking the breathlessness?' the doctor asked. 'What is it you do in the evenings?'

'I work, same as I do in the day. I monitor my social media. I answer emails. I check out my competitors' YouTube channels. I look for speaking opportunities.'

'Speaking opportunities?'

'I'm a PR consultant. I've been targeting big businesses but I'm not getting anywhere. I keep getting down to the final two but if it's me against a man, the man gets the gig.'

'That sounds frustrating, and stressful.'

'It is!'

The doctor shifted in her chair, crossing one leg over the other. 'Stress can cause asthma flare ups. Have you looked into relaxation techniques – meditation, yoga, mindfulness, that sort of thing?'

'Who's got time for that when they're trying to get a business off the ground?'

'It might help you. The breathlessness is obviously becoming a problem or you wouldn't have come to see me. Have you talked to anyone about how you're feeling – friends, family?'

Kate shook her head. Her dad was dead and her mother was a fragile creature who quivered at the sound of raised voices, cried at donkey rescue adverts and hadn't watched the news in over twenty years. Kate had friends, of course she did, but they were either hugely successful in their fields or happily ensconced in yummy mummy land, being puked on by babies or drawn on by toddlers or whatever it was they did all day. As far as they were concerned she was doing well and she wasn't about to correct them. She'd always prided herself on being independent and self-sufficient. And anyway, *she* wasn't the problem. Her lack of dick was.

She left the doctor's office feeling irritated. She didn't have time for mindfulness and all that crap. What she wanted, *needed*, was a quick fix to her problem. A pill she could pop whenever she felt like there was a lead weight pressing down on her chest. There was wine, that always made her feel more relaxed, but she couldn't be on top of her game if she spent every evening half cut. She googled for solutions when she returned home and ended up finding her way to a page about somatic symptom disorder. And that led her to Tom's Facebook group. She laughed when she read the description of his psychosomatic illness. What kind of utter basket case did you have to be for half your body to go numb when you weren't even ill? She rummaged in her handbag for her Ventolin, took two puffs and continued reading. The comments from the other people in the group were ridiculously effusive:

Tom has changed my life

I can't thank Tom enough. He's a miracle worker.

I was so fed up of being ill I considered taking my own life but my mum convinced me to go to Tom's group and now I can't believe I ever thought that way.

I feel like a new person. I'd be lost without this group.

It was like the second-coming, the way they exalted him. He was obviously a charlatan. Kate had watched enough YouTube clips of US preachers getting the wheelchair-bound walking and blind people seeing to know that all you needed to miraculously cure people was a charismatic and powerful personality, high expectations, a frenzied atmosphere and the power of suggestion. It was basically mass hypnosis and she was pretty sure Tom Wade knew all about that. The next group meeting was a Saturday lunchtime. She'd go along, she decided, for a laugh, if nothing else. And then her whole world was flipped on its head.

Now, as Tom splits the guests into groups, Kate slips quietly away. She puts her hand in her pocket as she walks down the corridor that leads to the bedrooms and folds her fingers around the keys the owner left in a locked box in the front garden. Each of the guests have a key to their bedrooms but what they don't know, is so does she. Not that she'd need them if she wanted to check up on Peter, Phoenix or Priyanka. They've all left their doors open; their possessions on display to anyone walking past. It's a good sign. They feel relaxed, secure and safe.

Geraldine's door is closed. Kate presses a hand to it and pushes. Locked. She glances back down the corridor then slips the key into the lock. She steps inside, leaving the door slightly ajar and scans the room. It's empty apart from a phone charger on the carpet and a navy blue suitcase on the bed. She unzips it, keeping one eye on the door. Taking care not to disturb Geraldine's packing, Kate moves her fingers through the items of clothing, feeling for anything unusual. She's not sure what she's expecting to find – maybe a recording device, a laptop, anything that doesn't fit with the information that Geri put on her form about being retired and grieving her late husband. She finds a washbag, which she quickly examines then replaces, a biography of Alan Turing, some medication, several pairs of socks, trousers, jumpers, underwear, pyjamas, a hairbrush and a reading light. And that's it. She feels around the lining of the suitcase then, certain nothing is being concealed, zips it back up again. She looks back at the phone charger, plugged into the wall. There's no mobile phone. If Geraldine did make a call to her editor she took her phone with her when she rejoined the group.

'Damn it,' Kate says softly then turns sharply, sensing she's no longer alone.

The door isn't just ajar now. It's wide open. And Renata is in the doorway.

'Everything okay?' Kate's question comes out more sharply than she intended but she softens it with a warm smile. 'You've spoiled the surprise.' She reaches into her pocket and pulls out a small bar of chocolate, then places it on Geraldine's pillow.

'Oh that's so lovely.' Renata beams at her. 'You're so thoughtful.'

'I thought you'd all need a bit of chocolate by the end of the day.' Kate tilts her head questioningly. 'The workshop hasn't ended has it?' A knot forms in her stomach. How long has Renata been watching from the door?

'Oh no,' Renata says brightly. 'It's still going. I left to use the loo. Too many cups of tea during the break.'

'The loo's at the other end of the corridor.' Kate moves to the doorway, forcing Renata to step out of the room. She steps out too and pulls the door closed. It locks automatically. 'I showed you where everything was earlier, remember?'

'Of course.' Renata runs a hand through her long blonde hair. The girl's loaded, or at least her parents are. She hasn't worked a day in her life as far as Kate can make out. She spends her life helping build orphanages in Cambodia and orangutan sanctuaries in Borneo, punctuating her 'charity work' with retreats, trying out every self-help technique there is. She's as vacant as she is beautiful.

'I thought I heard a noise,' Renata continues, 'when I left the loo but as you're okay I'll go back to the group and let you get on. I don't want to spoil Geraldine's surprise do I?'

'No,' Kate says, her cheeks aching from all the bloody smiling. 'No, let's definitely keep that to ourselves.'

Renata touches her on the shoulder. 'You can trust me, Kate. I hope you know that.'

Chapter 15

Now

FRAN

As Fran approaches the dining table she sees Phoenix making a beeline for her and tries to swerve out of his way but Joy and Renata are deep in conversation and despite Fran's frantic, 'Excuse me, excuse me please,' they remain stubbornly in the way. And then there he is, gesturing at two empty seats at the table, asking her to sit next to him. It's not that she dislikes Phoenix, but she finds his incessant chattering exhausting. They were paired up for the listening challenge earlier and he talked at her at double speed for a full five minutes. He described in minute detail the circumstances of how he came to meet his ex-boyfriend Gwyn (at a gay club in Swansea), how their relationship had progressed (quickly, by all accounts), the problems and obstacles en route (jealousy, insecurity, Gwyn's annoying best friend), Gwyn's dwindling sexual interest and subsequent cheating and Phoenix's refusal to accept the relationship was over and his eventual caution from the police. 'It wasn't stalking. I was just trying to stop him from ghosting me. I mean, we were together for eleven months and he owed it to me to tell me what I had done wrong. Don't you think, Geri? Just nod. Anyway, he totally destroyed my confidence and that's why I'm here . . .'

When it was Fran's turn to talk her brain was so overwhelmed all she managed to impart in the first thirty seconds was, 'My name is Geraldine. I'm fifty-one and I live alone.' She racked her brain for something suitably angsty that she could share with him but the truth was that, aside from Jenna's disappearance, she was perfectly content with her life. Her official story, her reason for being on the retreat, was that she was a widow unable to move on after the death of her husband but how was she supposed to talk about that at length? She'd had boyfriends in the past – the *very* distant past, as her last relationship ended when she was thirty-five – but none of them had ever broken her heart. Rather she'd only ever felt a vague sense of frustration when a relationship ended, that she'd given them her time and her company for what end? Some sexual fumbling, lacklustre intercourse and the occasional conversation that piqued her interest. There was only one boyfriend that she occasionally reminisced about – Gunnar Saevarsson, a fellow student at Cambridge University. He was Icelandic, the tallest man she had ever met, and astonishingly clever. Fran idolised him – she found his straightforwardness and lack of tact refreshing – but was pretty sure that his interest in her was almost solely intellectual. They would have the most fascinating discussions, sitting cross legged on his single bed, and when he did eventually lunge in for a kiss no one was more surprised than Fran. Then, when they had sex, the most incredible transformation occurred. Any self-restraint Gunnar may have shown in the day was thrown out of the window, along with Fran's knickers. Afterwards, as he lay curled around her, sticky with sweat and breathing heavily, his hand rested on her belly. When he gave it a little squeeze and said, 'No more beer for you!' she laughed with joy. It was so wonderful, meeting someone so like her. If he'd been the one with a fleshy little pot belly she'd have said something very similar. Their affair continued for seven happy months until Gunnar decided that Fran was distracting him from his studies and if he didn't achieve a first he'd never forgive himself. Fran agreed to the split. She'd found herself fantasising in the library about their sexual liaisons rather than actively studying her books and she knew she wasn't performing at her academic best. They parted with a hug and a smile but it took a while until the pang in her heart finally faded away.

But she wasn't going to tell Phoenix about Gunnar, most definitely not. Her relationship with her first boyfriend was a pleasant memory, not a source of trauma. In fact, the only trauma she'd encountered was the disappearance of her sister. She couldn't talk to him about that, but maybe she could discuss the nature of their relationship. There was a twelve year age difference and, with Fran at boarding school and her sister at home with her parents in an army camp in Germany, they only interacted in the school holidays, three times a year. Even then Fran spent most of her time in her room reading, only leaving for meal times and when her mother insisted she play a board game to entertain her little sister. It wasn't that Fran didn't love Jenna – she was a sweet, if dull, little girl who loved to draw – but they had nothing in common. When Fran left for university aged eighteen she'd send her six-year-old sister sweets in the mail and occasionally speak to her on the phone, but she rarely returned home, preferring to spend her holidays in her university bedroom instead.

Not that she was able to tell Phoenix most of this, as he continually interrupted her to ask questions or to draw parallels with his own life. At one point, Tom stepped in to ask Phoenix to just listen but then the buzzer sounded to signify that their time was up. Several people in the group were in tears by this point so Tom led a half hour mindfulness session during which Fran nearly fell asleep. On the upside, Phoenix didn't say a word, even when Tom asked them to imagine a beautiful lakeside walk and Fran sneaked a look to her left to see if Phoenix had his hand up, volunteering his idyllic vision. They broke for lunch then – a buffet affair that people either took to their rooms or ate on their knees in the living area (Fran chose her room). After lunch, they were summoned back to the heart of the house and then taken out to the garden where piles of bricks had been arranged with a slim piece of wood laid across the divide. They were invited, one by one, to approach the arrangement, shout, 'I can overcome my fears,' and then smash through the piece of wood with the edge of their hand. After watching several people break the plank on their first attempt Fran was dismayed when she failed to put so much as a crack in the thing.

'Believe,' Tom urged her. 'Visualise it breaking in two.' Fran made a second attempt, and a third, and when the plank failed to split on her fourth attempt Tom stepped forward and softly said, 'I think you may have an emotional blockage. We'll work on shifting it during our one-to-one session tomorrow.' Fran wasn't sure that she wanted an emotional irrigation, but she was aware that Priyanka was jiggling around on the spot, desperate for her turn, so she nodded and said, 'I'll be sure to brace myself,' and stepped aside.

Now, wedged between Phoenix and Damian, Fran dips her spoon into the leek and potato soup that Kate has served up and surreptitiously watches the other diners for any clue that they might be her mysterious note writer. Whoever wrote it addressed it to 'Fran', not Geraldine, so they know who she is.

Maybe it was Kate. Other than cooking meals she's been hovering around the group all day like a particularly irritating bluebottle. Could she be the mysterious note sender? Maybe Tom had sworn her to secrecy about Jenna's death and the burden was too great to bear?

Fran's gut instinct tells her that's unlikely. If Kate had something she was desperate to share she'd had more than enough time to find a way to contact her. So, who is it? Peter the grumpy old git? Damian, the sullen Scot who struggles to maintain eye contact? Or Priyanka, the mother of four who's sobbed her way through most of the day? It's most certainly not Joy – Mrs Rainbow Jumper – who's sitting so close to Tom she's almost on his lap.

The note writer was deliberately obtuse but if Jenna didn't kill herself there are only two possible alternatives – she's still alive, or someone killed her. Fran lowers her spoon, her appetite gone. Is that why Tom cried in the field earlier? Not because Jenna jumped to her death but because she was murdered? Fran feels sick. Learning her sister was so low she saw no alternative but to end her life was hard enough to come to terms with. When Geraldine rang to break the news, Fran swayed on the spot then grabbed at the kitchen sink to stop herself from falling. She couldn't breathe, couldn't think, couldn't move. Dead? How could Jenna be dead? She was thirty-seven. She'd barely lived. There had to be a mistake – a breakdown in communication between the Gozoian and British police. Jenna wasn't dead, she'd wandered off after the sweat lodge ceremony and got lost. She wasn't suicidal. She was beautiful and young with so much of her life ahead of her. She'd been bubbling with joy and champagne on her thirty-seventh birthday, surrounded by friends in a central London restaurant. 'It's my big sister!' she'd shouted as Fran approached the table. 'I *am* honoured!' She bounced to her feet, knocking her chair to the floor, and threw her arms around Fran's neck. Fran carefully extricated herself and handed Jenna a present.

She didn't stay long. Jenna's friends were rowdy and loud, there was too much talk about crappy ex-boyfriends, the food wasn't great and Fran had work the next morning. She excused herself after the main course, put forty pounds on the table to cover her share and a tip, and waved her sister goodbye. 'I'll see you at Christmas, if not before,' she told her. 'Enjoy the rest of your night.'

But she hadn't seen her at Christmas. They'd chatted, briefly, in the car park at work and the last words Fran ever said to her sister were, 'can't it wait?'

The guilt Fran felt consumed her. She took two weeks off work, drove the two hour round trip to visit her parents daily and sat silently in the living room as her mother sobbed and her father stood silently at the window until she could bear it no longer. She booked a flight to Gozo, secured a room in the same hotel that Jenna had stayed in and, after dumping her suitcase in her room, headed out to the scrubland outside the hotel boundaries. She expected to find police standing around the small stone circle where the sweat hut had been erected, or at least yellow and black tape, cordoning it off. But there was nothing, and no one, there. Three people had died eleven days earlier and there was no sign that a crime had been committed. As a bitterly cold wind blew off the sea, forcing her to wrap her cardigan tighter around her body, she inched her way to the edge of the cliff. She knew it was high – she'd circled around it on Google Earth, viewing it from every possible angle – but she hadn't anticipated how small and vulnerable she would feel as she dropped to her knees and, fingers quivering, reached for the edge. She craned her neck, trying to look down, but the angle of the cliff meant she could only see knuckles of white rock and moss, not the sea below.

The wind whipped at her hair, twirling and twisting it, as she shifted on her belly, pulling herself closer and closer to the edge. Gulls circled in the sky above her, shrieking and cawing, as though warning her that danger was near. Now it wasn't only Fran's fingers that were shaking, her whole body was juddering, her heart pounding. *It's not safe*, her brain screamed at her. *The cliff could crumble. You could die.* But another part of her, a bigger part, told her to keep moving. The Gozoian police had sent out boats as soon as Jenna was reported missing but no body was found in the deep, navy sea. The current was too strong and she'd probably been pulled into the depths. The chances were she'd never be found. But what if she could? What if, right now, Jenna's lifeless body was nudging the rocks below? As Fran weaved her fingers through the grass at the edge of the rock, searching for something solid that she could grip to pull herself closer to the edge, a deep male voice cut through the whistle of the wind.

'Hey! Hey! What you doing?'

She felt hands grab her ankles and twisted around to discover a tall, thickset man yanking her away from the cliff edge.

'So dangerous!' He barked as he released her ankles. He had a full beard, streaked with grey, a green bobble hat and a walking pole, abandoned on the ground beside him. 'What the hell were you thinking?'

His thick German accent gave his question gravitas and Fran couldn't help but feel chastised. What she had been attempting to do *was* dangerous.

'I was . . .' She sat up, wincing as her midriff sung with pain. Her T-shirt and cardigan had ridden up as the man had yanked her away from the cliff edge and the skin between her bra strap and waistband was red with scratch marks.

The man's expression changed in an instant. '*Mein Gott.* Sorry, sorry, one moment.' He shrugged his rucksack off his shoulders and rummaged around inside. He pulled out a compact green first aid bag, unzipped it and removed a handful of small white packets. He ripped the top off one, pulled out what Fran assumed was an antiseptic wipe and leant forward to wipe it over her stomach. She put out a hand to stop him but her objection dried up. Instead she sat quietly, not moving, as the man tenderly dabbed at her skin then applied plasters to the worst of the scratches.

'It hurts?' he asked, raising his eyes to hers.

She shook her head. 'Not especially.'

'But you're crying.'

She coughed to try and clear her thickened throat but her voice, when she spoke, was quiet and small.

'I came here looking for someone, but she's not here.'

The German man shook his head. 'Where is she?'

Fran looked out at the horizon where the inky black sea sliced across the white-blue sky. 'She's gone.'

Fran blinks several times as she steps out of the house, her eyes adjusting to the darkness. Out here, miles away from the nearest town, the sky is a black canvas, dotted with stars. The trees are shadowy figures, the shrubs and bushes crouching animals. Only the first few metres of garden are visible, illuminated by the lights of the house. A noise makes her glance towards one of the windows. It's thick with condensation but she can make out the shapes of three people, clambering into the hot tub. She moves away quickly, into the darkness at the side of the house and makes her way up the slope of the lawn. Her note sender didn't specify where she should wait but she's assuming they don't want to be seen. Whatever it is they need to tell her about Jenna, there's a reason they haven't pulled her aside in front of the others. It's a large garden and by the time Fran makes it to the boundary fence she's breathing heavily and sweating beneath her wool coat. She rests a hand on the fence and stares out into the darkness, listening to the drone of traffic in the distance and the low hoot of an owl. Earlier there were sheep in the field that butts against the garden but they've gone now, stowed safely away in a barn no doubt.

Fran turns to look back at the house. The lit windows look cosy and inviting and she thinks longingly of her duvet and a warm cup of tea. She scans the garden, squinting into the gloom, then taps a button on the side of her watch. 9.11 p.m. It would have been helpful if her note writer had specified a time. She could be out here for an hour, maybe more, and, in her haste to evade the others, she completely forgot her scarf.

'Fran?' She jumps as the bushes to her left rustle and a short, squat figure walks out of the trees.

'Joy?' There must be some kind of mistake. But she said Fran, not Geraldine.

'Caroline Harding.' Joy holds out her hand, returning Fran's handshake with a firm grip. 'I won't make this too long or we'll arouse suspicion, but I'm glad you're here. I'm a freelance journalist and I've been investigating the circumstances of your sister's disappearance.'

Fran is so astonished by Joy's transformation – her simpering voice replaced with a strong, confident tone, even her posture is different – that it takes her a moment to register the name.

'Caroline Harding? I recognise that name. You were one of the journalists who hassled my parents,' she says sharply. 'And now you've followed me here.'

Her family were inundated with media requests after Jenna's disappearance was ruled a suicide – by phone, email and then at home. Fran appointed herself the gatekeeper. Each time there was a knock on the front door she would fly through the house and throw the door open. Then, in her best teacher voice, she'd bellow at the waiting reporters that they should be ashamed of themselves for intruding on her family's grief.

Eventually, with no fuel to add to the fire of 'The SoulShrink Death Circle', the journalists finally gave up. All apart from Caroline Harding, whose name appeared in Fran's personal email inbox day after day after day. When Fran blocked her, Caroline rang her at work. Fran threatened to call the police. 'It's harassment,' she'd barked down the phone, 'plain and simple and I will not allow you vultures to pick over the bones of my sister's death.' She never heard from Caroline again. Until now.

'I didn't know you'd be here,' Caroline says, sparking a cigarette. 'Believe you me, I couldn't have been more surprised when you walked into the lounge earlier.'

'Is that so?'

'Look, Fran.' Caroline glances back towards the house. 'I know you don't trust me and I understand why but I genuinely want to help. Jenna didn't commit suicide. She was murdered.'

Fran stares at her, stunned into silence.

'I'm sorry.' Caroline touches her arm and, for once, Fran doesn't recoil. 'I know this will come as a shock and I'm genuinely sorry I'm having to break it to you like this. It's why I kept hassling you, I—'

'Who killed her? Why?'

'That's what I'm trying to work out.'

'But . . . the police, the Gozoian and the British police, they both agreed it was suicide.'

'Hmmm.'

'What's that supposed to mean?'

'Have you heard of Daphne Caruana Galizia?'

'Of course. She was an investigative journalist. She died when a bomb went off under her car.'

Caroline's hand falls away from Fran's arm and she glances around, checking they aren't being overheard. 'She didn't die. She was assassinated. Galizia had been exposing corruption at the highest level of government.'

'What's this got to do with Jenna?'

'Corruption isn't solely centred on Malta. No one wants there to be a murder on Gozo, not when so many tourists flood there every year. It's crime free, or so they claim.'

Fran waves a hand through the air, wafting Caroline's cigarette smoke away. It all sounds so preposterous, like some kind of spy thriller or one of her mother's outlandish theories.

'Blood was found on the ground where Jenna was last seen.' Caroline reads the shock on her face. 'I'm so sorry. Maybe I should have put that more sensitively.'

'It's fine. I'd rather know the facts.'

'Okay, well, blood was found, enough to suggest a violent altercation, but the evidence was misplaced.'

'Misplaced!'

'Along with most of the witness statements. The statements that were used as evidence were the ones suggesting Jenna took her own life. There's been a massive cover up, Fran, and I'm pretty sure Tom's part of it.'

'What did his statement say? "I don't know what happened because I ran away."'

Caroline laughs dryly. 'A fine leader he was, hiding in a church in the next town when people were dying.'

'You're sure it was murder?' Fran asks.

Caroline sucks on her cigarette then tips back her head and blows grey smoke upwards. 'More than sure. The blood . . . it's definitely your sister's. I saw the lab reports.'

Fran looks back at the house and remembers Tom at dinner, knocking back the wine and chatting like he didn't have a care in the world. 'Do you think he killed her?'

'That's what I'm trying to find out. I need to talk to the others.'

'What others?'

'Three of the guests who were at the retreat in Gozo are here.

You just had dinner with them. In fact—' She stops speaking and looks to her left.

'What is it?' Fran asks.

'I thought I heard something. A branch snapping or—'

'Never mind that.' Fran nudges her urgently as a figure walks up the garden towards them, a dark shape in the gloom. 'We've got company.'

Chapter 16

Then

JENNA

Jenna is still pressed up against the wall of the chalet, the cold stone under her palms, the sound of the slap ringing in her ears, when Tom appears at the end of the pathway. In the blink of an eye he's gone, sprinting down the path that runs alongside chalet number nine. She waits, and watches, then, when Tom doesn't return, she moves away from the wall. She needs to check on Kate.

The glass double doors to Tom's chalet are open. Kate is inside, sitting in one of the armchairs, staring at the floor, her arms crossed over her chest. She looks up sharply as Jenna draws closer. Irritation, or maybe anger, quickly dissolves into a smile.

'Hello!' She gets up and moves to the doorway, her long beige jersey skirt clinging to her thighs as she walks, her navy jacket sleeves turned back to reveal white cuffs, the same stark white as her top. There's an effortless elegance to her that makes Jenna feel scruffy and grubby.

'Everything okay?' Kate asks. 'Tom's just popped out. I'm waiting for him to return.' Her eyes are clear and white, lined with winged black eyeliner and thick, black mascara. The apples of her cheeks are pink and her lips shine with gloss. There are no tear tracks carving pale lines through her foundation, no panda smudges beneath her eyes and no red finger marks on her cheeks. Either she reapplied her make-up lightning fast after Tom hit her or he slapped her somewhere that didn't leave a mark. But it's Kate's demeanour, rather than her perfect make-up, that Jenna finds confusing. She heard the anguish in Kate's voice when she was arguing with Tom and the plaintive, 'Say you're sorry'. No sign of that now. She's all business as normal and 'how can I help?'

'I heard your argument,' Jenna says, 'with Tom. I know he slapped you.'

Horror flashes in Kate's eyes.

'He's gone,' Jenna says, 'and if we lock the doors he won't be able to get back in.'

As Kate slumps into an armchair, covering her face with her hands, Jenna rushes over to close the doors. She turns the key in the lock then looks back at Kate. She dithers, unsure what to do next. Fran would know what to do, she thinks ruefully. Fran with her no-nonsense personality and 'can do' attitude. She'd take charge of the situation in an instant. But Jenna isn't her sister and she feels completely out of her depth.

'Do you want a drink?' she ventures instead. 'Tea? Wine? Is there any?'

'There's red wine in the cupboard above the coffee machine.'

Jenna takes the bottle from the cupboard and roots around in a drawer for a bottle opener. When she finally pours the wine, Kate's moved from the armchair to the bed. She's perched on the edge, staring out through the patio doors; watching for Tom.

Jenna hands her a glass and sits on the bed beside her. 'Has he done that before?'

'Done what?'

'Hit you?'

'No.'

'Never?'

'Never.' There's an edge to Kate's voice, a full stop. *End of discussion.*

'What are you going to do?'

'Nothing.'

She looks at her in surprise. 'If you want to report it to the police I'll come with you.'

Kate takes a slug of her wine. 'That's not going to happen.'

'He hit you!'

'He tapped me.'

'It didn't sound like a tap.'

'Just let it go, Jenna.'

Jenna looks at her incredulously. She can't tell if Kate's in denial about what happened or if she genuinely thinks it's acceptable but she's a lot more together than Jenna would be in the same situation.

Kate twirls her wine glass between her fingers. 'I'm waiting for him to come back so we can talk.'

'And then what? Are you going to resign and go back to the UK?'

'No, of course not.'

'Cancel the retreat?'

Kate looks at her in horror. 'Why would I do that?'

'Because Tom's going to be alone with other women in this room. What if he hits them too?'

'That's not going to happen. Seriously, Jenna. Tom and I . . . we push each other's buttons, especially when we're under pressure. Running the retreat is stressful. We argued. It happens.'

Jenna tries to read the emotion in Kate's eyes. There's a defensiveness there, anger too. And something else. Something she can't read.

'I was angry with Tom,' Kate continues. 'I took it too far.'

Jenna tries to say that it's okay, that she understands, but the words stick in her throat. Kate's making excuses for him. 'It doesn't matter how angry you got. He shouldn't have hit you.'

'Like I said, it was a tap. But it shouldn't have happened and Tom will be tearing himself apart. If what you overheard got out he wouldn't be able to live with the shame. He's an emotional man, Jenna, and neither of us want to push him to a point where he heads out to the cliffs and . . .' She pauses and takes a steadying breath. '. . . and does something foolish. What you heard . . . it was utterly unprofessional, but I am absolutely as much to blame as Tom. It was a private matter and I would appreciate it if you would keep it to yourself.'

Jenna raises her glass to her lips, only to find that it's empty. She doesn't know what to think, nor how to feel. What Kate said was vile and what Tom did was worse. If Kate doesn't want to take it further there's nothing she can do to convince her. But it doesn't sit well, keeping it quiet.

'We all make mistakes,' Kate continues. 'I imagine you have too. Things you have done or said that you wish you could change? That you want to forget?'

Jenna glances at her. 'Of course I do.'

'Well then.' Kate's expression hardens. 'As Buddha said, "a person is destroyed by holding judgements about others". Wise words to live by, don't you think?'

*

Jenna hurries along the winding alleyway from Tom's chalet to the other guest bedrooms. She only left Kate a few seconds ago and regret is already gnawing away at her. It goes against everything she believes in, keeping quiet about a man hitting a woman. A slap was still a slap, regardless of how hard it was delivered. Kate had twisted what had happened. She'd made out she was as responsible as Tom, absorbed some of the blame. Jenna's anger builds as she reaches the end of the alleyway – with Tom, with Kate, with the situation, with herself. She trusted Tom. She flew eighteen hundred miles because she thought he could fix her but he's not the man she thought he was. He's another man pretending to be someone he's not.

As she bursts out of the walkway she stops abruptly. Damian's standing a few feet away, watching her with his eyebrows raised. He's naked from the waist up, a towel tucked tightly around his waist, his hair slicked back.

'Have you tried out the pools yet? They're great, particularly . . .' He pauses. 'You all right? You look stressed.'

'Tom hit Kate.' The words rush out of her before she can stop them.

'What the fuck?'

'Don't.' She grabs at his forearm as he tries to move past her. 'Tom's not there. He ran off.'

'He'd better fucking run because—'

'Don't. Please. Kate doesn't want anyone to know. She made me promise I wouldn't tell anyone.'

'You told me.'

She glances round, nervous she'll find Tom or Kate standing at the other end of the alleyway. 'Can we . . . can we talk about this somewhere quieter?'

Damian doesn't reply. He's staring over the top of her head towards Tom's chalet.

'Please. Let's talk about this first.'

'Fine.' He runs his hands over his arms, smoothing down the goosebumps that have appeared on his skin.

'You're freezing,' Jenna says. 'You need to get warm.'

He smirks. 'You could help me.' And there he is, the Damian of the plane, suddenly reactivated as though all he needed was for Jenna to press the right button.

'I meant you need to put some clothes on.'

His smile widens. 'Spoilsport.'

'Well?' Damian asks as they reach the gate that leads to the wasteland and the cliff path.

He listens, frowning as Jenna describes the conversation she overheard and the sharp sting of a slap. When she reaches the part about Kate asking Tom to say sorry he shakes his head in disgust.

'That's fucked up.'

'I know. But she doesn't see it that way. She made excuses for him: he's been under a lot of pressure, she pushed him too hard, etc., etc.'

'We're all under pressure. But we don't go slapping the shit out of people. I should take his head off.'

'Yeah, because the way to combat violence is with more violence.'

'I was joking.'

'Well I'm not. Kate said that Tom will be tearing himself apart about what happened. She's worried that if it gets out he'll do something stupid.'

'That's emotional blackmail.'

'But what if he did? What if he actually killed himself?'

'Jesus.' Damian zips up the hoody he grabbed from his room and pulls the hood over his head. 'I need a drink.'

'I've already had one. It didn't help.'

'Story of my life. To think I paid to come here when I could have gone to rehab.'

'Why didn't you?'

'Rehab was in Hertfordshire. SoulShrink was in Gozo. It was a no brainer. And I wouldn't have met you if I'd gone to rehab, would I?' He grins stupidly and raises his eyebrows suggestively. 'I'm guessing you've gone off Tom now you know he's handy with his fists?'

'I was never into him.'

'I'm no body language expert but I'd say you are approximately three Bacardi Breezers away from a shag. Were.' He corrects himself.

Something inside Jenna twists. 'You're totally off the mark.'

'If you say so. Anyway . . .' Damian looks back towards the hotel complex. 'What do you reckon? Get the rest of the group together, tell them what happened?'

'Yeah . . . fuck . . . no.' She tries to get the image of Kate's pleading face out of her mind but it's lodged there, along with the quote about judgement. 'No. We keep an eye on him. And if there's even the vaguest whisper of him touching one of the other women we'll shout what he did from the rooftops.'

'Do you know how dodgy that sounds? Let's wait until he beats someone else up before we speak up?'

'He didn't beat her up. It was more of a slap.'

He stares at her, incredulous, his mouth open. 'Did you seriously just say that? Fucking hell, Jenna. He's really got you under his spell. This is bullshit.'

She watches as he marches back towards the hotel. Who the hell does he think he is, talking to her like that? She isn't under anyone's spell.

'Who are you to judge?'

He stops in his tracks and turns back. 'What did you just say?'

She parrots Kate's words at him – about her relationship with Tom, the fact they'd both gone too far, her assurance that it had never happened before. When she reaches the part about Buddha and judging others Damian raises a hand. 'That's enough. It's bullshit, Jenna. All of it.'

'Maybe it is, but I made Kate a promise and whether that's right or wrong I have to keep it.'

'As I said, you told *me*.'

'And I'm really regretting that decision.'

Neither of them speaks as they wander back into the complex; doubt burying itself in Jenna's mind with every step she takes.

Chapter 17

Now

KATE

Even in the darkness of the garden there's no mistaking the look of horror on Geraldine's face as Kate draws closer. Joy drops her cigarette and stamps it into the grass. One more thing for Kate to tidy up, but she doesn't say anything.

'Hello, ladies,' she says, in the sweetest voice she can manage. 'Is everything okay?'

'Yes, fine.' Everything about Geraldine's body language, from the raised voice, to the way she angles her body away reinforces Kate's suspicions.

'Joy?' Kate asks. 'Everything okay with you?'

'Wonderful.' Joy beams at her. 'It's so lovely out here. It's not like London; you can actually see the stars.'

Kate gives them a cursory glance. 'We're very lucky.'

'Did you come out to see them too?' Kate stiffens at Geraldine's tone. She thinks she's so clever.

'Actually' – she smiles tightly – 'I noticed that Joy was smoking and came to remind you both that the smoking area is at the back of the house. We wouldn't want to set fire to anything, would we?'

'Unlikely,' Geraldine says. 'It's been raining.'

Before Kate can respond, Joy lets out a little squeal of apology, dips down and plucks her cigarette butt from the grass. 'I'm so, so sorry, Kate. I didn't think. I'll get rid of it now.'

She scurries away, her dumpy little legs moving faster than Kate would have thought possible.

'You've got good eyesight,' Geraldine says as Joy disappears round the back of the house. 'To see the light of a cigarette from all the way over there.'

Kate smiles. 'Eyes like a hawk.'

As much as Kate might want Geraldine to think she's all-knowing, it was luck, rather than some kind of ESP, that led her to spot the red tip of Joy's cigarette dancing at the far end of the garden.

She was in her bedroom. Tom was on the bed, flat on his back, headphones jammed over his ears, eyes closed and breathing heavily. She checked that he was asleep then carefully opened the desk drawer and took out the small, black key fob hidden at the back. She pressed a pin into the hole in its side and slid an SSD out of the tray that popped out. Once the card was in the adaptor, she slotted it into her laptop then sat down on the floor with her back against the wall, out of sight of the bed.

The video app opened, showing an empty room apart from two armchairs, facing each other, with a low table separating them. When she pressed play, nothing happened for several minutes, then two men walked into the scene and sat down. One of the men was Tom, the other Peter.

Tom's voice played in Kate's headphones. It was his normal spiel – the therapy session was confidential, nothing they talked about would be shared outside the room. Blah, blah, blah.

'To start,' Tom said, 'why don't you tell me what it is you're hoping to get out of this retreat?'

Kate stiffened as Peter's gaze drifted to the window. Had he spotted the key fob camera, nestling in a dish on the sill? She relaxed as he turned his attention back to Tom.

'I want to find out why I keep attracting unsuitable women.'

'Okay.' Tom nodded agreeably. 'Can you tell me a bit more about that? In what way are they unsuitable?'

'Well they don't seem unsuitable initially, when I'm taking them out for dinner and shelling out for ridiculously expensive bottles of wine. At that point in our relationships they're very pleasant, attentive and really quite fascinated by me.'

Kate raised an eyebrow.

'When we discuss hobbies they seem very keen for me to educate them about classical music, to show them the very best of art house cinema and to join me on hikes.'

'And then what happens?'

'They become irritable. They moan. And they stop listening.'

'And why is that, do you think?'

Peter turned his hands over, palms upwards. 'You tell me; you're the expert.'

'Do you . . .' Tom said delicately, 'do you ever join in with *their* hobbies?'

'Why would I want to do that? My own interests take up quite enough time.'

Kate pressed the fast-forward button. Peter was genuine. Everything about him screamed self-obsessed and narcissistic.

She watched the next video, skipping through Priyanka's

tearful session as she confided in Tom about the death of her husband. The next recording was Emily's. She was one of the willowy blondes from London. Kate scrutinised Tom's body language as Emily talked. He wasn't the least bit interested, other than in a professional capacity.

Kate stopped the video. It was excruciating, listening to hours and hours of other people's misery. God knows how Tom did it.

She copied the files into her secret cloud account then slotted the SSD card back into the spy cam and slid it into her pocket. Tom was still snoring lightly and most of the guests were in the living room or their bedrooms. No one would notice her slipping into the therapy room to put the key fob back in the dish.

As she returned the laptop to her desk she glanced outside. The garden, and the fields beyond it, were bathed in moonlight, barely a house to be seen. It was so different from London. There was so much space, so much room to breathe. A red dot, moving erratically at the end of the garden, caught her attention. Someone was smoking; after she'd stressed how important it was that smokers use the ashtrays in the back porch. So irritating. Why didn't people listen?

Tapping her pocket to check that the spy cam was still safely stashed away she grabbed her coat from the hook on the back of the bedroom door and hurried down the stairs.

'Excuse me, Kate!' Peter called from the living room. 'If you have a minute I'd just like to—'

But Kate was already halfway out the front door. She stalked up the garden, squinting to make out the two smokers as she drew closer. One was tall with cropped hair, the other shorter and wider. Geraldine and Joy, out for an evening stroll? Odd that the two women who were at each other's throats during the morning session had suddenly become friendly enough to spend their evening together. Was Geraldine trying to get Joy onside or was she quizzing her for the piece she was writing? Stupid bitch. She'd never get anything out of her. Uber fans like that were loyal to a fault.

'If you'll excuse me,' Geraldine says now. 'It's getting cold and I need to make a phone call.'

Of course you do, Kate thinks grimly. You've got an editor to report back to.

'You're excused.' Kate laughs, a horrible tinkling sound that, even to her ears, sounds fake. 'The fire's lit in the living area so you can warm yourself up there. And there are extra blankets if you're cold tonight.'

'Thank you.' Geraldine couldn't look more desperate to get away if she tried.

Kate watches as she plods back down the hill in her ugly old woman shoes. It's Geraldine's one-to-one with Tom tomorrow. Kate folds her fingers around the key fob in her pocket. That'll make for interesting viewing, assuming she doesn't spend the whole hour lying through her teeth.

She'll get it set up, then pull Joy aside for a word; see if there's anything Geraldine Rotheram would rather she didn't find out.

Chapter 18

Now

FRAN

Fran is assaulted by a wall of noise as she opens the door to the house. Wine was provided with dinner but, from the bottles and glasses crowded on the living room table, it seems most of the guests brought their own supply. In one corner of the room, Priyanka and the two well-spoken women, whose names she isn't sure of, are deep in conversation, while Renata, Phoenix and Peter are sitting cross legged on the floor like school children, playing cards on the carpet.

'Geri!' Phoenix raises a hand in greeting. His cheeks are flushed and his eyes are shiny. 'Where've you been? We thought you'd done a runner!'

'I was taking a walk.'

'In the dark? How was the view?' He laughs as though it's

the funniest thing anyone has ever said. Renata titters politely. Peter reaches for a new card.

'Want to play?' Phoenix asks. 'We've nearly finished this round. Peter's spanking us.'

'Maybe tomorrow.' Caroline's missing from the group but so is someone else. Fran mentally works her way around all the people at dinner then pauses as she reaches the man who was sitting to her left. Dark hair, top knot, made a couple of lascivious remarks about Emily, or was it Sophie, one of the young pretty ones. What was his name? Damian! When she was younger she'd prided herself on her ability never to forget a name. She'd zoom in on something about their appearance, voice, or character and tie it to their name. It was particularly useful for remembering the names of the children in a class – Cheryl might have pink cheeks like a cherry, Liam might be a big 'I am' and Archie might have pronounced eyebrow arches. She could normally find something to hook a name on. But yes, Damian with the black hair and the devilish glint to his eyes. That was how she'd chosen to remember him.

She heads off to Caroline's room, knocks on her door and waits. After a brief pause the door opens and Caroline ushers her inside.

'Where's Kate?' Caroline has removed her garish rainbow jumper and replaced it with a navy blue dressing gown. Fran still can't quite equate this short, rotund middle-aged woman with the investigative journalist she claims to be, but she appears to be fully informed about the situation in Malta, and she obviously has contacts if she knows about the missing witness statements and the blood on the rocks.

'I left her in the garden. I told her I had to make a phone call.'

'Excellent, take a seat.' Caroline gestures at the only chair in the room, a hardbacked chair by the desk, then sits down on the edge of the bed.

'Here.' She hands Fran a small white business card, which she tucks into the pocket of her fleece. 'Just in case they work out who I am and I'm kicked out. I need you to stay in touch. I want to know everything that happens.'

'Of course. So' – Fran can't keep the question inside her a moment longer – 'tell me. Who were the three people who were on the retreat?'

Caroline lowers her voice. 'Renata, Damian and Phoenix.'

'Phoenix?' The name comes out louder than Fran meant it to.

'Yep, Phoenix who zoomed in on you the minute you arrived and hasn't left your side since. Do you think he knows who you are?'

'He doesn't know the first thing about me. He barely listened to a word I said during the session this morning. He seemed far more concerned about imparting the minutiae of his relationship history.'

'He didn't mention Gozo or Jenna.'

'No.'

'Or his relationship with Tom?'

'He's barely mentioned him. He told me he came here to rebuild his self-esteem after his boyfriend cheated on him.'

'And you believed him?'

Fran shrugs. 'I had no reason not to.'

'And Renata and Damian? Have either of them spoken to you or singled you out?'

'Not particularly. Although I was sandwiched between Phoenix and Damian at dinner.'

'I noticed.'

'Neither of them said anything of interest. Did Tom? You were . . . very friendly.'

'Drama GCSE paying off, finally.'

'You were very convincing, very adoring. I found you highly irritating.'

Caroline laughs. 'Apologies, by the way, for earlier, when I sniped at you when you interrupted Tom. That was all part of the act. Although I did want to hear what he had to say for himself.'

'Do you think they know who I am? The Gozo three?'

'I wouldn't have thought so. It's Tom I'd be more concerned about. The only reason I even know what you look like is because I door stepped your parents and you answered. I remembered your face even if you didn't remember mine. There's absolutely no trace of you on the internet at all. No Facebook page, no Twitter, even your school staff listing doesn't have a photo.'

'I value my privacy.'

'Wise woman. It's scary how much you can find out about someone. It's the kids in their teens and twenties I worry about, spouting all sorts on Twitter, with no thought to the future. Some of them could be potential leaders of the country or industry heads and it only takes one poorly worded tweet to bring it all crashing down.'

'Quite,' Fran agrees. 'I try telling my students that but they never—'

A sharp rap at the door cuts her off.

'Shit,' she says under her breath.

Caroline presses a finger to her lips and gets up from the bed. 'Hello?'

'It's Kate,' says a familiar voice from beyond the door. 'Could I have a word?'

'Stay here,' Caroline hisses to Fran. 'Wait until it's safe to leave. We don't want her to know you've been in here.'

Fran nods in agreement. How much of their conversation did Kate overhear as she crept up the garden? She looked suspicious, no doubt about that. She glances at her watch as Caroline slips out of the door – 10.21 p.m.

She waits, watching the door, listening. After what feels like an age, she looks at her watch again to see it's 10.24 p.m. She eases herself up from her chair, crosses the room, and listens at the door. Nothing. No argument, no raised voices. But that doesn't mean they're not still in the corridor.

She moves over to the window, pulls back the curtains and, after some frantic fiddling with the ancient hook on the sash window, slides it up and steps out into the flower bed. Apologising to the snowdrop she crushed under her shoe, she makes her way back round the front of the house, keeping close to the wall. All the curtains are drawn and her breath slows as she reaches the back of the house. No one's seen her, she's safe.

'Hello, Geraldine.' Damian puffs a cloud of cigarette smoke in her direction as she approaches the porch. Before she can answer he whips out his phone and points it at her. The shutter fires and Fran raises a hand to her eyes, half blinded by the flash. When she lowers it again, Damian has gone.

Chapter 19

Then

JENNA

Dinner is the worst kind of hell. Jenna can feel Tom watching her from the other end of the table and she's steadfastly refusing to meet his eye. There was no avoiding Kate though. She zeroed in on her in the queue outside the restaurant and angled her away from the others. She kept their chat short and her voice low. Tom had returned to the chalet shortly after Jenna left, she said. He was 'heartbroken', 'a shell of a man' and 'utterly contrite'. He was going to cancel the course and get on the first plane to the UK to check himself into a rehab facility for anger management but she'd talked him down. Afterwards, they meditated and practised mindfulness. The last thing either of them needed, Kate said, her eyes roaming Jenna's face, was for him to fall ill again. When Kate asked her if she'd told anyone, Jenna shook her head. 'The world needs more people like you,' Kate said, then hurried to the front of the queue as the Maître-D opened the restaurant doors.

Jenna has barely raised her gaze from her place setting since they all sat down. As the waiter places a plate of steaming fish and sautéed potato in front of her she leans to her left. Her gaze flicks towards Tom. He's chatting to Erica and she's in full flow, gesticulating wildly, her eyes never leaving his face. He smiles and nods then, sensing he's being watched, glances in Jenna's direction. Her stomach hollows, just as it's done every time he looks at her, but now the sensation is accompanied by a wave of anger.

'Some people,' Damian bellows, from the other side of the table, 'are wolves in sheep's clothing.'

Kate, sitting at the head of the table, takes a sip from her wine, watching from above the rim of her glass.

'Who's a wolf?' Alan, sitting to Jenna's right, leans forward, sniffing gossip.

Damian laughs and sets his wine glass down. It's empty, and so is the bottle of red wine in front of him. Jenna shoots him a warning look. Subtly, she pinches her lips together with her thumb and index finger.

He raises his eyebrows. 'What?'

Jenna steals a look at Kate. Tim and Bessie have dragged her into their conversation about property prices in London. She didn't hear what Damian just said.

'Hey, waiter!' Damian waves his hand in the air. 'One more of these.' He points at the empty bottle of wine.

Beneath the table, Jenna grips her knees. Her heels bounce on the restaurant floor. Giving Damian more booze is like pouring petrol into a bottle and then setting it alight. And she doesn't want to be there when he goes off.

Alan nudges her with his elbow. 'Everything okay?'

'Fine.'

'You sure? You've barely touched your food. Should I get a waiter? Or I could tell Kate—'

'No, no. The food's fine. I've just . . .' She pushes back her chair. 'Excuse me a minute.'

If she's not at the table to give Damian the reaction he's after, he might let it drop. Or at least turn his attention elsewhere.

She stands up so quickly that her thighs nudge the table, making it shake.

'Oh god,' Alan shoots her a sympathetic look. 'You haven't got the shits have you? I didn't feel right after lunch at the cafe and—'

'I'm fine, honestly.' Out of the corner of her eye she sees Damian raise both hands in the air.

'Oi, Jenna! Where you going?'

He continues to call after her as she hurries through the restaurant but she doesn't look round. Instead, she opens the glass door, crosses the courtyard, and heads for the bar. The barman, polishing glasses behind the counter, looks up as she enters.

'How can I help you?'

'A bottle of red wine, please. Dry.'

Jenna zones out as he reels off several different types. She just wants a bottle of red wine to take somewhere quiet and hide. It's only the first day of the retreat and she hasn't had a single moment alone. Everything she does, everywhere she goes, there are people – talking, staring, overflowing with emotion. Normally, she'd take all that in her stride – she likes her clients to chat while she manipulates their limbs or shows them exercises. Too many quiet clients in a row and she starts to feel unsettled – but she couldn't stand another moment at the table with Tom looking quizzically at her, Damian shouting across the table and Alan nudging her arm.

'The first one,' she says.

'Malbec?'

'Yes, fine. You can charge it to Room 17. Thanks.'

She hovers at the bar while he uncorks the bottle. She can't go back to her room because she's sharing it with Erica and she'll head there after dinner, and it's too cold to sit around the pool. She could always stay here in the bar. With everyone else at dinner the place is deserted. She picks up her bottle and glass and carries them across the room to a chair that's tucked away in the corner, angled towards the window. The barman doesn't seem like the chatty sort but she's not taking any chances.

Jenna is on her third glass of wine and the tension she's been feeling all day is finally beginning to ease. Outside, the sky is black, the solar lamps around the pool puddling the ground with a warm, orange glow. She rests her head against the seat back and looks lazily at the painting on the opposite wall, her gaze soft, her thoughts hundreds of miles away, circling around the little world she made for herself: a rented studio flat in East London and a small room in a private physiotherapy clinic nearby. She thinks about Friday night drinks in Clapham Common, cinema trips and holidays, spending almost every penny she earns so she doesn't have to return to the tiny space she calls home. Her mum's been needling her for years, telling her to stop renting and buy a flat but Jenna keeps putting it off. She's done everything else her parents expected of her – she took the A levels they suggested, studied for a degree they approved of and moved to an area of London they felt was suitable – but buying a flat felt like putting a lock on the cage she was living in. She could never give up her job if she had a mortgage to pay, never throw caution to the wind and give it all up to travel the world with a single rucksack and the clothes on her back. Not that she would have done that because her parents wouldn't have approved.

What they wanted, what they *expected,* of her, was to do a respectable job, marry a respectable man and give them grandchildren. *Do what Fran didn't*, that was the implication; the burden of the second child.

Fran had escaped. She was carving her own path through life before Jenna had even pulled up the straps of her first training bra but there was a part of Jenna that relished the spotlight of her parents' attention. She eavesdropped their conversations and made mental notes as they bitterly complained about her sister's wilfulness, selfishness and independent streak. She would be nothing like Fran, she decided. She would be a good girl – kind, helpful and obedient. She'd never let them down.

But it was hot under the spotlight – stifling and suffocating – and she longed to creep into the shadows, just for a break. She staged small acts of rebellion – a tattoo of a ladybird on her left hip, binge drinking, one night stands with unsuitable men – but her parents never found out and Jenna's 'last great hope' halo remained.

She met Nick, her ex, at a family wedding. He had her in hysterics over dinner and then swung her around the dance floor later. She could see her parents at a table watching, judging, leaning towards their friends asking, 'Who is that?' When Nick tried to kiss her she moved her face away, aware that they were still being watched, but then she took him by the hand and led him out of the marquee. She shagged him in an adjoining field and got grass stains on her dress and sheep shit on her knees. When they returned to the marquee, her mother beckoned her to the table. Jenna braced herself for a lecture – 'you didn't just let the family down, you let yourself down too' – but the lecture didn't come. Instead she'd whispered hotly in Jenna's ear, 'His father's a surgeon, hang onto him.' Any lust Jenna may have felt for Nick was immediately extinguished. Her mother's approval was an anathema to desire. But Nick knew none of this. He bombarded Jenna with texts until she finally agreed to a date. Three months later and they were madly in love.

Geraldine began a new campaign then. Instead of hassling Jenna about buying a flat she started talking about marriage. A year of dating, she felt, was a suitable amount of time for an engagement to take place but, given Jenna was already in her mid-thirties, the sooner they got married the better. 'You don't want to be a geriatric mother,' Geraldine repeated almost every time they spoke on the phone. Jenna did her best to block her mother out and concentrate on her relationship with Nick but Geraldine's comments were always there, buzzing in the back of her brain: 'You're running out of time', 'You won't meet anyone as good as him again', 'Snap him up while you can'. Her self-confidence faltered. Maybe her mother was right. Maybe Nick was her last chance at happiness. She hadn't had much luck with men in the past and he did make her laugh more than anyone she'd ever met, plus the sex *was* amazing. She found herself making excuses for behaviours that normally would have had her questioning a relationship – Nick rolling his eyes when she shared her doubts about her career, his refusal to talk about past relationships, the guilt trips he'd spin if he didn't get his own way and his inability to apologise – and decided that what they needed, after eighteen months of seeing each other every weekend, was a holiday. They were both tired, she reasoned, and they needed to get away. A week touring the Greek islands would repair his short temper and her neediness.

In the run up to the holiday, Nick started making excuses. He'd hurt his ankle playing football so couldn't go to the cinema, he couldn't make dinner because he had to stay late at work. He hadn't answered her texts because his phone had run out of battery. She knew what was coming. It had happened to her so many times before, but rather than confront him, she blocked it out. He was going through a wobble, she told herself. They happened in all relationships. She just had to sit it out, give him space, and wait for him to remember how much he loved her. But it was hard to talk on the phone and pretend nothing was wrong when Nick yawned into her ear and told her he couldn't talk long because he needed an early night. Or when the only texts he sent her were in response to something she had sent him. She stopped texting, to see what he'd do and, for forty-eight unbearable hours, she watched and she waited, snatching up her mobile whenever it pinged. Nick was still using WhatsApp. She could see the last time he'd accessed it and it hurt knowing he had time to message other people but not her.

Finally, she caved and tapped out a message: *What's going on with us?* Almost instantly, two blue ticks appeared beside her question. She watched the top of the screen, waiting for the words *Nick is typing* to appear. But they didn't. And that night she went to bed with the phone in her hand and her heart empty.

There was someone else, Nick told her the next day. Someone from work. He hadn't meant it to happen – neither had she – and they couldn't ignore the chemistry. Jenna thought she couldn't possibly feel more hurt or betrayed . . . until she received a text from her mother. *What do you mean Nick has finished with you? What did you do?*

She threw her phone at the wall.

She was still hurting six months later, when she went out for a birthday dinner with her friends and got beautifully, riotously drunk. If Jenna's life was a line of dominos, all but one had been knocked to the floor. Her career bored her, her boyfriend had cheated on her and she'd lost her self-respect. But at least she still had her family, as dysfunctional as it was. And then Fran gave her a present and kicked the last domino down.

Now, she jolts in her seat as someone knocks against the high back of her chair. A dark head peers down at her and warm, red-wine breath fills her nostrils. Damian's found her.

'Hey, hey. I was looking for you. What are you doing sitting here all alone?' He clumsily loops an arm over the back of the chair and perches on the armrest, but then overbalances and tumbles into the chair, half-sitting on Jenna and pinning her up against the other arm.

She shoves at him but his size and his drunkenness make him impossible to shift. 'Damian, get off. You're hurting me.'

'Oh, oh. Sorry.' He tries to move, one hand grabbing the back of the chair, the other waving uselessly in the air but all he succeeds in doing is shifting more of his weight onto her. She tries to wriggle away but there's nowhere to go. She's wedged in.

She calls for help but no one replies and all she can hear are Damian's grunts and groans as he tries – and fails – to grip both armrests and heave himself up.

He slumps back again and rests his head on the chair back. 'I'm sorry. I only . . . I wanted to tell you . . . Tom didn't hit anyone over dinner.' He starts to laugh, his body jiggling against her.

'Damian.' She shoves at him again. 'Just get up, would you.'

He looks at her. 'Are you still here?' Then the laughter begins up again.

'Damian, get off me!' She punches him in the arm, hard, and his laughter dries up instantly.

'Hey!' He touches a hand to her face, cupping his fingers around her jaw. 'What was that for? I like you. I like you, Jenna and I think you like me too.'

'I'd like you a lot more if you'd just get off!' She pulls at his hand but his fingers snap back against her jaw as quickly as she releases them.

'I really like you,' he slurs. 'I think we are kin . . . something . . .' He lunges at her, his beard grazing her chin, his wet lips pressing against hers. She twists her head away then hits out at him, smacking him around the side of the head with her palm.

He reels momentarily, then he grips her wrist, anger flaring in his eyes. 'That was a stupid thing to do.'

Chapter 20

Now

KATE

Kate keeps the smile firmly fixed to her face as she ferries toast racks and plates, piled high with eggs, beans, sausages and bacon, from the kitchen to the dining room table. She's underestimated Geraldine Rotheram. She's cleverer than she looks. Joy couldn't have looked more surprised last night when Kate pulled her to one side for a chat.

'Did I do something wrong?' Joy asked, as Kate led her to the therapy room.

Kate gave her shoulder a friendly squeeze then sat down in Tom's chair and indicated that Joy should take the other one. 'Not at all. I just wanted to check that everything's okay.'

'It's wonderful. This is such a lovely place.'

'You had a bit of a falling out with Geraldine this morning?'

Joy's doughy face flashed with horror at the memory. 'She

was so rude. I was surprised Tom didn't ask her to leave.'

'And yet you took a stroll around the garden together this evening?'

'That wasn't my idea!'

'I didn't say it was.' Kate tried to keep her tone light. 'Did she . . . um . . . what did you talk about?'

Joy picked at her cuticles, digging at them with her short, stubby nails. 'Not much. She wanted to apologise.'

'Good, that's good. What else did you chat about?'

'What we're both hoping to get out of this week.'

Kate waited for her to continue then, as the seconds ticked by and Joy looked at her expectantly, said, 'You can always talk to me. You know that, don't you? If anyone at the retreat makes you feel uncomfortable or if you feel pressurised to talk about anything you're not comfortable sharing.'

'I'm not sure what you mean.'

Inwardly, Kate sighed. This was the trouble with people with a low IQ; you couldn't just dangle something in front of them, hoping they'd notice. You had to shove it, full force, into their face. 'Sometimes people take advantage of trusting people,' she said. 'You might assume someone wants to be your friend but their motives might not be as innocent as they appear.'

'Are you talking about Geri?' Joy asked.

And then there was no holding in Kate's sigh. For someone like Joy, who'd been so affronted when Geraldine had interrupted Tom that morning, to be taken in by her faux friendship was disappointing. Not that Joy had anything of interest to share with her. This was her first retreat. She'd been a huge fan of SoulShrink for years, according to her booking form, but had only been able to afford a place after her mother had died and left her a small inheritance.

Now, as Kate places an English breakfast in front of Phoenix, she widens her smile. 'Everything okay?'

He returns her smile. 'Wonderful.'

She had a word with the Gozo clients when they first arrived, ensuring they realised how hard she had worked to ensure the retreat could go ahead, and how precarious the situation was regarding future retreats. She didn't want to worry anyone by suggesting there might be an investigative journalist in the group – the sessions only worked if the attendees trusted each other – but she did stress that any discussions about what had happened in Gozo would be unhelpful and might cause upset. Her chat seemed to have worked. Other than Tom's brief mention of the sweat lodge deaths in his welcome speech, she hasn't heard anyone discussing it.

'Two poached eggs on toast,' Kate says as she rounds the table to where Geraldine is sipping her coffee. She's pretty sure Geraldine deliberately requested something that wasn't on the menu. And poached eggs no less – an absolute bastard to get right without any vinegar in the water. Is she going to review Kate's culinary skills in her article? 'Not only is Tom Wade a murderer, his wife is a shit cook too.'

'Hope you enjoy them,' she says as puts the plate down in front of her.

Then choke to death, she thinks as she walks away.

Chapter 21

Now

FRAN

Fran's poached eggs are the worst she's ever eaten. She dabs her mouth with her napkin and places it over the eggy abomination on her plate. She'll ask for toast tomorrow. With salted butter and apricot jam. She can't stand raspberry. She doesn't floss her teeth each morning just to get pips wedged in the gaps. Sitting back in her chair, her gaze flits from Caroline to Renata, sitting beside her, and Damian, on her other side. Interesting that two of the three Gozo survivors have chosen to flank Caroline, while Phoenix is ever present at her own side. Fran had hoped to have a word with Damian about the photo he took of her the previous night, and his motivations for doing so, but he was late to breakfast and she was already seated between Peter and Phoenix.

The first fifteen minutes of breakfast were interminable as Phoenix recounted, in excruciating detail, the dream he'd had last night. Initially, she paid attention, hoping for a nightmare that involved a sweat lodge or a grey-eyed man with shoulder length hair. Instead, he told her the world's most tiresome story about a bird on a rollercoaster and how he'd tried to rescue it from between his feet only to trample it to death instead. She zoned out and stared at the salt cellar in the centre of the table until he finally took the hint and fell quiet.

She glances at her watch. They've got half an hour until Tom tells them the itinerary for the day; she can either confront Damian or get an update from Caroline about her conversation with Kate the previous night. She deliberates, then gets to her feet, subtly signalling to Caroline to do the same.

'Back porch,' she mouths.

Fran raises her eyebrows as Caroline joins her in the porch. She hadn't been able to appreciate the sheer awfulness of today's jumper whilst Caroline was tucked up at the table. It's an enormous white tiger head on a black background.

'Good disguise,' she says.

Caroline looks at her quizzically. 'I'm sorry?'

'The jumpers. You look just like a middle-aged woman with emotional problems.'

'I always wear these jumpers.'

Fran's throat tightens and she coughs lightly. 'Oh. So, um, what news? What did Kate want to talk to you about last night? I'm guessing she hasn't worked out who you are.'

Caroline crosses her arms over the tiger's head. Because she's embarrassed or cold, Fran isn't entirely sure. 'She doesn't. But she made it very clear that she doesn't want me talking to you.'

'Because I asked about Jenna?'

'That's part of it, I'm sure. She's certainly got her suspicions. She couldn't say your name without grimacing.'

Fran shrugs. She's seen similar reactions in meetings at work.

'Talking of suspicious,' she says. 'Damian took my photo last night. After I left your room I headed for the back door and he was here, smoking. He took my photo with his phone and then scarpered.'

'Strange.'

'That's what I—'

She turns sharply as the door behind her opens.

'Oh, there you are!' Phoenix's eyes shine with excitement from behind his glasses. 'Tom's announcing what we're up to this morning. No spoilers, but I hope you can both swim.'

Fran tugs at the clips on her life jacket as she stares in horror as the large yellow dinghy on the edge of the river. According to Tom's morning briefing, they're going white-water rafting to get them out of their safety zones. They're also going to learn how to embrace fear, relinquish control and put their trust in their instructor. Oh, and it will be a bonding experience too. All absolute crap in Fran's opinion. She's fairly certain stag parties don't go white-water rafting for spiritual enlightenment. They do it for lad points, Facebook photos and half a dozen beers afterwards.

'Is it safe?' She addresses her question to Tom, who is shepherding four of the guests towards the second dinghy.

He pauses. 'Would I ask you to do something that isn't?'

The question hangs in the air between them and it takes all Fran's self-control not to state the obvious.

'It'll be fine.' Kate's hand lands on Fran's shoulder. She shoos Tom away with her other hand. 'We've been on umpteen white-water rafting expeditions and the instructors have done hundreds, haven't you, Evan?' She smiles at the thin young man standing nervously to the left of the group.

He steps forward, offering Fran what she assumes is supposed to be a reassuring smile but looks more like the kind of grimace one of her students proffers when she asks them a question.

'All you have to do is paddle when I tell you to and stop when I say stop. If anyone falls in we have Mark and Emma here, our safety canoeists, who'll rescue you and return you to your raft.'

'Return us to the raft? In this weather? We'll freeze to death!' Fran glances across at Caroline who's stamping from foot to foot and rubbing her arms. Even with helmets and waterproof jackets under their life jackets, it's bitterly cold.

'You won't be out there for long,' Evan says. 'Forty-five minutes, tops. There's a lot of thick undergrowth either side of the river and even if we did get you onto the bank it's miles from a road. Much safer to get back in the raft if you fall in the water and continue on to the end of the course.'

Fran blows out her cheeks. The only reason she agreed to go on the trip in the first place was because she was hoping to have a quiet word with Damian, but each time she approached him Kate sidled over and interrupted.

'All right then,' Evan says. 'Everybody ready? Let's get going then.'

To Fran's great surprise, white-water rafting is actually quite a pleasant experience. After a halting start they've got into a rhythm. She's sitting between Caroline and Damian, with Kate, Renata and Phoenix on the opposite side, and their instructor Evan perched on the end. They're moving at speed, skimming the surface of the water, working as a team. That was another of Tom's reasons for choosing this activity. The first day was about non-judgemental listening and now they're working on trust and communication. Not that Fran's communicating with anyone, she's too focused on the scenery to join in with the chat. Their river route really is quite beautiful, cutting through the

Snowdonian forests, huge great Norway spruces and beeches lining the riverbank, the water glistening in the weak February sunshine. It's nowhere near as relaxing as being punted along the Cam in Cambridge but the air is fresh and clean and she's enjoying the exercise.

'Okay then, guys,' Evan shouts. 'Once we get round this bend we'll meet some rapids. You're going to be thrown around a bit but don't panic. Just do as I say. When I shout at you to paddle, paddle!'

Phoenix, sitting diagonally opposite Fran, squeals. With excitement or nerves she's not entirely sure.

'Everyone ready?' Evan asks.

'Would it matter if we weren't?'

'What was that Geraldine?'

She shakes her head. 'Never mind.'

'Okay, here's the bend. All right! Everyone hold onto your hats. It's about to get bumpy!'

The dinghy isn't the only thing that lurches as it drops into the mass of swirling, churning water. Fran's stomach cannonballs between her lungs as she frantically paddles, beating the water with her oar as Evan roars, 'Go! Go! Go! Go!' As the dinghy tips to the right, it lifts Fran's side into the air whilst Phoenix, Kate and Renata dip closer to the water. Phoenix squeals with excitement and paddles harder while Kate, teeth gritted, repeatedly jabs her oar into the foam. Beside her, Renata, white-faced and bouncing on the edge of the inflatable, clutches her oar with one hand and grips the safety line with the other.

'Keep paddling!' Evan yells above the roar of the river. 'Everyone keep paddling!'

The dinghy rights itself, slapping Fran and the others back onto the water. Something in her stomach – probably undercooked poached eggs – surges back up her oesophagus, making her gag, but she dips her oar back into the river and drags it through the water. Her oar clashes with Caroline's and there's a brief moment when they're entangled but now isn't the time for apologies and they wrangle their oars free.

'Come on guys, come on!' Evan shouts as the dinghy rocks from side to side and a huge wave slaps up against the side, drenching Fran.

'You come on!' she shouts. 'We're doing all the work.'

'Can't we do that trust game instead? The one where you fall backwards on dry land?' Caroline asks, and everyone laughs.

And then they're free, drifting gently down the river, with Evan guiding them between the rocks, as though the rapids were a terrible dream.

'Oh thank god.' Fran slips off the edge of the dinghy into the belly of the boat. 'I never want to do that again for as long as I live.'

This time it's Damian who laughs.

'What?' She looks at him.

'We've got two more like that before we get to the end. And the next one is worse.'

'You're kidding me?' She looks at Evan who grins.

'Come on Geraldine,' Kate says curtly. 'Sit back up.' She seems to catch herself and softens her tone. 'Everyone finds their first rapid scary but we made it through by working as a team. The next one won't be nearly as bad.'

As Fran hoists herself back onto the side of the dinghy she notices that Damian is smirking. At her hippo-like manoeuvre or Kate's comment, she's not quite sure.

'Okay, guys,' Evan says, his gaze fixed further down the river. 'We're about thirty seconds away from hitting the next one.'

'Steer round it!' Fran says, as he angles the dinghy towards the small patch of brown swirling water further down the river. Only Caroline laughs.

'Here we go!' Evan shouts. 'We're going to need some hard-core paddling and when I shout hold on, hold on! Right, now paddle!'

Fran does as she's told, ignoring the part of her brain that's screaming at her to lie flat on the floor and just hold on. The dinghy picks up speed, the river foaming ahead of them, rocks and low hanging tree branches speeding past.

'Hold on! Hold on!' Evan shouts.

Fran holds her oar beside her, the paddle pointing upwards, and weaves her fingers around the safety cord. She's barely got a grip when the dinghy lifts into the air then slaps back down on the river. A wave of water arcs over the front of the boat, drenching them all. Evan deftly weaves the dinghy around a large flat rock. It twists in the water and they hurtle towards the far bank but he deftly swerves it away before it hits. Back down the river they hurtle, towards the churning water. Thirty seconds ago it looked unthreatening and surmountable. Up close it looks like there's a monster caught beneath the surface, thrashing and twisting and churning the water into a violent, muddy vortex. Fran swears under her breath. The dinghy turns sideways.

'Paddle!' Evan shouts. 'Paddle! Paddle, paddle, paddle!'

The dinghy leaps and falls, leaps and falls, and Fran fights for breath, inhaling in short sharp bursts as wave after wave bursts over the boat, battering her body and slapping her skin. She tries to paddle but the river pulls at her oar, trying to yank it out of her hands. She's not aware of Caroline and Damian either side of her or the three people opposite. She can't hear Evan. She can't hear anything other than the roar of the water and someone's scream. It's as though she's trapped in a dark, noisy void, hovering on the edge of life. It's terrifying, nauseating and interminable. She just wants it to—

The thought is obliterated as there is a slap, the thwack of a wave, and the dinghy tips violently to the left. Fran's right hand flies up into the air as she reaches for something, anything to latch herself onto, to stop herself from falling into the water, but there's nothing to grab and the last thing she sees as she's hurled out of the boat and into the dark, churning water is Kate rising above her and her wide, horrified eyes.

Fran plummets, the water enveloping her, wrapping her on all sides, sucking her down. The roar stopped the second she hit the water. Now all she can hear is a thick, muffled drone, a baritone hum, enveloping her, wrapping her on all sides. Her descent slows and she's suspended in the river, dark shapes swirling around her. Shock holds her there until her lungs begin to ache and instinct kicks in. She has to get to the surface. She has to breathe.

She stretches her arms up and flippers her feet but the river buffets her, keeping her under. She kicks harder, lungs burning. Time slows as she pulls herself upwards through the murky water. Every cell in her body is screaming at her to take a breath but she can't, she mustn't. She's so close to the surface, so—

Something hard smacks against the side of her helmet, ricocheting her head to one side.

She reaches up, tries to pull herself through the water. But it happens again. Another thump, a stamp, this time on the top of the helmet. Then another, and another. The impact travels from her head to her neck then judders its way down her spine. The others are above her; she can see legs waving through the water. Someone is stamping on her helmet, keeping her under the water, holding her down. She twists in the water, staring frantically around. Her lungs are empty and burning. If she doesn't get to the surface in the next few seconds she's going to breathe reflexively and drown. Out of the corner of her eye she sees a shape – small, squat, bloated – several feet to her right but in the blink of an eye it is gone. Fran swims to her left, fear propelling her away from the legs and up, up, up. But she can't do it. She can't hold her breath a second longer. She has to inhale. She has to. She can't fight it anymore. She tips back her head and her lips part.

Chapter 22

Then

JENNA

Jenna is still staring at Damian in horror, her palm stinging, when Alan rounds the chair and gawps down at them.

'Woah, sorry.' He backs away, palms outstretched, his face creased with amusement as Damian releases Jenna's wrist. 'Looks like I've interrupted something. I just wanted to check you were okay Jenna and um . . . it appears that you are.'

'Wa-hay!' Damian's mood switches in a heartbeat and he raises a fist in a victory salute. 'You all right, mate! Come to join the party?'

Alan smirks. 'You're all right, big guy. Looks like you're having a party all by yourself.'

'It's not what it looks like!' Jenna wriggles frantically and shoves at Damian. 'For fuck's sake, just get him off me. I can't get out of the chair.'

Alan jolts into action. 'Right. Shit, sorry. Course.' He grabs Damian around both wrists and leans back but Damian, at least six stone heavier, doesn't shift.

'Easy now, boyo,' Damian says as Alan transfers his grip to just one of his wrists. 'You can have your turn later.' He starts laughing again, his shoulder knocking against Jenna with each heaving breath.

'Everything okay?' The barman appears at Alan's shoulder and quickly assesses the situation. 'Can I help?' When Damian shrugs the waiter grabs him by the hand and gestures for Alan to do the same. 'Okay. Three, two, one. Pull!'

Jenna winces as Damian shifts in the chair, his shoulder knocking against hers as he's hauled to his feet. As he sways on the spot, one hand on the barman's shoulder, the other on Alan's, Jenna slips out of the chair and heads out of the bar. She hears someone shouting her name as she runs.

'Hey, Jenna. Wait!' She's halfway down the corridor when someone touches her shoulder.

She turns sharply, half expecting to see Damian lumbering towards her but it's just Alan, his glasses on the end of his nose, his curls clinging to his damp forehead.

'Damian just passed out. He took out a table on his way down.'

'And?'

'He's fine. The barman went to get some other—' He breaks off. 'Are you okay? What happened back there?'

'I don't want to talk about it. Honestly, Alan, I'm fine. I appreciate you coming to check on me but I just . . . I just want to go back to my room.'

'That's cool. I'll come with you.'

'No.' She turns to go. 'I'm fine, honest—'

'I'm coming with you.' He loops his arm through hers and smiles. 'Make sure you get back safely.'

Jenna hasn't got the energy to argue so she lets him guide her out through the glass door and into the cool night air. The change in temperature makes her head pound. She feels like shit, and not just because she finished off the best part of a bottle of wine. She hit Damian. She slapped him in the face, just like Tom did to Kate. She's no different. Or is she? Damian kissed her. He forced himself on her when she couldn't escape. She was justified in doing what she did. Wasn't she? But there were no witnesses. It would be her word against Damian's. And Tom's word against Kate's. Her thoughts weave and swirl, becoming tangled and dark.

'I'm so excited to be here,' Alan says as they walk arm in arm along the paving stones that run the length of the chalets. 'I literally can't wait for the sweat lodge experience. I've been dreaming about it. I'm even okay with cutting off my hair and my hair is literally my best feature.' He runs his free hand through his curls. 'I'll probably look like Grant Mitchell without it but, honestly, I'm not bothered. Have you picked out a name for your rebirthing?' He doesn't wait for her to answer. 'I'm trying to decide between a couple of names. I really like the name Leaf but I think that suits someone thin and' – he laughs ruefully – 'so not me. I thought maybe Maximus and I could be Maxi for short but I'm just asking for trouble with that name, looking like this. You know, Maximus Fatus. Can you imagine the comments I'd get on social media? But if I get the name right I could like, totally reinvent myself. Once my hair's grown back obviously. But just like, how cool would it be to introduce yourself to someone and they're like, "Hi, I'm Adrian or whatever," and I'd be like, "Hi, I'm—"'

He draws breath as Jenna stops walking. 'Oh, right. Is this your chalet? You're sharing with Erica, aren't you? I really like her. I think she knows some of the cast of *Made in Chelsea* but – oh holy crap, what's that?'

Finally, he's noticed what Jenna has been staring at for the last couple of seconds. Lying on the ground, just outside the closed door to her chalet, with its wings outspread and its guts strewn over the paved patio, is a dead bird.

Alan covers his mouth with his hands. 'The poor thing it must have flown into your door and killed itself.'

Jenna's gaze flicks upwards to the wooden slats of the door, gapped to allow air to circulate into the room. Birds don't fly into solid closed doors. They fly into glass.

'That's not what happened,' she says.

'Hey?'

'Look closer.'

Alan tentatively crouches then gags into his hands and turns away.

Maggots, crawling around in the bird's burst intestines and wriggling around on the ground. The bird didn't just die. It's been dead for a while. And it didn't put itself outside her door.

Chapter 23

Now

KATE

It's the fifth time Kate has been white-water rafting, and her third time on this particular stretch of river, but the adrenaline rush she feels each time the dinghy speeds towards the rapids hasn't lessened. It's the sheer power of the water she finds so intoxicating, the way it rises up around the boat and hurls its passengers out. Then it's just her and the river, locked together as she flails and thrashes, struggling to survive. The elation she feels, the triumph, when her head breaks the surface and she fills her lungs with cold, damp air is like nothing she's ever known. It's better than food, than wine, than sex. It feels like a victory, every time, to have come so close to death and twisted out of its grasp.

Now, she grips hold of the side of the dinghy and drags herself up and over the side, into its belly. A slow smile spreads over her face as she lies on her back, panting, gazing up into the cold, grey February sky. She did it again. And if she can do that, she can do anything.

The sound of laboured breathing forces her up and onto her knees. Damian, cheeks pink with cold above the dark line of his beard, has thrown his arms over the side of the dinghy. She reaches out a hand to help him but he shakes his head sharply and nods towards Phoenix and Renata who have just resurfaced and are also hanging onto the sides. Kate scoots towards Renata first. She grabs the back of her life jacket and pulls. Renata slips into the boat like an eel and lies on the bottom, gasping and shivering. Shortly afterwards Damian hauls himself back on board.

Kate and Damian have to work together to pull Phoenix up and over the side. As they haul him in his trousers slip down over his hips, revealing his red AussieBum underpants. He snatches at his trousers with one hand, grabbing them before they disappear below his knees and then drops into the boat. Kate doesn't pause to check on him. Instead, she scans the water, looking for any sign of Geraldine or Joy. Her eyes meet Tom's as his dinghy skims over the water a few feet away. There's six in his boat, including his instructor. They've all made it out of the river unscathed.

Kate holds out a hand, palm upwards, and with the other hand shows Tom two fingers. She shakes her head. Two of her crew are missing.

'There!' As Tom's shout rings out she spots a yellow helmet breaking the surface of the water, several metres in the other direction. Geraldine's pale face follows, lips parted, sucking in air. Each time she inhales a terrible barking sound fills the air.

'An oar!' Kate shouts, reaching a hand behind her. 'Give me an oar.'

Someone presses a pole into her palm.

She kneels against the side of the dinghy and stretches out her arms, her fingers wrapped around the paddle. 'Grab the end!' The river is starting to pick up speed again and if they don't get Geraldine back into the boat she'll drift downstream. As Geraldine splashes towards the oar, still honking like a seal, Kate glances around. Where the fuck are the safety canoeists?

'Holy shit!' Phoenix scrambles onto his knees, making the dinghy rock precariously, and points further down the river. 'Joy's . . . oh my god . . .'

Kate follows the direction of his finger and her breath catches in her throat. Lying on her back, arms crossed over her chest and hurtling into the distance, is Joy. Speeding after her, riding the current, are the two safety canoeists.

As Kate stares, transfixed, the oar is roughly snatched from her hands and she's shoved against the side of the dinghy.

'Geri!' Evan shouts. 'Hang on. I'm pulling you in.'

Kate retreats to the opposite side of the boat and squeezes herself up against Renata, Phoenix and Damian, as the rafting instructor pulls Geraldine closer to the boat and then heaves her up and over the side.

'Are you okay?' He crouches beside her as she rolls onto her side and coughs violently, each inhalation a noisy, scratchy wheeze.

Evan looks over at the instructor in the other boat and raises his thumb. 'She's fine.'

'I am not fine.' Geraldine props herself up on her elbow. 'Someone was stamping on my helmet.' Her gaze flicks from Renata, to Phoenix, to Damian, before settling on Kate. 'I could have died.'

Chapter 24

Now

FRAN

Fran stands by the window of Caroline's room, watching a robin grub around in the dirt outside. 'Go to my one-to-one and let Kate slip in here and finish you off? Absolutely not.'

Caroline sighs and pulls the duvet tighter around her shoulders. It's been several hours since they returned from the river and they've both showered and changed their clothes. Unlike Fran, who feels fine, save a strange taste in the back of her throat, Caroline is still bone cold and has been complaining that her chest aches.

'What makes you think we're any safer in here?' she asks.

'Well, she can't drown us, for one.'

'No, but she could petrol bomb us through the window and set fire to the house.' Caroline laughs dryly. 'Scratch that, Kate's sneakier than that. Did you watch the interviews she did after Tom was arrested?'

'One or two.'

'Hideous: the tears, the choked voice, the insinuation that she was as much of a victim as those poor people who died.' Caroline imitates Kate's voice, '"Oh poor me, sucked in by a handsome, charismatic, self-help guru. He exploited my vulnerability and love for him. He made me lie to the guests and pretend I was his assistant."' She shakes her head. 'She's quite the actress, that's for sure, but the media were all over it. "Wade's third victim" and all that shit.'

'Why would they do that?' Fran turns to look at her. 'Pretend they weren't together?'

'Your guess is as good as mine. I imagine it's that whole boyband thing – more women go along to a gig if they think the hot guy they fancy is single. Most of Tom's social media followers are women. Any inane shit he tweets is immediately retweeted, praised or turned into a meme. They lap it up! Not that he writes them. I've heard from several sources that Kate does that. You know she tried to set herself up as a self-help guru after he started his sentence?'

'I didn't.'

'She took over the SoulShrink Twitter account – put her own name in the tagline and everything – even got herself a few TV and radio interviews. But whenever she talked about herself, and how Tom wasn't the only one who'd suffered from somatic symptom disorder, the interviewers would swiftly turn the chat back to him. No one was interested in her. It was all *Tom Wade, a charlatan or a misunderstood guru?* But there was no wound licking for Kate. She set up a tour across dozens of towns and cities. It was billed as *The Truth About Kate Wade* but there couldn't have been more than fourteen people in her London talk – most of them journalists – and seven in Oxford. She cancelled the rest of the gigs.'

Fran perches on the edge of the bed. She'd been so sure that Tom was the dangerous one, with his tears, his woe-is-me story, and his inability to put a coherent sentence together when asked about Jenna. She'd dismissed Kate as his loyal but uptight wife with her strained, fixed smile and robotic Stepford Wife manner. But, if what Caroline was saying was true, then maybe Kate had been pulling the strings all along. It certainly explained why she'd tried to drown them both. Unlike Phoenix, Renata and Damian, who'd looked horrified as Fran floundered on the floor of the dinghy, Kate showed no emotion at all. Her face was a blank. At the time, Fran had assumed that it was shock – she was hacking like a forty a day smoker and Caroline was floating down the river – but it wasn't. Kate's empty expression was the cool stare of a sociopath who'd just tried to kill two people and failed.

'She's clever,' Caroline says. 'I've got to give her that. To frame it as an accident.'

'We need to call the police.' Fran taps her pockets then holds out a hand. 'Give me your phone. I've left mine plugged in in my room.'

'No.'

'Pardon?'

'What part of framed it as an accident didn't you understand? Those helmets are tough. There wasn't a single dent in mine, never mind a footprint. If we had died a coroner would have ruled it accidental drowning. We have zero evidence to give the police to support an attempted murder charge. And we can't be a hundred percent sure that Kate was the one kicking us. I couldn't see sod all but if your eyesight is superior to mine and you could tell the difference between all the legs then sure, let's ring the police.'

Indignation flames in Fran's chest. 'If you're going to be condescending—'

'I'm not.' Caroline holds up her hands. 'I'm sorry. I'm just frustrated. These people seem to think they can get away with murder. And they have! They whitewashed what happened to your sister and they nearly did the same with us. Kate's as bad as Tom. They're in it together. I don't know if he's pulling the strings or she is but they're dangerous.'

As Caroline continues to rant, Fran stares at her in awe. It's been a while since she's met someone with such fervour and passion, such a powerful drive to vanquish injustice and reveal the truth. It's really quite inspiring, despite Caroline's dubious taste in knitwear.

'And that,' Caroline says, 'is why I'm not going to let them drive me away. They might have found a way to cover up your sister's murder but they're not going to intimidate me into letting this drop.'

'No, but they could kill you.'

'Us. They could kill us. But the thing is—' Caroline covers her mouth with her hand as a cough steals her voice. As she continues to hack – a dry, brittle sound – Fran gets up.

'I'll get you some water.'

She heads into the en suite and turns on the tap. As the glass fills she sorts through her thoughts. Her initial reaction – her *logical* reaction – to what had happened was to ask someone to ring 999 from the riverbank so she and Caroline could be taken to the nearest hospital to be checked over. Caroline had poo-poohed the suggestion.

'I'm fine,' she told Evan. And, to be fair, she did seem to have weathered the experience relatively well. Her skin was pale and she was coughing intermittently but her pulse was strong and she was breathing normally. So was Fran. Her strange seal bark had disappeared after they swerved the last swirling rapids and the dinghy bobbed its way to the bank.

'I just inhaled a bit of water,' Caroline said. 'Everyone did when we capsized. The only difference was the fact I decided to be my own boat!' She smiled gratefully up at the canoeist who'd rescued her. 'Thanks for letting me hold on until we got to the bank.'

'Are you sure?' Tom hovered over her. 'I really think a doctor should—'

'No need,' Caroline snapped. 'I'm absolutely fine. And so is Geraldine.'

Her eyes locked with Fran's. 'You're fine.' She stressed the word *fine*. 'Aren't you?'

'Yes,' Fran replied, although she wasn't quite sure why.

Evan reluctantly put his phone away, then there was a flurry of noise and motion as Caroline and Fran found themselves surrounded by the other guests, gabbling and exclaiming and squeezing forearms and patting backs. For Fran, it was almost as excruciating as being stamped on the head.

Now, she turns off the tap and carries the glass of water out of the en suite. She hands it to Caroline and hovers by the side of the bed as she gulps at it.

'Do you want any more?' she asks as Caroline sets the empty glass on the bedside table.

Caroline shakes her head then settles herself back against her pillows. Dark circles have settled under her eyes and she looks pale and drained.

'I think it was a mistake,' Fran says, 'not to call an ambulance.'

Caroline flashes a weak smile at her. 'I just need a couple of hours of rest and then I'll be fine. We need to be here, Fran. There are only a few days left of the course. There's what, nine of us here? I'd be surprised if Tom and Kate hold another one; no one's interested in SoulShrink anymore. Do you want to find out what happened to your sister or not?'

'Of course I do.'

'Which is precisely why you need to go to your one-to-one with Tom.'

Chapter 25

Then

JENNA

A wave of nausea forces Jenna to stop walking. She presses a hand to her chest and takes a few shallow breaths. How the hell is she going to sit, alone, in the same room as Tom, without mentioning what happened the previous day? She was going to hide in her bedroom until her scheduled one-to-one session was over but Kate came looking for her.

'Please,' she begged as Jenna answered the knock on her chalet door. 'Go to your one-to-one or Tom will get suspicious that something is up, but don't mention what you overheard yesterday.'

Jenna protested – she didn't want to be anywhere near Tom – but Kate pushed her until she finally agreed; she'd go to her therapy session and she wouldn't mention a word about the slap. But now she's mere feet away from sitting alone in a room with him she doesn't see how she can. How can she look him in the eye, and say nothing, when she knows what he did? How can she open up to him when all she wants to do is scream abuse in his face?

Just yesterday she was in the sea with him, laughing and talking and swimming. She liked him. She respected him. She was attracted to him. And now here she is, standing at the far end of the alley, pressed up against the wall of his chalet, feeling sick with anger and fear.

You can do this, she tells herself, then she walks around the corner and into his room.

Tom's chalet is twice the size of Jenna and Erica's, with a double bed against the back wall with two armchairs in front, either side of a low table. The bed has been made and the pillows have been plumped but there's no sign of any personal items. No suitcase, clothes or books. The only sign that anyone lives in the room is an electronic key fob, lying on one of the bedside tables. She sniffs the air. Is that coffee she can smell?

The door at the far end of the room opens and Tom walks in with two steaming mugs in his hands. He jolts as he notices Jenna, hovering beside one of the armchairs, then smiles widely.

'Hi! You're here. Sorry, I wanted to have everything set up before—'

'I can leave.'

'No, no. Take a seat. It's all good.'

As Jenna sits down, Tom places the coffees on the table and she catches a waft of his vanilla, tobacco aftershave mixed in with the warm, rich scent of their drinks. She watches as he moves over to the patio doors and pulls them closed. They spent over an hour alone when they went swimming last night and he didn't so much as touch her, but she doesn't trust him anymore. What she overheard put paid to that.

'How are you doing?' Tom settles himself into the armchair on the other side of the table.

Jenna takes a sip of her coffee then sets it back on the table, deliberately avoiding eye contact.

'Everything okay?'

'Not really.' She can feel him watching her, his eyes roaming her face, reading her expression, but she can't bring herself to meet his gaze.

'Why's that?'

'I found a dead bird outside my room last night.'

'Sounds horrible.'

'It was.' She tries to push the image of the bloodied bird, its guts gaping, from her mind, but the more she tries not to think about it the more it hooks itself in her brain.

'You know men with violent tendencies often harm animals,' she adds.

'That's true. Particularly of serial killers. As children they'll often torture and abuse animals. It's not just men though. Child murderer Mary Bell throttled pigeons.'

'Well if any animal deserves to get throttled . . .' She tails off. 'That was a joke, by the way.'

'Glad to hear it.'

An uncomfortable silence settles between them. Tom reaches for his mug. Jenna does the same. She can feel his confusion weighing on her. He doesn't understand her change in mood.

'What colour was the bird?' he asks.

'What's that got to do with anything?'

'I was curious. Birds play an important part in mythology.'

'It was black.'

'Right.'

'Right what?'

She glances up at him as he sits back in his seat and crosses his legs, resting the ankle of his right leg on his left knee. 'Black is the colour of the unconscious, of the unaware. A black bird is said to be the spiritual representation of some unresolved tension within you that requires your attention.'

'That's bollocks.'

'Are you holding onto something that is hurting you, Jenna?'

'You know I am!' She sits forward so sharply her knees knock against the table and coffee slops over the sides of the cups. Tom jumps up and heads to the kitchenette. He returns with a tea towel and dabs at the spill.

'You're angry today.'

'People get angry' – she meets his eyes – 'even you.'

'Sure. I get angry, of course I do. But why you, why today?'

How did she get him so wrong? All this – these questions, this faux concern – he's so good at it. He makes her feel special, like he cares, but it's just play-acting.

Tom settles himself back into his seat. 'What are you thinking? Right now?'

'That I'm tired of people disappointing me. That I can't trust my own judgement. That maybe I should assume the worst of everyone so I'm not disappointed.'

'That's a cynical way of looking at life.'

'Is it?' She raises her eyebrows.

'Of course. In my experience, the majority of people in the world are good and decent.'

'And the ones who aren't?'

'Are often damaged.'

'But obviously you could fix them, couldn't you Tom? The SoulShrink can fix everyone.' She feels tense and twitchy. She wants to run until she's exhausted, or swim until she can't breathe. She wants to get as far away from this woman beating charlatan as quickly as she can.

'No. I can't. But I'd like to help you.'

'Bullshit!' She upends the table, sending the coffee cups scurrying towards Tom. He yelps as it splashes over his legs and pushes back his chair, scrabbling to stand up. Jenna gets up too. They face each other, the upended table between them.

Jenna braces herself. This is where Tom loses his temper and hits her. If he does then screw her promise to Kate. She'll shout it from the rooftops.

But Tom doesn't hit her. Instead, he rights his armchair, tips the table back into position, mops up the mess and removes the mugs to the kitchen. Then he disappears into a back room for a couple of minutes and reappears in a clean, dry pair of trousers. He retakes his chair and looks questioningly at Jenna, still standing beside her chair with her hands clenched at her sides.

'Shall we continue?'

To Jenna's horror, she bursts into tears.

Tom pushes the box of tissues across the table at the exact moment Jenna reaches for one. Her fingers slide over his and she pulls her hand away sharply.

'Sorry.'

'Don't be.'

He's still sitting forward in his seat, his hand resting lightly on the tissues. His gaze doesn't waver as their eyes meet. He looks straight at her, into her. She can feel him rooting around in her brain, reading her thoughts.

'Why did you do that?'

It takes her several seconds to process which 'that' he's talking about.

'I was angry with you.'

'For what?'

'I think you know.'

'No.' He shakes his head lightly. 'I really don't.'

'You were one more person to add to a long list.'

'Of what?'

'People who aren't who they appear to be.'

He puts a hand to his jaw, his thumb pressed into his cheek as he looks at her thoughtfully. 'Is it something I said or . . . or did?'

Jenna rubs at her arms, suddenly cold. She can't break her promise to Kate.

'Are you cold? I could get you a blanket.'

'No,' she lies.

'You're shivering. Let me get you one.'

As Tom disappears into the back room again Jenna looks past the glass doors, into the small, walled patio outside. A small black and white cat is stalking across the patio. Sensing it's being watched, it turns sharply and stares, its green eyes startled and suspicious. Jenna stares back, then, remembering something someone told her about making friends with cats, blinks slowly and deliberately. She's thirty-seven and animals are still a bit of a mystery to her: cats she finds unpredictable, horses are nervy and dogs are either over-friendly or aggressive. It's not that she doesn't like animals, she just can't read them. She was desperate for a pet as a child but her dad was in the army and they moved house every couple of years so animals were a no-no. She'd quite like a cat but every lease she's ever signed has said 'no pets'. She's so lost in thought that she doesn't hear Tom walk back into the room and when he gently places a blanket around her shoulders she shrieks in alarm.

'Woah.' He moves away, hands raised. 'I'm sorry I . . . I should have asked if it was okay to touch you.'

'You didn't ask Kate.' The words are out of her mouth before she can stop them.

'Sorry?'

'I know what you did, Tom.'

He shakes his head, bewildered. 'I don't . . . I . . .'

'I heard you. After we went swimming. You came back here with Kate. I was just around the corner when you were arguing. I heard you hit her.'

There's a beat of silence. 'That's not what you heard.'

'Isn't it? Because it sounded like a slap to me.'

Tom stares at her for the longest time, unblinking, then he lowers his gaze. When he finally speaks, his voice is so quiet she doesn't catch a word.

'What was that?' she asks.

Tom continues to stare at the terracotta floor tiles beneath his feet. 'You got it wrong.'

She bristles. This is where he makes an excuse; tells her that Kate goaded him into hitting her. 'Did I now?'

'Forget it. Forget I said anything.'

'No, you don't get to do that. You can't just brush it under the table.'

'Just leave it.'

'Is that what you said to Kate, right before you hit her?'

'She hit me. Okay?'

Jenna stares at him, too shocked to respond.

'Kate hit *me*. Not the other way round.'

Is he telling the truth? Or is this some twisted attempt to regain her sympathy? She doesn't know what to believe.

'For fuck's sake. This is why I . . . why I can't . . .' He covers his face with his hands.

'Why you can't, what?'

Tom says nothing but he's no longer just covering his face with his hands, he's holding the weight of his head in his palms. He's telling the truth, she suddenly feels sure of it. It's in his slumped posture, the beaten curve of his neck and the croak of his voice. He's curling into himself, hiding his humiliation in the hollow of his collarbone. This isn't a man who's ashamed of hitting a woman, it's a man ashamed of being hit.

Without thinking, she stands and wraps her arms around him, pulling him close. His arms close around her waist and he shudders against her, sobbing into her hair.

'It's going to be okay, Tom. Talk to me. You can trust—' The rest of her sentence is lost in an anguished screech from outside. A black and white blur streaks across the patio and a rock the size of a fist lands where the cat had been sitting just moments before.

'What the hell?' Jenna yanks open the patio doors and stares around, trying to work out where the rock came from, then she points straight ahead.

'There's someone behind that wall.' She looks back at Tom, bewildered, a foot or so behind her. 'There's a gap. Can you see? Between those two bricks. There's someone watching—'

A grey shape cuts through the air, striking her above the left eyebrow before she can twist away. A rock clunks onto the patio. And then there's blood. Blood on her temple, blood on her cheek, and blood on her hands.

Chapter 26

Now

KATE

Kate's been listening at Joy's door for the best part of five minutes and the only words she's caught are 'drowned', 'SoulShrink' and 'murder'. Everything else has either been too quiet to make out or obliterated by Joy's hacking cough. What exactly is Geraldine asking her? Any normal person would have taken themselves off to hospital for a check-up after nearly drowning white-water rafting but no, Geraldine insisted on returning to the retreat. Clever bitch that she is, she made it look like Joy's idea. She must have had a quick word in her ear when Kate's back was turned and Joy, being the dumb little sheep that she is, let herself be talked into it.

Geraldine's got her angle – SoulShrink Nearly Kills Again – she just needs some soundbites from Joy, 'the other woman who nearly drowned'. Her editor will turn cartwheels when she phones it in.

Kate balls her hands into fists. She wants – she *needs* – to hit something, to pound both fists through Joy's door and drag Geraldine out by the neck.

When the story comes out she and Tom will end up spending the rest of their lives stacking supermarket shelves. They'll never have a beautiful home again, never have a comfortable life. They're going to have to scratch and scrimp for the rest of their lives. Everything she's worked so hard to rebuild will be destroyed as soon as the story goes live. And it's all Geraldine Rotheram's fault.

She can't ask the woman to leave because she's got no proof. Well, she could, but that won't change anything. She'll still have her story. She'll still destroy Kate's life.

Think Kate, think. She rests her forehead on the cool painted wall. How can she turn this around? How can she stop Geraldine from filing her story?

How can she make her just disappear?

Chapter 27

Now

FRAN

Fran pauses in the doorway of the small room and glances around; not that there's much to look at – just two armchairs, facing each other, with a low table separating them. On the table there's a box of tissues, a jug of water and two glasses. And that's it, other than a couple of bland landscapes on the walls and a small wooden dish on the window sill. Oh, and Tom, sitting in one of the armchairs with a banal smile on his face. She remembers her mother's last text – *If you haven't got the truth out of that man yet I'll get Dad to wheel me onto a train to Wales and I'll do it myself* – and steels herself.

'Hello, Geraldine.' Tom rests his hands on the arms of the chair and makes a half-hearted attempt at rising, but doesn't actually stand. Fran feels a prickle of irritation. Gentlemanly behaviour doesn't impress her – she largely finds it antiqued and patronising – but there's a place for good manners in society. She opens doors for everyone, regardless of their gender, and expects the same courtesy in return. But Tom's attempt to acknowledge her presence was so decidedly lacklustre she'd rather he hadn't bothered at all.

'Hello, Tom.' She takes the seat opposite him, perches on the edge and looks at her watch. The session is tabled to last an hour but she's hoping she can be in and out in fifteen minutes. Caroline was insistent that she attend, in case Tom let anything slip about Jenna, but Fran isn't hopeful. If their last discussion was anything to go on he'll probably burst into tears the moment she mentions her sister's name.

'How are you?' Tom sits forward, his brow creased with concern. 'I wasn't sure I'd see you this afternoon, not after what happened earlier.'

Fran waves a dismissive hand through the air. 'It was an early bath.'

'It must have been scary, not being able to get to the surface.'

Interesting choice of words, Fran thinks. No hint that a murder was a lungful of river water away from being committed.

'Your wife was stamping on my helmet. Joy's too.'

Her words deliver the impact she hoped they would. Tom sits back in his chair and he stares at her incredulously. He gulps, his lips repeatedly opening and closing like a goldfish, before he finally finds his voice.

'I'm sure she didn't mean to . . . I mean, obviously everyone was trying to get to the surface. I'm sure she had no idea you were beneath her. I imagine everyone was kicking their legs, weren't they?'

No. It's on the tip of Fran's tongue but, actually, he's right. And Caroline said the same earlier. She shifts in her chair. Maybe going in with an attack wasn't the cleverest of moves.

If Tom's on the defensive he'll be wary for the entirety of their session.

'Of course they were.' She forces a smile. 'I'm sure I'd have stamped on someone's helmet too if I weren't so heavy and hadn't sunk deeper than everyone else. No harm done, no one died.'

'Quite.' Tom runs his fingers over the side of his face as he regards her. A comforting gesture, Fran thinks. Unwise of me to use the word *died*.

'What do you have in store for us tomorrow?' she asks, trying to swerve the conversation onto safer ground.

'A pole jump.' His lips prick up at the edges. A smile or a smirk? Fran's not entirely sure.

Oh lord, she thinks. Another opportunity for Kate to try and kill me off.

'Wonderful,' she says instead.

Tom continues to gaze at her, his eyes roaming her face.

'What scares you, Geraldine?'

She pauses to think. 'Failing,' she says eventually.

'In what way?'

'I'm a teacher, a good one, and if I fail, I fail not just myself but my students, too—' Fran catches herself. Bugger. She's done it again, brought up the fact she's a teacher not a retired whatever it was she was supposed to be. Mentally she slaps herself on the side of the head.

'Obviously I no longer teach,' she adds tartly. 'I'm retired. But I still think of myself as a teacher.'

Tom nods. 'It's a big part of your self-image.'

The man obviously hasn't bothered reading his notes.

'Yes,' Fran says. 'It is. Was.'

'So what scares you now? Now you no longer have a responsibility to your students?'

'Being without purpose.' The words come out of her mouth

without a moment's hesitation. It's true. The idea of retirement terrifies her, floundering around in the world with nothing to do.

'And what gives you purpose at the moment?' Tom asks.

Fran racks her brain. How would Geraldine answer? Her mind immediately flits to her mother. What's her purpose in life other than moaning about her husband? Gossiping about the other women in the local area? Judging her daughters and pouring scorn on their life choices? Fran rests her elbow on the arm of the chair and her gaze drifts beyond Tom to the naff painting on the wall. She's got that wrong. Her mother judges her, not Jenna. Whilst Fran was a brittle child who had the tears beaten out of her at boarding school, Jenna was softer, more malleable. With her parroty little expressions and her willingness to please it was no surprise that Geraldine had chosen to keep her at home rather than send her away.

'You're finding it hard to answer that question, aren't you?' Tom says, and Fran looks at him in surprise. She'd completely forgotten he was even in the room.

'Yes,' she says, although she can't remember what the question was.

'You're quite young,' Tom says, 'to retire. I imagine caring for your late husband gave you purpose too, in its own way.'

'Hmmm,' Fran says. Lying doesn't come easily to her. Nor does acting. There's a very good reason she was always cast as sheep, donkeys and trees during primary school productions.

'You're struggling, aren't you? With your grief.'

'It's hard to grieve when someone is taken from you unexpectedly.'

'His death was sudden?'

'Very sudden. I . . . I wasn't expecting it.'

'That must have been hard.'

'Very. You don't expect to lose people, particularly when they're so much younger than you.'

'There was an age gap?'

'Yes. Twelve years.' She searches his face, looking for a reaction, for a muscle twitch or a squint of the eye, some hint that he knows that she's talking about Jenna, not her fictitious late husband, but all she can see is concentration and compassion.

'It's the regret that's hit me hardest,' she says. 'All the things I didn't say, all the conversations we never had. I don't feel I knew . . . him . . . as well as I should. I didn't take the time to ask him how he was or what he was feeling. I was too caught up in my own life.'

'And where do you feel that regret?'

'I'm sorry?'

'In your body,' Tom clarifies. 'Where do you feel the regret?'

'In my brain, because that's where thoughts originate.'

'Close your eyes.'

Fran looks at him in alarm.

'I just want to do an exercise with you. Everyone holds their pain in different parts of their body. You may think it's in your brain but let's see if it's anywhere else.'

Fran deliberates, casting an eye over the room for any potential weapons that could be used to clunk her over the head while her eyes are shut.

'You're perfectly safe,' Tom assures her.

'Is Kate coming in?'

'Sorry?'

'Never mind.' She closes her eyes.

'Okay,' Tom says softly. 'With your feet flat on the floor and your arms resting lightly on your lap, tell me again about your regrets.'

Fran opens her eyes. 'I can't do this.'

'Why not?'

'It's not the sort of thing I do.'

'What isn't?'

Fran shifts in her seat. The air in the room feels thick and cloying and she feels the sudden urge to escape to the fields surrounding the house. She wants to draw cold air into her lungs, listen to bird song and let the wind blow the fog from her brain. Or to get in her car and drive back to London with the windows open and an audiobook playing. But she can't leave. If she has regrets now, how much greater will they be if she abandons her only hope of discovering what happened to Jenna?

'I don't like talking about my emotions,' she says flatly.

'Why is that?'

She sighs. It's the incessant questioning she finds so very wearing. It's like being poked repeatedly. Is that why he's doing it? To illicit some kind of reaction? Well, she'll save him the trouble and cut out the crap.

'Because it confers power to the other person.'

'Power?'

'Yes. Of course. If someone tells me politics makes them angry, cancer stories make them anxious or remembering their childhood makes them sad, they are effectively showing me where their weak spots are and giving me the ammunition to hit them where it hurts. And, before you ask, no, that's not something I would do.'

'But some people would?'

'Of course.'

'Has that happened to you?'

She looks at him steadily. 'Are you squeamish, Tom?'

'Not really.'

'Good. Let me share an analogy. I watched a documentary about ravens once. They stalked a ewe who was giving birth. The farmer was in a different field and the ewe was labouring and couldn't run. As the lamb's head was birthed the ravens pecked out its eyes. Even if it had lived it wouldn't have been able to feed, because they also consumed its tongue.' Tom presses a hand to his face in horror but Fran continues on. 'The ravens attacked the lamb when it was at its most vulnerable and the ewe couldn't protect it. A child sent to boarding school may as well be a lamb in a field full of ravens. No, not a field, a cage – because there's nowhere to run. And you can't fight back when you're outnumbered.'

'You were bullied as a child?'

'Mercilessly. Bored children will always look for entertainment, and I was theirs. Tears delighted them, retaliation fuelled them and silence was the only weapon I had.'

'You learned to suppress your emotions.'

She smiles wryly. 'An arrow can't pierce a house made of bricks.'

'Are your parents expressive people?'

'My mum threw a cup of tea in my face a few weeks ago. I'd say that was quite demonstrative.'

For several seconds Tom says nothing. Instead, he studies Fran's face so intently she can't bear it and looks away.

'I think I understand you now,' he says eventually. 'You came here because you're struggling with grief but the root cause of your pain is anger. You've suffered a great deal, Geraldine. You were sent away from home as a child, you were bullied and you developed a survival strategy to stop yourself being hurt ever again. And it's probably worked. You haven't let anyone close enough to hurt you. But you did love someone; you must have, to feel such intense grief and regret. Anger won't bring them back though. And self-recrimination won't help you heal. You have to forgive yourself. You did the best you could, Geraldine, with the life you've lived and the experiences you've been through. Love doesn't need words to be felt. The person you lost will have known how much you loved them.'

Fran swallows but her throat is tight and knotty and her chest is burning more than it did after she nearly drowned. She presses a hand to it and takes a shuddering breath.

'I wish that was true.' Her voice is a whisper. 'But I don't think they did.'

Chapter 28

Then

JENNA

Jenna smiles gratefully as the receptionist perches on the sofa beside her in the lobby, then winces as the woman dabs at her forehead with an antiseptic wipe. Over at the counter, Tom is deep in discussion with the manager. He's speaking confidently yet calmly, gesticulating with his hands as he describes what happened, all trace of the distressed man she held in her arms minutes earlier now gone. He was a quivering wreck and no one can be that good an actor. She is convinced that Kate hit him but she's got so many questions. Why did Kate go along with Jenna's assumption that Tom hit her? Why swear her to secrecy? Was she worried the truth would come out? And why didn't Tom sack her?

She catches herself. Kate's not the only one who's been violent towards Tom. Less than half an hour ago Jenna flipped a table over, spilling coffee all over him. She hit him too, yesterday, after their swim. She pummelled his chest with her fists and then sobbed in his arms. But he invited her to hit him, to ease her distress. Is that what he does? Let women take out their frustration on him? But that wasn't the situation between Tom and Kate; Kate was angry rather than upset. There was an argument, a slap, a gasp and then Kate forced Tom to say sorry. Why apologise when Kate was the one who lashed out?

Her gaze drifts to the ring finger of Tom's left hand. It's bare and there's no suntan mark where a ring could have been. She knows because she checked as they chatted after his seminar in London and she felt that first twinge of attraction. She found Kate irritating even back then, the way she hovered, listening in to Tom's conversations but she's been worse in Gozo, shooing him away from people, continually chasing and chastising him.

Jenna looks round at the sound of heels clacking on tiles; Kate's arrived. She heads up to reception and taps Tom on the shoulder, making him flinch.

'Tom, what's going on? Alan told me he saw Jenna running through the hotel with blood all over—' She catches sight of Jenna and heads over to the sofa. 'Oh my god. Are you okay? What happened?'

Before Jenna can answer, Tom joins them. 'Someone was throwing rocks into the patio. I think they were after a cat but they hit Jenna as she left her session.'

Jenna glances at him. Interesting that he told Kate it had happened *after* their session.

'Did you pass out?' Kate crouches beside the sofa and rests a hand on Jenna's knee. 'If you've got concussion we need to get you checked out.' She twists to look up at Tom. 'Have you rung for a doctor?'

'Of course.'

'And the police? Are they on their way too?'

Jenna sees the panic in her eyes.

'No. We're waiting for the porter to come back. He went outside to see if he could see anything.'

'Right, okay. Well . . .' Kate gets up and heads over to the manager.

Tom edges closer as the receptionist finishes up and gathers up the piles of bloodied wipes on the table. 'How are you feeling, Jenna?'

'I'm okay. I've got a bit of a headache but—'

'No one there!' A sweaty porter bursts through the open doors. 'I had a look but found nothing.'

The manager asks him a question in Maltese, then frowns at the answer.

'What is it?' Kate asks. 'What did he tell you?'

The manager, a thin man in his forties with a neat moustache, turns to address the group. 'He thinks it was probably kids from the local village. We have a lot of cats here and sometimes they come to throw stones at them.'

Jenna thinks about the gap in the bricks and the eye, watching her, unblinking, from behind the wall. It could have been a child but the cat was long gone when the second rock was hurled into the patio area.

'I still think the police need to be informed,' Tom says.

'No.' Kate shakes her head sharply. 'The manager just said it was children. What are the police going to do, arrest them?'

'They could put the fear of god in them.'

'No police.' Kate glances at her watch. 'Tom, you need to get going. You've got another session in five minutes. I'll wait with Jenna for the doctor to arrive.'

Jenna raises her hands in objection. 'You don't have to. I'll be fine alone.'

'If you're sure . . .' She hears the relief in Kate's voice. 'Come on then, Tom, let's go.'

'I heard you.' He doesn't move from Jenna's side. 'Next session in five minutes.'

Kate raises her eyebrows. 'Tom?'

'I do own a watch.'

'Of course you do.' She flashes a tight smile at Jenna, then stalks out of reception, her heels clacking on the tiles like a stopwatch counting down.

'Can we go outside for a bit?' Jenna asks Tom as the manager and the receptionist head back behind the counter.

He frowns. 'I'm not sure that's a good idea. I think you should sit down until the doctor gets here.'

'I want to talk to you, in private.'

'Okay.' He reaches out a hand to help her up and continues to hold it as they make their way out through the double doors and into the courtyard where two huge palms guard the archway and prickly pears and shrubs are crowded into the raised stone beds. When Tom pauses Jenna lets go of his hand.

'This way.' She gestures for him to follow her out towards the road then stops, her back against the wall that surrounds the hotel complex. Beyond the road, rough eggshell-coloured scrubland is edged by a patchwork of brown furrowed fields and lush green stretches of grass.

'You all right?' Tom stands beside her. 'What's going on?'

'Who's Kate?'

'Sorry?'

'Kate. She's not just your assistant, is she?'

'What . . . why . . . what makes you think that?'

'Just tell me, Tom.'

He slumps against the wall, his gaze fixed somewhere in the distance.

'Tom?' she says again. 'Is Kate your girlfriend?'

His lips tighten and he frowns. He looks torn. 'No.'

'But you're in love with her?'

This time he glances at her. 'No. Jenna, why are we having this conversation?'

She looks at him steadily. 'You tell me.'

Chapter 29

Now

KATE

Geraldine's a bloody good actress, Kate concedes as she clicks stop on Geraldine's recording, closes the program and removes the SSD card from her laptop. All that stuff about being bullied as a child would have been quite moving if it had been true. It obviously wasn't. No undercover journalist would have shared her darkest secrets with the man she was investigating. She must have lifted it from some poor sod whose story she'd covered. If Kate had been counselling her, rather than Tom, she'd have pushed Geraldine to say more and exposed the holes in her story. But, Tom being Tom, he'd lapped up every word.

Kate had placed the spy cam in a wooden dish on the window sill, centring it to capture the side profiles of Tom, and the client, for the duration of their sessions. When she'd first started recording client sessions, six years earlier when she'd decided they should keep their marriage a secret from the clients, it was to protect Tom's reputation and ensure he wasn't accused of impropriety. She'd seen some of the most successful speakers and self-help gurus in the States slapped with lawsuits – for sexual assault, molestation and even rape. She'd seen men destroyed, their reputations shredded. Most were sent to prison, and many killed themselves within hours of being locked up. She wasn't going to let that happen to Tom. She'd seen the way women threw themselves at him after his talks: the arm strokes, the hair flicks and the simpering smiles. All it would take was for one woman to take his rejection badly and concoct a plot to accuse him of something he hadn't done and his career would be over. She'd watched hours of recordings to ensure that would never happen, and all the time Tom had maintained a professional distance from the person sitting opposite him.

And then one day he didn't.

Kate slaps the laptop screen closed.

She needs to get some dirt on Geraldine: something so shameful and dark Geraldine would rather die than have it disclosed to the outside world. Something Kate can use to quash the story that Geraldine's penning about SoulShrink. But she's going to need a good recording, the camera zoomed in on Geraldine's face. She wants tears, regret, snot. She'll give her a choice – drop the story or the video gets shared.

She glances at her watch. There are only ten minutes until Tom's next one-to-one and she needs to get the SSD card back into the spy cam before it starts. She'll get it set up so it focuses in on Peter's face, to test it. Then it'll all be ready for Geraldine's next one-to-one tomorrow. Blackmail has worked for Kate before, and it'll work again. She just needs something good – a confession or a revelation that will destroy Geraldine's career.

And to get that out of her she'll need Tom's help.

*

Keeping one eye on the closed door of the therapy room, Kate moves the wooden bowl from the centre of the window sill to the edge. She places the key fob inside it, angles the camera towards the client's chair then places a handful of coins around it to keep it in place. She won't know if she's positioned it correctly until she checks the footage later but it's Peter's session and, if she's got it wrong, it won't matter. She's doesn't need an insight into his past to work out what makes him tick. He's a serial complainer, only happy if he's got something to moan about. No wonder he's been divorced three times. His ex-wives had a lucky escape.

Kate steps away from the window and checks the bin. Geraldine didn't cry in her session so there's nothing to empty and there's fresh water and glasses on the table. Her job is done.

The door clicking open makes her turn sharply.

'Kate.' Tom greets her with a nod, then looks at his watch. 'I've got Peter next, right?' Without waiting for a reply he says, 'Have you checked on Joy recently? I could hear her coughing as I walked past her room.'

'No,' Kate says, 'but I will.'

She doesn't mention that's she's heard Joy coughing too, or that she was listening at her door at the time. She looks at her husband, at the haggard sag of his skin, the five o'clock stubble on his jaw and the hint of grey at his temple. When they met he took good care of himself. He shaved daily, applied eau de toilette and did his hair for what felt like hours. She was shocked at his appearance when he came out of prison and assumed he'd jump into the shower and come out looking like a new man. He had showered – he'd insisted on washing the 'stink of his cell' off his body – but he didn't cut his hair. He used to glance at himself whenever he passed a reflective surface. Now he avoids mirrors. It's as though he no longer likes what he sees.

'How was your session with Geraldine?' she asks pleasantly. 'Everything okay?'

Tom slumps into his chair. 'Fine. There's some emotional blockages we need to work through but she's not resistant. She's quite self-aware. Intelligent too. Hardly surprising considering she used to be an IT teacher.'

'I'm sorry?'

Tom looks at her. 'Sorry for what?'

'I thought you just said she used to be an IT teacher.'

'She did. She's mentioned it several times.'

Kate rests a hand on the window sill, then snatches it up again as her fingers brush against the bowl. 'She's been lying to you, Tom. It says she's a retired receptionist on her form.'

'Does it?' He rolls back his shoulders then moves his head from side to side, stretching out the muscles in his neck. 'I need to get a massage when this is over. I don't know if it's all the sitting around or the white-water rafting but—'

'I think Geraldine's a journalist.'

'She's not. I already—'

'She is and she's writing a piece on us, on you. She's been prodding Joy for information. And god knows who else. I'm pretty certain she's going to sensationalise what happened this morning, claim we were negligent again.'

Tom slumps forward and rests his head in his hands. 'I knew we shouldn't have done this. I knew it. For fuck's sake, Kate, I told you.'

'Well we can't change that. What's done is done. What's important now is stopping her, minimising the damage. We need to get some dirt on her – *you* need to get some dirt on her. Otherwise you'll be crucified in the press.' She pauses. 'Why are you shaking your head?'

He looks up at her. 'I'm not the one she's gunning for. She told me that you tried to kill her this morning. I thought she was being dramatic but if you're right, and she is a journalist . . .' He sighs. 'If anyone's getting crucified here Kate, it's you.'

Chapter 30

Now

FRAN

Fran didn't return to Caroline's room after her session with Tom ended. Instead, she grabbed her coat from her room and took herself out to the field at the back of the house. Now she's marching around the perimeter, stomping through the long grass, swinging her arms and gulping down big lungfuls of air. There was a point, during her one-to-one with Tom, when she thought her emotions might overcome her. In front of that fraud! Somehow he'd wrong-footed her, tricked her into opening up and all the while she thought she was the one with the upper hand; that if she gave him the emotional nugget he was so desperately digging for she'd be able to turn the tables and reflect the conversation back at him. But that hadn't happened, had it? Instead of pressing him about Jenna's disappearance, she'd ended up examining her own feelings about her sister. Not that she'd shared them with Tom. She'd acknowledged that, yes, she did feel regret in her chest then, having been instructed to sit with her eyes closed and her hands on her chest whilst mentally repeating 'I forgive myself', she'd worked through her feelings instead. And what confusing feelings they were. She'd agreed to go to the retreat because her mother had needled her incessantly. And she'd only stayed in the hope she would find proof that Jenna had killed herself and stop their mother from bringing it up every time they talked. Or were those really her motives? If what Tom was implying was correct then Fran wasn't motivated by her own selfish needs. Rather, she was fuelled by anger and regret. She'd never bothered to get to know her sister and now she never would.

She could spend the rest of her life doing a double take when she saw women like Stella, the young woman from the tube, with a certain body shape and hair colour, because Jenna would never age. She'd never go grey, never wrinkle, never find sun spots on the back of her hands. She'd never move house or move jobs. Never travel, never fall in love. Never laugh or smile or hug. She'd remain frozen in time, like the photographs on Geraldine's mantlepiece.

Fran stops walking and rubs her hands over her face. If she discovers who murdered her sister, will it assuage her regret? Is that why she's teamed up with Caroline to discover what Kate and Tom are hiding? Normally she'd have rung the police. If a crime has been committed then it should be reported. But Jenna's death has already been investigated – by the Gozoian and the British police – and been ruled a suicide. But Caroline seems so certain it was murder: a source told her about blood on the rocks, destroyed evidence, missing statements. She's done so much work already, why not leave her to it?

Because it's about justice, Fran tells herself as she sets off again, the house in her sights. Someone took her sister's life. And she's going to find out who.

It's unusually quiet in the living room. Peter has taken the comfiest chair in the corner of the room, his book held at arm's length. He scowls as he turns the page. Fran raises her eyebrows. Who scowls when they read? The man's probably one of those terrible Amazon reviewers who gives one star to every book they buy. 'I purchased *How Not to Be an Arsehole* with the greatest of expectations. However, the missing full stop on page five ruined the reading experience for me. If I could give this book no stars I would.'

She turns away.

Priyanka, bent over a low table with a pen in her hand, catches her eye and smiles. 'Everything okay, Geraldine?'

'It's very quiet in here.'

'I think everyone's a bit worn out from the white-water rafting this morning.' Her smile fades. 'Are you and Joy fully recovered? I was horrified when your dinghy overturned, especially when you both took ages to come back up to the surface.'

'I'm fine.' Fran smiles tightly as a pang of guilt plucks at her heart. Priyanka is the woman she's pretending to be – knocked for six by her husband's death and as lonely as they come. She never stops smiling though and she's always the first to offer a hand if anyone needs help. But Fran's seen the cheery facade slip, when everyone else is chatting, and the most terrible sadness filling Priyanka's eyes. If Fran wasn't on a mission to find out who killed Jenna and why, she'd take the time to get to know Priyanka. She seems like she needs a friend. All the more reason for Fran to begin her interrogation of the Gozo three as soon as possible.

'I don't suppose you know where Renata is?' she asks.

'Oh yes,' Priyanka says brightly. 'Last time I saw her she was in the hot tub with Phoenix and Damian.' She smiles naughtily. 'Lucky girl.'

Fran sighs irritably as she opens the door to the hot tub room and finds it empty. She must have just missed them. Although, actually, maybe it's a blessing in disguise. It would have been tricky getting Renata on her own while she had company. Fran heads back through the door, pauses as she hears splashing from the hot tub and turns to see Renata's head break through the surface of the water, her blonde hair clinging to her face.

'Hi.' Renata reaches for her towel and dabs at her face. 'I was practising holding my breath. There's not much else you can do here.' She laughs. 'Want to get in?'

'No, thank you.' Fran closes the door and moves closer. She perches on a hard wooden chair beside the tub. 'I just wanted to say hello.'

She smiles in what she hopes is a warm friendly manner but suspects might look more like the fixed grimace of a fairground clown. 'One of the things that just came up in my session with Tom was that I need to be more open. He's believes that I'm emotionally repressed. He's absolutely right, of course. Even my own mother doesn't know me and . . . um . . .' She stumbles. The conversation is *much* harder than she anticipated. How do normal people open up to each other?

'Don't be nervous.' Renata smiles at her. 'I'm not a judgemental person. Anything you share with me won't leave this room.'

Interesting, Fran thinks. Renata's parroting some of Tom's favourite phrases. She shifts on her seat, her awkwardness and frustration increasing as she tries, and fails, to think of something to say.

'I might be a bit of a lost cause,' she says finally. 'I think perhaps I've embraced self-help too late in life. Is this your first retreat?'

Renata shakes her head. 'On no, I've been on loads, but Tom's the best. He's so incredibly warm and approachable, you know? I flew to America once to see one of their superstar motivational speakers but it was awful. I felt like I was at a rally or something. And any downtime you had you were hassled by sales people to sign up for this course or that. Tom's not like that at all. He does this to help people, not to make money.'

'Oh yes,' Fran says. 'Tom and Kate, the . . . goodness . . . just seems to flow out of them.'

Too much, she wonders? But her words have an almost transformative effect on Renata.

'Oh my god, yes. Goodness. Yes, that's absolutely it. Kate is just . . . oh, she's an absolute darling. She can't do enough for you. When I was in Gozo and' – she closes her eyes tightly and shakes her head – 'and tragedy struck, she took charge. She was amazing, comforting people, organising help. Honestly, the press destroyed her and Tom for what happened but it could have been so much worse. She actively saved people's lives.'

'And Tom?' Fran asks. 'Was he amazing too?'

Renata's left eye twitches. 'Tom . . .' She rubs her eye briskly. 'Sorry, I think there must be some chlorine in the water or something. Tom was traumatised by what happened. I'd never judge him. We were his responsibility. That's a lot of weight on one man's shoulders.'

Fran is on the edge of her seat. Literally. If she shifts any further forward she'll end up on the floor. But she can't help herself. Someone is *finally* talking about what happened that night. 'So what happened? What went wrong?'

The moment the questions are out of her mouth she regrets them. Renata closes like a crocus at night, pulling her knees into her chest and dropping her head.

Bugger, Fran thinks.

'Renata? Are you okay?'

Renata doesn't uncurl but the water around her tremors. She's shaking.

'Did I say something wrong?'

Still no response.

'I'm so sorry.' Fran looks at Renata's hands, gripping her calves, the skin on her knuckles pulled tight. 'Have I just . . .' She searches her mind for the kind of word her students use in this type of situation. 'Have I just triggered you?'

Renata nods into her knees.

'Should I . . .' She was going to say, 'Should I get Tom or Kate?' But they're the last people she wants involved. 'Should I get Phoenix or Damian?' she asks instead.

Renata nods again and as Fran leaves the room she hears the girl sob.

Fran knocks on Phoenix's door and waits. From the surrounding rooms she can hear people talking on the phone, watching TV and, faintly, the sound of someone snoring. With Tom's one-to-ones taking the best part of an hour each there isn't a great deal to do in the afternoons other than stroll around the countryside, lounge in the hot tub or read. In his welcome email, Tom had suggested they take that time to 'live mindfully without distractions' but it appears everyone's chosen to occupy their minds, or shut them down, instead.

'Hi!' Phoenix opens the door with a towel tucked around his waist and another draped around his neck. The strong, woody scent of his aftershave hits Fran full in the face. 'Oh! Geraldine, what a lovely surprise. I thought you were avoiding me. I've been talking about my ex too much, haven't I? Tom said I need to—'

'I need to ask you something,' Fran interrupts. 'It's urgent.'

Phoenix lights up but, before he can say a word, Fran continues, 'It's about Gozo. I was just talking to Renata and when the subject of Jenna came up' – she hadn't actually mentioned Jenna but she glosses over the lie – 'she became visibly upset and—' She breaks off, suddenly aware of the tears in Phoenix's eyes. 'Are you okay?'

He brushes the tears away. 'Sorry, but Jenna was lovely. I still feel terrible about what happened.'

'Why's that?'

'Guilt, I suppose.' He shivers then takes the towel from around his neck, unfolds it and wraps it around his shoulders. 'We knew she had her issues. But no one realised she was suicidal.'

Fran rests her hand on the door frame. 'So she didn't appear . . . upset? Depressed?'

'Not really. She never mentioned wanting to kill herself. In fact, the only time I saw her upset was the night she found the bird.'

'Bird?'

'The one outside her bedroom. I'd just rescued her from Damian. Actually, I didn't realise she needed rescuing at first. I thought she and Damian were . . . you know?' He raises his eyebrows.

'No.' Fran shakes her head. 'I don't.'

'Getting it together,' Phoenix explains. 'In the bar.'

'Damian?' Fran leans a little closer and lowers her voice. 'The same Damian who's here?'

'Yeah. Only I don't think they were, getting it together. I think Damian was sitting on her. He was drunk. They both were. Anyway, I helped him get up and then took her back to her room. That's when we found the bird. It was gross.' He shakes his head at the memory. 'Decayed, maggots. Really horrible. I think it upset her. I mean, obviously it upset me too, but—'

'Did Jenna and Damian spend a lot of time together?'

'No more than she did with anyone else. Well, not that I noticed anyway. It wasn't like I was keeping track of her every movement.' He laughs, his eyes no longer shining with tears.

'I see,' Fran says, although she really doesn't. The suggestion that Jenna and Damian were intimate has raised questions in her mind. Was it a lovers' tiff that led to Jenna losing her life? A tragic accident, hidden from view? Or was the truth darker than that? Had Damian killed Jenna in a violent rage fuelled by jealousy, anger or drink? Fran doesn't know the first thing about the man. Other than the fact he takes photos without permission. She had planned to speak to him about that after they went white-water rafting but what happened knocked him lower down her list of priorities. If what Phoenix is saying is true she needs to talk to Damian sooner rather than later.

'Was Jenna involved with anyone else?' Fran asks.

Phoenix shrugs. 'Like I said, I wasn't keeping track. There were a lot of people in our group and I made a lot of friends. Anyway' – he peers out of the doorway, looking back towards the living area – 'you said Renata was upset. Is she still in the hot tub?'

The question catches Fran off guard. She'd completely forgotten that Renata was her excuse for knocking on Phoenix's door. 'Yes, yes she is.'

'Then I'd better go see her.' He reaches behind the door for his dressing gown and pulls it on. 'I'm very good at comforting people. Seek me out Geraldine, if you ever need someone to talk to. I'm a good listener.'

Fran steps back from the door, suppressing a smirk. 'Thank you, Phoenix,' she says. 'I've enjoyed our chat.'

'Anytime!' He hurries off down the corridor, his flip-flops slapping on the wooden floorboards, leaving Fran beside his closed bedroom door.

She sniffs the air. She can still smell Phoenix's aftershave but it's mingled with another scent now. Smoke. Tobacco smoke. It's drifting down the corridor from the open back door. There are only two people who smoke on the retreat. One is recuperating in bed after a near drowning. And the other is Damian.

Unlike Phoenix, who greeted her with the unbridled enthusiasm of a Labrador puppy, and Renata, who jolted in surprise, Damian doesn't acknowledge Fran's presence at all. As she steps onto the porch he continues to puff on his cigarette, his back resting against one of the struts, his gaze fixed somewhere between the end of the garden and the horizon.

'Good afternoon,' Fran says, drawing alongside him.

'Hi.'

Fran looks him up and then down as he takes another drag on his cigarette. He's a big man. Six foot four at least and, in her estimation, well over twenty stone. He's heavily built but strong too, from the size of his biceps. Anyone who got into a fight with him would need their wits about them, or some kind of weapon, to come out of the altercation alive.

She decides to be blunt. 'Why did you take my photo yesterday?'

Damian blows grey smoke into the air. 'Wouldn't you like to know?'

'Actually,' Fran says. 'I would.'

'Ah well.' He shrugs and takes another drag on his cigarette.

An unsettling thought hits her. Might Tom have asked him to take the photograph? Perhaps Tom finally looked through his notes and noticed it didn't say IT teacher on her form. But how would a photo help him reveal her true identity? Caroline's already told her there aren't any photos of her on the internet. Fran racks her brain. Why else would Damian take her photograph? They're not friends and she hadn't seen him taking anyone else's photo so it's unlikely to be for a future Facebook post – *Here are all the nutjobs I went on a retreat with*. She decides to stop worrying about it. Unless he's a serial killer who takes photos of his future victims she's unlikely to come to any harm.

'Have you come to terms with what happened in Gozo?' she asks, changing the subject. And there it is again, the smirk pricking at the edges of Damian's dark moustache.

'What are you digging for, Geraldine?'

'I'm not digging for anything. I'm . . . being caring.'

Damian's roar of laughter catches her by surprise.

'What is so funny?' she asks

He shakes his head, a smile still playing on his lips. 'You'd be a shit detective.'

He takes another puff of his cigarette. He hasn't tapped it once since Fran joined him and a tower of ash is balancing precariously on the end. He glances to his left and flinches. The ash on his cigarette tumbles to the floor.

'Tell me about Jenna,' Fran says. 'Phoenix said you were close.'

Even as she formed the sentence in her head she knew he wouldn't answer, but what she didn't anticipate was the oddness of his response. He looks to his left again, then hurls his cigarette into the gravel that edges the garden.

'Don't mention Jenna's name again.' His expression is stony as he turns back towards Fran. 'Seriously. You need to shut up—'

He breaks off, and she's suddenly aware that there's someone else in the garden. Standing at the edge of the house, staring at her with undisguised contempt, is Kate.

Chapter 31

Then

JENNA

As Jenna steps onto the patio, her gaze flits towards the wall that separates Tom's chalet from the waste ground beyond. The space in the stones, where an eye peered in at her, is no longer there. It's been filled so seamlessly she can't work out where it was. She touches a hand to her forehead, feeling the rough texture of the skin closure strips under her fingertips. The doctor told her the wound wasn't deep enough to require stitches but she might develop a scar. Tom wasn't with her when the doctor arrived. He fled after she confronted him about Kate, saying he was late for his next session. Had she insulted him by insinuating that there was more to his relationship with Kate than a professional relationship? Had she come across as unstable and jealous? It would explain why he'd avoided her for the rest of the day, seating himself at the far end of the dinner table and disappearing before dessert. Conversely, Kate couldn't have been more attentive. She took the seat next to Jenna and fussed and faffed throughout the meal, grabbing up the water carafe the minute Jenna's glass emptied, insisting the waiter gave her her meal first, and generally gnawing her ear off with question after question. Was she feeling okay? Had she napped? Was there any dizziness? On and on she went until, finally, Jenna had had enough and excused herself to the toilet.

Kate was waiting when she came out.

'I'll refund the cost of the retreat,' Kate said, grasping one of Jenna's hands with both of hers, 'as recompense for what happened. I wouldn't want your SoulShrink experience to be tarnished by the actions of a couple of bored children.'

Her deep red nails dug into Jenna's skin. 'I want you to be able to sing our praises, not . . .' she tailed off.

Jenna almost laughed at how transparent Kate was being. She wasn't concerned about her wellbeing, she was worried about SoulShrink's reputation.

'Thank you,' she said. 'That would be very helpful.'

And it would. She hadn't paid her rent for that month in order to afford the retreat.

'I can rely on your discretion, can't I?' Kate said. 'We wouldn't want the other guests running to me for refunds if they stub their toes on a door.'

'Of course.' Jenna smiled sweetly. 'Your secret is safe with me.'

That one, anyway.

Now, as she walks through the doorway into Tom's chalet, unease flutters like moths in her stomach. Is Tom going to bring up what happened when they were in the same room yesterday? Should she?

'Jenna!' He gets up from his armchair as she walks into the room. 'How are you?'

'I'm okay.' She sits down. 'I didn't think we had another session until tomorrow but Kate said I should come today, seeing as yesterday's session was cut short.'

'We didn't exactly get started, did we?' He smiles warmly. He seems happy and relaxed, as though a weight has been lifted from his shoulders. 'Water?' He pours her a glass and pushes it across the table.

'Okay then.' He sits back in his chair. 'Let's get back to why you're here.'

Jenna rubs her palms over the arms of the chair, remembering the birthday party when she'd unwrapped Fran's present.

'It was buy one get one free,' Fran said as Jenna looked at the ancestry test in her hands, trying, and failing, to hide her smile. How like Fran to put zero thought into her present. 'Our results will be identical, of course, but I thought it might inspire you to visit the parts of the world our ancestors came from, like the countries in Scandinavia and Southern Europe. Or you could mark them on a map.'

Jenna thanked Fran and joked, 'This is where we discover we're not actually sisters.'

All her friends laughed. It was a standing joke, that either she, or Fran, was adopted. Other than inheriting their mum's hooded eyes, they were about as different as two people could be – looks wise and otherwise.

Once she got home, Jenna ignored the test for several weeks then, one quiet weekend before payday, she dug out the test, spat into the test tube, filled out the form and sent it all off.

By the time the email arrived, saying her results were ready, she'd forgotten she'd even sent the test off, but she dutifully logged onto the website to check her results. Her genetic ancestry results were more interesting than she'd expected them to be. She was sixty-one percent British, nine percent Scandinavian, twenty-one percent Southern European and nine percent North

African. She sat up a little taller in her chair. North African! Now *that* was unexpected. She clicked on the 'compare family tree' icon, the link refreshed, and there, on the screen, was her sister's name – Frances Fitzgerald. Beneath it was one word:

Cousins.

Cousins? She half laughed. The test was useless. No wonder they'd been giving them away for free. She opened a bottle of wine, turned on the TV, and put it out of her mind.

The next day, at work, as she pushed on her client's arm, her mind wandered back to that word on the screen.

'Have you ever done one of those ancestry tests?' she asked Juliet. She was a regular customer, a gardener who was suffering from frozen shoulder. 'The DNA ones.'

'Not personally.' Juliet gasped as Jenna moved her arm to a different position.

'Sorry.' She lowered the arm. 'Have you been doing the exercises I showed you?'

'Mostly.'

Jenna raised her eyebrows questioningly.

'Not as often as I should have, sorry. I've been busy. Anyway, what was I saying? DNA tests. Yes, my friend Brita discovered a half-brother she didn't know about.'

'Really?'

'Yep. No idea he even existed. She thought he might be a cousin at first because that's what the website said but it all came out when she confronted her dad about it. It turned out he'd slept with someone six months before he got together with Brita's mum and she fell pregnant. She didn't tell him about the baby and she brought their son up alone.'

Jenna let the words sink in as she gently moved Juliet's arm out to the side, watching her face for any sign of pain. 'Why did the website say he was her cousin?'

'I'm not sure. Weird though, isn't it?'

Somehow, Jenna managed to hold it together long enough to finish the session but she snatched up her phone the moment Juliet had dressed and was out of the door and typed a question into Google. And there it was, in black and white: *If the amount of shared DNA between half-sisters falls into the range of expected DNA between first cousins, then there is a chance that they will be labelled as first cousins on the match list.*

She rang Fran's number but it went straight to voicemail so she hung up and called the ancestry hotline instead. It was a mistake, it had to be – some kind of screw-up in the lab. That's what Fran would have told her if she'd managed to get through to her.

But that's not what Barbara, the customer services lady with the sympathetic voice told her. She said the tests were ninety nine percent accurate. It was very unlikely that a mistake had been made.

'I'm so sorry,' Tom says as Jenna finishes her story. 'I can't begin to imagine how shocked you must have been. Did you ever talk to your sister about it? Fran? Is that her name?'

'Yes, I did but she was abrupt and dismissive and I just . . . It wasn't the right time. She wasn't the right person to tell anyway. She can be quite abrasive and I knew she'd go barging in, all guns blazing, demanding answers. She'd get Mum and Dad on the defensive.'

'So you told them yourself?'

'I tried to talk to Mum. Dad had a stroke six months ago. It knocked him for six, affected his memory, his speech, everything really. He's still re-learning how to walk.'

'A stroke? That must have had a big impact on the family.'

'Massively. Dad was always this big, loud, imposing figure. You know, the sort of person who can fill a room even before he steps into it. He had that kind of energy. He commands respect. I guess that's why he did so well in the army. We were that typical "wait until your father gets home" family. That's not to say that Mum was a wallflower though.' She shakes her head, remembering how her mum would puff out her feathers the moment her dad stepped out the front door. 'She was his second in command, always backing him up, never, ever taking anyone's side against him. If Dad was a tank, barrelling everyone out of his way, then Mum was a sniper on the sidelines, taking people out before they even knew she was there.'

'That sounds like a challenging environment for a child.'

'You adapt, don't you? If there's a tank and a sniper roaming around you make yourself small, so you're not a target. And you make out you're on their side. You don't want to be the enemy.'

'Was Fran the enemy? Your sister?'

Jenna looks at him thoughtfully, mulling over the question. She's never really thought of Fran like that before. Fran didn't break ranks and desert the family, she dug a hole under the fence and escaped.

'I don't know,' she says eventually. 'Maybe once. Not anymore though, they just let her get on with her life.'

'Do they let you get on with yours?'

She laughs dryly.

'Okay . . .' Tom nods. 'We'll come back to that. Let's go back to you confronting your mum about the results of the ancestry test. How did that go?'

'Not well.' Jenna reaches for her glass and takes a sip of water. 'Have you got anything stronger? I'm not sure I can do this without booze.'

'Stay with the feeling. It's important.'

'But it's horrible.' She balls a hand into a fist and jabs herself in the diaphragm. 'It really fucking hurts.'

'I know it does. But you need to work through this if you're going to heal.'

There's a part of Jenna that wants to tell him that she's never going to heal. Instead, she says, 'She denied it, at first. She said of course Fran and I were full sisters and then I pushed the printout across the table and she laughed.'

'She laughed?'

'At the bit where it said we were cousins. She said it was rubbish and I should throw it in the bin. So then I told her what the customer support woman had said. She stopped laughing then.'

Tom nods for her to continue.

'She sent me twenty-one texts the day I flew over here. Not to ask how I'm doing or to check I'm okay. She wanted to make sure I was going to keep it quiet. What was it she said? "There's no need to cause a fuss." A fuss? I found out that my dad's not my dad and she acts like I found a hair in my soup?' Jenna can hear her voice rising but she can't stop it. All the pain, hurt, and shock that she dialled down as she sat across the kitchen table from her mum, because her dad was asleep on the sofa in the living room, is exploding out of her. 'What Mum meant was: Don't tell anyone. She cared – cares – more about the family's reputation than she does about me.'

'Did she tell you what happened?' Tom asks. 'Was it an affair or—'

'Swinging.' She watches his face carefully, for any hint of amusement or surprise but his expression doesn't change. 'Of course she didn't use that word. She said that before Dad became an officer they'd go to parties with other army couples and they'd have a meal, a couple of drinks and swap partners. It was normal, she told me. Army life could be boring, especially abroad and it was a way of' – she makes quotation marks in the air – 'spicing things up. When I asked her if she'd been forced into it she laughed and said of course she hadn't. It had been Daddy's idea but she'd gone along with it because she loved him and she wanted to make him happy.' She pauses to swipe at her eyes. 'She just . . . she sat there and she told me that like it was the most normal thing in the world. She didn't apologise. She didn't ask me if I was okay. She didn't hug me. She was . . . she was defensive. She acted like I was attacking her.'

'I'm sorry, Jenna.' Tom pushes the tissues towards her. 'I'm genuinely sorry that happened to you.'

'The worst thing' – Jenna takes a tissue and blows her nose noisily – 'or one of the worst things, is that Dad doesn't know.'

'That you're not biologically related?'

'Yeah, well . . . I don't know that for sure, but Mum made me swear not to bring it up with him. She said he had enough to deal with. She emotionally blackmailed me and now I'm complicit too.'

'Oh, Jenna.'

'And it hurts.' She presses a hand to her chest. 'It hurts so much that all this time I've done everything they asked of me, I've been the daughter they could be proud of and I'm not their child at all. It was a lie, all of it – the respectability, the family name, everything. My whole life is a lie. I don't even know who I am.'

'Jenna.' Tom crouches beside her and presses a hand to her arm as she sobs. 'You will get through this. You'll never feel this much pain again. I promise you that.'

She peels the hair from her face to look at him. She wants to believe him but she's not sure she can.

Chapter 32

Now

KATE

Just looking at Geraldine, stepping into the harness and pulling it up her body, makes Kate feel sick. She can't stand the way the woman's been making comments about how unattractive the harness is whilst quizzing the instructor about its sturdiness. Now, the poor man's being bombarded with questions about the number of accidents per year and the rigorousness of the testing procedure for the equipment. Kate's almost certain Geraldine's mentally adding everything he says to the article she's penning – 'As well as trying to drown their guests, SoulShrink attempted to humiliate them by getting them to leap to their deaths whilst revealing their gussets to the world.'

All she has to do is climb up the pole and jump off it, for god's sake. Although, Kate thinks idly, if the harness *is* faulty, then Geraldine won't be around to write her bloody story. Hoorah.

Sighing, she reaches for the pile of coats the guests have thrown over a nearby log, grabs an armful, and trudges back to the Woodland Adventures lodge. General skivvy, that's her. At least she doesn't have to jump off the bloody pole. Once the coats have been hung up she'll be able to grab a cup of tea and sit down for five minutes. She's been running around for days, ushering guests to their one-to-ones, preparing the therapy room, tidying the living area, cooking the food, serving it up, double checking the morning activities are booked and reviewing the spy cam footage. She hasn't stopped. Last night, heading out to her car to retrieve a book for Tom, she spotted Phoenix and Renata chatting in the hot tub room. Renata, perched on the edge of the tub in a tiny bikini, was sobbing into her hands as Phoenix hovered awkwardly beside her. Kate hurried over to find out what was wrong. Surprise, surprise, Geraldine Bloody Rotheram had been sniffing around and she'd upset Renata. She'd quizzed her about Gozo, demanding she tell her exactly what had happened on the final evening of the retreat and then she'd headed off to question Phoenix too.

'I'm starting to think she's a bit obsessed with Gozo,' he told Kate. 'I can't get a word in edgeways about my own life experiences. It's all Gozo this and Gozo that.'

Fuming, Kate stalked out of the room. It was obvious what Geraldine was up to – she was targeting previous guests and prodding them for soundbites. If she'd already interrogated Renata and Phoenix there was only one person left to chat to. Damian wasn't in his room – she'd walked past his open door minutes earlier – and if he wasn't in the living room there was only one place he could be.

Rather than head back through the house and down the corridor to the back door, Kate left from the front. Outside, she'd be shrouded by darkness and if she could creep close enough she might be able to overhear what Geraldine was asking him. But they were talking so quietly she couldn't hear a word. When Damian laughed at something Geraldine said Kate took a step closer, and they spotted her. Seconds later Geraldine disappeared back into the house. Damian was about to follow her when Kate called his name. He turned slowly.

'Yes.'

'What did she want?'

'Good afternoon to you too.'

She stared up at him, frustrated. Unlike Renata and Phoenix, who were open books, Damian was impossible to read. She'd watched his therapy recordings but an insight into his past – as a child he'd witnessed the murder of his older sister – didn't give her an insight into the man he was now. On the Gozo trip he was bawdy, loud, sexually inappropriate and a heavy drinker. Now, two years and nine months later, he was an entirely different person – reserved and anti-social with only the occasional inappropriate comment. In his most recent session with Tom he was practically monosyllabic. There was something dangerous about Damian's silence that unsettled her.

She decided on the direct approach. 'Did Geraldine just ask you about Gozo?'

'No.'

He was lying. Geraldine hadn't just cornered him for a chat about the weather.

'What did she want then?'

He smirked. 'Nosy, aren't we?'

'I'm not . . .' She stopped herself. He was trying to push her buttons. Well, he'd have to press them a damned sight harder than that. 'She upset Renata. I'm trying to find out why.'

'Why don't you ask her? Or does she intimidate you?' He bent at the waist so that his face was level with hers. 'That's it, isn't it, Kate? That's why you're creeping around in the dark. Snooping. What is it you're so scared of?'

She glared at him, fighting the urge to hit back, to use his past against him, to pluck the scab off his vulnerability and plunge her nails into the fresh wound. She could destroy him if she wanted but she was better than that, cleverer. If he wanted to play, she'd win.

'You're right.' She tossed back her head and laughed. 'Absolutely right. I'm terrified of the woman. Have you seen the scowl she pulls when I announce the next day's activities? And her face when she doesn't like her food? She's a monster and I hold my hands up, I'm absolutely terrified. You got me.'

Damian's smirk slipped but he didn't straighten up. Instead he continued to meet her eyes, his gaze unwavering. 'I think you might have met your match, Kate. No wonder you're scared.'

'Stupid fucking arsehole,' Kate mutters now as she hangs the coats on the hooks in the small wooden lodge that serves as a guest reception area for the activity centre. She could feel Damian watching her at dinner the night before, as she served up steak and ale stew with mashed potatoes and roasted carrots. She heard his laugh as she took her seat directly opposite Geraldine; but she didn't look at him. She couldn't bear to see the twisted smirk on his face. She forced herself to make small talk with Geraldine – each question like a knife in her chest. Where do you live in London? Have you been there long? What made you choose SoulShrink over similar retreats? Geraldine batted answers back at her – North London, several years, I'd heard of it. To other questions – do you have family? Any children? What did you do before you retired – Geraldine took longer, forking food into her mouth, chewing interminably slowly before answering. And then dinner was over and Geraldine took herself off 'to check on Joy'. Loyal, long-suffering Joy, who was still in bed, insipidly pale, and hadn't been able to attend the afternoon's activities.

Kate hangs up the last of the coats and heads across the room to the pitiful 'refreshment area' – a sink, fridge, kettle, two cupboards and little else. She fills the kettle and turns it on then takes a teabag from the metal caddy in the cupboard. She drops it into a tannin stained mug and crouches to open the fridge. Her hand falls away from the handle as a thought hits her. Across the room is a wall of coats. Geraldine's is in the middle – a horrible green fleece, the material bobbled from over-use. As the kettle bubbles, Kate slips her hand into the pocket of Geraldine's coat. She grimaces as her fingers fold around a used tissue. When she can't find anything else she moves her hand into the other pocket, feeling sure she won't find anything. If Geraldine was clever enough not to pack anything that gave away her real identity there's not going to be anything in her coat.

Or is there?

Kate's forefinger grazes something solid and thin. The edge of a train ticket maybe? She plucks it out, fully expecting to be disappointed.

She holds it at arm's length, squinting to make out the text on the small, white card.

'Gotcha,' she says.

Chapter 33

Now

FRAN

The queasy feeling in Fran's stomach is still there, despite a packed lunch in the cramped back room of the Wilderness Adventures lodge, a two hour lie down back at the retreat, two pints of water and several antacids. It began when she reached the summit of the twenty-five foot pole and ventured a glance down. Her stomach roiled and her knees weakened. There was no way she could stand on the tiny, circular ledge at the top, without anything to hold onto. She crouched, straddling it, her feet on the metal climbing pegs, her fingers gripping the edge.

Tom shouted up words of encouragement. 'Stand up!' 'Trust your partner.' 'Relinquish control!'

Fran wanted to tell him to stick his control up his arse but she was too terrified to speak. As for trusting her partner –

Phoenix was so easily distracted he'd probably let go of the safety rope to do up his shoelace at the exact moment she leapt off the pole.

'Face your fear and jump!' Peter called up to her. He was next in line to experience the 'leap of faith' and was growing more and more exasperated the longer Fran refused to let go of the pole and step off the small platform.

'If you can't do it for you,' Tom shouted, 'do it for someone else. Do it for someone you love, to turn back time . . .' He paused. '. . . To say sorry.'

Fran glared down at him. How bloody unprofessional. Their conversation in the therapy room was supposed to be confidential and there he was, telling everyone that she had regrets.

'I'll do it!' she shouted back. 'If you all just shut up.'

'Does being told what to do make you feel uncomfortable?' Damian shouted back. 'Maybe you need to discuss that in your next session with Tom.'

Fran was too far off the ground to see his face, but she could hear the smirk in his voice.

'Geraldine,' Tom shouted, 'I want you to—'

The rest of his sentence was lost as Fran launched herself off the platform, her eyes tightly closed. She screamed like she'd never screamed before.

'You didn't give the speech,' Renata commented later as Fran picked herself off the ground. 'About leaving behind your fears and relinquishing control.'

Fran groaned.

'The only thing I just left behind . . . was my dignity.'

'Not hungry?' Kate leans between Fran and Caroline to take Fran's bowl. In a tight little voice she adds, 'I could make you something else if it wasn't to your taste. Some fruit perhaps, or a yoghurt?'

'No, no,' Fran says hastily. 'I've just lost my appetite. Leaps of faith disagree with me.'

'You finished all yours, I see . . . Joy.' Kate turns to look at Caroline.

There's something about her intonation and the way she stresses the name 'Joy' that makes Fran frown.

'It was delicious.' Caroline rubs her belly over-enthusiastically and not for the first time, Fran marvels at what a great actress she is. It's almost as though 'Joy' and Caroline are two entirely different people. 'Yum, yum.'

'Well I'm glad you enjoyed it,' Kate says, and there it is again, that tight little voice.

Strange, Fran thinks, she normally reserves that for me.

'Best apple crumble I've ever had.'

'And I'm sure you've had a few.'

Before either Caroline or Fran can respond Kate is halfway across the room, a pile of plates in her hands.

'Charming!' Fran says.

Caroline doesn't respond. She's coughing into her hand and staring down at her phone. She lifts it to her ear. 'One sec,' she mouths.

Fran takes a sip of her water, watching as the other guests excuse themselves from the table and drift off to the living room or their bedrooms.

'Withheld number.' Caroline tucks her phone back into her pocket. 'Probably PPI.'

That's what she'd said during dinner, when it rang as they tucked into their main course. She'd ended the call without answering it and apologised to the group for bringing her phone to the table.

'Anyway—' Caroline coughs into her hand again then swears loudly. 'I swear, if I've got some kind of lung infection from drinking all that river water I'll sue. Anyway, I haven't seen you all day. Tell me all.'

'You were asleep,' Fran says. 'I knocked on your door when we got back. Did you know that you snore like my parents' dog?'

Caroline laughs. 'It may have been mentioned. So go on, have you had chance to speak to the Gozo three?'

'Yes, with varying results.'

Caroline listens intently as Fran recounts the details of her conversations with Renata, Phoenix and Damian, then raises her eyebrows when she mentions Kate's interruption.

'Was she listening?'

'I don't think she could have overheard but she was most definitely skulking around.'

Caroline dabs at her mouth with her napkin. 'I'd have loved to have been a fly on the wall during Renata and Phoenix's chat. They might be nervous about opening up to you but I bet they talk about the sweat lodge deaths amongst themselves. Or when they're drunk . . .'

She raises her eyebrows at Fran, who has no idea what she's hinting at.

'How good are you at games?' Caroline asks.

'I'm quite good at Cluedo and I'm excellent at Scrabble. I can't remember the last time—'

'Drinking games.'

'Oh. Never played one.'

Caroline looks at her incredulously. 'Never? Not even spin the bottle? Not at university?'

'No, at university I mostly spent my free time . . .' Fran's cheeks burn as faded memories of Gunnar's naked body flash up in her mind. 'I did a lot of studying.'

'Of course you did. Anyway,' Caroline leans back in her chair and looks towards the living room area, 'here's the plan.'

*

As far as new experiences go, playing a drinking game with two twenty-somethings, a thirty-something and Caroline is about as excruciating as they come. In fact, the only thing getting Fran through it is the drink itself. She rests her weight into the sofa, takes the shot glass Phoenix is proffering, and braces herself. She's done shots before – she's not a total square – but not for twenty-odd years and, after three in a row, or is it four, just the smell of the tequila makes her stomach twist.

After an hour or so of general chatting and drinking they began the games night by playing two truths and a lie. Fran proved herself to be the world's worst detective. Not only did she fail to spot the lies told by Phoenix (that he was on the *Big Brother* shortlist), Renata (that she was distantly related to Princess Michael of Kent) and Damian (that he went to the roughest school in Glasgow), but she completely messed up her own turn, going into far too much detail about her truths (completing the Greek Cyclades swimming challenge when she was thirty-two and the urban fox she fed from her match-box sized garden in London) whilst being far too brief about her lie ('I am an ordained priest').

'Right,' Phoenix says, 'neck that and we'll get on to the next game, Fuzzy Bunnies.'

'Noooo.' Caroline groans from the floor where she's sitting cross legged between Damian and Renata. 'That's boring. Let's play I Have Never.'

Fran frowns. 'I have never what?'

Caroline rolls her eyes. 'You're what, five years older than me and you've never heard of I Have Never?'

Fran shakes her head. Phoenix gets up from the floor. 'Neck your shot and I'll get you some wine.'

Fran knocks it back then shudders. Her stomach clenches horribly as she hands the glass back to Phoenix. Whatever's been making her feel nauseous all day really doesn't like the addition of alcohol. 'That's the last shot.'

'Don't be a killjoy.' Caroline gives her a steely look. 'Anyway, this game isn't about shots. You just need to sip, or gulp, from whatever you're drinking.'

This is their one, possibly *only*, chance to get the truth out of the Gozo three. Most people are more likely to open up when they're drunk, Caroline had said earlier, and if she and Fran were clever with their questions one of the others might let something slip.

'Fine,' Fran says. 'Now someone tell me what the rules are.'

She listens as Renata explains how the game works.

'So I drink if I have done something the other person has never done?' Fran asks.

'Yes,' Renata tucks a strand of blonde hair behind her ear. Her cheeks are pink, her eyes are shining and the bottle of gin on the carpet in front of her is half empty. 'But you can say I have never even if you have done it.'

'Right. Clear as mustard.' Fran pauses. That's not right, is it? What's the phrase she's looking for? She attempts it again 'Clear as . . .' She shakes her head. Why can't she think of the word?

'What is it as clear as, Geraldine?' Damian asks, smiling as he strokes his beard.

Fran waves a hand through the air, her irritation growing. 'I know this. It's clear as—'

'Your wine, madam.' Phoenix presses a glass into her hand.

'Are we ready to play?' Caroline asks. 'I'll go first. I have never . . . skinny dipped.'

'Boring.' Phoenix plonks himself back on the ground beside Fran's feet. He takes a sip of his drink, as do Renata and Damian. 'Hasn't everyone?'

'Mud,' says Fran.

Phoenix twists round to stare at her. 'Have you genuinely skinny dipped in mud?'

'Nooooo.' The word rolls around on Fran's tongue as her

brain scrabbles to keep up. 'No, I just . . . I just thought of the word. Mud?' Her brain is foggy and slow. Oh god, she's drunk. She looks desperately at Caroline for help.

'Clear as mud,' Caroline says, then launches into a coughing fit.

'What is?' Fran asks and Damian's booming laughter fills the room.

'Right,' Phoenix says. 'Renata, it's your turn.'

The next few questions pass in a blur. Someone mentions sex on a bench, someone else says the word 'anal' and then everyone falls around laughing when Phoenix says something about naughty thoughts about Tom. Fran's desperate for a glass of water but the sink is too far away and she hasn't got the energy to get up so she sips at her wine instead. She wants to go to bed. It's noisy in the living room and every time she announces that she's tired everyone starts laughing. 'That's three times now.' 'Four!' 'Seven.' 'I think she's tired, everyone!'

'I have never . . .' Caroline's East London tones cut through the noise. 'Hit someone.'

Fran rests a hand on the arm of the sofa and grips it, trying to anchor herself, but the room continues to spin.

'You hit someone?' she hears someone say, then Damian's bass reply, 'Aye, and they asked for it, too.'

'Geri?' Caroline says. 'Geri? Are you still with us? It's your turn.'

Fran rests her head on the sofa back and surveys the room, her eyes half closed. She hears the stress on the words 'your turn' and a thought crawls out of the thick fog in her brain. Jenna, that's why she's doing this. That's why she's so drunk. Someone in this room knows what happened to her sister. Her stomach lurches again as she forces herself to sit upright. She looks from Phoenix to Renata to Damian. They're all looking at her expectantly, smiles playing on their mouths.

'I have never . . .' Fran pauses to take a sip of her wine then looks at her glass in surprise. It's empty. 'I have never . . .' she says again, her head moving like a lead weight on a spring. She squints. She needs to see the Gozo three's expressions when she finishes her statement. 'I have never . . . seen a dead body.'

No one answers, but there's a sea change in the room. She feels the weight of it pressing down on her and the air feels thick and cloying. Damian's eyes burn into her. Renata stares at the carpet. Phoenix's smile droops and then vanishes. Even as drunk as she is, Fran can sense the guilt and regret. One of them knows. They saw Jenna's body. They were there.

Damian lifts his glass of water to his mouth and sips. Renata, head bowed, does the same with her gin. Phoenix knocks back his cider and cradles the empty glass in his hand.

Jubilation burns in Fran's chest – she's done it, she's solved the mystery. One person didn't murder Jenna, all three of them did. They've as much as admitted it. She taps her pockets, clumsily feeling for her phone. She's going to call the police, have them taken in for questioning. Why isn't Caroline smiling jubilantly at her? It's done. It's over. Jenna can finally rest in—

'To Tim Chambers and Bessie Grange.' Phoenix raises his empty glass.

Renata swipes at her eyes. 'To Bessie and Tim.'

'Bessie and Tim,' Damian repeats.

Fran shakes her head. What are they talking about? Who are Tim Chambers and Bessie Grange? What are they talking about? She screws her eyes shut and digs around in her brain. She knows those names. Why does she know them?

Her blood runs cold.

The Gozo three didn't drink because they killed Jenna. They drank because they dragged Tim and Bessie's bodies out of the sweat lodge. They watched their friends die.

'I'm . . . I'm . . .' She tries to say she's sorry – for asking something so insensitive, for putting them through so much pain – but before she can finish her sentence, her stomach twists violently and she vomits all over her thighs.

Chapter 34

Then

JENNA

Jenna can't sleep. She's been lying beneath the cool, starched hotel duvet for hours, twisting and shifting, unable to get comfortable as Erica snuffles softly in her sleep in the next bed. Just a few hours earlier, Jenna felt light and happy as she left her session with Tom. After she opened up about her family situation, Tom got her to do a breathing exercise to make her feel more grounded, then a visualisation where she had to imagine blowing all of her fears into a balloon and then letting go of it. Finally, he had her relive the experience of finding out that she wasn't related to her dad whilst Tom moved his fingers in the air and she followed them with her eyes. It was Integral Eye Movement Therapy, he told her afterwards, and when she dug into herself, searching for the deep pain that had been weighing her down for months, she couldn't locate it. It wasn't gone for good though, Tom told her. She'd need more sessions and there was more work Jenna would have to do outside of the retreat to help heal herself.

He thought it would be a good idea to have a family meeting when she returned to the UK; to get everyone together and talk through what she had discovered. Jenna disagreed. That wasn't going to happen, not with her family. They swept emotions so far under the carpet they became embedded in the foundations of the house. There was absolutely no way she was going to sit down with her explosive mother, her abrasive sister and her shadow of a father and have a frank conversation. It could never happen.

Tom didn't push the suggestion. Some families, he said, were too embedded in their roles and beliefs to ever change, and it wasn't Jenna's responsibility to try and fix that.

The relief she felt, hearing that, was so overwhelming she started to cry again.

For years, she'd felt like it was her fault that her family was so dysfunctional. With Fran away at school, and then at university, she'd sat crossed legged on the carpet listening as Geraldine listed Fran's faults and all the ways she'd disappointed her. Jenna resolved that she would be different. She'd wouldn't be anything like Fran; she'd be the daughter her mother had always dreamed of. And for a long time she was. She was Geraldine's shadow, her mini-me, in thought, word and deed. She followed the rules – don't raise your voice, don't voice opinions and never disagree with Daddy. Men didn't like women who thought they were clever, Geraldine told her. That's why Fran didn't have a husband; with her brutish ways, inelegant attire and harsh voice she was the exact opposite of what men found attractive. Jenna absorbed her mother's advice, believing every word. Didn't Daddy adore Mum? Didn't his eyes light up when she walked into a room? Didn't he pull her into his arms and call her 'my little Twiggy'? Geraldine was Jenna's role model, in every single way.

When Jenna reached thirteen, she told some of her friends about the rules her mother had instilled in her and they laughed in her face. That was crap, they said, Geraldine was stuck in the dark ages. Women didn't have to be quiet and keep their opinions to themselves, they had to shout them from the rooftops. Women's voices had to be heard. Her friends were feminists and proud. That afternoon, when Jenna returned home, she told her mum that she'd decided to become a feminist.

Geraldine slapped her round the face.

It was the first time her mother had ever raised a finger to her and Jenna's heart stung more than her cheek. She crept off to her room but, instead of crying into her pillow, she trashed the place. It felt good, finally setting her emotions free and destroying every trace of her neat, orderly life. The next day, when she returned home from school, her mother didn't say a word as Jenna walked into the living room to say hello. Instead, Geraldine raised her newspaper so it obscured her face and Jenna went up to her room. Every trace of the devastation she'd wrecked the previous night was gone. Anything broken had been removed, the carpet had been hoovered and the bed had been made. There was one addition to the room, a note on the pillow:

No one is more ashamed of you than me.

It stung at the time but now, twenty-four years later, Jenna feels a rush of rage when she thinks about that slip of paper and her mother's words. Geraldine must have known that Jenna wasn't Henry's daughter. She'd moulded the little girl into her own image so everyone would say how alike they were. That way they wouldn't focus in on the fact that Jenna looked nothing like her dad.

In her session with Tom, he'd told her that there was a very real possibility she might never discover the identity of her biological father and that they'd have to do some more work together to let go of that pain.

Jenna pushes back the covers and sits up. It's so hot she can't breathe. She thinks about the sea, the cold, sharp shock of the water. She remembers the freedom she felt, sculling in the water, gulls squawking overhead. But it's too dark to go down to the sea now, too dangerous.

She swings her legs out of bed. She'll go to the pool instead.

The path is cold under Jenna's bare feet, her dressing gown little protection from the May wind. She doesn't care. She just wants to get into the pool and feel the sweet sting of the cold water on her arms, legs and face. The lights are off in all the chalets she passes but the path is illuminated by softly glowing LEDs, embedded under glass. As she turns the corner, the pool stretches before her, an azure ellipse, framed with palm trees and bathed in pools of warm light. Her heart sinks. Someone's got there before her. She can see them, a pale blur, moving underwater along the length of the pool. She turns to go as they surface.

'Jenna?'

Tom props himself up on the side of the pool, his elbows on the tiles, his hair slicked back from his face.

Jenna lifts a hand in goodbye. 'I'll leave you to it.'

'Don't go.'

The plaintive note in his voice makes her pause.

'Come and swim,' he says.

She is paralysed by indecision. The pool looks beautiful, the water so cool and clear, but she wanted to be alone.

'We don't have to talk if you don't want to,' he says, reading her thoughts.

Before she can change her mind, she throws off her dressing gown and dives into the water. She doesn't arch towards the surface. Instead, she continues to swim, pulling her arms through the water, eyes open, vision blurred, until her lungs ache for air and she lifts her chin out of the water and takes a deep breath. She dives back down again and swims lap after lap along the bottom of the pool, popping up for air then diving back down again, until her mind stops buzzing and her legs start to ache. Then she rests in the shallow end, her legs extended, her arms stretched across the tiles.

Tom, swimming a lazy breast stroke, stops a metre or so away. 'Feeling better? Sorry.' He pulls a face. 'I said we didn't have to talk.'

'It's fine.' She smiles. 'I just . . . I needed to do that.'

'I get it. I love this time of night. Everything's so still.'

'It never happens in London. So much light and noise, even at four or five a.m.'

He touches his forehead, in the same place Jenna was hit by the rock. 'How's the head?'

'It's okay, aches a bit. But at least I know nothing else can go wrong now.'

'What do you mean?'

'Well, bad things come in threes, don't they? First, someone else's nail varnish came open in my suitcase, then I found a dead bird outside my room and now this.' She touches a hand to her forehead. The plasters are wet. Swimming was a stupid move, she'll almost definitely scar.

'Are you superstitious?' Tom asks.

She laughs. 'Is this an official session? Are you going to make a note in your pad?' She drops her feet to the bottom of the pool and mimes writing in a notepad. 'Jenna Fitzgerald tells lies when she gets nervous. She is also obsessively superstitious.'

Tom laughs. 'I didn't say that.'

'But you read people. It's your job.'

'I don't judge them though.'

'No one said anything about that but it's human nature, isn't it? To watch, to make assumptions? It happens within seconds of meeting someone.'

'Of course. But there's a difference between my . . . human . . . side and my professional side.'

She mimes writing in her imaginary notebook again. 'Tom Wade has a split personality.'

He laughs again.

'I do it all the time,' Jenna continues. 'When someone walks into my clinic I assess their posture, their gait and their balance. All before they even open their mouths. Ninety-nine percent of the time I know which part of their body they want me to focus on, even before they tell me.'

'People are much better at masking their real selves than they are their physical ailments.'

They both fall silent. As it stretches into awkwardness Jenna wonders if she should say something, but Tom speaks before she does.

'I owe you an explanation.'

'Do you?' She looks at him quizzically.

'Kate,' he says. 'I know you were shocked that she hit me.'

'It's none of my business what goes on between the two of you.'

'Can I . . .' He gestures at the space between them. 'I don't want to be overheard.'

'Sure.'

She keeps a hand pressed to the side of the pool as he moves closer, to steady herself, not because she's scared.

'It's complicated.' Tom's eyes search hers. He's inches away from her now and the air between them feels loaded, weighted with emotion. 'The situation with me and Kate. It's not a healthy . . . working relationship.'

'Can't you just sack her?'

'Like I said, it's complicated.'

'Really? If one of your clients told you they were working somewhere where they were bullied, controlled and hit' – Tom blenches at the word 'hit' – 'would you advise them to stay?'

'No, I wouldn't. But Kate's more than just an assistant. She helped build SoulShrink. It's her baby. It was her idea. She's grown it, made it what is. I'm just a figurehead, really. I can't sack Kate because . . . fuck.' He looks away, towards the chalets on the other side of the pool.

'What is it?' Jenna asks.

'I can't . . . I shouldn't . . .' He rubs his hands over his damp face and growls in frustration. 'I shouldn't be telling you any of this. You're a client and it's not professional. We shouldn't even be in the pool together but . . .' He slides his hands down his face and looks at her.

Jenna's stomach hollows. There it is again, the expression in his eyes – the same one she saw when they met, when they talked on the plane, when they swam in the sea. It's not compassion or kindness or caring. It's not professional. It's longing. And despair.

'I know,' she says softly. 'I know.'

'Yes, you do.'

His eyes are so full of desperation and pain she feels as though she's absorbing it, pulling it inside of her and wrapping it tightly around her heart. She feels suffocated, excited, scared. It's as though they're suspended in time. It's just her, and Tom, and the black inky sky and the warm pools of light and the shimmering water.

His hand is on her shoulder and his thumb is rubbing minute

circles over the top of her arm. She wants to reach up and lay her hand on his but she can't move. All she can do is gaze up at him, her eyes moving from his face to his throat – his Adam's apple rising and falling as he swallows – to the droplets of water pooled in his collarbone, and then back to his face, to his eyes, to his lips. She is no longer aware of where she is, or why. It's just her, and Tom, and the space between them.

Kiss me.

She looks from his lips to his eyes, but his lips draw her back.

Kiss me.

The air is so charged she's breathing shallowly, her chest rising and falling.

Kiss me.

She wants to wrap her arms around his neck and pull him towards her. It's unbearable, this waiting, this wanting, this needing.

Kiss me.

Tom's gaze shifts from her eyes to her lips as he moves towards her. It's the tiniest motion, a dipping at the waist that brings his face a fraction of an inch closer. Jenna slides a hand through the water. She wants to touch him, to cup her hand around his jaw, to feel the roughness of his stubble under her fingertips, to feel his lips against hers. Tom's hand slides across the top of her back and he pulls her closer. She twists in the water and reaches for him, to close the space between them. Tom lowers his face to hers and she can't bear it, this terrible, wonderful longing and—

'Evening!'

They spring apart, pool water sloshing around them as Damian steps out of the shadows on the opposite side of the pool, a cigarette glowing between his fingers. He raises it to his mouth, inhales and holds. Not once does his gaze flick towards Tom. Instead, he watches Jenna, his eyes not leaving her face. She shivers, the water that was so cool and refreshing just minutes ago now feels icy cold. Damian puffs a plume of grey smoke into the air then turns and walks back into the shadows. The smoke remains, twisting and shifting like a ghost.

Chapter 35

Now

KATE

The sound hits Kate first, then the smell. One of the guests in the living room has just vomited loudly and the others are rushing around, cooing, exclaiming and sympathy gagging. Kate descends the last few stairs and glances around the banister. She can see the hulking shape of Damian, Phoenix's wild woolly hair, Renata's short blonde bob and the back of Joy's – no, Kate catches herself – *Caroline*'s pink fluffy jumper.

They're all gathered around someone on the sofa, offering water, tea towels and sympathy.

'I think I need my bed.'

Geraldine's low gravelly tones carry across the living room.

'I'll take you,' Kate hears Caroline say.

'I'll get water and some washing up liquid,' Renata offers. As she heads for the kitchen area, Kate takes several steps back upstairs, hiding out of sight in the curve of the staircase. A silent rage builds in her chest as she listens to Caroline taking charge and the others kowtowing to her every instruction. They still think she's Joy – sweet, bumbling, fat little Joy with her stupid jumpers and her simpering smile. Kate tightens her grip on the small, white card in her hand until the edges bite into her palm. She found it in Geraldine's coat – a business card bearing the name Caroline Harding and, in a smaller font beneath it, the word 'Journalist'. The urge to say something, to shove the card into Geraldine's face when the group returned to the lodge for their packed lunches, was almost more than Kate could bear. She'd had to take a walk, after doling out the paper lunch bags, so she could scream into her coat in the woods.

Afterwards, she began to think more clearly. Confronting Geraldine was a terrible idea. Not only was it bad form to confront a guest in front of the others, but there was also a very real chance that Geraldine would simply deny that the business card was hers. There were social media links in the bottom left hand corner – Twitter and Facebook – but the photograph on Twitter was of a woman with a hat tipped over her face and on Facebook the photo was of a small, black cat. Googling didn't help. No photos of Caroline in the search results and her LinkedIn profile had a blank space where the photo should have been. No, Kate decided, a much better idea was to put Geraldine in a position where she couldn't deny the fact that she was journalist Caroline Harding. There was a mobile number in the bottom left of the card, above a Gmail email address. She'd ring the number, Kate decided, but it had to be at the right time, when she could see the expression on Geraldine's face.

Back at the house, she delved deeper into Caroline's life. She read some of her articles, including one about the financial perils of being freelance. Maybe she could buy her off to stop her publishing her story? Depending on how much Caroline demanded it could mean they wouldn't make a penny from the retreat and Kate would have to temp for the next few months just to pay the rent. But it would be worth it if it meant SoulShrink wasn't completely destroyed.

She decided to ring Caroline's number at dinner. She'd seated herself opposite Geraldine. They were halfway through their main and Renata and Phoenix, on either side of Kate, were deep in conversation with other people as she slipped her mobile onto her lap. She'd already stored the number in her contacts so all she had to do was hit 'call'. She watched Geraldine as she moved her fork from her plate to her lips.

And then she heard it; a tinkly, happy tune from directly opposite her. She kept her eyes on Geraldine, willing her to answer her phone. But it wasn't Geraldine who dug around in her pocket and lifted her phone above the level of the table cloth. It was Joy. She jabbed at the screen, ending the call, then apologised profusely for bringing her mobile to dinner.

Kate's phone, sheltered from view by the table cloth, stopped vibrating, jolted once, then lay still in her hand. It couldn't be a coincidence, could it? That Joy's phone had gone off at the exact moment Kate had called Caroline's number? No, it couldn't. The reason the card was in Geraldine's pocket was because Joy – Caroline – had given it to her. It wasn't Geraldine who'd suggested a walk in the garden on the first night, it was Caroline. Geri's comment about Jenna must have prompted Caroline to take her to one side to find out how much she knew.

Fuck. How could she have got it so wrong? With Geraldine's bombastic tone, clipped vowels and ugly shoes, she'd assumed she was the journalist, not Joy.

Beneath the table, Kate twisted the skin on the back of her hand until it stung. Focusing on the pain was the only thing that stopped her from picking up her plate and slamming it into Caroline's face.

*

Kate took herself off to her room after dinner, leaving the plates soaking in the sink. She couldn't trust herself to be around Caroline, not until she'd calmed down. She had to be clear-headed and in control of her emotions. And she needed a plan.

She sat at the dressing table and played a film on her laptop – staring through the screen, rather than at it – while Tom read a book on the bed. When he finally fell asleep she dug out the SSD card, slipped it into the slot on the laptop and watched Caroline's therapy sessions with Tom. There had to be *something* that bitch had confessed that she could use against her, some dark little nugget she could hold over her head. But there was nothing. Caroline's session was a bullshit splurge about body consciousness and self-esteem. Watching the recording again it was obvious the woman was acting. She hadn't cried once.

It was the sound of laughter from the living room – and a burst of terrible paranoia – that had driven Kate out of her bedroom and down the stairs. Was Caroline behind it? Was she slagging off the retreat and making the others laugh? Or was the laughter hers and Geraldine's? Had she missed her chance by retreating to her room? Had Caroline already destroyed her reputation? Was it too late?

Kate freezes as Caroline and Geraldine pass the bottom of the stairs. Geraldine is slumped against Caroline, her arm around her shoulder, her head resting on the top of Caroline's head.

'I think the wine was bad,' Geraldine slurs. 'I never . . . I never norm . . . is fine . . . I can walk by myself.'

As they disappear in the direction of the bedrooms, Kate walks down the stairs. She stands at the bottom, watching as Caroline and Geraldine stumble along the corridor. When they enter Geraldine's bedroom and disappear she hurries after them and waits, out of sight, near the open door. If any of the other guests spot her she's got an excuse. She's come to help but she doesn't want to intrude, not until Joy's got Geraldine into her nightclothes and into her bed.

She hears the slump of Geraldine falling onto her bed, a low groan then the double clunk of shoes being dropped to the floor – all accompanied by Caroline's voice:

'Can you undo the button on your trousers? No, okay. I'll do it. You push them down.'

'Do you feel sick? I've put your bin directly by the bed.'

'There's water on the bedside table.'

'Okay, I think we're done. Get some sleep and I'll see you in the morning.'

Kate takes a few steps back into the corridor. Seconds later, Caroline emerges from Geraldine's room and gasps.

'Kate!' She presses a hand to her heart and in that split second reaction Kate sees Caroline, and not Joy. 'You gave me a shock.'

'Geri all right? I heard she'd been sick.'

'Yeah, yes.' Effortlessly, Caroline slips back into her bumbling smiling Joy persona. 'I think we got carried away with the drinking games.'

'How funny,' Kate says, smiling sweetly as rage flares through her like wild fire. 'Can we have a chat? In the therapy room where we can have a bit of privacy?'

Joy gives an exaggerated yawn. 'Sorry,' she says as she removes her hand from her mouth. 'Can it wait until tomorrow? I'm still not quite recovered from white-water rafting and it's very late.'

Didn't stop you from chucking my wine down your fat little throat, Kate thinks. They won't have put any money in the honesty box. They never do.

'It won't take long,' she says. 'Then you can get yourself off to bed.'

She leads the way down the corridor towards the therapy

room with Caroline padding behind her. She can almost hear the woman's brain whirring with excitement.

'So,' Caroline sits forward in her seat, the dark circles under her eyes belying her cheerful tone, 'how can I help you, Kate?'

Whilst 'Joy' is straight-spined and eager, Kate is recumbent and relaxed – or at least that's the impression she wants to give. She crosses one leg over the other and looks her adversary in the eye.

'I think it's time we were honest with each other, Joy.'

Caroline tips her head to one side. She's modelled herself on a fucking Labrador, Kate thinks irritably. Greedy, largely confused, but eager to please. 'In what way?'

'Why don't you start by telling me who you really are?'

'I'm sorry, I'm not sure what you mean.'

Kate crosses her arms over her chest. 'Just cut the shit, Caroline.'

'Who?'

'Caroline Harding, journalist.'

'I don't know what you mean?'

'No?' Kate slips her phone out of her pocket and taps at the screen. Seconds later Caroline's pocket rings. As she touches a hand to it Kate ends the call. 'The phone in your pocket has the same number as the business card I found in Geraldine's coat. Don't insult me by denying it.'

Caroline sits back in her seat. The simpering smile has gone, replaced by an amused grin. 'I wouldn't dream of insulting you, Kate.'

'You already have, by coming here.'

Caroline shrugs. 'You reap what you sow.'

'And what is it you think I've sown?'

'There's no point in telling you because you'd only deny it.'

'Try me.'

'You killed Jenna Fitzgerald.'

'What?' Kate stares at her, aghast.

'You act surprised.'

'And that's why you're here? Because you think I killed Jenna? She committed suicide. An official inquiry—'

'Yeah, yeah, yeah.' Caroline waves a hand through the air. 'We both know that was bullshit. What did you do? Pay off the Gozoian police? Is that how the blood went missing? And half the witness statements?'

'What . . .' Kate's heart pounds in her chest. 'What blood?'

Caroline laughs. 'You're good. And I thought I was the actress.'

'I didn't . . . I don't . . . I don't know what you're talking about?'

'Course you don't.'

She can't take it in. She'd summoned Caroline to the therapy room to stop her selling a story about the white-water rafting accident and now she's being accused of murder.

'How much?' she asks.

Caroline raises her eyebrows. 'How much what?'

'How much do you want?'

'Wow.' Caroline looks at her incredulously. 'You're quite something.'

Kate lurches forward in her seat, rage boiling in the pit of her stomach. 'I'm quite something? You're threatening to destroy my life, you piece of shit. How can you sleep at night, doing the job you do – door stepping grieving people, hassling the innocent, grubbing around in the ashes of people's lives for a story? You're scum.'

Caroline lifts a hand and, for a split second Kate thinks she's telling her to stop, but then she pulls down the cuff of her jumper, revealing the mobile phone in her sleeve. 'Would you like to repeat that? My recordings are normally pretty good but, just in case a few words were missed, could you say that again?'

'Fuck you.' Kate leaps out of her chair and heads for the door. It's over. There's nothing she can do to stop the story. Caroline's got everything she needs.

She slams the door behind her and stalks through the corridors, heading for the back door. Unless . . . she pauses as a thought hits her.

Unless Caroline's dead.

Chapter 36

Then

JENNA

Jenna kicks a leg out from under the duvet and twists onto her side. She stretches out, resting her elbow on the pillow and her head on her hand.

'You okay?' Tom rolls lazily towards her.

'I could go off you if you don't stop asking me that all the time,' she says with a smile.

'But' – he plays it dumb – 'how will I know how you are if I don't ask?'

'You could use your intuition. Maybe read my body language or the expression on my face.'

'I might be lacking in those skills.'

'Liar!' Laughing, she leans in to kiss him then squeals as he flips her onto her back and straddles her, pinning her wrists up by her head.

'Are you okay?' he asks, his eyes shining as she squeaks and wriggles and tries to escape. 'Are you okay? Are you okay? Are you okay? I'm not letting you go until you answer me. Are you okay? Are you—'

'Happy!' she shouts. 'I'm happy. Now stop being a dick and kiss me.'

Thirty minutes earlier, as Jenna made her way to Tom's chalet for her third therapy session, there were no nerves, no sick feeling in the pit of her stomach, no doubt in her mind that they'd end up having sex. The night before, after Damian's interruption, neither of them said a word for several seconds then Tom pushed himself up so he was sitting on the edge of the pool, his legs dangling in the water.

'Do you think he'll tell anyone?'

'Tell them what?' Jenna raised an eyebrow. 'Nothing happened.'

A look passed between them then – knowing, loaded.

'You've got your final session tomorrow haven't you?'

Her eyes didn't leave his. 'I do, yes.'

He got to his feet, water clinging to his legs. 'I guess I'll see you then.'

'I guess you will.'

Tom wasn't sitting in his armchair when she walked into his chalet. Nor was he strolling out from a back room with two mugs of tea. He was perched on the edge of the bed in jeans and a grey T-shirt, cleanly shaven, hair wet from the shower, his bare feet on the floor. He stood as Jenna entered the room, gave her the briefest of smiles then, without saying a word, pulled the wooden shutters closed and locked the glass doors. When he did, finally, walk towards her, Jenna's heart was beating so powerfully she could feel it in her throat. He was as nervous as she was. She could see it in the rapid rise and fall of his chest, the dark swell of his pupils and the thumb of his right hand, rubbing circles into the denim of his jeans.

'Kiss me,' she said.

Now, as they lie together under the blankets, warm and naked, their limbs entwined, Tom strokes Jenna's hair as she rests her head on his chest, her eyes closed.

'I'm going to give up SoulShrink,' Tom says quietly. 'I'm going to walk away.'

'What?' Jenna shifts up onto her elbow so she can see his face. 'I thought you said—'

'I've been thinking about it for a long time and I've realised that I can't keep living like this. This will be last retreat I ever do and then' – he shakes his head – 'then I reclaim myself. I just want to be Tom again. I never wanted to be famous, respected or rich. I didn't want a monetised YouTube channel or a huge Twitter following or a book deal or a tour or any of the other stuff that Kate's been pushing for. Those are her dreams, not mine. But I tried, I really tried, because I felt like I owed her. And I wanted to make her happy. But I'm not happy. I've not been happy for a very long time.'

'I think that's the right decision,' Jenna says as she pulls the blanket up over her shoulder. 'I could see you were troubled, the other day on the cliffs. I didn't know why though. But it makes sense now. You've got to put your own happiness first.'

'Yeah.' He smiles but the wistfulness doesn't leave his eyes.

'What?' she asks. 'What is it?'

'If I gave all this up . . . started a new life . . . Would you . . . could you, imagine being part of it?'

She searches his face, trying to make sense of her feelings. The attraction between them has been building since they met but it could just be an electrical storm of a relationship where all the excitement is in the build-up, when the atmosphere is charged with desire. Then, when the lightning bolt finally discharges, it's over: the air clears, the tension dissipates and all that's left is two people wondering what the hell just happened.

But they've had sex now and he still wants her. More than that, he's imagining a future together and she loves the idea of casting off their old lives so they can start anew somewhere no one knows them. It's something she's dreamed of doing for years but never had the guts to go through with. With Tom by her side it would be easier, less scary.

Could she have a relationship with him though? A healthy one? He gets her, understands her like no one else, she knows that much, and there's definitely a connection between them, as well as a physical attraction. But should she? That's the real question. In his own way he's as screwed up as she is and two broken people do not make a whole. She touches a hand to his face, allowing herself to be drawn back into his eyes, and her chest aches with longing. Tom Wade is a good man. She can trust him. And that's all that matters right now.

Chapter 37

Now

KATE

Two cups of coffee and Kate still feels as though she's been run over by a tractor. She could hear them, rumbling past as the weak morning sun peeked from between the gaps in the curtains. She hasn't slept a wink and now she's got to do an aerial walk, twenty feet above the ground, with the clients.

After her conversation with Caroline, she stalked around the garden, shivering with rage, as the lights in the house went out, one by one. Fuck Caroline Harding and her story. This isn't about damage control anymore, this is her life Caroline's threatening to destroy. It's libel, accusing her of murder, but how can she fight it? Her bank account is empty and there isn't a legal team in the country who'd take it on for a share of damages, not when her name's already associated with the sweat lodge deaths.

Now, Tom sidles up to her as she steps into her harness. 'Are you sure about this?'

'I've decided to challenge myself and face my fears. We ask the guests to do that and we should lead by example.'

Tom raises an eyebrow. 'That's a sudden change of mind after years of refusing to do any activities involving heights.'

Kate glances round to check none of the guests are close enough to overhear their conversation then hisses, 'Fuck off you sanctimonious twat.'

'Wow.' He shakes his head. 'Still a bitch. Some things never change.'

Kate watches as he sidles off to join the clients, and, not for the first time, she wonders what the hell she's doing, staying married to him. She's spent nine months trying to rebuild his confidence, to turn him back into the man she first met, and while he can still charm a crowd, he's also weak, spineless and directionless beneath the facade. Everything good about SoulShrink comes from her – the drive, the ambition, the determination and the resourcefulness. She's the one that crafted the SoulShrink Instagram posts that became memes. She's the one who combed the news to spin into a SoulShrink soundbite. She's the one who courted the media and tipped off the paparazzi to follow Tom into London and take photos of him giving a fifty pound note to a homeless man. She *created* SoulShrink. Tom may be its figurehead but she's the power behind the throne. The only time Tom grew a backbone was when he threatened to leave her in Gozo, but she wasn't going to let that happen. Not after everything she'd done, not when she'd worked so hard. SoulShrink is hers.

She tried to keep it going after Tom was sent to prison. She arranged interviews and press appearances. She anticipated the questions she knew she'd be asked and recorded herself answering them; zooming in afterwards to check that the 'pain' in her eyes matched her words from her mouth. She'd express regret for what had happened in the sweat lodge but she wouldn't denounce her husband. Instead, she'd talk about his mental health. She'd demonstrate her compassion, her insight and her deep, deep empathy for those who struggle with their own mental health. The interviewer would regard her with silent admiration. She wasn't just Tom Wade's wife: she was a force in her own right.

Only none of that happened.

Instead of letting her talk, the interviewers interrupted her, angling the conversation back to Tom: how had the sweat lodge deaths affected him? How was he coping with prison life? Tom, Tom, Tom. It was all she could do not to scream. What was the media's obsession with men? Six years had passed since she'd given up her PR business to work on the SoulShrink retreats full time and nothing had changed. No matter how good she was, how professional, how informed, how educated, she was never going to be accepted as the face of SoulShrink. Because she wasn't a man.

So where did that leave her? She could leave Tom, go it alone and grub around in the dirt of London's temping agencies, earning precisely fuck all, or she could resurrect SoulShrink. She didn't need Tom's help for that. How many puppets pull their own strings?

'Okay, everyone!' A deep male voice cuts through Kate's thoughts. It's Thomas, one of the instructors, standing on an empty oil barrel, waving his hand in the air. 'If you could all line up we're ready to go.'

'I can do this,' Kate tells herself as she heads towards the ragtag group congregated around her husband.

'Don't be scared,' Phoenix says as she draws closer. 'It'll be over before you know it.'

She looks past him to Caroline, chatting animatedly with Geraldine in the centre of the throng. 'Yes,' she says. 'It will.'

Kate hastens her pace, stepping from one unsteady, swinging plank of wood to another, her palms sore from the rough support ropes. The gap between her and Caroline is widening and she needs to reduce it before they reach the platform. Kate glances behind her to check on Geraldine's progress but she can't see her. Geraldine lost her footing on the first obstacle and had to be winched back to the beginning by the instructor. Peter, who was in the queue before Caroline, has also disappeared. He's making quick work of the course, striding confidently and barking orders to poor Priyanka ahead of him. She's moving tentatively and slowing him down.

Kate takes another wobbly step, then another. There are only four planks between her and Caroline now and the other woman has paused, gauging the leap between the end of the bridge and the platform. It's deliberately wide, forcing the participant to jump and Caroline's shaking so much that the plank she's standing on is swinging back and forth.

Kate takes another step closer, her gaze flitting to the metal carabiners attaching Caroline to the safety rope. There are two to ensure safety and the instructor was very clear in his briefing: One clip *must* remain attached at all times.

'When moving between bridges, walkways and obstacles, unclip one carabiner at a time and attach it to the safety rope before unclipping and re-attaching the second.' Kate's witnessed multiple aerial walks and, ninety-nine percent of the time, she's witnessed the participants carefully following protocol, unclipping and clipping one carabiner at a time. That said, she once watched a man – an overly protective, verging on mothering, sort – try to help his girlfriend out by unclipping her second carabiner at the exact moment she unclipped the first one, leaving her teetering on the edge of a walkway with nothing attaching her to the safety rope. It was only thanks to an instructor screaming up at the man to take his hand off the clip that the woman didn't plunge to her death.

Lucky indeed.

But Caroline won't be as fortunate. The trees are dense in this part of the wood and, because of the time of year, there's a tangle of branches beneath the next platform that haven't been cut back. Anyone who jumps from the bridge to the platform and makes their way round the pole to the next walkway can't be seen from the ground.

Not until they jump.

Kate glances behind her as the bridge shakes beneath her. Geraldine is falteringly crossing it, one of the instructors following close behind.

Fuck.

Almost as though she can read Kate's thoughts, Caroline looks round too. Her eyes meet Kate's and narrow, warningly.

'Come on,' Kate says. 'Make the jump! There's going to be a traffic jam here in a minute.'

'You like giving orders, don't you?' Caroline laughs – a short, sharp 'ha!' – then turns away. One second she is facing the platform and the next she's midair, arms spread like a squirrel monkey. The two safety carabiners slide down the rope behind her and she lands heavily, wrapping her arms around the pole, hugging it close.

'Fuck,' Kate says again.

She moves quickly, striding across the remaining two planks, all the while watching Caroline as she inches her way around the platform, still hugging the pole close. Kate reaches the last plank and takes a steadying breath. She *has* to make it onto the platform *now.* If she unclips the second safety clasp as Caroline unclips the first and then pushes her it'll be over. A troubled client whose darkness engulfed her. A tragic suicide. There was nothing she could have done to help.

Caroline is now halfway around the platform.

Don't look down, Kate tells herself. Don't look down; just jump. She tightens her grip on the ropes and bends her knees. Jump, she tells herself. Jump!

And she is! She's moving through the air and the pole is a brown blur rushing towards her. The toes of her boots hit the edge of the platform and she reaches . . . reaches. The pole is half a foot away from her outstretched fingers. But she's not close enough and her body rocks backwards; her heels, then her toes, then her whole body leaves the platform and she drops, the ground rushing towards her.

The safety ropes tighten and she's jerked upwards, and then she's just dangling, swinging back and forth twenty feet above the ground.

Chapter 38

Now

FRAN

Fran dips her spoon into the steaming tomato soup, blows on it lightly and takes a sip. Her phone vibrates in her back pocket but she ignores it. She texted Geraldine with an update half an hour ago and she's pretty certain that: *Still working on Tom. He's giving nothing away at the moment, other than the fact he knew Jenna and he's sorry she's dead* won't have elicited the most polite response.

'Not enjoying the soup?' Caroline asks as Fran lowers her spoon.

'I feel horrendous.' She presses her hands to her head and massages her temples. 'I thought I felt bad this morning but it's getting worse. I need to lie down in a darkened room, possibly forever.'

'It could have been worse; you could have ended up swinging

from a rope like Kate. Oh my god, the look on her face as she fell, and that scream!'

It's a conversation they've had multiple times but Fran still feels a jolt of glee at the memory of Kate launching herself at the platform, wobbling on her toes and then tipping back like a felled tree.

'Couldn't have happened to a nicer woman. Where is she anyway?'

Caroline cranes her neck to look back towards the kitchen area. 'Vanished. Hopefully disappeared into a well of her own despair.'

Fran looks at her friend admiringly. The woman has balls the size of watermelons. Not only had Caroline insisted on returning to the retreat rather than going to the hospital after their near drowning, she'd also turned down a bribe that would have significantly eased her financial situation. She'd told Fran about the previous evening's conversation with Kate in hushed tones when they were squeezed together on the back seat of the minibus, en route to the Woodland Adventures site. Caroline hadn't actually disclosed how much money Kate had offered her to put her story to bed, but it said a lot about her moral fibre that she'd refused.

'Hangover or no hangover,' Caroline says, putting down her spoon. 'You still have to go to your one-to-one.'

'Again?' Fran groans so loudly that Phoenix, sitting beside her, asks if everything's all right.

She dismisses him with a wave of her hand and leans in towards Caroline. 'What difference will it make if I go or not? Surely you've got enough on them both now.'

'Have I?' Caroline raises her eyebrows. 'Kate's a devious bitch who tried to buy my silence but there's no evidence pinning her, or Tom, to Jenna's murder.'

Fran flinches at the word murder. It's the image it conjures in her mind that's so distressing: of her sister, standing on the cliff edge, dehydrated and disorientated after having survived the sweat lodge, only for someone to sneak up behind her and attack her. She only hopes it was swift, that she would already have been lost to the world as she tumbled into the sea.

'You're shivering.' Caroline touches a hand to Fran's arm. 'Would you like my jumper?'

Fran stares in horror as Caroline plucks at the hem of the white, fluffy monstrosity she's wearing. 'No, no. I'll get a wrap from my room.'

'Geri,' Tom calls from across the table as she stands up. 'Don't forget our session in fifteen minutes.'

Fran smiles tightly. 'No danger of that.'

Despite Tom's reminder about their post-lunch one-to-one, Fran is the first to arrive. She settles herself into the armchair and crosses her arms over her chest, then swiftly uncrosses them again. When Tom arrives she needs to appear open and receptive. No, receptive is not the right word. It has *all* the wrong connotations.

Open and communicative?

Better.

Not that she expects to get anything out of Tom. The last time she attempted that he twisted the conversation back to her and she found herself so swept along by his questions that, before she knew what she was doing, she was talking about her feelings.

She gives a small shudder and reaches into her pocket for her phone. Her message folder is bound to be bursting with texts from her mother..

She smooths her hand over the flat line of her pocket. No phone. Checks the other pocket. Also empty. She must have left it in her room. Again. She stands up and heads for the door, pauses, then wanders back into the centre of the room. There's no point getting her phone; not least because she'll get sucked into her mother's neurotic vortex and she'll probably end up spending the entirety of her session with Tom talking about *that*.

She gazes idly out of the window until she grows bored then paces around the room, her gaze sliding from the beige walls, to the bland painting, to the leather armchairs, to the table with the glasses and the jug and the tissues, to the key fob on the—

She stops walking. The last time she had a one-to-one the key fob was in a dish in the centre of the window sill. Now it's pushed up to one side. She picks up the dish and pours the coins into her hand. As a child, bored in her grandmother's house, Fran would often dig around in the dishes and pots on the cluttered shelves and sideboards. More often than not, she'd discover old pennies, big and brown and heavy in her palm. There was something so satisfying about clutching one in her hand. She felt like Jack after he'd climbed up the beanstalk and raided the giant's house.

But there are no weighty pennies in this dish. Just a handful of tarnished coppers and a few tiny five pence pieces. She tips them back into the dish then picks up the key fob. She turns it over, running her thumb over the matt, black surface. It's as weighty as her own key fob but there's something cheap about the plastic and there's a ridge, just below the keychain hole that runs all the way around. Unusual. She presses her thumbnail into it and is about to lever it open when she hears the click of the door opening.

'Sorry I'm late.' Tom runs a hand through his hair. He's dressed casually in jeans and a sweatshirt and he's forgone shoes in favour of a pair of grey and navy stripy socks. 'I got caught up talking to—'

'Is this yours?' Fran opens her palm to show him the key fob.

He squints. 'What is it?'

'A key fob. It lives in this dish.'

'Nope.' He lowers himself into an armchair, letting out a little groan of satisfaction as he settles back into it. 'Our car key is in the bedroom.'

'Oh.' Fran places the key fob back in the dish, in the same position as she'd found it, piling the coins either side. Then she takes the seat opposite Tom. 'The cleaner must have moved it.'

Tom laughs. 'I'm not sure Kate would take kindly to being called "the cleaner".' He mimes quotation marks with his fingers.

'There's no cleaner?'

'No. No, Kate's the only one who comes in here other than me . . . and the guests, obviously.' He indicates the table. 'That's why we have tissues, fresh water and glasses.'

'Right.' Fran glances back at the window sill. It's dusty. Why move the dish unless you were cleaning? And why leave a key fob and a pile of coins in a house you're renting when the rest of the place is uncluttered and pristine? She pushes the thought away. It's a displacement activity, focusing in on a small annoyance in order to delay her session with Tom.

But as the session gets started and Tom begins delving into her past, Fran is continually distracted by the small, black object on the window sill. It's pointed directly at her. Almost as though it's watching. She shakes the thought off. She's becoming paranoid. Kate is the threat at the retreat, not a small piece of plastic on a window sill.

She looks back towards Tom. 'How's your day been so far? Did you enjoy the aerial walk?'

He dismisses her question with a swipe of his hand. 'Nice try. Let's talk some more about your mother, as I think you have some unresolved issues there. How would you describe your relationship with her?'

'Awful. How's your relationship with your mother?'

He shakes his head. 'Come on, Geri. You can do better than that.'

And on it goes, Tom pressing her to open up and her rebuffing his question with one of her own. Tom becomes more and more impatient as the hour ticks by: his sighs become longer, he shifts in his chair, he almost empties the jug he drinks so much water. Finally, he holds up his hand and says,

'What is it, Geri? What's this about?'

She shrugs. 'I don't know what you mean?'

'Yes you do. You're feeling emotionally vulnerable, aren't you? We made good progress in our last session and that's scared you. You've closed right up.'

Fran suddenly becomes aware of her crossed arms and ankles and slowly, deliberately, unfolds herself. 'No I haven't.'

'I've noticed a pattern,' Tom says. 'Whenever I turn the conversation to your mother you try and swerve it away.'

Fran shrugs. 'You'd swerve too if she threw hot tea at you.'

Tom doesn't laugh. 'Humour is also an attempt at deflection. You mentioned earlier that your mother told you you needed to get help for your grief. That this retreat was her idea and you weren't keen. The actual phrase you used was "she bullied me into it".'

Fran shrugs again. She can see where he's going. He's going to draw a parallel between her bullying mother and the bullying she suffered at school.

'Do you find it hard to say no?' Tom asks.

Fran grins. 'No.'

'Do you find it hard to say no to your mother?'

This time Fran doesn't respond. She stares out of the window, at the trees bending and bowing in the wind.

'Why is that?' Tom asks. 'Why is it so hard to say no?'

'Imagine a glacier being dropped on you from a great height,' Fran says, looking back at him. 'That's what my mother's disapproval feels like.'

'And yet you still want her approval?'

Fran squirms in her seat. All this emotional dissection is unbearable. 'Perhaps. She's a much nicer person if you do what she says.'

Tom scribbles in his notepad. 'What's your relationship with your father like?'

'It's hard to say.'

'In what way?'

'He's not the most communicative of men, particularly after his stroke, but even when I was a child he wasn't really one for expressing himself, not the emotions he deemed feminine anyway – things like warmth, compassion, sensitivity or love. When he was relaxed and happy, often after a drink at the Mess, that's the only time he'd pull me in for a hug. But more often than not he was a force of nature, a whirlwind; the air would change in the house when he got home from work. It was interesting, and somewhat perplexing, watching the change in my mother when he'd return home. She'd shrink so far into herself it was almost as though she physically diminished. Her tone would soften and she'd become giddy and ineffectual and tasks she could do perfectly well herself suddenly become too difficult: "Henry, darling, could you open the jam?" "There's a spider in the bedroom, could you catch it for me, please?" I was never really sure which person she was – the one before Dad came home or the one after.'

'Interesting, interesting.' Tom continues to make notes. 'I'm wondering if perhaps your mother felt so dominated by your father that she dominated you in return. Maybe it was her way of retaining some control.'

Fran raises an eyebrow but says nothing. She's trying to imagine the look on her mother's face if she passed *that* titbit of psychoanalysis on.

'So, Geraldine.' Tom looks up from his notepad. 'When you think about your parents where do you feel that emotion in your body?'

Oh for goodness sake, a voice shouts in the back of Fran's head but, instead of voicing it, Fran finds herself pressing a hand to her chest.

'That's the same place you touched when we talked about regret in the last session,' Tom says sagely. 'What is it you regret, Geraldine?'

'How long have you got?'

Tom smiles and then glances at his watch. 'On that note, our time is up, I'm afraid. Are you okay?'

Fran shrugs agreeably. 'Fine.' Compared to the last session, when she'd left the room feeling emotionally bulldozed, she feels remarkably chipper.

'Right then.' Tom stands up and gestures for Fran to leave the room. As she eases herself out of her armchair Tom crouches to grab the jug and glasses from the table. 'I said I'd do the water this afternoon. Kate's having a lie down. She's not feeling great.'

'Did the harness chafe?'

Tom glances up. 'Sorry?'

'Nothing.'

They leave the room, Tom first and then Fran. She closes the door behind her and pauses, watching as Tom disappears down the corridor then, as soon as he turns the corner, she ducks back into the room. She grabs the key fob from the plate and tucks it into her pocket, then she hurries back out again, closing the door behind her.

Tightly clutching the key fob, Fran hurries along the grassy path that leads from the house to the car park. She turns frequently, to check she's not being followed. Her eyes are drawn to Kate and Tom's bedroom; the curtains are closed. It's a first, Kate retiring to her room after serving up lunch. Is she plotting her next move? The thought makes Fran nervous. Kate's already attempted murder and bribery. What's left?

She hurries on. There isn't time to unpick the inner workings of Kate's mind.

There are ten cars squeezed together in the car park, one of which belongs to her. She casts an eye over it to check nothing is untoward then points the key fob at the Alfa Romeo parked beside it. She presses the button on the key fob in her hand. No match. The Alfa Romeo doesn't flash its lights. She moves on to the next car, a black Range Rover. She presses the key fob again. Nothing. On to the next car, and the next, and the next. The key fob fails to open any of them. Fran turns the fob over in her hands. Could it belong to the owner of the house? But why leave it behind, and nothing else? Not even the car it opens?

The sensible part of Fran's brain tells her that she's being silly and paranoid and that taking things that don't belong to her is immoral. The other part of her brain shouts louder – the key fob doesn't match any of the cars, it doesn't feel right, there's no car badge on the back, she found it in the therapy room and someone moved it so it was pointed towards the chair she was sitting in.

'Sod it,' she says aloud as she lowers her reading glasses from her hair to her nose.

She examines the key fob from every angle, then runs her thumbnail around the indent under the keychain hole. Is it a lid of some sort? She grits her teeth and pushes against it with her nail.

Pop! A piece of plastic leaps into the air and drops to the ground. Fran stoops to pick it up. She examines it – nothing exciting of note – then takes a closer look at the innards of the fob. Inside is a USB port, the same size as a mobile phone charger and, beside that, what looks like a tiny disk drawer with a pin hole in the side. Interesting. She removes one of her stud earrings and presses the metal stalk into the hole. The drawer pops open and reveals an SSD card. Also inset into the plastic is what looks like a lens.

Well, well, well. Someone's been covertly recording the therapy sessions.

She pushes the drawer back into its slot and clicks the two pieces of the key fob together. She's got two choices – put it back, or find out what's on the card?

She snorts softly. That's not a choice at all.

Caroline pinches the SSD card between her thumb and forefinger and stares at it in wonder. 'This is . . . wow. Who do you think's behind it – Kate or Tom?'

Fran perches on the end of Caroline's bed. 'Well, I'm no body language expert but Tom didn't look the slightest bit bothered when I asked him if the key fob was his.'

'Kate's then?'

'Looks that way.'

'Hmmm.' Caroline twiddles the card back and forth. 'I could just take this with me when I return to London . . .'

'I'd rather you didn't.' Fran holds out a palm and raises her eyebrows in the direction of the card.

'I won't watch your session, I promise.'

Fran isn't entirely sure whether she believes her. It's not that she doesn't trust her new friend – she's entirely convinced that she wants to solve the mystery of Jenna's murder – but she is a journalist. In Caroline's shoes, she'd want to examine every last second of the footage.

'I think we should watch it now,' she says.

'How? We've both got iPhones and neither of us has got a laptop.'

'Kate has. I saw it on the first day. She was carrying it under her arm.'

Caroline sits up taller. 'Where does she keep it?'

'I don't know. In her room, I imagine.'

'And I bet she keeps her door locked.'

'I'd imagine so.'

'We can't ask to borrow it. The minute she sees the spy cam is missing she'll know why.'

'So we put it back,' Fran says. 'Minus the SSD card.'

'Too risky.' Caroline drums her fingers against her cheek as she stares at Fran, lost in thought.

Fran thinks too. At that very moment, Kate is in her room upstairs, pretending to have a migraine. In that room is the laptop. How to separate one from the other and ensure that she doesn't lock the door behind her when she leaves? Her gaze settles on Caroline's bedside table. And the lighter, lying on top of a packet of Marlboro Lights.

'I've got an idea,' she says.

Chapter 39

Now

KATE

Kate paces the small stretch of carpet between the base of the bed and the dressing table.

She's been hiding away in her room for what feels like days but can't be more than a couple of hours, and she's still no closer to finding a way to stop Caroline's story from getting out. She feels like an idiot for even thinking about murdering the woman. It was a rash idea, born of desperation and it probably would have failed, even if she hadn't fallen off the walkway.

And it was humiliating, dangling from the rope like a tampon, swinging back and forth. As Kate fell she heard a gasp, then a gale of female laughter. It was enough to make her want to unclip her harness and drop.

Later, when everyone had finished the walk, Kate asked Tom if they could have a quick chat. He wasn't keen but she managed to talk him into leaving the group. She told him how scared she felt, how vulnerable, how she thought she might die. It was a huge exaggeration but she wanted some sympathy, for her husband to look at her with warmth and love, not anger and dread. But, Tom being Tom, he couldn't even manage that. Instead, he stared at her with his dead eyes and said, 'It was your choice to do it.'

She slapped him then, only her palm didn't connect with his cheek. He gripped her wrist and held it tightly.

'You don't get to hit me again.'

Then he walked away, leaving her standing there, shaking with rage.

She can't keep doing this. She can't keep playing this fucking game where Tom strains at the leash and she yanks it back in. Why is he so blind to everything she's done for him? All the sacrifices she's made? There's no point discussing the Caroline situation with him because he simply doesn't care.

She stops stalking back and forth and sits back down at her dressing table. She wiggles the mouse to wake her laptop up and, for what feels like the hundredth time, enters Caroline's full name into Google. There *has* to be something grubby she can use against her. If she can track down friends or ex-boyfriends with grudges against her then maybe—

She stops typing and listens. Beyond the closed bedroom door she can hear someone calling her name.

'Kate!' Phoenix pounds at the door. 'Kate, come quickly. There's a fire!'

Chapter 40

Now

FRAN

Fran stands very still as Kate opens her bedroom door. She's obscured from view but she's breathing so rapidly she feels sure Kate must be able to hear her.

'What is it?' Kate barks at Phoenix, standing on the other side of the door.

He begins to explain but is cut off by the wail of the fire alarm.

'For fuck's sake!' Kate shouts and she's off, speeding down the corridor with Phoenix hurrying behind her and her bedroom door wide open.

Fran grabs it before it can close and slides into the room, closing the door behind her. There's a laptop on the dressing table, its screen dimming. Fran launches herself at it and jabs at a key.

Please don't have locked, please don't have locked.

As the screen flashes to life Fran checks her watch. She's got five minutes, ten minutes tops to get the SSD card into the laptop and delete her therapy session from the recording. When that's done she'll give the card to Caroline and she can do what she wants with it (with the proviso she doesn't share any of the other guests' private conversations, even the irritating ones like Peter).

There's no sign of an adaptor to plug the SSD card into so Fran yanks open the drawers. It's not there.

Breathe, Fran tells herself, as she casts an eye over the dressing table for a second time. She lifts papers, and the laptop, then she checks the drawers again. And there it is, lying in the corner, a small, black adaptor. She snatches it up, slots the card into place, then pushes it into the side of the laptop. As a notification pops up on screen, asking her what she'd like to do with the drive, the fire alarm stops. The walls of the house are thin and she can hear shouts and bangs from downstairs. If Kate's got any sense she'll turn off the electricity, put out the fire, chuck the toaster outside and return to her room.

There are two folders on the card. One labelled Wales and the date of the retreat, the other labelled Gozo. Fran catches her breath. If Kate has been recording all the therapy sessions then there's got to be one of Jenna. Frantically she scans the folder names:

Alan
Alison
Bessie
Damian
Erica
Jenna!

There are three files in Jenna's folder. Fran double clicks on the first and inhales sharply as her sister walks into frame. Jenna's in a bedroom just like the one Fran stayed in when she went to Ta' Cenc in Gozo, but it's bigger. There's a double bed with two chairs in front of it, separated by a table. Tom's in one of the chairs. He stands as Jenna walks into the room and holds out a hand. Jenna doesn't shake it. Instead she slumps into the empty chair and she . . . Fran squints, despite her glasses, it's so hard to make out the expression on her sister's face because she's so far away from the camera . . . Is Jenna glaring at Tom? The urge to keep watching is almost more than she can bear but there are two more files with her sister's name on and she hasn't got much time. Kate could come back in at any moment; the smell of burnt toast is already starting to fade.

Fran clicks on the next file and fast forwards through the session. Is Jenna crying? She's got her head in her hands and Tom is pushing tissues towards her. She looks distressed and Fran wasn't there. She doesn't even know what Jenna was upset about. What she'd give to be able to rewind time, to have made one phone call or sent an email. Jenna might never have gone to Gozo. She might still be alive.

Tears burn behind the sheen of Fran's glasses as she double clicks the third file. How long had Jenna been so unhappy? What caused her so much pain? The final recording begins and Jenna walks into shot. There's Tom, sitting on the edge of the bed this time. He's getting up and he's . . . he's hugging her and . . . they're kissing. They're kissing? Fran taps further along the timeline and there's Tom and Jenna on the bed and they're naked, twisted together, kissing and—

Fran freezes. There are footsteps in the corridor. There's a cough, directly outside the door. As the handle turns, she jumps to her feet, slaps at the laptop lid to close it and darts into the en suite. Seconds later, Tom walks into the room.

She can see him, through the 3mm gap where the door is hinged to the door frame, searching through a pile of papers on the bedside table on the left hand side of the bed. He swears under his breath and crosses the room. Fran stares in horror at the laptop. She didn't slap the laptop lid hard enough: the footage is still playing and Tom and Jenna are naked and screwing on the Gozoian hotel bed.

She holds her breath as Tom steps closer to the dressing table. *Please don't see it,* she prays, *please don't—* But it's too late. Tom's staring at the screen, his mouth open, his eyes wide. Slowly he lowers himself onto the stool and pushes back the laptop lid so the full screen is exposed.

'No,' he says softly.

He continues to watch, transfixed, then he jolts back to life, snatches up the laptop and storms out of the room, slamming the door behind him.

As Fran creeps out of the bathroom she can hear him in the corridor shouting, 'Kate!' at the top of his voice.

Chapter 41

Now

KATE

Even with the back door shut Kate can hear the commotion in the house: footsteps, slamming doors, and shouts, 'How do we get rid of the smell?' 'Where's Kate?' 'It stinks in here!' Any minute now one of them will come barrelling through the door, jabbering away, demanding her attention. It was just a bloody toaster fire. You would have thought a nuclear bomb had gone off for all the screaming and waving of hands. Did none of them have any common sense?

She dealt with it in a matter of minutes – unplugging the toaster and smothering the flames with a fire blanket then, when it was cool enough to touch, she wrapped it in a tea towel and deposited it in the skip in the car park. When she returned, the stench of burnt toast hit her even before she opened the front door, and when she stepped into the house she discovered the guests, crowded together in the kitchen, arguing about who put breakfast muffins in the toaster when they were told on the first day that the toaster slots were too small for anything larger than a slice of bread. Kate had sailed past them, down the corridor and out the back door.

Now, she steels herself. She's going to have to go back in.

As she makes her way down the corridor she hears classical music coming from one of the bedrooms. She pauses beside Geraldine's open door. She was told not to play music without headphones, as were all of the guests. Does no one listen to a word she says? Sighing, she snatches up the source of the noise, a mobile phone, lying on the carpet. It's ringing, rather than playing music, and she's just about to hit the red 'end call' icon when something prompts her to hit green instead.

'Hello?' She holds it to her ear.

'Is this Fran Fitzgerald?'

Her first instinct is to reply 'No,' but she catches herself. 'Yes,' she says tightly. 'Who is this?'

Even as the words leave her mouth she's running the name Fran Fitzgerald through her brain.

'This is DS Marchant,' says the voice in her ear. 'I'm following up on a sexual assault that took place on the London Underground last year. I understand you witnessed—'

Kate jabs at the 'end call' button and stares at the phone in her hand, breathing shallowly. Fran Fitzgerald. That's what the DS said. Why is that name familiar? Fran . . . Fran . . .

She stares around, searching the walls, the corners, the bed, the carpet, as though the answer lies somewhere in the fixture and fittings of the bland, beige room. Fitzgerald? She squeezes her eyes tightly shut. She knows someone with that name. Who? Who?

Jenna. Her eyes fly open. Jenna's last name was Fitzgerald and she'd mentioned a sister called Fran in one of her sessions. That explains it – why Geraldine mentioned Jenna in the first group meeting, why she's been sneaking around with Caroline, why she regularly gives Kate dirty looks.

Geraldine Rotheram is Fran Fitzgerald, and she's helping Caroline with her story.

She needs to talk to her, to try and unpick the damage Caroline has done. She needs to—

'Oh!' She gasps in surprise as she steps into the corridor. Tom is two feet away, his eyes dark, his expression unreadable.

'Oh my god, Tom,' she says. 'You'll never guess what I've found out.'

And then she notices the laptop he's clutching against the side of his body. *Her* laptop.

'Tom?' Her voice drops to a whisper. 'Tom, what is it?'

She's never seen him look this angry.

'Outside,' he says. 'Now.'

Kate has to jog to keep up with her husband, her heels sinking into the ground, as she follows him up the wet, marshy field.

'Tom!' she cries. 'Could you just stop? Whatever's wrong, we can sort it out.'

He stops so suddenly she nearly runs into him.

'Can we? Because I think you've outdone yourself this time, Kate.'

'I don't know what you mean.' But she does; the laptop clutched to his chest, the expression on his face. She knows exactly what's wrong.

'Why?' His face twists with disgust. 'Why would you do something so vile?'

'To protect you! Against accusations of sexual harassment, of inappropriate behaviour, of . . . of . . . anything that could be used against you.'

He stares at her in disbelief. 'What the fuck are you talking about?'

'The clients! I recorded your sessions with them in case they . . .' She pauses, a cold chill running through her body. Tom's not talking about the client one-to-one recordings. Somehow he's accessed her other recordings, the ones of him and Jenna. 'Those aren't the videos you're talking about, are they?'

Tom stares silently down at her, his eyes searching her face. 'How long have you known?'

Her only option now is to go on the attack. 'Since I watched the video, the day after you fucked her.'

He flinches.

'Nearly three years. You've known that long and you never—'

'Said anything? Why would I?'

Tom says nothing but his eyes don't leave her face. It's unsettling, this sudden change in her husband's mood, the reluctance to speak after his burst of anger. Confrontation she was equipped for, but this – this strange stillness – feels cloying and loaded, like the hours before a storm.

'You told me' – he says it slowly, deliberately – 'that if I ever cheated on you you'd leave me; that would be it, no second chances, no forgiveness.'

'People change and after what happened in Gozo . . .' She flounders. 'It didn't feel that important.'

'You must have watched the recording before we set up the sweat lodge. And you didn't say a word.'

'And ruin the experience for the guests? Unlike you, Tom, I've got self-control. I don't react to every emotion, every urge that I feel. I was going to confront you about it once we got back to the UK but then everything . . . everything went wrong and then you were arrested and' – she shakes her head – 'and there was no right time. What was I going to do?' Her voice grows more shrill. 'Have a go at you about it when you were in prison? When you got out?'

'I got out nine months ago.'

'And you had sex with me.'

'Only because—' He catches himself.

'Because what?'

'Because I knew that's what you expected me to do.'

A beat passes as his words sink in.

'That's base.'

He looks at her steadily. 'Why did you keep the video?'

'I didn't. I forgot it was even on there.'

But *you* found it, she thinks. Somehow you logged in and you dug around in my files until you unearthed whatever it was you were looking for.

'What is it?' she asks. 'Why are you looking at me like that?'

He hands her the laptop. 'Thank you.'

'What for?'

'For making this easier.'

'I don't know what you're talking about.' She clutches the laptop to her chest.

'I think you do. You weren't the only one who wanted to have a conversation after the Gozo retreat ended.'

'Tom—'

'Let me speak.' He pushes his hands into his pockets and stares down at the ground, his tongue playing over his teeth as he searches for the right words. 'I loved her.' Her glances up to gauge her reaction. 'And you knew that. That's why you screamed at me that she was dead, in this exact spot, a couple of days ago.'

'She wasn't the only one who loved you, though,' Kate says quietly.

Her husband closes his eyes, inhales slowly through his nose, then opens them again, all emotion extinguished. Kate's chest tightens. He's going to ask her for a divorce.

I can pull this back, she tells herself, as she reaches into her pocket for her inhaler. I've done it before, I can do it again. Her fingers close around the cool plastic but she doesn't remove the inhaler from her pocket. It's not a real asthma attack. It's a physical response to stress.

'I forgave you,' she says. 'I stood by you. Through everything. I could have left you after I found out about Jenna but I didn't. I could have testified against you in court but I didn't. I could have found another man to take care of me, but I didn't. I've never stopped loving you Tom, not for one second.'

He's weakening. She can see it in the sag of his face and the slump of his shoulders. He needs her, whether he admits it or not.

'I need you,' she says softly. 'You're a part of—'

'What did you say to Jenna in the sweat lodge?'

She jolts at the change of subject. 'Sorry?'

'You said something to Jenna that made her get up and leave.'

'No.' She shakes her head lightly. 'I didn't. She needed water. I told her that if she was struggling she should go.'

'Are you sure about that?'

'Of course.'

'You didn't say anything to her about what you'd watched the night before?'

Kate stiffens but she continues to meet his eye. 'No. I didn't.'

'Why did you follow me after I left to check on her?'

'To see if she was all right, same as you.'

A slow smile spreads on Tom's lips. 'And you kissed me because . . .'

'I knew you were stressed.'

'Not because you were marking your territory?'

Kate flinches.

'Had Jenna just told you I was going to leave you to be with her?'

'Don't be ridiculous.'

'Because I was. Once the retreat was over I was going to ask you for a divorce and Jenna and I were going to start a new life somewhere. Maybe in Gozo, maybe somewhere else. Somewhere quiet. Somewhere we could be alone.'

Kate turns away. Her husband's new backbone is serrated and it's puncturing her self-control. She wants to fly at him, to scream at him that he's a cheat and a fantasist. But she won't. She can't. She's going to have to suck it up and play the victim, turn the knife back on him.

'Tom . . .' When she turns back to look at him her eyes are wet with tears. 'Please don't do this.'

His face remains a blank.

'I love you.'

Nothing.

'I can change.' She forces a sob into her voice. 'I know you don't like how brittle I can be, how argumentative, but I can get help.' She reaches for him but he moves away. 'Please, Tom. We can put things right. I love you. I've always loved you.'

'I'm sorry, Kate.'

She feels light-headed but she's not going to reach for her inhaler. She can still regain control. There's only one weapon left in her arsenal; using it will be risky, but it's all she's got left.

'If you leave me I'll kill myself.'

Her arrow finds its target and Tom gasps.

'It's true.' She pushes on, shoring up her advantage. 'I can't live without you, Tom. If you leave me, I've got nothing. My life is over.' She throws herself at him, latching herself onto him like a limpet, her arms around his waist, her head against his chest. Then, dredging up her most painful childhood memories, she bursts into tears.

Tom doesn't respond. He doesn't wrap his arms around her, nuzzle the top of her head or murmur in her ear. He doesn't comfort or console her. She may as well be hugging a lamppost for all the love she can feel. She pulls away so she can see his expression, and so he can see the tears on her face.

A smile pricks at the edges of Tom's mouth and he lowers his chin to look at her. 'Just when I thought you couldn't sink any lower, you plumbed the depths. Nice try Kate, nice try.'

Kate takes two short, sharp puffs on her inhaler then she flies around the bedroom in a fury, snatching up her make-up bag, hairbrush, toiletries and clothes. She hurls them into her suitcase, zips it up and slams out of the room.

'Kate?' Renata steps out of her bedroom, blocking her escape route down the stairs. 'Kate, what's wrong?'

'Tom is.' She moves to push her way past then changes her mind. It's about time her husband's adoring minions knew the truth. 'I wouldn't advise you to spend any more time alone with him.'

Renata gives her a bewildered look. 'I'm not sure I know what you mean.'

'Good. That's one less person he's fucked.'

'I'm sorry?'

'My husband's in love with Jenna.' She laughs at the disbelief in Renata's eyes. 'Yes, I know. She's dead, and yet he's still divorcing me.'

'But . . . but . . .'

Kate pushes past her. 'Don't bother booking another retreat. It's over. I'm done.'

Chapter 42

Then

JENNA

In a patch of wasteland at the back of the hotel, over a low stone wall, fifty metres from the rough track that leads to the cliffs, is a large circle of pale rocks. Some are limestone, dug out of a local quarry and shaped into bricks, others are rubble, placed loosely on top. It looks to Jenna like the remains of a large animal pen but now it's become the perimeter of the sweat lodge, a curved, tarpaulin roof like a turtle's back rising above the grey stones. Her hair whips around her face as she walks past it, to the small marquee that's been set up to give them shelter from the wind before the ceremony takes place, and to prepare.

Erica, trudging behind her, looks impossibly young without her make-up. Erica *is* impossibly young. Jenna isn't wearing make-up either; none of the women are. No jewellery either.

They have all showered and shaved and, under their white dressing gowns, they're in bikinis and swimsuits. In ancient cultures, Tom told them that morning, participants in a sweat lodge ceremony would be naked; partly to allow the whole body to be cleansed, along with the mind, but also to complete the symbolism of the rebirthing at the end. They would squirm and stumble, naked, through the flaps of the tent, leaving behind the warm womb and entering the world cleansed and renewed. Damian laughed so hard at the word 'flaps' that he had to leave the room.

Jenna looks for him now, scanning the sea of people clambering over the wall or traipsing alongside her, their flip-flops slapping against the rough ground and their white dressing gowns billowing in the wind, but there's no sign of him. He hasn't said a word to her since he saw her and Tom in the pool two nights ago but she's felt his dark eyes on her, at every meal and in every meeting: silently judging her, subtly shaking his head. If he had seen their near kiss he hadn't told anyone about it, of that she's pretty sure. No one else has given her sly looks or talked about her behind their hands and Kate, well, Kate's just been Kate, bouncing around from person to person with a clipboard in her hands and a sour look on her face. Other than mealtimes, Jenna has only seen Tom twice since they first slept together. The first time they crossed paths she was heading to the spa. Aware that other people might see, or overhear them, Jenna nodded and smiled but kept walking. Tom touched her elbow as she passed, making her pause.

'You okay?' he asked. The tense expression on his face evaporated as she started to laugh. 'I'll take it that's a yes.'

'Yes.' She smiled up at him. 'I'm happy. I'm good.'

'Are you still okay with the . . . the plan?'

She nodded. Their plan was devised after the third time they had sex – a hurried, desperate, clawing, grabbing shag in the last few minutes of her session. They would avoid each other for the rest of the retreat, they decided, then, when they returned to London, Tom would tell Kate that he wasn't going to be part of SoulShrink anymore. Then he'd ring Jenna and they'd arrange to meet up.

'Or we could just . . . you know . . . just fuck off together now,' Tom had joked. 'Do the sweat lodge and then jump on the next ferry out of here. Get a job in a bar in Madrid or . . . I don't know, be a gardener in Morocco. Not that I know the first thing about plants.'

She'd liked the sound of that, running away and never going back to the UK. They could create a new life, a cocoon that would protect them from the outside world. She wouldn't have to tell her dad what she knew, wouldn't have to deal with her mum's wrath. Fran wouldn't notice if Jenna lived in a different country. Neither would her friends; they were so busy with their own lives they mostly communicated by WhatsApp anyway. Her clients might miss her but they'd find other physiotherapists. There was nothing to stop her from running away with Tom. Nothing at all.

The second time she saw him was that morning. She'd woken up to find Erica sitting on a chair in the corner of the room, staring straight at her, her knees hugged to her chest, her face blotchy from crying. When Jenna asked what was wrong Erica had buried her face in her knees.

'What's the matter?' Jenna had asked gently. 'What is it?'

When she'd reached out a hand and touched her lightly on the calf Erica jumped as though she'd been burnt.

'You know what I've been through and you still betrayed me.'

'Betrayed you?' Had Jenna said something she shouldn't? Shared something Erica told her in confidence? She'd searched her memory and come up blank. 'How?'

'Just go away,' Erica had screeched. 'Just leave me alone.'

Jenna went in search of Tom. She'd eventually tracked him down to the waste ground behind the hotel where he was stripped down to a black vest and cargo shorts, lugging bits of timber around as a couple of local carpenters helped him build the sweat lodge out of tarpaulin, plastic sheeting and wood. He hadn't looked the slightest bit surprised when Jenna had told him that Erica was hysterical. Instead, he'd thanked her for telling him and, after a brief word with the carpenters, he'd headed back to the hotel.

Now, as Jenna joins the others in the centre of the marquee, Erica takes herself off to one corner. She gathers her long blonde hair in her hands, twists it into a pony tail and pulls it forward over one shoulder. She strokes it, moving her hands from root to tip: a repetitive, self-soothing motion Jenna's seen her do many times before. Just a few hours ago she'd looked and sounded distraught, but she seems calmer now, more focused. Her breakdown had come from nowhere, or at least that's the way it had appeared to Jenna. Erica had been fine at bedtime the night before, chatty and excited about the sweat lodge ceremony the next day and then suddenly, in the morning, there were sobs and tears and a rant about Jenna betraying her. Was she upset because Jenna had gone to the spa alone the day before? Did she feel rejected because Jenna hadn't asked her to join her? Had it brought up memories of Erica's dad walking out? Jenna heads towards her, squeezing through the crowd. She's only a couple of metres away when Alan cuts in front of her, his curly hair a halo around his pink, sweaty face and his chest hair peeping through a gap in his dressing gown.

'Jenna! Can you believe it's finally happening? The sweat lodge. We're finally going to get to do it!'

Out of the corner of her eye she sees Erica drift away.

'Do you think you'll do the whole thing?' Alan asks. 'Stay in there until the end?'

'I hope so.'

Alan lifts himself up onto his toes and jiggles up and down. 'I feel like today is the first day of the rest of my life. I've chosen my new name. Did I tell you? Phoenix, like the bird that rose from the ashes. I'm going to be a new me, a better me. It's like, this is literally what I've been waiting for for the last twenty-two years of my life and—'

A shadow looms over them.

Damian, dressed in black jeans and a grey hoody, nods at Jenna. 'Could I have a word?'

She shakes her head, but then a thought hits her. The sweat lodge ceremony is about healing, gaining new wisdom and purifying the mind, body and spirit. When she steps inside she wants to leave her old life behind, and that includes all the crap with Damian.

'Okay,' she says. 'Let's go outside.'

They draw to a halt behind the marquee, Damian with his arms crossed over his body and Jenna with her hands buried in the pockets of her dressing gown. Standing between the marquee and a low wall, they're partially sheltered from the icy wind but she can't stop shivering.

'What are you doing?' he asks.

'I would have thought that was obvious.'

'I'm not talking about the ceremony.'

She can hear the slur in his voice, see a shine to his eyes that isn't caused by the wind.

'What are you talking about, Damian?'

'Why him? A man who beats his assistant. Why would you go there?'

'He didn't hit her. It was the other way round.'

'And you believe that?'

'Yes. I do.'

And she does, unequivocally. Before she left her last session with Tom, the one where they made love, she'd asked him why he'd used the word 'complicated' to explain his friendship with Kate.

Kate was unlike anyone he'd ever met, he'd said, as he pulled on his clothes. She was strong but broken, feisty but vulnerable. Back when she was just a member of his little self-help group she'd confided in him about her childhood and it was one of the most traumatic stories he'd ever heard. Her parents had separated when she was ten but her father had struggled to come to terms with the break-up. Jim was a volatile man, a drinker and deeply paranoid. He'd go through the bins, tearing correspondence and bank statements into tiny shreds because he was convinced the neighbour would go through their rubbish and discover how much debt he was in. Kate's mum, Annabeth, couldn't cope and fled to her sister's with Kate.

Her dad demanded visitation rights and it was agreed that he'd have Kate every other weekend. The first few weekends were lovely. Her dad didn't drink, he showered her with presents and he took her to the zoo. But then, one weekend, a couple of months after the separation, Kate realised something was wrong the minute she walked into her dad's house. There were cans everywhere, overflowing ashtrays, and STUPID BITCH was written in red paint on the living room wall. Her dad opened the fridge, took out a beer and told Kate to sit at the kitchen table.

Then, for the next hour, he ranted at her. He loved her mum, her told her, but she wouldn't take him back. She'd met someone else and betrayed them both. It was the first Kate had heard about a new boyfriend and she burst into tears. Her dad hugged her then, holding her head against his chest. He smelt of booze and cigarettes. He'd look after her, he told her. He'd love her until the day he died. And then, that night, as Kate slept in her childhood bedroom, Jim doused the house, and himself, in petrol, and set the place alight. Kate survived, coughing and spluttering but otherwise unharmed, but only because the neighbour, the same one her dad had been so paranoid about, returned from a nightshift at four a.m. and saw the smoke.

'That's why Kate has control issues,' Tom told Jenna as she stared at him in shock. 'She's doesn't trust anyone, not even me. I thought that I could make her well. If she hit me I told myself it wasn't me she was angry at, it was her dad. I knew why she was doing it so I was able to separate her behaviour from who she is.'

'That makes her sound like a child.'

'In many ways she is. She hasn't moved on from what happened that night, not emotionally. I suggested she see a psychiatrist, but she refused. Our relationship had moved on by then, we were . . . business partners, really . . . and it wasn't right that I treat her. In her mind, because she'd overcome her stress-related asthma attacks, she could overcome anything. But she wouldn't confront what had happened to her. She threw herself into making SoulShrink a success. And I was so grateful. She was doing it because she respected and believed in me and that was a heady combination but . . .'

'But?'

'When someone continually chips away at you there comes a point when they're not just taking chunks out of your self-esteem, they're destroying you bit by bit. I realised that if I stayed, I'd become as damaged as she is. I had to walk away, while I still could.'

'And that's now?'

He'd nodded. 'Yes, it is.'

'And that makes it better, does it?' Damian asks, jolting her from the memory.

Jenna's so lost in her thoughts she can't be sure what he's asking her.

'That she hits him,' Damian clarifies, 'not the other way round?'

'Yes, it does.'

'And you want to be with him?'

'It's none of your business what I want.'

'Maybe it's not, but someone has to point out that what you're doing is fucking stupid. The man's a master manipulator. Him and Kate.'

'And yet you still paid two grand to come here.'

'And what a mistake that was. What can I say, I was desperate. I would have paid Derren Fucking Brown to come to my house if I thought he could help me. And yes, I am an alcoholic. I've never denied that, but I'm not stupid—'

'So you keep saying.'

'I've got eyes!' He slaps the side of his face. 'I've seen what he's doing to you. He's got you under his spell and you're too screwed up to see it. I tell you, Jenna. No good will come of shacking up with him.'

'Who said anything about shacking up with him?'

'Ah for fuck's sake.' He rubs his hands over his face then rests them behind his head and stares up at the sky. 'Look, I'm a screw-up, I know that – I'm the first one to admit it. But you'd be better off with me than with him.'

There's a part of Jenna that wants to tell Damian to fuck off and another that wants to give him a hug. *Now* she understands what he's trying to tell her. It's not that he doesn't trust Tom, although that's part of it. In his own clumsy drunken way he's trying to tell her that he has feelings for her.

'Damian . . .' She waits for him to lower his chin and look at her. 'We need to talk about what happened on the first night—'

He growls, low in his throat. 'I fucked up.'

'Yes, you did. You can't do that, Damian. You can't kiss women who don't want to be kissed. And yeah' – she holds up her hands – 'maybe I shouldn't have hit you, maybe that makes me no worse than Kate, but you gave me no choice. It was the only way to stop you. You were pinning me in the chair. You're a big man. I know you were drunk and you thought it was funny but I couldn't escape and that was scary. *You* scared me.'

Her words hit their target and he crumples, his head in his hands, his chin on his chest.

'I wasn't going to say anything,' Jenna continues, 'but I've spent my whole life biting my tongue and I like you, I do, but I had to tell you. You can't do that again, not to me, not to anyone.'

As Damian sobs something inside Jenna cracks and she moves closer.

'You're a good man. But you need to get help. Promise me that when you get back to the UK you'll go and see someone.'

He doesn't reply but there's a pause between sobs. He's listening. But will he remember when he sobers up?

'Go get some sleep,' she says softly. 'I'll come and find you after we're done here. We can talk again. '

Damian takes a long deep breath and straightens back up. 'Can I ask you something?'

'Sure.'

'Do you love him? Tom?'

She rakes through her feelings as he waits for her answer. She's attracted to Tom, she's drawn to him, she enjoys being in his company, but is it love? It's too soon to say, but there are embers that could turn into flames given enough time, enough space, enough air. But she can't tell Damian that. Not when there's so much hope in his eyes. She can't let him walk away believing he has a chance with her.

'Yes,' she lies. 'Yes I do.'

He stares at her for a beat then shakes his head sadly. 'Jenna, I—'

He breaks off, his gaze flicking from Jenna to a spot somewhere behind her. She turns, sensing they're no longer alone.

Erica is standing at the corner of the marquee, her hands hanging loosely at her side. As Jenna's gaze flicks to her head, bald and pale in the weak May sun, Erica gives her a defiant look.

'Kate's waiting for you,' she says. 'It's time to say goodbye to your hair.'

Chapter 43

Now

FRAN

'Caroline!' Fran raps excitedly on her friend's door. 'Caroline!'

She knows she's in there, because she's looked everywhere else, but Caroline's taking her sweet time answering the door. And there's so much to tell her; not just what Fran discovered on the SSD card but Kate's disappearance. She's gone. Possibly for good, if Renata is to be believed.

'Caroline!' She knocks again. 'I've got something important to tell you.'

When the door finally opens Fran leans away in alarm. Caroline looks terrible; her skin is grey and there are deep dark circles below her eyes. When she opens her mouth to speak she coughs instead. Fran waits patiently for her to stop but when Caroline starts gasping for breath Fran ushers her back into the room and into bed.

'I should get Tom,' she says as she straightens the duvet.

'No, don't. I'm fine,' Caroline's voice is a dry rasp as she collapses against her pillows. 'I just . . . I just need some more sleep. I'm very . . . I'm very tired.'

Fran presses a hand to her friend's forehead. She's burning up.

'I'm going to get Tom,' she says decisively, then adds needlessly, 'stay where you are.'

A hush falls over the guests gathered in the living room as Tom walks into the house. His expression is grim as he gets closer. His gaze sweeps the group, resting on each of them in turn. Fran stiffens as Tom's eyes meet hers. It's bad news, she can see it in his face.

'So.' He forces a tight smile, his hands twisting in front of him. 'Um . . . first things first. Joy won't be returning for the last couple of days of the retreat. The doctors suspect she is suffering from secondary drowning and they want to keep her in for observation.'

'What—' Phoenix says but Tom cuts him off.

'She's got fluid in her lungs. It can be fatal but, thanks to Geraldine's swift action, Joy should make a full recovery. She's being given oxygen and various medications and she's being well looked after.'

'Oh thank goodness.' Priyanka, perched on the edge of her armchair, slumps back against the cushions. 'I was so worried.'

'We all were,' Peter says, and everyone nods in agreement.

'Can I see her?' Fran asks.

Tom shakes his head. 'Probably best to just let her rest today but I'm sure we can sort something out for tomorrow. The . . . er . . .' He clears his throat. 'The other thing I know you'll all want an update on is . . . um . . . Kate.'

Phoenix, sitting beside Fran, gives her a nudge. In the two

hours Tom's been at the hospital the house has been abuzz with rumours. No one is entirely sure where Kate disappeared to but Emily and Sophie saw her charge down the stairs with her suitcase and when one of them (Fran still struggles to tell them apart) asked her if everything was okay she totally blanked them. Peter, who was in his and Phoenix's bedroom on the first floor, said he saw Kate dragging her suitcase up the path to the car park and Damian, who'd been smoking round the back of the house, said he'd seen Kate and Tom arguing a few minutes earlier, in the field.

'Kate's um . . .' Tom runs a hand through his hair. 'Kate's had to leave for personal reasons but she's . . . er . . . she's left me with strict instructions not to let anyone touch the toaster.'

Several of the guests laugh, but it has a strange, nervous timbre to it that doesn't ring true.

'Seriously,' Tom continues, 'Kate's done such a good job organising this retreat that it should run itself. I've got her itinerary and tomorrow morning's group activity is all booked.'

Phoenix raises his hand. 'What is it?'

'Now there's a question! Um . . . I couldn't tell you off the top of my head but I suspect it won't involve water.'

Fran cringes. Tom's attempts to lighten the mood are hideous. A natural-born comedian he is not.

'I may need some help at meal times,' Tom adds. 'Mostly so what's served up at lunch and dinner isn't burnt.'

Fran buries her head in her hands and groans quietly as Sophie, Emily, Priyanka and Peter all volunteer at once, swiftly followed by, 'I'm happy to step down if there's too many of us' and 'We pair up, take one meal each' and 'Is there any flour? I make a lovely quiche.'

As they continue to squawk and squabble, Fran gets up from her seat and leaves.

*

Fran pushes off her duvet and swings her legs out of bed. Someone's turned the heating up to 'incinerate all human life' and her body is prickled with sweat. She unlatches the window and inhales the cool, clear air that billows into the room. Outside, a storm is brewing; trees are bending in the wind, a line of dark clouds scuttle across the dusky horizon and an eerie silence has replaced the chirping of birds.

She plucks at the neckline of her pyjama shirt and wafts it back and forth, letting the air get to her skin. It's 12.35 a.m. She can't have slept more than an hour and now she's awake.

She found it almost impossible to drop off, and not just because Sophie/Emily's over-salted bean casserole was churning in her stomach. There's one day left of the retreat and she's no closer to discovering what had happened to Jenna than she was the day that she arrived. She is fairly certain that her sister didn't take her own life but that's no comfort, and although Kate's recordings prove how underhand she is, they're not evidence that she murdered anyone. And now she's gone, the one person who may have been able to shed light on Jenna's fate. No Caroline either, the only person Fran can trust.

She moves from the window to the en suite, uses the toilet, then stares at her reflection in the mirror as she washes her hands. Her reflection looks as haggard and as exhausted as she feels. She thinks about her sister, and how she'll never age; how she'll always be thirty-seven. It still doesn't feel real, Jenna being gone.

Two months after the official suicide verdict they had a small memorial for Jenna in a little church in their parents' village, but only a handful of people turned up, bunched up together in the first few pews. It felt wrong for Jenna's life to be reduced to something so small – a handful of words, half a dozen bent heads and then tea and sandwiches in a local pub.

Fran dries her hands then lies back down on her bed. She

gets up again, almost immediately. She can't do it. She can't sleep. And she certainly can't drive back to London with so many questions unanswered. The only option left to her now is to disclose her true identify to Damian and see if *that* guilts him into telling her exactly what happened to Jenna and why.

Fran pads down the corridor, her slippered feet stepping lightly on the floorboards, her dressing gown belted tightly at her waist. Normally, she'd never dream of waking someone up at this hour, but needs must. And besides, there's a chance some of the house might still be up, given the amount of noise that seeped under her bedroom door for a good hour after she turned in.

As she reaches the bottom of the stairs, low voices drift down from the first floor and she stops to listen.

'Now Kate's gone I can tell you . . .' Renata says clearly then she lowers her voice and Fran misses the rest.

'No,' Tom says. 'That can't be true.'

'Sssh. It is.'

'Jenna's alive? I can't believe it.'

Fran grips the banister.

'Tom, please, keep your voice down or you'll . . .' Renata fades out again.

'So where is she?'

'My parents' holiday home.'

'Where's that?'

'Abersoch. I'll take you but . . .'

Fran screws up her face, trying to make out the rest of the sentence but the only words she catches are, 'no police'.

'Fine. Whatever. Can we just go?'

'Okay. Wait for me by my car . . . black Range Rover. I'll just grab a few things.'

As the floorboards creak above her, Fran takes off. She hurries into her room, grabs her car keys from the bedside table and clambers out of the window. By the time Tom has put on his shoes and his coat and stepped out of the house, Fran's already halfway up the path.

Chapter 44

Now

KATE

Kate indicates right, manoeuvres the car onto the M6, and pushes down hard on the accelerator. As the car leaps forward she screams, releasing all the tension that's been building for the last couple of hours. What was she thinking, threatening to kill herself? It was crass and she'd cheapened herself, just by saying it aloud. She hadn't regretted it at the time, not when Tom had gasped. At least *something* she'd said had provoked a reaction, only it wasn't the reaction she'd been hoping for. He'd looked at her like she was scum. He'd won and she'd lost. It was the most infuriating, humiliating conversation of her life.

Her phone, lying on the passenger seat, pings with a new message. She ignores it. It's been pinging and ringing on and off for the last fifteen minutes but she's not picking up. If those twats back in Cân-y-gwynt need someone to complain to, they can whinge at Tom.

Who did he think he was? Kicking her off the retreat. *Her* retreat, the one she'd put everything into: her money, time, passion and creativity. The retreat she'd organised for *him,* to reinstall his confidence and ease him back into what he enjoyed most: fixing other people. While he'd sat on his arse in their South London hovel, snivelling about poor dead Jenna and eighteen months in jail, she'd been stuck at her computer, rebuilding their lives. When did she get to fall apart and have someone else pick up the pieces? Never, that was when. And now she was driving back to London . . . to do what? Wipe the arse of some snot-nosed graduate solicitor for ten pounds an hour? Fuck that. She's not going to spend the rest of her life walking to and from filing cabinets in cheap shoes so someone else can live a life of luxury. She doesn't need Tom to make SoulShrink a success. He was the figurehead, nothing more. As long as his face is on the Twitter account she can keep doing what she's been doing, pumping out inane tweets about self-worth, happiness and joy. She'll turn them into tote bags, or tea towels, or T-shirts, or whatever the fuck it is the public will pay for. She could license the SoulShrink name, set up new groups across the country, like Slimming World, but for the needy and depressed. All she needs is for Tom to sign the company over to her.

A sign for the M40 flashes by. Once she's on the M40 it's only another two hours until she reaches London. Will Tom come back to their flat after the retreat ends, or will he slope off somewhere else to lick his wounds? Yes, she's pretty sure that's what he'll do. He'll ignore her calls and she'll spend her days sitting on their grotty sofa leaving him voicemail messages and waiting for him to walk through the door. She spent eighteen months waiting for Tom to come home. Eighteen months she put her life on hold and she's not going to do it again. She signals left and turns off onto an A road. She's not going back to London. She's going to return to Wales to make her husband a deal: a quickie divorce in return for his resignation as a Director. And she won't leave until she gets what she wants.

Chapter 45

Then

JENNA

Jenna runs her fingertips over her head, stroking the soft stubble that is all that remains of her hair. There's a charged, manic atmosphere in the marquee. The other guests are milling around like shorn sheep in their white bath robes, bleating in excitement.

'Oh wow, you look so different.'

'Short hair really suits you.'

'I barely recognise anyone.'

Kate didn't say a word as she stood behind Jenna's chair and took the clippers to her hair but Jenna could sense a change in her energy. It was as though the veneer she wore over her emotions was so tightly stretched it was fit to burst.

A couple of hours ago, Jenna wasn't sure if she'd be able to go through with the head shaving.

Her chat with Damian convinced her otherwise.

Only it wasn't a chat, was it? It was a directive: 'Don't trust Tom.' It wasn't about her at all. It was about him, and what he wanted from her. How he felt. It was like talking to her mother: the disapproval, the warning, the judgemental stare.

But now isn't the time to trudge around in old memories and resentments. The purpose of the sweat lodge is to cleanse herself of all that, to let go of the negativity and emerge anew. She hasn't chosen a new name for herself and she's not entirely sure about the whole 'rebirthing' element but she likes the symbolism. Earlier in the morning, they set out as a group, onto the wasteland. They were to find a rock, Tom told them, that represented their pain and hurt. It didn't take Jenna long to find hers. It was black, with sharp edges, and riddled with holes. As instructed, she carried her rock to the cliff edge and stood with the others in a line.

'Transfer all the anger, the pain, the hurt, the betrayal, the guilt and the sadness you are feeling into the rock,' Tom shouted into the wind. 'Feel it grow heavier in your hands as you become lighter. Transfer all your negative emotions into that rock: all the things you've talked to me about and all the things you haven't. And when you're done, hurl it into the sea and scream. Throw it as far away from you as you can. Let it go!'

Jenna stared at the rock in her hands and she imagined all the dark threads that were wound around her heart – her mother's confession, her father's true identity, her sister's apathy, her ex-boyfriend's infidelity and her own feelings of listlessness, worthlessness and loss – slowly unfurling. She felt them journey across her chest, down her arms, out of her fingertips and into the rock. It grew hot and heavy in her hands – the sharp edges pricking at her skin as though her emotions were trying to escape – and she hurled it away. Several of the others launched their rocks at the same time, their screams filling the air as the rocks soared up into the pale blue sky and then dropped, hurtling towards the sea, disappearing from view.

Alan, beside her, bounced on the spot, one fist in the air, shouting with glee. Alison, on her left, sobbed with emotion, Erica dropped to her knees, Bessie hugged herself as she stared up at the sky, Tim rocked back and forth on his heels. Everywhere she looked there was emotion – relief, jubilation and joy – but when she looked inside herself, all the old painful feelings were still there.

'Okay everyone!' Tom shouts now. 'We're going into the sweat lodge.'

Jenna's nerves build as Tom leads them out of the marquee and across the small stretch of waste ground to the sweat lodge. Standing at the entrance is Kate, her long hair twisted into a bun on the top of her head, a bowl of burning sage in one hand and a bunch of lavender in the other. As Tom approaches she taps him on both shoulders with the lavender then runs it down the length of his dressing gown. He nods at her then disrobes, slips off his flip-flops and crawls inside the flaps of the tent.

One by one, the group follow him until only Alan and Jenna are left. Alan steps forward first.

Kate taps him with the lavender. 'I cleanse you of negativity.'

Alan undoes his dressing gown and drops it onto the pile at the entrance of the sweat lodge then lifts the flaps and ducks inside.

Jenna steps forward. On the one hand she feels sorry for Kate; what happened to her as a child was breath-takingly awful, but as an adult she finds the woman overbearing, controlling and cruel. As their eyes meet, Jenna catches her breath at the undisguised loathing in Kate's eyes. In a blink the emotion is gone and Kate taps her on the shoulder with the lavender.

'I cleanse you of negativity.'

The scent of burning sage wafts into Jenna's nostrils. It smells of weed or cigarette smoke. Kate taps her other shoulder then bends at the knees to move the lavender down the length of her body. Her eyes meet Jenna's again, just for a split second, as she straightens back up then she nods for Jenna to make her way into the sweat lodge.

Jenna slips her dressing gown from her shoulders and shivers as the wind whips at her skin. She can feel Kate watching as she drops the dressing gown onto the towering pile, peels back the tent flap and ducks to go in.

The heat is like nothing Jenna has ever known; her eyes sting, her skin, slick with sweat, feels like it's peeling from her body and each breath blisters her throat and burns her lungs. She'd give everything she owns for a sip of water, a lungful of cool May air or a cold towel on her skin but there's no respite.

'Suffering is part of life,' Tom announced earlier. 'This is the hardest thing you will ever do but if you can make it through, if you can last until the end, you will be rewarded. You will find peace.'

Everyone clapped and a rousing chorus of 'we can do this!' went up.

They were all so excited when the sweat lodge ceremony began. Tom poured water onto the hot stones in the centre of the tent and a fizzing sound filled the air. Seconds later, Kate edged through the flaps with a Bucara-style drum tucked under her arm. The flaps closed behind her as she picked her way through the cross-legged guests, and then they were plunged into darkness.

'Room for a little one?' Kate asked as she squeezed into the gap between Erica and Jenna.

Jenna edged away, but with Alan on her other side and twenty-two bodies wedged tightly into the small circle around the hissing stones, there was nowhere to go. Alan abandoned his cross-legged pose a while ago and now he's stretched out behind her, groaning quietly. Kate beats on her drum to drown it out. She's been doing that intermittently for the last hour. Two? Three? Jenna lost track of time a long time ago. Initially, she focused on her breathing – inhaling, holding, exhaling, holding – but instead of calming her it made her panic. There wasn't enough air in the room and she couldn't hold it in her lungs, not when it stung so terribly. Claustrophobia came in waves, crashing over her. It was a battle between mind and body. Her body was screaming at her to scrabble over the sweating, moaning bodies and make a break for freedom but she remembered what Tom had said about conquering her fear and she forced herself to remain.

She hadn't been able to see anyone's expression since the tent flaps were closed but she could hear them suffering, their low moans, their sobs, their sighs. Every now and then someone would complain about wanting to leave but they'd be shot down by shouts of, 'Don't give up yet, you've come so far!' and 'We're in this together!' At one point, maybe an hour or so ago, Bessie complained that she was struggling to breathe.

'I've got asthma,' she said. 'I need to use my inhaler.'

'No you don't. You're panicking,' Kate bit back, her voice ringing out in the darkness. 'Release the tension in your body. Unhunch your shoulders. If your tongue is pressed against the top of your mouth let it go flaccid, rest it against your bottom teeth.'

Tom called out words of encouragement too, telling Bessie to stay strong, that he believed in her. He reminded her that if she could overcome this she could do anything.

She fell silent and an uneasy quiet descended on the group, punctuated only by the dull beat of Kate's drum. Sometime later, Tim called out that he was feeling light headed, only to be met by a chorus of 'lie down, it will help.' When Bessie said she was still struggling, Kate told her to remember why she was doing this, that her children and grandchildren would be proud of her, that it would make her a better mum.

All around Jenna, people are talking softly, reassuring and encouraging each other, stressing how important it is to succeed. There's no fence keeping them in and no lock on the door but the sweat lodge has become a prison with the guests acting as guards. It's palpable, the pressure to see it out until the end. Jenna closes her stinging eyes and trawls through her memories, looking for something, anything, that will help lift her out of the hell hole she's found herself in. She thinks about the sea on the first night, and that first, sharp, intake of breath. She thinks about the pool and the way the water rose up to meet her as she dived down to the bottom. She thinks about Tom and how she ached for his kiss.

'Keep away from my husband.' Kate's words are hot in her ear, making her jump.

'What?' Jenna turns towards her, searching the darkness for the face she knows she can't see.

Kate grips her forearm and leans in again. 'I'm his wife. He missed that little detail out when he was fucking you, didn't he?'

Jenna smothers a gasp with her hand.

'Tom's a liar,' Kate hisses, 'and a cheat.'

'I . . . I didn't . . .' Jenna stutters. Her mind's whirring, picking through what Kate has just said. How does she know she slept with Tom? 'I didn't know.'

Somewhere, on the other side of the tent, separated from her by a pile of red-hot steaming rocks, is Tom. But Jenna can't see him. She can't meet his eye, can't gesture that she needs his help.

'We keep our marriage quiet,' Kate continues, 'because of women like you. Sad, lonely, desperate women who latch onto him like limpets.'

Jenna tries to pull away. Her arm is slick with sweat but

Kate's grip is pincer strong and the more she pulls the tighter it gets.

'You're not running away with him.' Kate laughs softly as Jenna stiffens. 'Yes, I know about that. Surprised, are you? Tom tells me everything. How else would I know you'd had sex?'

'Please.' Jenna wriggles and squirms, her voice rising as she tries to escape. 'I want to go. I can't breathe.'

'Everything okay, Jenna?' Tom calls from the other side of the tent.

'She's fine.' Kate's nails dig into Jenna's skin. 'Just a bit panicky. Why don't you do some square breathing exercises with everyone, Tom?'

There's a chorus of 'yes!' and 'please!' and several seconds later Tom's voice fills the small space. 'Everyone exhale, then gently inhale through your nose to a slow count of four. Hold now for a count of one . . . two . . . three . . . four. Now gently exhale through your mouth for one . . . two . . .'

As he continues to instruct the group Jenna feels Kate's hot breath in her ear again.

'When I let you go you're going to leave the tent and you're not going to make a fuss. You're going to return to your room, pack a bag and ask the concierge to call you a taxi to the ferry. You're going to go back to wherever it is you came from and you're never going to contact my husband again.'

'And if I don't?'

'I'll tell the press all about your dad, the highly decorated Colonel. Well, I say "dad", but we both know that's not true. They'd have a field day with a story like that. Swinging Soldiers Sex Scandal – I can see the headline now. Do your parents read the tabloids at all?'

Jenna lurches away from her, smacking into Phoenix's legs, then she scrabbles to her feet, hitting out at Kate as she yanks her arm free. There are shouts of 'Who is that?' 'What's going on?' 'Who's leaving?' as Jenna scrabbles over and around hot, slippery bodies until, finally, she makes it across to the other side of the tent. As she claws at the tarpaulin, searching desperately for the loose flap of material, the drum starts up again. She can still hear it – boom, boom, boom – pounding in her ears as she drags herself out of the sweat lodge and onto the cold, hard ground outside.

Chapter 46

Now

FRAN

Fran drives in the dark, sitting low in her seat, headlights off as she follows Renata's black Range Rover at a distance as it winds through the narrow country lanes. After her initial burst of excitement that her sister might still be alive and hiding out on the coast of Wales, doubt has set in and the adrenaline that coursed through her body as she ran up to the car park has worn off, leaving her exhausted and confused.

How could Jenna be alive when her blood was found on the cliff edge? Was she attacked and then she ran off? How could she have done that without her flip-flops? Anyone walking barefoot on those rocks would cut their feet to shreds. Is that why there was blood – because Jenna ran from someone? But Caroline hadn't mentioned a trail of bloodied footprints, she'd specifically mentioned blood on the rocks where Jenna was last seen. Did Jenna have a spare set of shoes with her and she'd left the flip-flops and blood to make it look as though she'd been murdered? Did she murder someone else and stage her own death?

Fran shakes off the thought.

All she knows for sure is that Jenna's suitcase, her purse – containing all of her credit cards, her passport, her clothes and her mobile phone – were found in her hotel room. They were couriered to Geraldine and Henry's house after the British police had examined them. There was nothing unusual or worrying on Jenna's mobile and, other than some nail varnish on some of her clothes, no sign anything untoward had happened. Even if Jenna had staged her own death she wouldn't have got very far without money, a phone and a passport. If she is hiding out in Renata's parents' house nearby, how did she get back from Malta without her passport? And what was so terrifying that she decided to fake her own death? The only thing Fran can come up with is that she was smuggled onto a ship to escape some kind of Maltese or Gozoian criminal gang, but that's so ridiculously OTT she can't countenance it.

Did Renata help Jenna get out of Gozo undetected? She heard from Caroline that the girl's parents are rich. Maybe they're friends with senior officials in the British Embassy, or perhaps they know someone with a yacht? Fran isn't au fait with customs checks at British marinas but she supposes there's a chance someone could be smuggled back into the UK.

She turns on her headlights as she joins the A497. There's one car between her and Renata's Range Rover and she drives in silence, watching out for road signs that might give her a clue as to where they're heading. She passes a holiday park then, ten minutes or so later, spots a sign for Abererch Sands Holiday Centre. They're heading west, along the A499. Is Jenna hiding out in a house by the sea?

Fran checks her watch as the road bends into Abersoch. She's been following Renata for nearly forty minutes. Could Jenna have been so close the whole time? The car in front turns off and now it's just Fran trailing Renata and Tom as they weave their way through the narrow streets of the small Welsh village. It's stuffy and airless in the car so Fran winds down the window. She smells the sea air before she hears it – the low drone of the waves, beating against the beach.

As Renata's Range Rover slows, so does Fran. Then, as Renata indicates left into what looks like a track or possibly a private driveway, Fran deliberates. If she follows her and it is the entrance to her parents' house, she'll blow her cover. If she keeps driving and goes back on foot she might lose them. The track is too narrow to allow two cars to pass each other and if it doesn't lead to Renata's parents' house it can't be much further away.

Fran decides to drive on, finds a space by a gate to pull over, and gets out of the car.

She walks down the track, stepping slowly, listening hard. Out here, away from the streetlamps in the centre of the village, the only light is the faint glow of the moon. She stops walking as she hears a car door shut, then another. Seconds later Tom says, 'Are you sure she's here?' If Erica replies, Fran doesn't catch it.

She inches forward, keeping close to the bushes that flank the driveway. As the path curves to the right she spots Renata's Range Rover and, looming behind it, a house. When Renata said, 'holiday home', Fran had imagined a two or three bedroom cottage with low ceilings and doorways you'd hit your head on but there's nothing small about this place. It's detached, four or five bedrooms, with a stone porch and wide windows on either side. The lights come on in the room to the right of the door then, seconds later, in the room to the left.

They're looking for Jenna.

Fran darts out from the darkness of the driveway as one of the lights in the upstairs rooms is flicked on. She rounds the Range Rover, runs up to the porch and pushes at the door. It's heavy and well-made but it opens easily – in their hurry to get into the house Tom and Renata must have left it unlocked. Beyond the porch, filled with welly boots and umbrellas, is another door, also ajar. Fran moves silently into the porch and listens at the hall door.

She can hear footsteps pounding back and forth above her head and doors being opened and shut. Tom's voice rings out above the noise.

'Jenna! Where are you?'

'She must be hiding,' Renata shouts back. 'She probably got scared when she heard the car pull up. Jenna! It's okay! You can come out now.'

More footsteps, then the house goes quiet. Are they searching under the beds? Looking in the wardrobes? Fran's grip tightens on the hallway door – should she go in and help them? She feels torn. There's still a part of her – a dominant, logical part – that believes what Caroline told her: that Jenna was murdered. But the other part – the emotional, grieving part – is hoping for a miracle, for her sister to be alive, for the blood and the rocks and the flip-flops to all be a terrible mistake. If Jenna is in the house she wants to be the person to find her, to throw her arms around her before anyone else.

Before she can open the door, footsteps thumping down the stairs make her freeze.

'Jenna!' Tom shouts. He's a dark pixelated shape, twenty feet away, beyond the mottled glass of the hallway door.

Fran takes a step backwards but she can still see him as he edges closer to the front door. Then, in a blink, he darts into a room at the front of the house and disappears.

'Renata?' He shouts, his voice more distant, 'Where—'

There's a thwack – like a cricket bat hitting a ball – then a thump.

The house falls silent: no footsteps, no creaking floorboards, no doors opening and shutting, no shouts. Fran reaches for the hall door handle, then pauses. Something's telling her not to go into the house. Instead, she slips outside and moves silently towards the window of the room that Tom went into.

And then she sees him, lying on the floor, face down, arms outstretched. Kneeling beside him, and sobbing like her heart is breaking, is Renata. Did he collapse? Have a heart attack? It would explain why everything went so quiet. Ambulance, Fran thinks, running her hands over her dressing gown pockets. They're both empty; her phone's back at the retreat, plugged in on the floor.

There should be a phone in the house though. She taps on the window to get Renata's attention, completely forgetting she's not supposed to be there.

Chapter 47

Then

JENNA

Jenna drags a dressing gown from the pile at the entrance to the sweat lodge and wipes it over her face as she gets slowly to her feet. The wasteland is deserted and the only light is a slither of sun on the horizon. She slips her feet into the nearest pair of flip-flops and takes an abandoned bottle of water from an upturned oil drum, unscrews the lid and empties the bottle in a couple of gulps. She pulls on the dressing gown, pockets another bottle and, hearing shouts from the sweat lodge behind her, panics and runs. She clambers over the wall that separates the wasteland from the path back to the hotel then deliberates. She doesn't want to see anyone. She just wants to be on her own, to calm down, to think. She could go back to her room but she wouldn't be alone for long. Erica would be out of the sweat lodge soon and want a shower. The bar? Too many people. And she doesn't want to risk bumping into Damian.

Damian. Just thinking about him makes her stomach twist. He warned her. He told her not to trust Tom and she ignored him, told him she was in love. Maybe she shouldn't go anywhere. Just wait for Tom to come out and confront him about what Kate said. But how had Kate known about her dad? Had she coerced Tom into telling her what they'd discussed in their session? Hit him until he told her?

Kate knew they'd slept together too. How was that possible unless he'd told her? The hole in the patio wall had been repaired and Tom had made sure to pull the shutters closed before they went to bed together. He had to have told her; but why?

Kate's words echo in her mind: 'We keep our marriage quiet because of women like you. Sad, lonely, desperate women who latch onto him like limpets.'

Was it all a lie? A sick joke? Maybe Tom was sleeping with lots of the women, whispering sweet nothings into their ears and making them promises. She'd assumed that the warm, compassionate, softly spoken man she'd got to know was the real Tom Wade. But what if he wasn't? What if that was the persona he adopted to seduce his clients? When they'd gone for a sea swim on the first night and stopped at the cliff edge Tom had looked troubled. Was that an act? Was he just mimicking her mood so she'd feel a connection with him? She was vulnerable, broken, needy – he barely needed to try.

Was she part of a long line of conquests that Kate tolerated for the sake of the business? Did she warn them off when they fell for Tom, when he took it too far?

He'd lied to her. She'd given him the opportunity to confess that Kate was more than just his assistant but, instead of admitting she was his wife, he'd fudged the conversation and made excuses for her behaviour.

Jenna reaches into her pocket for the water bottle and takes a long, desperate gulp. She's exhausted and dehydrated, not thinking clearly. She needs to go back to the sweat lodge and wait for Tom to come out. She'll know by his reaction if Kate was telling the truth.

As she turns to climb back over the wall, the water bottle falls from her hands.

Tom's left the sweat lodge, but he's not standing by the entrance shouting Jenna's name or looking desperately around for her; he's entangled with a dark-haired woman, their half-naked limbs entwined. The woman he's kissing is Kate.

Chapter 48

Now

KATE

Kate pulls into the retreat car park a little after three a.m. She turns on the torch function on her phone and makes her way down to the house; the lights are off and all the curtains are closed. She lets herself in then climbs the stairs to the room she shared with Tom. She's buzzing with adrenaline, braced for a fight. For the last hour, she's been mentally rehearsing every possible permutation the conversation could take; preparing come-backs for any verbal obstacles Tom puts in her way and arguments to shoot him down. She opens the door to their bedroom and turns on the light.

'Tom?'

There's no one in the bed and the duvet's smooth, untouched.

'Tom?'

She taps on the en suite door.

'Tom?'

She tries the door handle. It opens but there's no one inside.

'Oh for fuck's sake.' She looks at her watch and sets off down the corridor, then jumps as one of the closed bedroom doors opens and Phoenix sticks out his head.

'Oh, Kate!' He runs a hand through his hair. His face is sleep lined and tired. 'I thought I heard someone moving around out here. Peter's been snoring and I've barely slept a—'

'Where's Tom?'

'I dunno.' He shrugs. 'In his room?'

Kate tries hard not to roll her eyes. 'Never mind, go back to bed.'

She makes her way downstairs and checks all the rooms for her husband. Tom's not in the living area, dining room or kitchen, and he's not in the therapy room either. She drops down into one of the chairs and digs around in her handbag for her phone. There's no way she's going to traipse around the fields to see if he's gone for a walk. She'll just ring him instead.

As she taps the button on the side of her phone the screen flashes with notifications. She's missed several calls. She holds the phone to her ear, maybe one of the messages is from Tom? The first voicemail is from Peter, asking if he can have Caroline's room seeing as she's in the hospital. Kate deletes it before he's even finished speaking. The second is from Renata.

'Hi Kate, I hope you're okay. Just to let you know that Tom's come with me to my parents' holiday home in Abersoch for a bit of a time out. I think you two need some time apart from the group to sort things out. I don't know if you're staying somewhere locally or if you've decided to drive back to London but I think it's important you come back tomorrow. You and Tom need to talk face to face and I think I'd make a good intermediary. Anyway, have a good sleep, get some rest, and I'll see you in the morning, hopefully. The address is Cas-bach, Lon

Traeth, Abersoch, just in case you've forgotten. Take care, Kate. Love you! Bye.'

As the message ends Kate stares around the room in confusion. Who the hell does Renata think she is, stepping in to try and save their marriage? And that closing 'love you' was totally bizarre. And Tom went along with it? He disappeared off with her, leaving the other guests to fend for themselves? Jesus Christ. She jabs at his number and holds the phone to her ear. The man's a liability. The sooner she gets him to sign over the company the better. Anything could have happened while they've both been away. Their insurance wouldn't cover them for something happening to an unattended guest.

'Tom,' she snaps as the call goes to voicemail. 'Ring me as soon as you get this. I can't believe you left the guests alone. What were you thinking, asking Renata to stage some kind of . . . some kind of mediator situation. It's un-fucking-believable.'

She ends the call and calls Renata's number instead. It rings out then goes to voicemail. Not exactly surprising given it's 3.21 a.m.

Kate rubs her hands over her face. What should she do – put out the breakfast stuff now and leave the guests a note so she can take off for Abersoch before they get up, or wait until they all come down and then go? Option one means she gets about four hours sleep, if she can actually sleep, and option two means five hours sleep and dozens of questions from the guests.

Option one it is.

She makes her way to the kitchen area and starts ferrying cereal, bowls and cutlery to the dining table. She sets out the table mats then sits down to write a note:

Dear guests, I'm sorry you're waking up to find that neither Tom nor I are here but—

She balls up the note.

Dear guests, I'm sorry there's no cooked breakfast this morning but—

She screws it up and hurls it across the room.

Fuck it. Why should she be the one who apologises? Tom's the one who's screwed everything up. Why does she have to shoulder the responsibility for his actions? Let him explain what's going on for a change.

She pushes back her chair and stands up. She's not going to wait until the morning. She's going to confront him now.

Chapter 49

Then

JENNA

With the sun so low in the sky it's almost as though a fire is raging on the horizon; darkness stretching for miles and then an explosion of orange and red. It's beautiful, but all Jenna can see is the image in her mind of Tom and Kate kissing. Any doubt she may have had about what Kate had told her vanished the moment she saw them together. Tom had never had any intention of leaving his wife; how could he, when he'd shared every private detail of Jenna's life with her? She imagines them, last night, cosied up in the bed she'd shared with Tom, gossiping and laughing. Rage bubbles inside her. She was used, a play toy for a bored couple.

The wind whips around her, making her dressing gown flutter like a flag. It pulls at her, taunting her: *Step closer to the edge.*

She doesn't want to die. If she can live with the fact that her dad isn't really her dad and she may never find out who is, she can live with the fact that Tom Wade is a liar and his wife is a blackmailer. What other secrets has Tom told Kate over the years? How many other people's lives have they ruined?

Gulls dip and glide, still fishing in the last of the light, and shouts from the sweat lodge are carried to the cliffs on the wind. Jenna pulls her dressing gown tighter around her body. The other guests have shed the skin of their old lives like snakes and they're celebrating the birth of a new future. Sorrow fills the well of her rage. She should be with them; excited, optimistic and fizzing with joy. When she lay in bed with Tom two days ago she'd seen their future shimmering like a mirage: a new start, a new life somewhere new. If she returns to London she has two options: confront her family about what she knows, or keep it to herself. She imagines going to work, visiting her parents at Christmas, the occasional awkward coffee with her sister. How can she continue to do those things, knowing what she does? She can't step back into the life she had when the shadow of her secret will follow her everywhere.

What if she doesn't return? What if she stays in Gozo or gets the ferry back to Malta? She could get a job in a bar or a restaurant, surround herself with strangers and create a new Jenna. She doesn't need a sweat lodge to start a new life. But what she does need, she realises, her heart sinking lower than the sun, is money. She's got two hundred euros in her purse. Even if she found a youth hostel on the mainland she wouldn't be able to survive for more than four days, if that.

The shouts from the sweat lodge grow louder, then a scream cuts through the noise.

Jenna turns to see what's going on and catches her breath. Standing a couple of feet in front of her, swamped in a dressing gown that's so big the arms obscure her hands and the hood falls to just above her eyes, is her roommate.

'Hello, Jenna,' Erica says.

'How are you, Erica?' Jenna asks wearily. She's really not in the mood to listen to her roommate gleefully warble on about what a transformative experience the sweat lodge was and how great she feels now.

Erica gives her a strange, twisted smile. 'Renata.'

'Sorry?'

'It's my new name. It means reborn.'

Of course it does. Every conversation Jenna overheard before the sweat lodge ceremony was about the new names people were going to give themselves and the majority were either mythical or some kind of synonym for birth, positivity or starting again. But there's something unnerving about the way Erica is looking at her. There's a nervous energy radiating off her that makes Jenna feel uncomfortable. 'What is it?' she asks her. 'What's happened?'

'Why do you insist on hurting people?'

'Sorry?'

Erica's eyes thin. 'Why can't you leave Tom alone?'

'I don't . . .' Jenna shakes her head lightly. 'I don't know what you're talking about.'

But she does, and she feels sick, even as the words leave her mouth. Erica's found out what's going on between her and Tom. She must have overheard the conversation Jenna had with Damian behind the marquee. How many people has she told? Does everyone know?

Erica takes a step closer. 'You've really hurt me, Jenna. You're not the friend I thought you were. I was so quiet yesterday and you didn't once ask how I was.'

Jenna thinks back to the day before. She slept through breakfast, read for a few hours in the hotel lounge, grabbed some lunch and then went back to their chalet to grab her things for the spa. Erica was sitting on her bed looking at her phone; they exchanged pleasantries and then Jenna headed out again. That's when she ran into Tom and they had a brief chat. She used the spa for an hour or so and then went back to the chalet. Erica was still on her bed, lying on her side, facing away. Jenna had assumed she was asleep and left her alone.

'I'm sorry,' she says. 'This is about dinner isn't it? I didn't wake you up but I—' Erica holds up a hand, shushing her.

'I heard you, you and Tom, planning your escape.'

'Erica—'

'When you didn't invite me to the spa I thought I'd go anyway. I was standing in the porch and I overheard your whole conversation.' She stares at Jenna, her eyes dark and haunted beneath the hood of the dressing gown. '*That's* why I was so upset this morning, Jenna. Because I stayed awake all night, unable to sleep while you didn't stir once. You have no conscience, no moral compass and—'

'Woah! Enough.' Jenna raises both hands. Erica's reaction is completely over the top. She's acting as though she's Tom's wife, not Kate. Has she got a crush on him? Is that what it's about? 'Stop. Just stop. I'm sorry you overheard that conversation and that it upset you but things have—'

'I tried to warn you.'

She narrows her eyes. 'About what?'

'In fact, I gave you multiple warnings.'

Jenna takes a step back. Erica's standing too close and she feels smothered. 'What warnings? What are you talking about?'

'The nail varnish, the bird, the rock.'

Erica did those things? Erica who held her hand during the flight, nearly crying with fear? Erica who slept in the bed beside her and wished her sweet dreams every night?

'Why?' Jenna asks, 'why would you do that?'

'To protect Kate.'

'From what?'

'You. I knew you'd try and steal Tom away from her.'

Jenna feels a jolt of surprise. 'You know they're together?'

'Of course I do.' Erica looks gleeful. 'I saw them kissing, in private, on the first retreat I went to. Tom didn't know what to say when I knocked on the window but Kate took me to one side and confided in me. She told me that they were married but they were keeping it a secret. They didn't want their relationship to make the guests feel awkward about confiding in Tom. She made me promise not to tell anyone and I never have. She trusts me.' Her expression darkens. 'You're not the only woman to fall for Tom. It happens on every retreat – the flirting, the hair flicking, the long looks. I make them stop.'

'What do you mean you "make them stop"?'

'I warn them off. Just like I warned you.'

Jenna stares at her incredulously. 'By throwing a rock at my head? What the fuck? You need help.'

The accusation glances off her roommate. Erica's stopped listening, locked in her own little world, talking at a hundred miles an hour, her cheeks pinched pink from the cold, her huge, dark eyes looking not at Jenna, but through her.

'I respect Kate. I think she's incredible. She's the strongest woman I know and she works so hard. Tom's great too, obviously, he's really helped me with . . . a lot of things . . . but Kate's the one who cares, who looks after us, who makes the retreats so amazing.'

Jenna glances past her, to the sweat lodge in the distance. The noise levels have dropped but there are people everywhere, scurrying around like ants. She catches glimpses of them, lit by the orange glow of torches that sweep the wasteland. The light darts around, catching the wall of the sweat lodge, the roof of the marquee, the hard, dry ground.

'Kate would never do anything to jeopardise the SoulShrink retreats.' Erica's still talking, firing out thoughts, machine gun fast. She's not well; Jenna can see it in her eyes. 'But Tom's weak. That's why he needs my help and I will always—'

'Stop it.' Jenna grabs her by the shoulders and shakes her. 'Erica, stop it.'

'Renata.'

'What?'

'My name's Renata.'

Jenna crouches so her face is inches from Erica's. 'You need help, Renata. What you're doing – what you've done – isn't right. Putting nail varnish in someone's luggage, leaving a dead bird outside their door, throwing a rock at them, listening to conversations, bursting into tears, confronting people . . . You need to see someone when you get back to the UK. Not Tom, a medical professional. Go and see your GP. Tell him how you've been feeling and . . .' She pauses and draws a sharp breath. She just saw a stretcher, back at the lodge, lit up by a flashlight. She follows the beam as it lands on a couple hugging, half a dozen people standing alone and a dark shape on the ground. Two of them. She squints, trying to make sense of what she's seeing, then covers her mouth in horror. They're bodies, lying side by side.

'What's happened?' She looks back at Erica. 'What's going on?'

'You've ruined everything. That's what I came to tell you. Tom and Kate were arguing about you, screaming at each other outside the tent. Everyone inside started complaining, saying they wanted to leave, but I told them not to. I said we weren't to leave until Tom said the ceremony was over. Some of the others backed me up. We said everyone should stay where they were and stop moaning and crying. But it was ruined. They didn't want to do it anymore and they pushed past us and left. There was no celebration, no joy, no singing. You ruined it, Jenna, you ruined it all.'

Jenna's barely listening; she's watching people congregate around the dark shapes on the ground. A flashlight bounces off a neon strip on someone's jacket.

'Erica,' she asks, unable to tear her eyes away, 'why are the police here? Why are people lying down?'

'Because they're dead.'

Jenna's heart misses a beat. She swerves around Erica, adrenaline surging through her, ready to run, to help, to do CPR. She's so focused on the scene of devastation in the distance that she doesn't notice Erica push back the sleeve of her dressing gown. She doesn't see the large, weighty rock in her hand. But she feels it, smashing against the base of her skull, catapulting her head forward, knocking her off balance. As she falls, the ground rushes up towards her and the world darkens.

Chapter 50

Now

FRAN

When Fran taps on the window, Renata looks up sharply, panic in her eyes, her face pale and blotchy. She stares at Fran, both hands resting on one of Tom's shoulders then, with a sharp shake of her head, she snaps out of her trance and frantically beckons her in. Fran doesn't think twice; she heads back to the porch and pushes open the door to the hall. She's a First Aider at work and though she's never actually given someone CPR before, the procedure has been drummed into her. She'd certainly be capable of performing it while they wait for an ambulance to arrive. She just hopes Renata has rung one, because every minute that Tom's not breathing is a minute his body and brain are being deprived of oxygen.

She sprints along the hallway and into a large, open room. In a flash, she takes in the decor: a large, tan leather sofa to her right and another smaller sofa with its back to the window. There's a gilt mirror above the fireplace and a log burner in place of an open fire. The place looks tired and dated with its floral wallpaper, opaque glass light fitting and a mottled grey rug. It's this rug that Tom is lying on, his face turned to the side, eyes closed, his arms spread above his head. But there's no sign of Renata.

'Renata?' Fran calls as she crouches beside Tom's prostrate body. 'I'm going to give him CPR okay? Tell the ambulance crew I'll keep doing it until they arrive.'

She reaches for Tom's wrist and moves her fingers over the veiny underside, searching for his pulse. It takes her a couple of seconds then she feels it, pounding against her fingertips. It's a good sign. She lowers her face to Tom's and feels his warm breath on her cheek.

'He's breathing!' she shouts. 'I need to get him into the recovery position. When you've finished on the phone I could use your help.'

She gets to her feet and puts both hands around one of Tom's arms. She grimaces as she tries to lift him. He's not a large man but he's heavier than she anticipated.

'Renata!' she calls again. 'I could really—'

She doesn't hear Renata creeping up behind her, barefoot on the carpet, but she feels the blow, connecting with the back of her head.

The first thing Fran becomes aware of as she opens her eyes is how dark it is; the second, that every part of her body aches. She tries to reach a hand up to the base of her throbbing skull but she can't. Her hands are bound tightly behind her back, her ankles are tied, and there's tape across her mouth.

'You're awake, then,' says a voice.

Fran struggles to move into a sitting position. Renata is on the sofa near the window; clutching a cushion, her legs tucked to one side, a knife resting on the arm of the sofa. Behind her, the blinds are closed and the only light in the room is from two large, white candles, flickering on the mantlepiece. The light catches the steel of the knife, making it glint.

'Hngh.' Fran grunts. She nods her head towards Renata then grunts again when the young woman doesn't move. Why isn't she using the knife to free her? Is she scared? Is that why she looks so expressionless? It there someone else in the room?

A low grunt from Fran's right makes her shuffle around. Tom is lying on the carpet a couple of metres away, his wrists and ankles trussed, his mouth sealed with tape.

He strains to sit up and slumps against the second sofa, breathing noisily through his nose, his damp hair clinging to his forehead. Somehow he manages to place both feet on the floor, but as he straightens his legs they give out beneath him and he tips sideways, landing with a thump. He gives a guttural moan of frustration then lies still.

'Please don't struggle, Tom,' Renata says softly. 'It's important that you listen.'

Tom closes his eyes.

'You can block me out,' Renata says, and this time there's an edge to her voice, 'but I know you can hear me.'

Her attention is so entirely focused on Tom that Fran risks a glance around the room. Beside the wood burner is a cast iron fireplace tool set. The broom, shovel and tongs are still hanging in place but the poker is lying on the hearth. It would explain the thwack she heard from the porch and the thump as Tom hit the ground.

There's little else of interest in the room – a carriage clock on the mantlepiece, a television on a glass and wood stand, two wicker chests arranged on top of each other in the corner of the room and, on the window sill behind Renata's head, what looks like a replica oil lamp. Nothing Fran could use to pick away at the tape around her hands, not unless she could get to the poker, or the knife.

'Geraldine!'

She jolts as Renata barks her name.

'You need to pay attention, too.'

Fran raises her eyebrows then grimaces as the base of her skull starts to throb painfully.

'I'm sorry I had to do this to you, Tom,' Renata says, pulling the sleeves of her jumper over her hands. 'I did try to talk to you in the car but you weren't interested in talking about Kate. Finding Jenna was more important to you than mending your marriage and that . . . that really hurt, Tom. And if it hurt me, imagine how Kate would feel?

'I've always felt,' Renata continues, 'that you don't appreciate how much Kate does for you, how much she does for all of us. I think you did, once; back when I started coming to SoulShrink retreats and I saw you kissing, I thought you two were the perfect couple. You were so much in love and I' – she falters – 'I wanted that so much for myself. You and Kate were my role models. You were both so warm, kind and caring, and I felt like part of the family. You were like the parents I'd never had.'

Inwardly, Fran rolls her eyes. God only knows how bad Renata's home life must have been if she thought Tom and Kate would make better parents.

'I'd get so angry' – Renata pulls the cushion tighter to her chest – 'seeing women flirt with you. It was horrible. I could see you were just being nice to them but it worried me, that maybe one day you might not be so strong, that someone would come along and lure you away. My father was lured away from my mother countless times and it broke her heart. She forgave him because she loved him, just like Kate loves you, and then he left us and destroyed our lives. I couldn't sleep, worrying what would happen if the same happened to you. SoulShrink saved my life, Tom. You and Kate have saved so many people's lives but you were prepared to throw it all away and abandon us all.

'Jenna!' Renata screeches, making Fran start. 'All the wonderful people who come to your retreats and you chose her? I saw you, Tom. I saw the way you looked at her, the way you touched her, even the first time you met.' She swings her legs over the edge of the sofa and sits forward, her eyes fixed on his face. 'What was so special about her? She wasn't strong like Kate, she was weak, pathetic, lost. She wanted to destroy SoulShrink and I couldn't just sit back and let that happen.' She pauses, her chest rising and falling, her breath coming in short sharp gasps, the candlelight catching the tears in her eyes.

Fran can't stop staring at her. Has Renata just admitted to killing Jenna? Is that why she broke down in the hot tub? Is that's why she's crying now? Fran glances at Tom, writhing around on the ground, smashing his feet against the sofa, grunting and growling, twisting his hands back and forth, trying to work himself free.

Renata's gaze switches to Fran.

'Missing your friend, are you?' she asks. 'Poor old Joy, laid up in hospital. With any luck she'll die.'

Fran's eyes widen with horror.

'Don't tell me you're surprised?' Renata continues. 'Who do you think kicked you both when you fell out of the raft? I heard you two, plotting to bring down SoulShrink, huddled together in the garden like a couple of old women. I waited for this retreat for nearly three years. Three years!

'I thought I'd never be happy again when Tom was sent to prison. I missed SoulShrink, Tom *and* Kate, and the way they made me feel. I went travelling, I did some voluntary work. I did everything I could to put myself back together but I was still so lost. I emailed Kate because I knew she was hurting too. She'd tried so hard to save Tom from himself, even harder than me. I was sitting next to her in the sweat lodge when she told Jenna to leave him alone.'

At this, Tom stops thrashing and lies still.

'Yes.' Renata turns her attention back to him. 'That's why Jenna left, because Kate was onto her. She wasn't going to let her run away with you.'

'Ngh.' Tom shakes his head. 'Nggh nggh.'

'You can protest all you like, Tom. Jenna's feelings for you weren't real. It was all a game to her.' Her expression hardens. 'Do you have any idea how hard it was to get the others to stay in the lodge after you left? I had to do your job for you.' She jabs at her chest. 'It was down to me to complete the ceremony. I tried to do the right thing, but then people started screaming, saying Tim and Alison had stopped breathing, and then they all rushed out. Kate was crying and you'd gone and then I saw her . . . Jenna . . . standing on the edge of the cliff, like nothing happened, like it was nothing to do with her. I was so angry. I was *so* angry.' She rocks back and forth as her gaze darts, unfocused, around the room.

She's reliving it, Fran realises. Renata's standing near the stone circle and she's looking out towards the sea, seeing Jenna silhouetted against the dying light. Fran stood in the same place, trying to imagine what caused her sister to leave the sweat lodge and head, not for the hotel, but to the windswept cliffs.

She glances at Tom. He's stopped grunting and he's staring at Renata with huge, haunted eyes. The only sound in the room is the steady beat of the mantlepiece clock; tick, tick, ticking, like a timer counting down a bomb.

'She hadn't learned her lesson.' Renata's whispery voice makes Fran shiver. She can't bear to look at her anymore, with her taut pale face and her strange distant eyes. 'She was going to go running back to Tom and I had to stop her. I had to use the rock. I hit her on the back of the head to protect Kate.'

A tear rolls down Tom's cheek, curving its way over his cheekbone then disappearing into the stubble on his jawline. Another joins it, then another, and all Fran can do is watch as Renata's words slice through her, tearing through her heart, hollowing it out.

Fran shuffles on her knees across the carpeted living room and out onto the wooden floor of the hallway. She moves slowly and carefully, having already overbalanced and hit her chin once, only to be yanked up by the arms.

A couple of minutes earlier, Renata decided that she was tired of talking and wanted to go to sleep.

'You need to think about what I've said and how you're going to apologise to Kate,' she told Tom before she looked at Fran. 'As for you. I'll decide that tomorrow. Now, off to the basement you go.'

She instructed them to get up onto their knees and move into the hallway. When Tom shook his head and grunted in objection, Renata picked up the knife and held it to Fran's throat. Tom made his way, stumbling on his knees, to the door.

'There we are!' Renata says now, pointing at a small door under the stairs. She ducks around Fran to pluck the key from the lock. She tucks it into her pocket then opens the door, revealing a steep, dark staircase.

'Down you go,' she tells Tom. 'On your bum if you don't want to get hurt.'

'Nggh nggh.' He moves his mouth from side to side under the tape.

'No,' Renata snaps. 'I'm not taking it off. We're not going to be asleep for very long. Kate should be here in four or five hours. You'll survive without food and water until then.'

'Nggh.' Tom tilts his head towards Fran then stares in the direction of the front door.

'No! I'm not letting her go and if you keep this up I'll just push her down the stairs.'

Fran gives Tom a stoic nod. There's something dangerously erratic about Renata's moods, and she's still got the knife. Rather than continue to bargain with her, they need to get into the basement, out of sight. Then they can formulate an escape plan.

Tom tips himself to one side so he lands on his buttocks then carefully sweeps his legs in front of him. He digs his heels into the ground then 'walks' towards the open basement door on his tail bones. Carefully he drops down onto the top step, then the next, and the next. When he disappears, Fran feels Renata's shoe nudging her side.

'Now you.'

Copying Tom, Fran shifts onto her bum and shuffles towards the door. She's barely made it down the first step when Renata slams the door shut behind her and the basement is plunged into darkness.

Fran screeches into her masking tape as she bumps her way down the last step and collides with something large and warm.

The large, warm lump grunts in response.

It's just Tom.

'Nggh.' He grunts again and Fran realises he's moved. He's above her and sounds as though he's facing away. 'Nggh,' he says as his hands touch her face. She holds herself very still as his fingers move clumsily over her cheeks and nose, his nails digging into her skin, searching for the edge of the tape. Fran closes her eyes and braces herself. He's trying to pull it off.

Tom grunts in frustration. With his hands tied behind his back he's having trouble getting purchase on the tape and each time Fran feels a slight tugging his fingers slip away.

She loses count of how many attempts he makes at pulling it; somewhere around the dozen mark. Her skin is sore from all the poking and prodding but she hasn't groaned once or pulled away. If they can just talk to each other they can formulate a plan.

She gasps as the tape is finally ripped from her mouth and runs her tongue over her throbbing, raw lips. They are wet with blood.

'Nggh,' Tom says, and she feels him drop down beside her. It's her turn to take his gag off now.

Several minutes later and it's Tom who winces in pain.

'Oh thank god.' Fran breaths heavily. 'I thought I was never going to get it off.'

'Well done.' Tom rests his head against her, a gentle knock of solidarity. 'Let's get our wrists undone now.'

They move around on their bums, shuffling like infants, their fingers splayed, spider-like, on the floor as they search the cold, dark basement floor for something, anything to rip through the tape. Fran smacks into a chair leg, several cardboard boxes and something hard and metallic.

'Fuck,' Tom swears from the other side of the room.

'You okay?' Fran asks.

'I' – he breathes loudly through his teeth – 'I overbalanced and smacked my elbow on the floor. I'm okay it just . . . it just bloody hurts.'

They fall silent again, the only sound the shuffle of their bottoms on the floor and the occasional low groan of dismay. Fran touches something behind her then doubles over when it smacks her on the top of her head.

'You okay?' Tom calls softly.

'I will be.'

There's a pause then, 'Jenna used to laugh at me for that.'

Fran sits up again and feels behind her, trying to work out what had just hit her. 'For what?'

'Asking if she was okay all the time.'

She can feel prongs, hard, metallic, evenly spaced out with a long length of wood above them. A rake. The handle was what clunked against her head. 'Jenna hated people implying she couldn't look after herself.'

'You knew her well?'

Pressing her head back against the wooden shaft of the rake, Fran rubs her wrists against one of the prongs. 'She wasn't my physiotherapist; she was my sister. My name isn't Geraldine, it's Fran.'

'Fran.' There's a beat, then Tom says, 'Yes . . . yes of course you are. Yes, that makes sense.'

'Was what Renata said true?' Fran asks, changing the subject. 'Were you planning on running away together?'

'Yeah, we were.'

Fran uses one of the rake's prongs to pierce the tape on her wrists. 'Did Jenna know you were married?'

She can feel the tape start to give and moves her hands up and down more fervently.

'No,' Tom says quietly.

'You didn't tell her?'

He sighs. 'She asked me outright once if Kate and I were in a relationship and I lied. We were getting really close at that point and I didn't want her look at me differently, or pull away. I was so attracted to her, and not just physically. I regret the fact that I lied; every single day since.'

Fran sighs. She wants to like Tom, or at least to understand what her sister saw in him, but there's something cloying and self-pitying about him that gets under her skin.

'Have you got your hands untied yet?' she asks, changing the subject.

'No.'

'Well get a move on or Renata's going to take that poker to my head again.'

There's a pause, then Tom says, 'Do you have any regrets, Fran?'

Images flash through her mind – Gunnar, the backpacking trip to Asia with a friend that she turned down in favour of doing her PGSE, the slightly larger flat in London she didn't buy because it would have stretched her budget, not standing up to her mother and for not letting Jenna talk when she'd needed Fran most.

'Yes,' she says. 'Of course I do. Anyway, oooooh.' She tentatively rolls her shoulders forward and feels the sweet sting of her muscles stretching. 'I've got my hands free. Shuffle this way and I'll untie yours.'

Fran gets to her feet and stretches out her body. From Tom's low groans beside her she's pretty sure he's doing the same.

'Right,' she says. 'This is the plan. I sit at the bottom of the stairs, with the tape back on, or at least it needs to look that way. You need to be against that back wall over there' – she points into the darkness – 'beyond the stairs, where Renata won't be able to see you.'

'Okay.'

'Face the wall and pretend to be dead. When she tells us to get up, or move or whatever, you stay completely still. Then, when she comes over to check on you, I use that plank of wood you found and I hit her round the back of her head. Then we get the hell out of here.'

Tom doesn't reply.

'What is it?' Fran asks. 'Is there a problem?'

'No.' She hears the smile in his voice. 'You're . . . you're very refreshing.'

'I've heard that before. Anyway, are we set?'

'Yes, Fran. We're set.'

'Okay then. I've gathered all the tape I need. You go and lie over there.' She gestures, again, in the dark. 'And I'll sit at the bottom of the steps.'

There's a beat. 'Thank you, Fran.'

'For what?'

'Just . . .' She hears Tom move quietly away. 'Just thank you.'

Chapter 51

Now

KATE

Kate pulls up behind Renata's black Range Rover, turns off the engine and looks up at the house. All the lights are off and the curtains are drawn. The rage she felt on discovering that Tom had abandoned the guests hasn't abated. If anything, the forty minute drive through the dark has made it worse. Over the course of their marriage she's forgiven Tom for so much – for lacking ambition, being a flake, having no backbone and for letting her do all the hard work.

She even forgave him for sleeping with Jenna.

She knew the woman was needy – she'd had to prise Tom away from her on the plane to Malta – but she'd never seen her as a threat to her marriage. For all Tom's faults, she'd never once suspected him of infidelity. In the early days of their relationship she'd been suspicious about the motives of a couple of women in Tom's group, but when she checked his phone she didn't find anything incriminating. In fact, if anyone in the group texted him anything even remotely flirty or suggestive he'd either ignore it or call it out for being inappropriate.

It was Kate's idea that they keep their marriage secret. She knew women were drawn to him and if they thought he was single it would only increase his allure. And it had worked. Not only did his YouTube videos attract a huge number of marriage – and more lascivious – proposals, they raked in money. Kate became obsessed with analysing the drop off graphs and she began editing the videos to concentrate on what the viewers were interested in: his face, torso and eyes. Tom found what she was doing amusing. He didn't care who found him attractive, he'd tell her, as long as she still wanted him.

She'd never dreamed that he'd cheat on her.

Okay, so they weren't having sex very often, he rarely gave her compliments and it had been a long time since they'd looked lovingly into each other's eyes, but didn't that happen in all relationships? The first time she realised something was amiss was when Tom took Jenna for an ocean swim. She'd watched from the shadow of the hotel as Jenna had hit out at her husband then collapsed into his arms. There was something so tender about the way he stroked Jenna's hair that set off alarm bells in Kate's head, something so intimate about the shape of their bodies as they clung to each other that made her feel sick. Later, when Jenna came to her, telling her she'd heard the slap, Kate had lied about it. She wanted to turn Jenna against Tom and make herself the victim, that way she'd get Jenna onside.

For a while, Kate breathed easily as Jenna actively avoided Tom – she could barely bring herself to look at him at meal times – but when she refused to go to her sessions, Kate had to step in and tell her to go. She didn't want Tom to become suspicious.

After Jenna was hit by a rock, Kate checked the recording. It was the first time she'd caught Tom out in a lie. He'd told her Jenna was hit by a rock *after* their session but she'd clearly seen them break off from a hug to rush outside. A hug. He wasn't supposed to touch the clients in any way, shape or form.

The next video she watched broke her. It wasn't so much the sex, although that made her want to put her fist through the screen, it was the tenderness afterwards, the soft caresses, the radiant expressions and the lingering looks. Tom had looked at Kate that way once, stroking her cheeks, kissing her lips and gazing into her eyes like he was disappearing inside her. Tom was in love with Jenna. Looking at them, naked and intertwined, hurt so much Kate wanted to claw her eyes from her face. The pain was like nothing she'd ever felt before. It fizzed like poison under her skin, burning through her. She felt rejected, used and abandoned; betrayed, humiliated and defiled. She wanted to drink, to fuck, to get high – she would have done anything to block out the pain. She lifted the laptop above her head. She would smash it to pieces on the hotel room tiles then she'd go after Tom. She'd fly at him, claw his skin from his muscles, rip his hair from his head and tear his heart from his chest. She'd destroy him the same way he'd destroyed her. She'd tweet about his infidelity, put out a press release and rip his reputation to shreds.

Her arms shook as she gripped the laptop, preparing to hurl it to the ground. She would humiliate the pair of them. She'd announce what they'd done at the next group dinner. The guests would be shocked, embarrassed, then horrified. They'd look at Tom with disgust and they'd gather around Kate, consoling her, cosseting her, comforting—

No. She lowered the laptop to the table. No. That wasn't what she wanted. She didn't want sympathy. She'd never be a victim again. She'd had that millstone hang around her neck for long enough – Katherine Armstrong, the little girl whose dad tried to kill her. She'd heard the whispers of the other kids in the playground, shrunk beneath the looks people gave her in the street.

As tempting as it was, public shaming was not the answer. It was a cheap shot that wouldn't just wound Tom, it would also destroy SoulShrink.

An idea formed as she clicked on Jenna's final video and a slow smile spread across her face. Here, on screen, was a way of hurting both of them – Tom and Jenna – and bringing him back. She'd be there to pick up the pieces when Jenna disappeared, never to be seen again.

The hardest part of her plan was acting naturally around Tom. If she was too sweet, or too icy, he'd grow suspicious. What she had to do was harness her emotions, wind back the clock and pretend she'd never clicked on that video, never seen what she'd seen. The first time she met Tom's eye she felt sure he knew that something was wrong. But no, Tom being Tom, he was too wrapped up in himself to notice. Her husband had stopped caring how she felt a long time ago.

The conversation with Jenna in the sweat lodge was sweeter than Kate could have imagined. She heard the pain in the other woman's gasp when she told her what she knew. Kate smiled into the darkness as she continued to turn the knife, one barbed revelation after another.

She smiles now, too, as she opens the car door and swings her legs outside. She'll get what she wants from Tom. There's nothing she can't do.

She walks down the drive to the entrance and, using her phone as a torch, points the beam at the small lock safe attached to the wall. She'd ignored almost all of the emails from past guests when Tom was in prison – they could write to him if they needed counselling, she had better things to do – and she'd almost deleted Renata's email until she saw the subject line: 'I can help'. It wasn't an offer of money but it was almost as good. Renata's parents had a 'cottage' in Wales, she wrote, and it was Kate's for a week, free of charge, if she wanted a break. Naturally cynical, Kate had assumed there'd be a catch but there didn't appear to be. The house was hers if she wanted it and god did she; a big house again, not a dingy one-bedroom London flat. For one glorious week she felt like she had been transported back into her old life – a huge house with room to move, to think, to breathe.

She taps out the code, opens the door and takes out the key.

She lets herself into the house, slips off her shoes and steps quietly through the porch and into the hallway. She doesn't turn on the lights, her phone gives her all the light she needs. She just wants to wake Tom, get him into the car and get him back to the retreat with minimal fuss, and definitely no audience. Renata may want to play the role of moderator but that's the last thing Kate needs.

She climbs the stairs, stepping softly in her socks. The house is a new build, the carpets thick and soft and the floorboards don't creak under her weight. She ignores the bathroom at the top of the stairs and opens the door to the first bedroom instead. She sweeps the beam of her phone across the room. The bed's empty. Leaving the door ajar she continues along the landing to the next bedroom. She almost doesn't open it – it's a twin room and who'd choose to sleep in a single bed when there are doubles available – but she turns the handle anyway. Again, the room's empty, the beds untouched. She tenses as she approaches the third bedroom on the long landing. This has to be where Tom is sleeping. Renata will surely have taken the final bedroom, the master – huge, light and airy with a beautiful en suite – for herself. It was the room Kate chose, too.

She steadies herself outside the door. Tom's going to be confused when she wakes him and he'll probably tell her to go. She's going to have to tread carefully to stop him from raising his voice, maybe mention something about how vulnerable Renata is and how it will cause her unnecessary trauma if they involve her in their marital woes. It's worked before, shifting the attention onto someone else. She exhales softly, opens the door, slips through it and closes it softly behind her. She angles the beam of her phone from the carpet to the base of the bed.

'Tom?' she whispers as the torch illuminates the edge of the duvet, a pale grey cotton embroidered with white flowers.

She takes a step closer. More of the duvet is revealed and a hint of white pillow. Then another pillow and more duvet: flat, smooth and untouched.

'For fuck's sake.'

Has he already left? How? Renata's car is still in the driveway and Kate drove their car. Tom couldn't have got a taxi back to the retreat, surely? Or is he still in the house? Sleeping on the sofa downstairs? Maybe he got drunk? Passed out?

She steps back out of the room and moves to head back down the corridor, then stops and turns back to look at the closed master bedroom door. A thought – ridiculous, unconscionable – flits through her head. Is Tom in there, with Renata? Mentally, Kate rewinds the voicemail Renata left. 'Tom needs some time out. I've taken him to my parents' holiday house in Abersoch. You need to talk face to face. I'll see you in the morning.'

She'd assumed Renata meant she and Tom needed to sort out their differences. But what if she didn't? What if, for the second time, something has been going on right under her nose? Has Tom replaced Jenna with Renata? Do they want to break the news that they're in love with each other, away from the other guests?

Kate moves silently towards the master bedroom, clutching

her phone, her thoughts racing. Her hand shakes as she reaches for the handle and opens the door.

There's someone in the room. She can hear the slow, rhythmic sigh of sleep the moment she steps through the doorway. She steps closer, her thumb over the end of her phone, smothering the beam. The curtains are cracked open an inch and a slither of moonlight casts a pale puddle of light onto one half of the bed. There's Renata, her blonde hair sucked of colour in the half-light, a grey shadow on the white pillow. She's lying on her side, the duvet tucked under her armpit, her pale arm thrown over a lump in the bed. Kate blinks into the gloom, trying to work out what she's seeing but her brain is in rewind, cycling back to Gozo, to her hotel room, to her laptop, to the video, to Tom and Jenna naked and fucking, writhing and twisting, grabbing and bucking and kissing. And there's the pain again, the humiliation and the hurt and the betrayal and it's ripping through her and she wants to lash out, to scratch and bite and slap and tear. She lurches forward, roaring with anger and tears back the duvet. How dare he? How dare he do this to her again?

Her thumb slips away from her phone and in a flash she sees a pillow, an arm wrapped around it, a knife hanging loosely from the fingertips and then she sees Renata, blinded by the light in her eyes, rising up from the bed. And then there's pain, slicing into her stomach, and everything goes black.

Chapter 52

Now

FRAN

Fran is asleep, curled up on the concrete floor of the basement, her head resting on a deflated paddling pool, when the door is slammed open and the light comes on. It takes her sleep-startled brain a second to work out where she is and why the back of her head is throbbing, but then she sees pale ankles and slippered feet hurrying down stone stairs and a voice screams, 'Tom! Tom!' Fran sits up sharply, squinting under the harsh glare of the strip lights, one hand curved over her eyes.

Shit, she thinks, feeling around on the floor for the tape that's fallen away from her cheeks, wrists and ankles. Shit!

But if Renata notices that Fran is no longer bound and gagged she doesn't care. She stops at the bottom of the stairs and screams Tom's name again. He's sitting up too, his face sleep crumpled, his hair wild and ruffled, his hands and feet unbound.

'Help me!' Renata screeches. Her face, hair and chest are spattered with blood, there's a deep red stain on the front of her nightdress and her hands and arms are coated up to the elbows. She looks like Carrie, blood-drenched at the prom. Fran blinks up at her, trying to make sense of what she's seeing. Is she injured? What the hell has she done?

'You have to help me.' Renata ducks down and pulls at Tom's hand. 'She's bleeding. I can't get it to stop. Please, be quick. I'm scared she's going to die.'

'Who?' He gets slowly to his feet. 'Who? Who are you talking about?'

Renata bursts in tears. 'I didn't mean to stab her. I didn't . . . I didn't know who it was . . . I couldn't see . . . the light was . . . it was so bright.'

Tom's expression switches from confusion to urgency. 'Who?' He shakes Renata's shoulder. 'Who? Who did you stab?'

'K . . . K . . .' Renata struggles to get the name out. 'Kate. I stabbed Kate.'

Fran jumps to her feet and follows Tom and Renata as they speed up the basement steps, through the hallway, up the stairs to the first floor and across the landing to the bedroom at the far end. Tom enters the room first then stops abruptly. The sound he makes – a gasp that shudders in his throat then turns into a whimper – is like nothing Fran's ever heard. It's so chilling, so unnatural, that all the hairs on her arms go up.

She tries to look round him but Renata's in the way. They're all bunched up in the doorway and she can't see into the room.

'Help her.' Renata shoves at Tom. 'Please, please help her. I don't want her to die.'

Her words break the spell that's frozen Tom to the spot and he staggers into the room. As he moves, a space between him and Renata opens up and Fran sees her – Kate – stretched over the bed, her dark hair covering her face, one hand outstretched. She's covered in blood.

As Tom screams her name Fran darts back down the landing and flies down the stairs, her heels catching and slipping as she runs.

'Phone . . . phone . . . phone . . .' She stares around the living room, searching for a landline. Nothing. She can't see anything, just the gas lamp and the baskets and the TV. She hurries back into the hallway and opens another door. Kitchen. Her eyes flit from the work surfaces, to the cupboards, to the table to French doors that lead to a beautifully manicured garden, and back to the walls. Where the hell is the phone? Back to the living room she runs. She can hear noises from above: Renata screaming and crying and Tom saying his wife's name over and over again. Where is the phone?

Focus, she tells herself. Focus, calm down. She moves around the room, forcing herself to look properly, and then she sees it, sitting in a cradle to the side of the TV, a black cordless landline phone. She snatches it up and dials 999.

'Police,' she barks before the operator can finish her sentence. 'Ambulance too.'

Fran is sitting on the sofa in the living room, her hands on her knees and a sick taste in her mouth. The police officer sitting beside her is writing something in a notepad. Periodically, she pauses and asks Fran if she's feeling okay. Each time she asks, Fran says yes.

Everything happened so quickly after she made the 999 call. She rushed upstairs to see if she could be of any help and found Tom cradling Kate in his arms. He'd bound a towel around her midriff, but it was soaked in blood. Kate's eyes were still closed and her skin was grey.

'Is the ambulance coming?' Tom met Fran's eyes. 'She's lost a lot of blood.'

'Yes, it's coming.' She didn't mention the police. Instead, she glanced at Renata, sitting on the floor, her back against the radiator, her knees pulled to her chest and her face buried in her arms.

'Tom.' Still watching Renata, Fran drew closer. The smell of the blood, metallic and strong, made her stomach turn.

'Where's the knife?' She kept her voice low.

'I kicked it under the bed.'

'How's Kate?'

'Her pulse is weak but she's holding on.'

'Are you going to be okay in here? If I go downstairs to wait?'

He nodded. 'I don't think' – he inclined his head in Renata's direction – 'she's going to try anything. Not now.'

Looking at the frail creature, curled into herself by the window, Fran couldn't imagine her driving a knife into Kate's stomach. Then again, she couldn't imagine such a small, light girl wielding a poker or smashing a rock into Jenna's head. The thought – of her sister's skull being smashed in – made her stomach clench violently and she tasted bile at the back of her throat.

'Renata?'

Tom looked at Fran warningly but she ignored him. Once the police turned up Renata would be arrested. She might never get this chance again.

'Renata, what happened after you hit Jenna with the rock?'

Renata didn't lift her head, didn't speak, didn't move. She gave no indication she'd even heard Fran at all.

'What happened after you hit Jenna? Where did you put her body?'

Still nothing. A nerve twitched in Fran's eyelid and she rubbed at it irritably. Renata didn't get to do this. She didn't get to sob her heart out about Kate and keep quiet about Jenna. She didn't get to pretend that Jenna's death meant nothing at all. Fran walked slowly around the bed. She stopped a foot away from Renata and looked down at her.

'WHAT DID YOU DO?'

Renata flinched and hugged her knees more tightly, refusing to look up.

'Fran,' Tom said softly. 'Fran—'

'This isn't about you.'

'Fran, the police are here.'

She heard them then, thundering up the stairs, shouting 'Police', and then they were in the room and they were asking questions and radios were buzzing and Tom was talking and Kate was groaning and still Renata wouldn't look at her. Someone placed their hand on Fran's arm and she swatted at it irritably. Then it was on her elbow, angling her away, moving her away from Renata, shifting her out of the room, telling her everything was going to be okay. She wanted to scream, to hit out at the man with his hand on her arm, to tell him that her sister had been murdered, that she'd never get to see her again, never say she's sorry, never put things right. She couldn't speak for crying.

'It's okay,' the police officer said, 'it's okay.'

But it wouldn't be okay. It would never, ever be okay.

Jenna was dead.

'Let's get you to the hospital,' the policewoman says now.

Fran shakes her head. 'No. I don't need—'

'We need to get you checked over. Check that blow to your head, see if you've got any other injuries.'

'I'm fine,' Fran insists. 'I just . . . I just want to go home.' A thought hits her and she sits up straighter. 'I need to go back to the retreat. My bag's there and my house keys. And my phone. I need to—'

'We can take you back there afterwards,' the policewoman says. 'But it's really important that—'

'Kate's the one who needs to go to hospital, not me.'

The living room door is shut but she'd watched through a gap in the blinds as Kate was carried on a stretcher to a waiting ambulance by two paramedics. Tom traipsed behind them like a broken man. Following him was a uniformed officer and a grim-faced detective in a suit.

'As well as getting you checked out,' the policewoman continues, 'we'll need to take some photos, professional ones, of your injuries, and then we need to get a written statement.'

Fran looks impassively at her wrists, at the twisted red skin she only noticed when one of the officers took out a camera and asked her to show him her hands. He photographed them from every angle then did the same with her ankles, her face and the back of her head.

'It's all evidence,' the police officer says. 'You were imprisoned and held against your will.'

'Yes I know but—' Fran stiffens. A uniformed officer has appeared between the gap in the blinds. Wedged between him and a colleague, with her hands handcuffed behind her back, is Renata.

The female officer follows Fran's line of sight and gets up to close the blinds. As she crosses the room Fran gets up too.

'I need the toilet,' she tells the officer guarding the door. He looks across at his colleague. When she nods the okay he opens the door. Fran holds her breath as she steps through it then, as soon as she's out of sight, she runs, down the hallway, through the porch and out the front door. Renata has reached the waiting police car.

'Renata!' Fran barrels down the driveway. 'Where's my sister? What did you do with her?'

Out of nowhere a police officer steps in front of her, blocking her path.

'Renata!' she screams, ducking and twisting to try and get

closer but the officer's got her by the arm now and more are closing in, telling her no, asking her to return to the house. She watches, her heart twisting in her chest as one of Renata's minders puts a hand on the top of her head, pushing her down and towards the open car door. Renata's still not looking at her. She's blocked Fran out, pretending she doesn't exist.

'You killed my sister!' Fran shouts, straining against the men holding her. 'She didn't deserve to die.'

It's as though someone has pressed pause on a film. Or maybe it's just Renata that stops moving, because she's the only person Fran's looking at, a character in close up, freeze-framed in the scene. Then she's looking directly at Fran and her lips are moving, her voice is amplified and every other sound is muted.

'I wasn't the only one who hated Jenna. I hit her, but I didn't kill her.'

'Who?' Fran shouts. 'Who killed her?'

A slow smile spreads across Renata's face.

'Damian,' she says, then she ducks her head and climbs into the car.

Chapter 53

Now

FRAN

The door to the retreat opens as Fran pushes it. She steps into the house and then stops, listening for signs of life. It's just after nine o'clock in the morning and, normally, the place would be buzzing with guests pulling on their shoes and coats, excitedly speculating about the morning's adventure. But there's no sign of Peter in the kitchen area, impatiently drumming his fingers against the counter top as he waits for everyone else to get ready, no Priyanka stepping from foot to foot by the door, no Phoenix jabbing at his phone in the living area and no stragglers hurrying down the stairs. The house is silent and clean, stripped of shoes, coats and boots. Other than six mugs and plates on the draining board and the faintest whiff of toast in the air, there's no sign that anyone has ever been there. A police officer, a softly spoken man in his early twenties, dropped Fran back to Abersoch after she'd given her statement at the police station. She sat in the passenger seat, watching as he spoke to one of his colleagues. Then he nodded at her and she got out. Together they walked down the lane to her car.

'Is anyone here?' Fran asks, even though she already knows the answer. Hers is the only car in the retreat's car park. She's not sure whether Tom rang them from the hospital or, more likely, they got up, realised that four members of the group were missing, including the retreat leaders, and simply packed up and left. She had worried that she might run into Damian but his car has gone too. The police will catch up with him. She made sure of that. As well as telling the officer who interviewed her about the events of last night, she also told her about Jenna. The officer made notes as Fran told her what Renata had said about hitting Jenna with a rock, and that Damian had killed her. The policewomen laid down her pen at the first mention of Gozo. It wasn't their jurisdiction, she said. If Jenna had died abroad the new information would have to be shared with the police force who'd investigated her disappearance. Frustrated, Fran explained that there'd been a cover up and the Gozoian police would simply ignore any new information. The police officer gave her a sceptical look then glanced at her colleague. 'We'll pass it on to the governor,' he said, but Fran didn't believe he'd do any such thing. She'd get in touch with Caroline, she decided, once she was out of the hospital, and find out who they needed to contact to kick up a fuss.

Now, she stifles a yawn and heads for her bedroom. She's barely slept in twenty-four hours and she's been prodded, poked and questioned by doctors. There were no signs of concussion, the doctor said when he examined her, but there was some pretty violent bruising on her neck and the base of her skull.

She pushes at her bedroom door, still ajar from when she crept out last night, and looks longingly at the bed. All she wants to do is crawl under the duvet and sleep, but not here. She wants to be at home, in her own bed; she'll stop at a service station once she's on the motorway and buy a coffee and some sweets to keep herself awake. She strips off her pyjamas, deliberates about whether or not to take a shower, then decides against it – too much faff – and pulls on a pair of jeans and a jumper instead. She pulls a hairbrush through her hair then packs it in her suitcase, along with her pyjamas and her toiletries, adds her book and medication then zips it up. She unplugs her charger and picks up her phone. There's a text from Caroline complaining about hospital food and asking for news, one from Fran's mother demanding an update and then another, three minutes later, all in caps, accusing Fran of being callous and cruel. Sighing, she tucks the phone and the charger into her handbag. As she turns to pull her suitcase off the bed she sees a flash of black in the doorway.

'There you are,' Damian says.

Fran clutches her handbag to her body, desperately wishing she could rewind time thirty seconds so her phone would be in her hand, not nestled in her bag. She could unclip it, dig her hand in and grab her mobile. She could call the police. It would take her seven, eight seconds tops from opening the catch to hitting 999, but Damian's tall, with long legs. He could cross the room in a lot less.

'Damian.' She looks him in the eye but her throat is dry and as she swallows his gaze drifts to her throat.

He's so wide he fills the doorway. She could escape through the window but it's closed. There's no way she could turn the handle, push it open and climb out. Not when it would take him seconds to grab her. She'll have to talk her way out – of the room, if nothing else.

'We're the only ones here,' he says.

'Can we talk?' she asks. 'Out there, in the lounge.'

Damian shrugs. 'I suppose so, aye.'

He doesn't turn to go. Instead, he waits in the doorway until she draws closer and then he steps into the corridor and gestures for her to go first. As she walks through the corridor, past the kitchen area and into the living room Fran digs desperately in her bag. There's so much stuff in it, so much unnecessary crap, and her fingers slide over pens, notebooks, packs of tissues, a comb, receipts, coins, but not her phone.

'Take a seat.'

She jumps, knocking her knee against the side of the armchair. The bag flies out of her arms and hits the rug, spewing its contents all over the ground.

'I'll get that for you.'

As Fran stands beside the armchair, her knee pulsing, her heart racing, Damian drops to his knees and scoops her notebooks, her pens, her tissues, her comb and her phone and drops them back into her bag.

'Take a seat,' he says again, and she does.

He places the bag on the ground beside her then sits down on the sofa. Fran looks at the bag. Is it a trick? If she reaches for it will he know she's going for her phone? Should she ignore it? Play along?

'So.' Damian leans forward, his forearms on his knees. 'Finally, just you and me, all alone.'

Fran nods but says nothing. She's trying to read his expression but his features contradict each other: his brow's rumpled and his eyes are dark and serious but there's the hint of a smile playing at the edges of his mouth.

'You all right, Fran?'

Her lips part then close again. 'You called me Fran.'

'That's your name isn't it? Fran Fitzgerald?'

'Yes,' she says warily. 'Yes it is.'

'Where is everyone?'

She casts her eyes over the furniture and around the room as though one of the other guests might suddenly pop up from behind an armchair. Not because she thinks they might be there but to buy herself time to think, to work out how she's going to get out alive.

'No idea,' she says and then, because she's still play-acting that everything's normal, 'I thought you might know.'

He shakes his head lightly. 'I got up late and they'd all buggered off. I thought maybe I'd missed the activity or something. I drove over to the adventure place in the woods but they said no one had turned up.'

'Oh.'

'So where are they? Where is everyone?'

Fran's lips open and close again. Is this deliberate – his confusion, his . . . innocence? Is he lulling her into a false sense of security with his 'It's just me and you and where are all the others?' Should she play along? Say she overslept too, make her excuses and then go back to her room for her suitcase? Would Damian let her out of the house? Maybe he'd let her get as far as her car, thinking she's home free, before he launches an attack.

'I . . . I genuinely don't know.'

A frown forms between Damian's dark brows. 'Why are you lying?'

Fran glances at her handbag, six inches to the left of her feet. 'I'm not.'

'I think you are. What's going on, Fran?'

She swallows nervously. 'How do you know my name?'

'I wondered when you'd ask me that.'

'So?'

'How about you tell me what's going on first?'

She's not sure if it's the fact his eyes have softened but when Fran mentally flips a coin it lands 'tell him everything' side up. So she does. Or at least a version of the truth. She tells him that she woke in the night and overheard Renata telling Tom that

Jenna was hiding out at her parents' holiday home. That she ran up to her car and she followed them. She speaks quickly, her gaze fixed on her hands. If she pauses she'll give Damian the opportunity to ask her why she was bothered about Jenna's whereabouts, and she doesn't want to do that. She tells him about Tom, dropping to the ground in the living room and how, when she went to help him, Renata hit her over the head. She speeds through the hours spent in the basement, Renata's bloodied appearance, Kate's slumped body and calling the police.

'Then they turned up,' she said. 'Renata was arrested and Tom went to the hospital with Kate.'

She risks a glance at him. *There you go*, she mentally adds, *no one knows that you murdered Jenna. You don't have to kill me now.*

'Wow.' Damian stares at her, his eyes wide, his mouth too. 'Holy fuck. I knew she was a psycho but . . . Jesus.' He shakes his head. 'Is Kate all right? Will she live?'

'I don't know. I think so. The police couldn't tell me much but they did say she'd gone into surgery.'

Damian rests his head in his hands and groans loudly. 'Fucking, fucking, hell.' He looks up again. 'Is Tom all right? Are you?'

'Tom's okay. I'm . . .' She frowns as Damian reaches into his back pocket and pulls out his mobile. 'What are you doing?'

He taps away at the screen, completely ignoring her, then looks up. 'Sorry. She's been texting me all morning. She was worried when I said you'd disappeared.'

Fran searches his face. Who's he talking about? Did he swap numbers with Caroline? They barely even spoke.

'Who?' she asks. 'Who was worried about me?'

'Your sister.'

A chill passes through Fran like a ghost. 'Jenna?'

Damian touches her lightly on the hand. 'Shit, I'm sorry. I didn't mean to tell you like that. But it's true, Fran. Your sister's alive.'

Chapter 54

Now – two days later

JENNA

Jenna checks her phone for what feels like the hundredth time. It's 3.21 p.m., two minutes since she last checked it. She stands up, crosses the room, picks a speck of fluff from the thin carpet and drops it into the bin. She turns in circles, trying to see her flat through a stranger's eyes. It's small, tired and threadbare, but it's safe, it's warm, it's filled with love and it's home. She moves towards the living room doorway then stops. There's no need to check her reflection in the bathroom mirror again. She'll look exactly as she did twenty minutes ago – tired, pale and scared. She looks at her watch again – 3.23 p.m. Is it too late to send a text saying not to come? Or maybe she could go out? She doesn't *have* to answer the door.

Yes she does.

She sits down, jiggles her feet on the carpet, watches as her hands bounce around on her knees. A light tapping at the front door makes her jump.

Heart pounding, she slips out of the living room and walks through the narrow hallway to the front door. She pauses, breathing through her fear, then turns the handle.

'Jenna!' She only catches a glimpse of her sister – her short grey hair, her navy jumper, her wide, disbelieving eyes – before Fran reaches out and pulls Jenna close. Jenna's hands flounder on her sister's back as she's hugged tightly, desperately, like she's one step from falling and she's been pulled back from the edge.

'Let me look at you.' Fran moves her grip to Jenna's shoulders. Her eyes are shining behind her glasses, glinting with tears.

'I can't believe it,' she says. 'I can't believe it's really you.'

Sitting on the small sofa, their knees pressed together, Jenna gently extricates her hand from Fran's.

'Sweaty.' She wipes it on her skirt then laughs as Fran does the same. 'Isn't this killing you, all this . . . touching?'

Now it's Fran's turn to smile. 'You have no idea how many times people touched me on that bloody retreat. I'll always hold it against you, you know, for putting me through that.'

'I'm sorry.'

The two words hang in the air between them. It's not the first time she's apologised to her sister – their first phone call that final day of the retreat, on Damian's phone, was eighty percent tears and strangled sobs and twenty percent 'I'm sorry' – but it's the first time she's said it in person.

She searches her sister's face. It's been nearly three years since she last saw her and the lines around Fran's eyes and between her eyebrows have deepened; the stress and lack of sleep forever etched on her face.

'No.' Fran shakes her head lightly. 'I'm the one who should apologise. If I'd . . . if I'd been a better sister then you wouldn't have felt so alone. You should have been able to turn to me. No . . . no that's not it. I should have picked up that something was wrong. I should have known.'

Jenna bows her head. She can't bear it, seeing the ache in her sister's eyes, the regret.

'It wasn't your fault, Fran. I let you believe I was dead.'

'You were in a dark place.'

This time Jenna doesn't contradict her.

'Damian saved my life,' she says instead.

She didn't lose consciousness after Erica smashed a rock into the back of her head, but she was dazed from the blow and weak from four hours in the unrelenting heat of the sweat lodge. She lay on the ground, a jagged piece of rock beneath her cheekbone, and blinked in the darkness as the last slither of light dropped off the horizon and turned the world slate grey. The gulls stopped cawing and circling and the only sounds she could hear were from the camp behind her, shouts, orders and cries of distress. She tried to lift her head, to shift up onto her elbow but everything hurt and she was too weak to move. She gave up trying and closed her eyes but the darkness brought memories – Kate's voice, warm and damp in her ear, the bird, red and rotten, the nail varnish spilled over her clothes, Tom moving above her, pushing into her, his eyes fixed on hers, Kate and Tom kissing, Erica sneering 'I tried to warn you', her voice melding with Damian's: 'He's got you under his spell.'

'Jenna? Jenna?' Damian's voice grew louder, more insistent. She screwed her eyes tighter as she tried to block it out.

She could feel a hand on her shoulder, shaking her, making everything ache. She groaned as his fingers probed the base of her skull.

'What the hell happened?'

'Erica. She attacked me.'

She heard him swear as he dug his fingers beneath her armpits and under her knees, felt her flip-flops fall as he lifted her into the air. 'We need to get you to a medic.'

'Where's Tom?'

'Gone.' Damian's face was slick with sweat, his cheeks and forehead grubby with dirt. 'He did a runner, took off in the direction of the town. The police are here.'

'The others.' She twisted in his arms, trying to get free. 'I need to help. I can do CPR. I can—'

'No. You can't. You need someone to check you over.'

He started to walk then and she juddered and jolted as he carried her away from the cliff edge and back towards the sweat lodge. With every step, her mind cleared and her anxiety increased. Could she be the part of the reason that two of the group were dead? Several people had been struggling to breathe, even while she was in the tent, and then she'd left and Tom and Kate had followed her. Erica wasn't well but she was right about that. She could be there now, colluding with Kate, creating an alibi for the attack, turning the others against her, telling them that Jenna was the reason that two people were dead – Jenna, who'd slept with a married man and tried to steal him away from his wife. Shame surged through her. He'd manipulated, seduced and tricked her. And then he'd run away from the people who needed him most.

She squeezed Damian's arm. 'Put me down.'

He slowed his pace and looked down at her. 'You all right?'

'I need to get out of here.'

'No problem. I'll take you back to your room after you've seen a medic and talked to the police. You need to tell them what Erica—'

'No, Damian. Listen to me. I don't want to see a medic or the police. I don't want to see anyone. I just want to leave. Here. Gozo. I need to go.' She could no longer see his face in the darkness but she could tell by his breathing that he was listening.

'You were right about Tom and Kate. It was all a game and I'm not going to play it anymore. Please, just help me get out of here.'

She felt his arms tighten around her as he deliberated and she tensed too. If he insisted on carrying her back to the sweat lodge to see a medic she'd have to hurt him to get free. She didn't want to but—

'I've got a car.' His voice cut through her thoughts. 'I rented one yesterday when you lot were dicking around doing one of Tom's bullshit tasks. I'll drive you wherever you need to go.'

She sighed with relief. 'Thank you. Oh Damian, thank you.'

'So, where are we going?'

'To the ferry. I need to get some stuff from my room first though.'

'No problem.'

Instead of walking back towards the sweat lodge then along the track to the hotel, Damian carried her the long way round. As soon they were off the rough ground Jenna asked him to set her down.

'What kind of car is it?' she asked him.

'A blue Nissan Micra.'

'Okay.' She nodded. 'I'll grab some stuff and meet you round the front of the hotel. I can't . . . I can't thank you enough.' In the light of the hotel she could see his face again. He looked pale and drawn and there was worry in his eyes. 'I mean it.' She touched him on the arm. 'You've saved my life.'

He shook his head dismissively. 'Get going, and make sure you don't run into Erica.'

Back in the hotel room, Jenna didn't turn her back to the door once. She could hear voices outside and footsteps thundering down the path that led through the chalets. Every few seconds a burst of light from a torch would flare in the window and her heart would leap into her throat. Was Erica looking for her? Were the police?

She tore off her dressing gown, grabbed a pair of jeans from the floor and pulled them on. She didn't bother with underwear. Instead, she pulled a jumper over her bikini top, yanked on her trainers and snatched her day bag from the bed and slung it across her body. She looked at her suitcase, wide open in the corner of the room, the contents spilling onto the floor. Taking it with her would be too risky. She'd be too conspicuous, dragging it behind her as she made her escape.

Damian started the engine as Jenna slid into the seat next to him. 'Are you all right? Not feeling woozy or dizzy or anything?'

The worry in his eyes hadn't dimmed and she knew he thought running away was a bad idea but she didn't have the strength to justify her decision. He thought she should go to the police to report Erica but she was too spent to sit in a police station and tell a stranger what had happened. They'd want to know why Erica had attacked her, and then she'd have to tell them about Tom. She didn't want to have to pick through the bones of his lies.

She looked across at Damian, gripping the steering wheel. 'Are you still drunk from earlier?'

'Do you care?'

'No. Let's go.'

As they drove through the darkness, Damian did all of the talking. He'd woken from his nap, he told her, and headed out to the sweat lodge to see what was going on. It was like nothing he'd ever seen: shaven headed people lying strewn on the ground like broken dolls, sobbing and gasping or else stumbling around looking confused, waving away the water bottles that were pressed into their hands by hotel staff. He'd found Alan, sitting on his own on a low wall, but when he asked him what had happened the Welshman didn't make any sense. He just kept repeating, 'I'm Phoenix. I'm Phoenix now.' As Damian tried to convince him to get some water there was a scream from beyond the sweat lodge, a sound so hysterical, so grief-stricken, it tore straight through him. He sprinted back across the waste ground as men and women dropped to the ground where they stood, too exhausted to take another step. Someone must have alerted the hotel because the area was flooded with staff, their smart, dark uniforms incongruent with the half-naked guests, grubby and pale in their bikinis and swim shorts, their panicked shouts punctuating the wails and sobs of the guests. One shout, in English, cut through the rest: 'Someone help, Bessie's not breathing!' Damian's breath caught in his throat as he rounded the sweat lodge. Lying spread-eagled on the ground with her mouth agape and her eyes closed, was Bessie. A woman he recognised from the reception desk was crouched on the rough ground beside her, her locked hands pounding at Bessie's chest. Sensing she was being watched, the receptionist looked up. Her eyes were flooded with terror, her skin grey with fear.

'Get an ambulance!' she screamed then she lowered her mouth to Bessie's. But Damian didn't call an ambulance. He didn't move. He didn't speak. He watched, transfixed, his arms hanging loosely at his sides, as Bessie's chest rose with each forced breath then fell, and didn't move again until two clasped hands pounded at it. He knew he should get help but he couldn't look away. He couldn't process what he was seeing, couldn't make sense of it, couldn't draw on past experience and leap into action. All he could do was stare. And then someone brushed past him and a shout sucked the white noise from his brain.

'Tim's dead! I think he had a heart attack. Please, someone, help me!'

And then he saw him – Tim – several metres away, slumped and lifeless in another man's arms, being cradled like a baby, his heels resting on the ground. Damian hadn't even noticed them when he'd rounded the sweat lodge but they must have been there the whole time. All he'd seen was Bessie, collapsed on the ground, a grey shell of a person, all trace of the vibrant pink-haired woman he'd known gone. Something sparked in him then, not sadness but anger. How had this happened? What had gone wrong? And where the fuck was Tom?

'Tom!' He turned away from Bessie and Tim and searched the gloom for a tall, fair man. 'Tom!'

No one replied. No one even looked at him.

He saw Kate, crouched by the entrance of the tent, sobbing into her hands.

'Kate!' He shook her by the shoulder. 'What happened? What the fuck happened?'

But she didn't reply, she just kept crying.

'And that,' Damian said, glancing across at Jenna for the first time since he'd started speaking, 'is when I searched for you. I looked everywhere. I even went into that fucking tent, terrified I'd find you dead, but you weren't there. You weren't anywhere. It was as though you'd vanished. I kept shouting your name, shouting and shouting. I saw Erica, walking back towards the sweat lodge from the cliffs and I asked her if she'd seen you. She gave me this weird little smile and said no. I knew she was lying but I didn't know why . . .' He swallowed. '. . . until I found you.'

Jenna didn't reply. None of it felt real. She didn't feel real. She felt as hollow and as disassociated as she had on the plane. Only when they pulled up at the ferry terminal did she speak.

'Could you turn the light on?' she asked as she rooted around in her bag.

'Lost something?'

Wordlessly she held up a small cloth purse containing two hundred euros.

'What is it?'

'It's all I've got. This is my day bag. I didn't think. I just grabbed it. Everything else is in my suitcase: my passport, my credit cards, my phone.'

'Ah, fuck.' Damian started the engine.

'No.' She touched his hand. 'I'm not going back.'

'Well you're not getting back into the UK without a passport.'

'I'm not going back to the UK.'

'Where are you going then?'

She shrugged. 'I don't know.'

'Jenna.' He gave her a long look. 'Do you want me to come with you? Because I would, you know. I've got nothing to go back for either.'

Her heart splintered at the look in his eyes: the loneliness, desperation and longing. But she wasn't the life buoy he could cling onto. She was flailing around in the water and if he clung to her they'd both go under.

'I—' she began, but Damian stopped her.

'You don't have to say it.' He rooted around in his pockets and pulled out a mobile phone and a wallet. 'Here . . .' He took out a credit card and three hundred euros and pressed them into her hand. 'You won't get far with what you've got.'

'I can't take that.' She pushed them back at him. He ignored her and tapped at his phone.

'Damian, please. It's really kind of you but I can't take your money. I don't know when I'll be able to pay you back.'

He held out his phone. 'I've unlocked it. If you open the notes app you'll find my credit card pin and my email address. Send me an email when you get to wherever it is you're going. Just let me know you're okay, please.'

'I can't take it.'

'Look,' Damian said. 'You might find porn in the browser history and . . . maybe in the video gallery . . . but don't hold it against me. I've been single a while.' He laughed. 'That's supposed to be funny, by the way. You're supposed to smile. Seriously though, just . . . just use what you need. You can pay me back when you're back on your feet. Or I can cancel the contract and the card and send a hitman after you. That was a joke too.'

Tears welled in Jenna's eyes. 'Why are you doing all this for me? I don't deserve it.'

He shrugged. 'I was hoping for a shag but friendship will have to do.'

'Was that a joke too?'

'No, but feel free to laugh.'

She leaned towards him then and wrapped her arms around his shoulders. 'I can never thank you enough.'

'Just email me to let me know you're safe. Promise me you'll do that?'

She nodded into his shoulder. 'I promise.'

He pulled away and reached into the side compartment of the car. 'Here . . .' He handed her a baseball cap. 'If you're planning on disappearing, you might want to hide your shaved head.'

'So Damian's always known,' Fran says, sipping at her tea, 'that you were here, in Valletta?'

'Yes. I figured the least I could do was keep my word so I emailed him when I checked into a hotel. I didn't know where else to go. When I got off the ferry and the taxi driver asked me where I wanted to go it was the only place I could think of. It was either Valletta or the airport and I . . . I couldn't come home.'

Fran looks at her thoughtfully and Jenna feels another pang of guilt.

'Is Damian in love with you?' Fran asks, changing the subject.

She's different, Jenna realises; it's not Fran's face that's changed. Three years ago she would have marched into her flat – side-stepped a hug – and demanded answers. She's less abrasive than she was, softer somehow.

'I think he might have been,' Jenna says, 'and that makes me feel sad, but he's happy now. He's engaged to a woman called Grace and we're friends – me and Damian, I mean. I've paid him back for the phone and the use of his credit card. But I owe him more than money.'

'What I don't understand,' Fran says after a pause, 'is why he would sign up for the retreat in Wales after everything you both went through?'

'He was scared someone would get hurt again. He was horrified when the advert was posted and he wanted to keep an eye on Tom and Kate. He had no idea Erica . . . or whatever her name is now . . . would be there. When I realised you were there too I nearly jumped on the first plane to the UK. Damian talked me out of it. He promised he'd look out for you. He sent me daily updates.'

Fran frowns. 'How did he know who I was?'

'He texted me on the first night. He said there was a woman who'd interrupted Tom's welcome talk to ask what had happened to me. I asked him to take a photo and when your photo popped up on my phone I felt sick. I tried to ring you but you'd changed your number. The only way to get hold of you was to ring Mum and I . . . I'm sorry Fran . . . I couldn't do that. I asked Damian to look out for you instead, to keep you safe.'

'That's why he told me not to mention your name.'

'I guess so. He was probably worried about Erica coming after you.'

A silence settles between them and Jenna shifts on the sofa.

'I'm sorry,' she says again. 'I owe you an explanation.'

'It's fine. You've already explained—'

'Not about Damian and the retreat; about me, and what I did. I let you think I was dead, Fran. For nearly three years. I . . . I didn't think you cared or, at least, I convinced myself that you didn't. It made it easier.'

'To do what?'

'To hide. To disappear.' She stands up and crosses the room to the window. She's been dreading this moment, where she has to try and make sense of what she did. Thinking about who she was three years ago is like thinking about a different person, but it still aches like a bruise, remembering what a dark place she was in.

'I was a mess when I got here, Fran. Worse than a mess. Looking back now, I'm pretty sure I was having a breakdown. I checked myself into a hotel and I . . . I didn't unpack. I didn't put on the TV. I drew the curtains and got into bed and I didn't get out for days other than to drink water or use the toilet. I'd run from Gozo because I wanted to escape but I couldn't escape from what was in here.' She places a hand on the side of her head. 'I was depressed. I didn't want to eat, I couldn't sleep. I couldn't look at myself in the mirror.' She runs a hand over her hair, remembering the prickle of her shaved head. 'I cried and cried. I'd never felt so alone. I had Damian's phone and I could have reached out to someone but there was nothing anyone could have said that would have made things better. I just wanted to . . . to . . . to not be here anymore.'

'Oh Jenna,' Fran says softly and the compassion in her voice makes Jenna want to cry.

'Eventually, I had to get up because I was so hungry that my stomach hurt. I went out in Damian's baseball cap and the clothes I'd been wearing for days and I was scared. I thought people would look at me and laugh. I scurried into a shop and I grabbed . . . god knows what . . . I paid and I left. When I got back to the room I burst into tears. I ate some of the food and got straight back into bed. Damian kept sending me texts, asking me to let him know I was still alive.'

'You never told him how you were feeling?'

'No. He'd already done so much and I . . . I didn't want to be a burden. I didn't want to put all that on him. I knew he was suffering too. He'd watched two people die.'

She peels back the curtain, watching as an elderly woman makes her way down the street, leaning heavily on a cane. She sees the same woman every day, creeping down the street then creeping back with a grocery bag.

'I went back to the store, after my food ran out. I wasn't as scared as the first time. I didn't shake as I handed the assistant the money. The third time I went, I didn't just grab things and rush out. I looked around and that's . . . that's when I saw the front page of the newspaper and Tom's face, staring out at me in black and white. What had happened had made the news. I had no idea. I hadn't bothered going online. My brain was enough of a mess without social media adding to the noise. I realised that Mum and Dad were probably wondering what had happened to me but I couldn't ring them. I wrote letters instead, dozens and dozens, and they all ended up in the bin. I couldn't find the right words. I was so angry about the DNA test. I still felt betrayed.'

She hears Fran inhale noisily through her nose and then grunt irritably. 'And I'm still so cross with myself. If I'd have just checked . . . if I'd have logged onto that site to look at your results . . . I'd have seen what you saw. I'd have understood what you were going through and why you wanted to talk to me. I can't stand the thought of you here, dealing with everything alone.'

Jenna looks back at her sister. 'It was the only way I could deal with it. I started going for walks. I'd walk round and round the city until I was exhausted – mentally and physically – and then I realised where I'd gone wrong.'

'What do you mean?'

'I'd spent my whole life trying to be what other people wanted me to be, Mum and Dad especially. I didn't want to let anyone down or be a disappointment so I went along with things instead of saying no. There was a lot of pressure on me, after you left home, to be the perfect daughter. That's not a criticism of you,' she adds quickly. 'I would have left, too, if I were you. But I was young and I loved them and I felt like their marriage, their life, was perfect. I thought Mum was impossibly glamorous and Dad was this . . . this big, strong, powerful man. They had their faults but people looked up to them, they were respectable and they were honest. I tried to be the person they wanted me to be and I only realised how cruel Mum could be when we fell out in my teens. But I never stopped wanting them to be proud of me, even though it made me unhappy and then . . . then you gave me the genealogy test . . .' She tails off, aware that her older sister has slumped down on the sofa.

'Fran' – she sits next her and takes her hand – 'none of this is your fault. It's no one's fault. I'm glad the truth came out because this life, the one I chose for myself, makes me happy but I was devastated for the longest time. I felt like I'd been lied to my whole life, tricked into being someone I never wanted to be. Behind the gloss of Mum and Dad's "perfect" marriage was this huge, grubby secret. Mum dressed it up like it was all a bit of drunken fun but I'm pretty sure it wasn't her idea. She went along with it because Dad suggested it, or because everyone else in their circle was doing it, because someone had drummed it into her that, in order to be a good wife and a good person, she had to be subservient, agreeable and attractive – all the things she tried to drum into me as a child.'

'Do you think Dad knows the truth about' – Fran shifts uncomfortably – 'you?'

'I don't think so. I think that's part of the reason why Mum insisted I keep it quiet. Not just to preserve their reputation but to stop Dad finding out.'

'Will you tell him? When you go back?'

It's a dilemma Jenna has battled with since she first spoke to Fran on the phone. By not telling their dad, she and Fran would be complicit in their mother's lie. But telling him might ruin what was left of his health, and destroy his marriage.

'I don't know,' she says. 'I really don't. Just seeing them again is going to be hard enough. One step at a time.'

'Of course.' Fran touches her on the back of the hand. 'Of course.'

It's not going to be easy, explaining to her parents why she let them believe she was dead. It's something she hasn't really explained to Fran either.

'I'm sorry,' she says again, 'for doing what I did, for dropping off the face of the earth. I was still such a mess when I saw the papers and I couldn't pick up the phone or send the letters I'd written. I wasn't strong enough. And the more time that passed, the harder it became. One week became two became a month, became six months. How could I pick up the phone and say, "Hi, it's Jenna! I know you've grieving for me but it's okay now because I'm alive!" How could I explain why I'd let you all believe the news reports that I'd committed suicide and put you through so much pain? Eventually I convinced myself you were all better off without me. That it was better for everyone if you thought I was dead.'

As Fran's face crumples, Jenna's heart breaks. 'I didn't think you cared. I was wrong and I hurt you. I'm so, so sorry, and I don't blame you for hating me. I'd hate me too.'

'Hate you?' Fran swipes at the tears on her cheeks. 'Of course I don't hate you.'

'But you must resent me. I've put you through so much. You had to deal with—'

'Nothing, not a thing, not compared to you.' Fran reaches for a tissue and blots her eyes. 'I have regrets too. For not being the sister you deserved, for not caring for you or protecting you, for being so wrapped up in my own little world that I wasn't there when you needed me. But the fact is . . .' A tendon above her eye twitches. 'Oh gosh, why is this so hard to say? I love you, Jenna.' The words come out in a rush. 'I'll get better at doing that. I promise. It'll come more naturally. I'll say it daily.'

'Don't go that far!' Jenna laughs and then her expression grows more serious. 'I love you too, Fran. I didn't say it to you either but I do. I love you.'

Her older sister plucks another tissue from the box on the table, dabs at her eyes and then loudly blows her nose. Afterwards, she gets up, crosses the room, drops the tissue into the bin and stands by the window, looking out into the street. Jenna's eyes fill with tears. Fran's so forgiving, so understanding, and what she did was selfish. She put Fran – and their parents – through so much pain.

Fran sighs softly and turns away from the window. 'Is there another reason why you decided not to come back?'

Jenna shakes her head. 'I'm not sure I know what you mean.'

'There was a wooden train in the hallway, there's a baby gro on the radiator and a' – Fran gestures behind her, to the window – 'a framed photo of a baby on the sill.'

Jenna's eyes dart towards the radiator and the blue and white spotty baby gro lying across it. She thought she'd hidden everything away. Not because she wanted to keep her son from

Fran but because she wanted the moment to be right, before she shared the most precious thing in her life.

'Is the child Tom's?'

The question hangs in the air between them, weighty and loaded.

'No. He's not.'

Fran lets out a breath. 'Good.'

Jenna joins her sister at the window, takes the baby gro from the radiator and holds it to her chest. It's warm with the soft scent of washing powder. 'I didn't plan on getting pregnant. But when it happened . . .' She smiles to herself, remembering the way her stomach had lurched when she saw the second line on the pregnancy test – she wasn't married, her parents would be horrified. She sat on the closed toilet lid and gazed at the small stick of plastic in her hands. And then it hit her, no one need ever know about the baby. It was hers. Tristian's, too, if he wanted to stick around. They'd met in the bar where she worked. He was a local who worked for the Valletta Film Festival. He asked her out five times before she finally relented and agreed to a coffee on a Saturday morning. She liked how passionate he was, how fired up he got when he talked about funding cuts and how important it was to support the work of local film-makers, how oblivious he was to the glances of nearby coffee drinkers when his voice grew a little too loud. He wore a fedora that had belonged to his grandfather and a worn, brown leather jacket. He dressed for himself, not other people, and she admired that. And he was interested in her, not her past or what was going on in her head, but what drove her, the dreams she had and the things she felt passionately about. When she told him she'd always wanted to study art he shrugged and said, 'So do it. Buy materials, learn on YouTube.' He was straight talking, uncomplicated and emotionally solid. She didn't need Tristian the same way she'd needed Tom or Nick – she wasn't broken anymore. She didn't need his approval, or his love, or anyone else's. But he did love her, he told her, after three months together. Still, when she'd discovered she was pregnant she'd been prepared to embrace life as a single mother if Tristian decided to walk away; she'd got through worse. When she told him the news he'd punched the air and said, 'Marvellous news, the best!' and happiness spread through her chest like honey.

'When it happened . . .' She looks across at Fran. 'It felt right. And it . . . it strengthened my resolve, to stay here, to keep quiet. My son is the most precious thing in the world to me and I didn't want that tainted. I didn't want it spoiled by criticism or questions. I didn't want Dad to ask why I'm not married or to grill Tristian about his job. I didn't want Mum to lecture me about the right and wrong way to feed or care for my child. I didn't want them to take over and spoil everything.'

'You know Mum wanted to be here today,' Fran says. 'She screamed blue murder at me down the phone when I said I was going alone. So I screamed blue murder back at her and I told her that if she ever threw tea at me again I would throw some back.'

'I don't imagine that went down well.'

'She went unusually quiet. It was very pleasing. I'll have her apologising to me next.'

Jenna smiles then a wave of regret washes over her. 'When I decided to keep Tama to myself I wasn't just robbing Mum and Dad of a grandchild, I was robbing you too.'

'Well,' Fran says, crossing her arms over her chest. 'I have two points to make about that; actually I have three. Firstly, do not feel guilty for the choices you made. We're done with guilt, I've decided. It's not helpful and frankly it serves no purpose other than to cause pain and insomnia. Secondly, we need a plan of action. If, or when, you go back to see Mum and Dad, I'll be by your side. If either of them wage war, we wage it right back. A united front, so to speak; probably for the first time in our lives but it's well overdue. Thirdly, when do I get to meet this little nephew of mine?'

Jenna puts the baby gro back on the radiator and smiles. 'He's in the other room with Tristian.' She glances at her watch. 'He's not due to finish his nap for another twenty minutes but we can go and see him.'

'No, no.' Fran shakes her head. 'Let him sleep. We have lots more catching up to do. Nearly forty years, by my calculations. Shall I make some more tea?'

Chapter 55

Now – six weeks later, April

FRAN

It's a Sunday morning, the sun's shining and Fran's thrown open all the windows to let in some air. She's sitting at the desk in her living room tapping at her keyboard. It's been six weeks since she visited Jenna in Valletta and four since Jenna, Tristian and Tama flew over to be reunited with Geraldine and Henry. Fran met them at the airport and drove them to Buckinghamshire, Tristian and Tama in the back and Jenna in the front.

Jenna was almost green with fear; her skin was so pale and she fidgeted in her seat, rolling down the window for air, doing it back up, having a drink, putting it in her bag, taking it out again to have one more sip. Old Fran, the one whose sister hadn't gone missing, would have been irritated. New Fran reached out and gave her sister's hand a tight squeeze. She kept hold of it as they walked into their parents' house, leaving Tristian and Tama in the car. Neither Fran nor Jenna wanted them to witness one of Geraldine's meltdowns or risk the baby getting covered in tea. But it wasn't their small, slight mother who greeted them in the kitchen. It was their father. He got up from his stool, a cup of tea steaming on the breakfast bar beside him, and gave them a nod.

'Girls,' he said, then burst into tears.

It was the first time in her life that Fran had seen her father cry. Even when a family liaison officer had visited to update them on the investigation into Jenna's disappearance and confirmed that the Gozoian police had ruled it a suicide, Henry's eyes had remained dry. He was an ex-Colonel, a man from a generation that believed that men didn't cry.

Fran remained in the doorway as Jenna rushed towards him and threw herself against him like a child. It was simultaneously the most joyful, and the most heartbreaking thing that Fran had ever seen and she removed her glasses and dabbed at her eyes.

'Jenna,' Henry said softly, his good arm wrapped around her. 'You have always been, and will always be, my daughter.'

He knew the truth – Geraldine must have told him – but there was no mention of the DNA test, parentage or swingers parties. No recrimination, castigation or blame. Just a man holding his daughter, crying into her hair. Fran retreated into the porch. She'd come to support her sister but this reunion, this sweet, tender, loving reunion, wasn't one she should share.

'Where's my Franny?' Her father's voice rang out. 'Franny, you brought Jenna back to us. Don't hide.'

Fran crept back into the kitchen. In an instant she was twelve again, abandoning the television at the sound of his call. It had been so strange, almost otherworldly, seeing her big, strong Daddy standing in the middle of the kitchen cradling a small, mewing baby. She'd inched closer and peered into his arms, scared and excited in equal measure.

'Hello,' she had said tentatively. 'Welcome to the family.'

Jenna's eyelids had flickered and opened. They were so big, Franny had thought, so round, almost too large for her face but they were the most beautiful eyes that she'd ever seen. She'd always wanted a sister, and she was finally here.

Fran accepted a couple of seconds of her father's embrace then squirmed out from beneath his arm.

'Shall I put the kettle on?' she asked.

Hugging Jenna had been one thing but there was still something about the pressure of someone else's body against hers that made her skin crawl.

'Where's Mum?' Jenna asked as Fran set down the mugs.

Their father raised his gaze to the ceiling. 'She's waiting upstairs. I thought it might be best if I gauged the lay of the land first.'

Fran raised an eyebrow.

'Your mother and I have been talking,' her father continued. 'She took some of the things you said on the phone to heart, Franny. Wait' – he held up a hand as Jenna and Fran both interrupted – 'let me finish. Your mother does love you both very much and she's realised that perhaps she hasn't been the best at expressing that love. And I'm as guilty of that as her. There's to be no fighting today. We don't want to upset anyone and, in turn, we don't want to be upset.'

'You're telling us to be nice to Mum,' Fran commented.

'I'm not telling you anything.' Her dad raised his eyebrows, a smile pricking at his lips. 'I wouldn't dream of it; you're both grown women. But today is special. It's important that we're gentle with each other, that we're kind.'

'Oh for goodness sake,' Fran said. 'Let's not overdo it, Dad.

Anyone would think you'd just lifted that speech from a SoulShrink tweet.'

She shared a look with her sister, and smiled.

Fran inputs her details into the Facebook sign up screen and presses enter. It goes against everything she believes in, joining social media. She's read about data mining and targeted advertising and the last thing she wants is for some Russian oligarch to know what size knickers she buys from M&S and which newspapers she reads. She's already sneaked a look at the Guardian Online and speed read an article about the demise of SoulShrink. Apparently, Kate's recovering from her stab wound, Tom's moved out of their flat, the SoulShrink Twitter account has been disabled and Erica/Renata's trial date has been set.

But needs must. Jenna has created a private Facebook group for the family and some of her very closest friends to share photos and videos of Tama and there's no way Fran's going to miss out on such precious gems. Little Tama has captured the hearts of everyone he's met, even his prickly grandmother, whose demeanour became almost marshmallow-like when she held him in her arms.

Fran searches for the group name, clicks to add herself and then sighs as a message appears on the screen saying something about moderator approval. She reaches for her phone to text Jenna, asking to be let in, then looks back at her screen. Facebook is telling her there are people she may know. Would she like to add them as friends?

Curious, she scrolls through the faces, raising her eyebrows at some of the suggestions. She's not entirely sure how the algorithms have chosen her friends given she used her 'throwaway' email account to sign up (the one she uses to order shopping online), but a couple of the suggestions aren't entirely wide of the mark. There are a couple of fellow teachers from school, her violin tutor and a woman who looks not dissimilar to her local florist. Did she give them her throwaway email for some reason? Facebook must have mined their contacts. Sneaky little thing.

She puts a hand to her laptop lid to close it then changes her mind. Would it hurt to enter someone's name into the search bar at the top of the screen? Just to see a face from the past? It's not that she's lonely, per se, but if there's one thing recent events have taught her it's that life's too short to live with regret.

Gunnar Saevarsson.

She types the name quickly and clicks on the magnifying glass before she can change her mind. Four Gunnar Saevarssons fill the screen but she spots her Gunnar right away. He's grey, like her, balding a little at the temples and there's a ruggedness to his once smooth skin. His smile's not changed though, nor has the light in his eyes. Fran presses a hand to her chest, surprised by the flutter of emotion below her ribcage. Gunnar's probably married, happily so. He's probably forgotten who she even is. She clicks on his profile and scans his page.

Gunnar Saevarsson.

Works at: Professor of Epidemiology at London School of Hygiene and Tropical Medicine

Studies: Mathematics at University of Cambridge

Lives: London

Relationship Status: Divorced

She reads the last two lines again and the fluttering in her chest grows.

'Stop it,' she tells herself. 'You're being ridiculous. You're fifty-one years old.' But she moves the mouse over the message icon, clicks and types into the little box that pops up. *Hello, old friend. How are you?*

She clicks send before she can change her mind then almost jumps out of her skin as her laptop speakers ping with a notification. He can't have replied already, surely? She's barely drawn breath. No, of course not. It's a notification from her throwaway email account telling her she's received a new message from the genealogy site.

Fran eyes the notification suspiciously. Logically, she knows it's probably spam, telling her to buy more testing kits for her family, as if that hasn't caused enough problems already. Emotionally, something inside her stirs. She clicks on the notification and watches the screen as a new browser window pops up and an email message opens.

Dear Frances Fitzgerald

You don't know me but I think we might be related. Having recently completed a DNA ancestry test the site is telling me that I have four half siblings on this site. Needless to say, this came as something of a surprise as I've spent my whole life thinking I'm an only child. Could you tell me a little about yourself? I'm thirty-nine, married with two children. I live in Leeds and am an accounts officer. My parents are Sally and Dennis Broadfoot.

I hope this email hasn't come as too much of a shock and I look forward to hearing from you soon.

With best wishes
Gary Broadfoot

P.S. My dad was in the army. We were stationed in Germany and Cyprus for a lot of his career. I'm not sure if that helps.

She reads the message again. Old Fran would probably delete the email and sweep what she just read under the carpet; it is a family trait after all. But new Fran does things that make her feel uncomfortable, like talking back to her mother, saying I love you, and allowing people to hug her.

Dear Gary Broadfoot, she types. *How are you?*

Chapter 56

Now – two months later

KATE

Kate shifts in her hard, plastic seat, runs her hands through her newly blonde, bobbed hair and looks idly around the cavernous church hall she's found herself in. She had hoped to be the first to arrive but there were three people already seated in the circle – a frail pensioner with her handbag clutched to her chest and her feet neatly crossed at the ankle, a scruffy middle-aged man in a faded blue and white stripy jumper, and a man in his early thirties in a white shirt, suit jacket and pin-striped trousers. She smiled expectantly at the man in the suit, but he wasn't the one who got to his feet, ambled over to her and held out his hand – it was the scruffy one in the jumper. Her spirits plummeted as he held out his hand.

'A new face! Welcome, welcome.' He pumped her hand up and down. 'You've done a brave thing today. I know how difficult it is, just walking through those doors. I'm George, by the way. It's my group. Well, I say that. It's everyone's group. It wouldn't be much of a group if I were the only one here!'

'Kate.' She extricated her hand from his grip.

'There's tea and coffee over there' – George gestured in the direction of an ancient trestle table – 'for a fifty pence donation. Do take a step back from the urn when you pull on the lever. It can spit a little.'

'Right, thank you.' She sidled away, towards the instant coffee and own brand tea bags, fighting the urge to walk straight out the front door. Instead, she made herself a black coffee, carried it back to the circle of chairs and chose a seat opposite George. Before she gave him up as a lost cause she wanted a very good look at his face.

He wasn't, she realised, as more people trickled into the hall and all the chairs filled, a complete twat. Rather, he was a high-energy person with a nervy initial vibe. Once all the 'Welcome, welcomes!' were done and everyone was seated he seemed to settle back into his skin. He was well spoken, likely highly educated and, beneath the terrible jumper and appalling 'pulled through a hedge backwards' hair style, not a completely unattractive man.

'So here we are,' he said, opening his hands wide. 'For those who are here for the first time' – his gaze fell on Kate – 'welcome to the Survivors of Violent Crime group. We are not a therapeutic group, not in the medical sense anyway. We are more of a community. We share stories, discuss coping techniques and any fears or worries we may have. Everyone, this is Kate. She's joining us for the first time today.'

There was a smattering of applause and half a dozen cries of 'Hi Kate!' and 'Welcome!'

'As usual,' George continued, 'we'll go around the group to see who'd like to share their story but, as you're new Kate, I'd like to give you the opportunity to go first.'

Kate sat straighter in her seat. She was ready for this; she'd spent several hours practising earlier in the day.

'Hello, everyone.' She smiled, letting her eyes travel around the group, making sure that each person felt the warmth of her attention (and to gauge whether they recognised her with her newly blonde hair), then let her gaze rest on George. 'My name's Kate and I'm here because I am the survivor of a vicious knife attack that left me scarred, not only physically' – she pressed a hand to her belly – 'but also mentally and emotionally. I lost my home, my livelihood and my marriage as a result of what happened.'

George's eyes softened with compassion and, inwardly, Kate gave herself a high five.

'I may have lost everything,' Kate continued, 'but I am no victim and neither are any of you. When your life is destroyed you can either weep over the wreckage or you can rebuild it. When your worst fears come true you can either cower in a corner or rise up stronger. And when your body is striped with scars you can either view them as imperfections or as medals. We didn't fight a battle when we were attacked, we won!'

She paused for breath. Was the last line too cheesy? When she was practising earlier she nearly took it out.

The applause began before she could say another word of her speech. First George, then the elderly woman, then the man in the suit and then the whole circle was clapping and nodding and calling out words of appreciation. One woman, with tears in her eyes, even got to her feet.

'Well,' George said, when the noise finally died down. 'That was one hell of an introduction. Thank you, Kate. I think we all needed that.'

Now, as the meeting ends, half a dozen people make a beeline for Kate. They pat her shoulder and tell her that it's lovely to meet her and that she did herself proud. Kate smiles and nods and says, 'thank you very much,' but the compliments and the niceties glance off her. It's not the group's approval she came in search of; what good is the plankton when you need the whale?

As the room empties she gets to her feet and joins George at the refreshment table where he's counting out the coins from the honesty pot.

'Hello, hello.' He gives her a warm smile. 'Well, you certainly made a good impression tonight. You really gave this group their fighting spirit back and a lot of them needed that, believe you me.'

Kate returns his smile. 'Did I? That's so lovely to hear.'

Mentally, she's restyling him; cutting his hair, shaving his stubble and replacing his clothes and his shoes. There's something about George, with his Home Counties accent and his bonhomie vibe that would appeal to a lot of middle-aged woman. He's a very safe man; totally unassuming with zero sexual magnetism, but that's not a bad thing. He's someone you'd want to mother, to share a big bear hug with. And there are lot of women who'd go for that. Some men, too.

'I thought um . . .' She produces her business card. 'I thought I'd give you this. I'm really keen to help you spread the word about this group and help you reach others who might find it useful.'

George raises his eyebrows as he looks at the card. 'Kate Sheridan, Happiness In An Unhappy World. Sounds intriguing.'

'It's my new business,' Kate says. 'I'm very good.' She gives him a long, lingering look. A little flirtation never hurts.

George's neck colours. 'I imagine you are.'

'Give me a ring,' Kate touches the back of his hand, making him start; a fifty pence piece drops into the pot with a clang. 'Let's chat.'

'Will you be back next week?' he asks, swallowing.

'Of course. I couldn't think of anywhere else I'd rather be.'

She smiles prettily then turns and strolls out of the church hall, feeling the weight of his gaze as she leaves. Only when she's out of eyeshot does she glance at her watch. That's 'Survivors of Violent Crime' done, along with 'The Other Side of Divorce', earlier that evening and 'Childlessness Through Choice' that morning. If she jumps in a cab she should make it to the 'Wives of Prisoners' meeting with a couple of minutes to spare and then tomorrow she's got 'Living With Toxic Friendships' and 'Rebuilding Trust After A Relationship Ends'. She smiles and stretches her arms above her head. SoulShrink may be no more but that was only a tower block of a business. She's going to build a self-help self-empire, and crown herself Queen.

Acknowledgements

A quick author note before the acknowledgements. Please don't read them if you haven't read the book yet as they may contain spoilers:

Firstly, any legal types who have read this book may be querying the sentence that Tom Wade received for the sweat lodge deaths. I spoke to a barrister about a charge of gross negligence manslaughter and the UK guidelines were so specific they would have had a significant impact on my plot so I had to use a little artistic licence in awarding Tom Wade a two-year sentence.

Secondly, whilst the comments in the book about the murdered journalist Daphne Caruana Galizia are based on reality (you can read about the case in the news), I didn't come across any cases in my research where the police in Gozo covered up a crime – that was pure fiction on my part. Gozo is an absolutely beautiful island and a very safe place for tourists to visit. Please don't let this novel put you off visiting, it really is magical.

Thirdly, those who know me well will realise that there are similarities between Fran's past and my own – we both went to boarding school, we both had fathers in the army and we both have significant age gaps between us and one of our siblings. That is where the similarity ends – there was no swinging or tea swilling in the Taylor household and we are nowhere near as dysfunctional!

So, on with the acknowledgements . . .

A huge thank you to everyone at Avon and HarperCollins who work so very hard on my books. The term 'superstar editor' is bandied around a lot in publishing but it really does apply to Phoebe Morgan who is so incredibly hardworking, dedicated and efficient it makes me tired just thinking about how much she does and all the different authors and job roles she juggles. I couldn't have asked for a better editor while my regular editor, Helen Huthwaite, was on maternity leave. Welcome back Helen and thank you for all your enthusiasm and excitement as you took *Her Last Holiday* to publication.

Thank you also to Sabah Khan my publicist, whose energy levels and enthusiasm are unmatched, and to the incredibly hardworking and innovative marketing team: Hannah O'Brien and Ellie Pilcher. My books wouldn't be available in the shops and supermarkets without the drive and dedication of Caroline Bovey. Huge thanks to Claire Ward for my stunning cover, to Rebecca Fortuin and Claire Corbett for producing and narrating such wonderful audio books, to the digital team for all their hard work, to Bethany Wickington, and to the teams in HC Ireland and HC ANZ for spreading the word about my books.

Very excitingly this book, and my next, will be published in the United States and Canada by the team at HC360 and I'd particularly like to thank Jean-Marie Kelly, Emily Gerbner, Alice Gomer and Peter Borcsok for everything they have done to introduce transatlantic readers to my books.

Big love to my world class agent Madeleine Milburn who is a spinner of dreams and the most savvy agent in the business. Huge thanks for your wisdom, your excellent advice and your insights. Thank you to the rest of the team at the agency for everything you do. I really appreciate you spreading the word internationally about my books.

Thank you to the international publishers who continue to buy, translate and sell my books and the readers who love them. I'm so thrilled that people all over the world are reading my stories.

Huge thanks to authors Tony Kent and Neil Lancaster. Tony is a barrister as well as an author of excellent crime novels and I really appreciate the fact he took time out of his very busy day to answer my questions about gross negligence manslaughter and sentencing. Ditto Neil Lancaster, a retired detective who is also an excellent crime author (it comes in very useful knowing crime authors!), massive thanks for your input on the last few chapters of this book where the police, finally, get involved. I really appreciate it.

All the love in the world to my wonderful family who will no doubt read this book and think, 'I hope she's not referring to me here!' No, I most definitely wasn't referring to you, it's fiction and I love you all very much. Much love to my parents Jenny and Reg Taylor who read all my proofs and provide me with a list of typos I've missed (thank you!) and are always quick to celebrate or commiserate, no matter what life throws at me. Love too to my little brother Dave who is the only other person in the world as obsessed with analysing my sales figures as I am! And to my sister Bec, the celebrity stalker, who would tell the whole of Brighton about my books if she could. Love and thanks to my wonderful sisters-in-law (accident prone) Lou Foley, Sami Eaton (best mum in the world), Ana Hall (hello

Ana's students – yes, she is famous!) and Angela (sit Mildred, sit!). Also Steve and Guinivere Hall, James Loach, and my nieces and nephews Sophie Taylor, Frazer Eaton, Rose Taylor, Oliver Eaton and Mia Taylor. To my 'boys' Chris and Seth, you are my everything. Thank you for putting up with me when I hole myself away or moan about not getting any alone time. I couldn't be without you.

A massive thank you to Laura Barclay who travelled to Gozo with me so I could research the setting for the wellness retreat. Thank you for traipsing around the wasteland at the back of the hotel while I took videos and photos and muttered to myself, and for chatting to the taxi driver on our tour of the island while I looked out of the window and took notes. Thank you to the other friends who have been a huge support over the last year, particularly Joe Rotheram (sorry for stealing your surname for horrible Geraldine!), Kellie Turner, Kate Harrison (who came up with the title *Her Last Holiday* during a brain storm and I absolutely loved it), the Knowle school mums, the Ellerslie girls and my criminally good author family (you make me laugh like no one else).

And finally a huge thank you to everyone who spreads the word about my books – the retailers, the book shops, the reviewers, the librarians, the bloggers and, most of all, my readers. Thank you for reading my books. I don't know if this is the first book of mine that you've picked up or whether you've read them all but THANK YOU. I couldn't be an author without you.

To keep in touch with me on social media follow me on:

http://www.facebook.com/CallyTaylorAuthor
Twitter: http://www.twitter.com/CallyTaylor
Instagram: http://www.instagram.com/CLTaylorAuthor

And if you'd like to receive quarterly updates with all my news and book recommendations then do join the free C.L. Taylor Book Club. You'll receive THE LODGER for free, just for signing up.

cltaylorauthor.com/newsletter

Her Last Holiday Book Club Questions

1. How did your opinion of Kate change as the story progressed? Did you feel sympathy for her at any point?

2. Geraldine kept a secret from her husband and daughters for a very long time. If she'd revealed it earlier do you think it would have altered the family dynamic in any way?

3. Much of Fran and Jenna's ire was directed towards Geraldine. Was it deserved? Do you think relationships between mothers and daughters are inherently more fractious than between fathers and daughters? Why?

4. How do you feel about Tom? Was he a browbeaten victim of Kate's ambition or a self-absorbed, responsibility-shirking cheat? And were his feelings for Jenna real?

5. Fran and Jenna barely had a relationship when Jenna disappeared. Was that the fault of circumstances, their age gap, their personalities or something else?

6. After Jenna discovered that Tom was married and that he'd fled the scene after the sweat lodge deaths she decided to walk away from him forever. Could they have had a relationship or do you agree with her statement that two broken people can never make a relationship work?

7. Do you think Jenna was justified in letting her family believe she was dead?

8. In the one-on-one sessions Tom spent a lot of time talking to Jenna and Geraldine about their pasts. Do you think his sessions helped either of them? What's your view on self-help and therapy? Do you need to come to terms with your past in order to have a happy life?

9. What did you think of Fran? In what ways did she change over the course of the novel? And what kind of future would you like for her?

10. Damian was the true hero of *Her Last Holiday*. Discuss.

Seven guests. Seven secrets.
One killer.

The gripping Richard & Judy psychological thriller from the *Sunday Times* bestseller.

Sometimes your first love won't let you go . . .

The sensational, gripping thriller from the *Sunday Times* bestseller.

What do you do when no one believes you . . .?

The gripping, twisty thriller from the *Sunday Times* bestseller.

She trusted her friends with her life . . .

A haunting, compelling psychological thriller to have you hooked.

Keeping this secret was killing her . . .

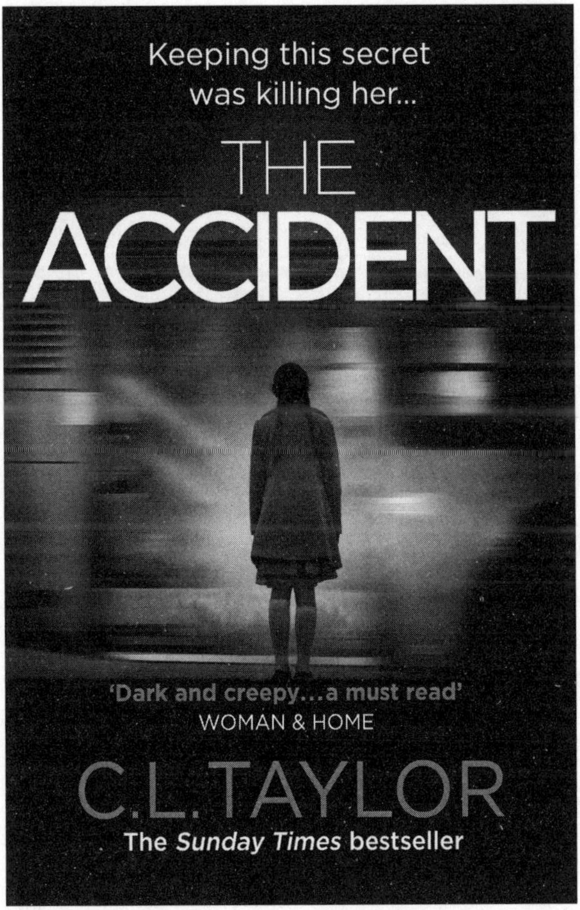

A gripping psychological thriller from the *Sunday Times* bestseller.